Praise for #1 *New York Times* bestselling author

NORA ROBERTS

"America's favorite writer."

—*The New Yorker*

"You can't bottle wish fulfillment, but Nora Roberts certainly knows how to put it on the page."

—*New York Times*

"When Roberts puts her expert fingers on the pulse of romance, legions of fans feel the heartbeat."

—*Publishers Weekly*

"Nora Roberts is among the best."

—*The Washington Post Book World*

"You can always count on Nora Roberts to deliver outstanding, character-driven novels that are destined to be bestsellers."

—*RT Book Reviews*

"Roberts' bestselling novels are some of the best in the romance genre."

—*USA TODAY*

SF

NORA ROBERTS

WHEN WE MEET

Silhouette Books

Published by Silhouette Books

America's Publisher of Contemporary Romance

SILHOUETTE BOOKS

When We Meet

ISBN-13: 978-0-373-28249-4

Recycling programs
for this product may
not exist in your area.

CONTENTS

THE LAW IS A LADY

To all the experts at R&R Lighting Company.

Chapter 1

Merle T. Johnson sat on the ripped vinyl seat of a stool in Annie's Cafe, five miles north of Friendly. He lingered over a lukewarm root beer, half listening to the scratchy country number piping out from Annie's portable radio. *"A woman was born to be hurt"* was the lament of Nashville's latest hopeful. Merle didn't know enough about women to disagree.

He was on his way back to Friendly after checking out a complaint on one of the neighboring ranches. Sheep-stealing, he thought as he chugged down more root beer. Might've been exciting if there'd been anything to it. Potts was getting too old to know how many sheep he had in the first place. Sheriff knew there was nothing to it, Merle thought glumly. Sitting in the dingy little cafe with the smell of fried hamburgers and onions clinging to the air, Merle bemoaned the injustice of it.

There was nothing more exciting in Friendly, New Mexico, than hauling in old Silas when he got drunk and disorderly on Saturday nights. Merle T. Johnson had been born too late. If it had been the 1880s instead of the 1980s, he'd have had a chance to face desperados, ride in a posse, face off a gunslinger—the things deputies were supposed to do. And here he was, he told himself fatalistically, nearly twenty-four years old, and the biggest arrest he had made was pulling in the Kramer twins for busting up the local pool hall.

Merle scratched his upper lip where he was trying, without much success, to grow a respectable mustache. The best part of his life was behind him, he decided, and he'd never be more than a deputy in a forgotten little town, chasing imaginary sheep thieves.

If just *once* somebody'd rob the bank. He dreamed over this a minute, picturing himself in a high-speed chase and shoot-out. That would be something, yessiree. He'd have his picture in the paper, maybe a flesh wound in the shoulder. The idea became more appealing. He could wear a sling for a few days. Now, if the sheriff would only let him carry a gun…

"Merle T., you gonna pay for that drink or sit there dreaming all day?"

Merle snapped back to reality and got hastily to his feet. Annie stood watching him with her hands on her ample hips. She had small, dark eyes, florid skin and an amazing thatch of strawberry-colored hair. Merle was never at his best with women.

"Gotta get back," he muttered, fumbling for his wallet. "Sheriff needs my report."

Annie gave a quick snort and held out her hand, damp palm up. After she snatched the crumpled bill, Merle headed out without asking for his change.

The sun was blinding and brilliant. Merle automatically narrowed his eyes against it. It bounced off the road surface in waves that shimmered almost like liquid. But the day was hot and dusty. On both sides of the ribbon of road stretched nothing but rock and sand and a few tough patches of grass. There was no cloud to break the strong, hard blue of the sky or filter the streaming white light of the sun. He pulled the rim of his hat down over his brow as he headed for his car, wishing he'd had the nerve to ask Annie for his change. His shirt was damp and sticky before he reached for the door handle.

Merle saw the sun radiate off the windshield and chrome of an oncoming car. It was still a mile away, he judged idly as he watched it tool up the long, straight road. He continued to watch its progress with absent-minded interest, digging in his pocket for his keys. As it drew closer his hand remained in his pocket. His eyes grew wide.

That's some car! he thought in stunned admiration.

One of the fancy foreign jobs, all red and flashy. It whizzed by without pausing, and Merle's head whipped around to stare after it. *Oo-wee!* he thought with a grin. *Some* car. Must have been doing seventy easy. Probably has one of those fancy dashboards with— Seventy!

Springing into his car, Merle managed to get the keys out of his pocket and into the ignition. He flipped on his siren and peeled out, spitting gravel and smoking rubber. He was in heaven.

* * *

Phil had been driving more than eighty miles non-stop. During the early part of the journey, he'd held an involved conversation on the car phone with his producer in L.A. He was annoyed and tired. The dust-colored scenery and endless flat road only annoyed him further. Thus far, the trip had been a total waste. He'd checked out five different towns in southwest New Mexico, and none of them had suited his needs. If his luck didn't change, they were going to have to use a set after all. It wasn't his style. When Phillip Kincaid directed a film, he was a stickler for authenticity. Now he was looking for a tough, dusty little town that showed wear around the edges. He wanted peeling paint and some grime. He was looking for the kind of place everyone planned to leave and no one much wanted to come back to.

Phil had spent three long hot days looking, and nothing had satisfied him. True, he'd found a couple of sand-colored towns, a little faded, a little worse for wear, but they hadn't had the right feel. As a director—a highly successful director of American films—Phillip Kincaid relied on gut reaction before he settled down to refining angles. He needed a town that gave him a kick in the stomach. And he was running short on time.

Already Huffman, the producer, was getting antsy, pushing to start the studio scenes. Phil was cursing himself again for not producing the film himself when he cruised by Annie's Cafe. He had stalled Huffman for another week, but if he didn't find the right town to represent New Chance, he would have to trust his location manager to find it. Phil scowled down the endless stretch of road. He didn't trust details to anyone but himself. That, and his undeniable talent, were the reasons for his success at the age of thirty-four. He was tough, critical and volatile, but he treated each of his films as though it were a child requiring endless care and patience. He wasn't always so understanding with his actors.

He heard the wail of the siren with mild curiosity. Glancing in the mirror, Phil saw a dirty, dented police car that might have been white at one time. It was bearing down on him enthusiastically. Phil swore, gave momentary consideration to hitting the gas and leaving the annoyance with his dust, then resignedly pulled over. The blast of heat that greeted him when he let down the window did nothing to improve his mood. Filthy place, he thought, cutting the engine. Grimy dust hole. He wished for his own lagoonlike pool and a long, cold drink.

Elated, Merle climbed out of his car, ticket book in hand. Yessiree, he thought again, this was some machine. About the fanciest piece he'd seen outside the TV. Mercedes, he noted, turning the sound of it over in his mind. French, he decided with admiration. Holy cow, he'd stopped himself a French car not two miles out of town. He'd have a story to tell over a beer that night.

The driver disappointed him a bit at first. He didn't look foreign or even rich. Merle's glance passed ignorantly over the gold Swiss watch to take in the T-shirt and jeans. Must be one of those eccentrics, he concluded. Or maybe the car was stolen. Merle's blood began to pound excitedly. He looked at the man's face.

It was lean and faintly aristocratic, with well-defined bones and a long, straight nose. The mouth was unsmiling, even bored. He was clean shaven with the suggestion of creases in his cheeks. His hair seemed a modest brown; it was a bit long and curled over his ears. In the tanned face the eyes were an arresting clear water-blue. They were both bored and annoyed and, if Merle had been able to latch on the word, aloof. He wasn't Merle's image of a desperate foreign-car thief.

"Yes?"

The single frosty syllable brought Merle back to business. "In a hurry?" he asked, adopting what the sheriff would have called his tough-cop stance.

"Yes."

The answer made Merle shift his feet. "License and registration," he said briskly, then leaned closer to the window as Phil reached in the glove compartment. "Glory be, look at the dash! It's got everything and then some. Those French guys are something."

Phil sent him a mild glance. "German," he corrected, handing Merle the registration.

"German?" Merle frowned doubtfully. "You sure?"

"Yes." Slipping his license out of his wallet, Phil passed it through the open window. The heat was pouring in.

Merle accepted the registration. He was downright sure Mercedes was a French name. "This your car?" he asked suspiciously.

"As you can see by the name on the registration," Phil returned coolly, a sure sign that his temper was frayed around the edges.

Merle was reading the registration at his usual plodding speed. "You streaked by Annie's like a bat out of—" He broke off, remembering that the sheriff didn't hold with swearing on the job. "I stopped you for excessive speed. Clocked you at seventy-two. I bet this baby rides so smooth you never noticed."

"As a matter of fact, I didn't." Perhaps if he hadn't been angry to begin with, perhaps if the heat hadn't been rolling unmercifully into the car, Phil might have played his hand differently. As Merle began to write up the ticket Phil narrowed his eyes. "Just how do I know you clocked me at all?"

"I was just coming out of Annie's when you breezed by," Merle said genially. His forehead creased as he formed the letters. "If I'd waited for my change, I wouldn't have seen you." He grinned, pleased with the hand of fate. "You just sign this," he said as he ripped the ticket from the pad. "You can stop off in town and pay the fine."

Slowly, Phil climbed out of the car. When the sun hit his hair, deep streaks of red shot through it. Merle was reminded of his mother's mahogany server. For a moment they stood eye to eye, both tall men. But one was lanky and tended to slouch, the other lean, muscular and erect.

"No," Phil said flatly.

"No?" Merle blinked against the direct blue gaze. "No what?"

"No, I'm not signing it."

"Not signing?" Merle looked down at the ticket still in his hand. "But you have to."

"No, I don't." Phil felt a trickle of sweat roll down his back. Inexplicably it infuriated him. "I'm not signing, and I'm not paying a penny to some two-bit judge who's feeding his bank account from this speed trap."

"Speed trap!" Merle was more astonished than insulted. "Mister, you were doing better'n seventy, and the road's marked clear—fifty-five. Everybody knows you can't do more than fifty-five."

"Who says I was?"

"I clocked you."

"Your word against mine," Phil returned coolly. "Got a witness?"

Merle's mouth fell open. "Well, no, but…" He pushed back his hat. "Look, I don't need no witness, I'm the deputy. Just sign the ticket."

It was pure perversity. Phil hadn't the least idea how fast he'd been going and didn't particularly care. The road had been long and deserted; his mind had been in L.A. But knowing this wasn't going to make him take the cracked ballpoint the deputy offered him.

"No."

"Look, mister, I already wrote up the ticket." Merle read refusal in Phil's face and set his chin. After all, he was the law. "Then I'm going to have to take you in," he said dangerously. "The sheriff's not going to like it."

Phil gave him a quick smirk and held out his hands, wrists close. Merle stared at them a moment, then looked helplessly from car to car. Beneath the anger, Phil felt a stir of sympathy.

"You'll have to follow me in," Merle told him as he pocketed Phil's license.

"And if I refuse?"

Merle wasn't a complete fool. "Well, then," he said amiably, "I'll have to take you in and leave this fancy car sitting here. It might be all in one piece when the tow truck gets here. Then again…"

Phil acknowledged the point with a slight nod, then climbed back into his car. Merle sauntered to his, thinking how fine he was going to look bringing in that fancy red machine.

They drove into Friendly at a sedate pace. Merle nodded occasionally to people who stopped their business to eye the small procession. He stuck his hand out the window to signal a halt, then braked in front of the sheriff's office.

"Okay, inside." Abruptly official, Merle stood straight. "The sheriff'll want to talk to you." But the icy gleam in the man's eye kept Merle from taking his arm. Instead he opened the door and waited for his prisoner to walk through.

Phil glimpsed a small room with two cells, a bulletin board, a couple of spindly chairs and a battered desk. An overhead fan churned the steamy air and whined. On the floor lay a large mound of mud-colored fur that turned out to be a dog. The desk was covered with books and papers and two half-filled cups of coffee. A dark-haired woman bent over all this, scratching industriously on a yellow legal pad. She glanced up as they entered.

Phil forgot his annoyance long enough to cast her in three different films. Her face was classically oval, with a hint of cheekbone under honey-toned skin. Her nose was small and delicate, her mouth just short of wide, with a fullness that was instantly sensual. Her hair was black, left to fall loosely past her shoulders in carelessly sweeping waves. Her brows arched in question. Beneath them her eyes were thickly lashed, darkly green and faintly amused.

"Merle?"

The single syllable was full throated, as lazy and sexy as black silk. Phil knew actresses who would kill for a voice like that one. If she didn't stiffen up in front of a camera, he thought, and if the rest of her went with the face... He let his eyes sweep down. Pinned to her left breast was a small tin badge. Fascinated, Phil stared at it.

"Excess of speed on Seventeen, Sheriff."

"Oh?" With a slight smile on her face, she waited for Phil's eyes to come back to hers. She had recognized the appraisal when he had first walked in, just as she recognized the suspicion now. "Didn't you have a pen, Merle?"

"A pen?" Baffled, he checked his pockets.

"I wouldn't sign the ticket." Phil walked to the desk to get a closer look at her face. "Sheriff," he added. She could be shot from any imaginable angle, he concluded, and still look wonderful. He wanted to hear her speak again.

She met his assessing stare straight on. "I see. What was his speed, Merle?"

"Seventy-two. Tory, you should see his car!" Merle exclaimed, forgetting himself.

"I imagine I will," she murmured. She held out her hand, her eyes still on Phil's. Quickly, Merle gave her the paperwork.

Phil noted that her hands were long, narrow and elegant. The tips were painted in shell-pink. What the hell is she doing here? he wondered, more easily visualizing her in Beverly Hills.

"Well, everything seems to be in order, Mr.... Kincaid." Her eyes came back to his. A little mascara, he noticed, a touch of eyeliner. The color's hers. No powder, no lipstick. He wished fleetingly for a camera and a couple of hand-held lights. "The fine's forty dollars," she said lazily. "Cash."

"I'm not paying it."

Her lips pursed briefly, causing him to speculate on their taste. "Or forty days," she said without batting an eye. "I think you'd find it less…inconvenient to pay the fine. Our accommodations won't suit you."

The cool amusement in her tone irritated him. "I'm not paying any fine." Placing his palms on the desk, he leaned toward her, catching the faint drift of a subtle, sophisticated scent. "Do you really expect me to believe you're the sheriff? What kind of scam are you and this character running?"

Merle opened his mouth to speak, glanced at Tory, then shut it again. She rose slowly. Phil found himself surprised that she was tall and as lean as a whippet. A model's body, he thought, long and willowy—the kind that made you wonder what was underneath those clothes. This one made jeans and a plaid shirt look like a million dollars.

"I never argue with beliefs, Mr. Kincaid. You'll have to empty your pockets."

"I will not," he began furiously.

"Resisting arrest." Tory lifted a brow. "We'll have to make it sixty days." Phil said something quick and rude. Instead of being offended, Tory smiled. "Lock him up, Merle."

"Now, just a damn minute—"

"You don't want to make her mad," Merle whispered, urging Phil back toward the cells. "She can be mean as a cat."

"Unless you want us to tow your car…and charge you for that as well," she added, "you'll give Merle your keys." She flicked her eyes over his furious face. "Read him his rights, Merle."

"I know my rights, damn it." Contemptuously he shrugged off Merle's hand. "I want to make a phone call."

"Of course." Tory sent him another charming smile. "As soon as you give Merle your keys."

"Now, look—" Phil glanced down at her badge again "—Sheriff," he added curtly. "You don't expect me to fall for an old game. This one—" he jerked a thumb at Merle "—waits for an out-of-towner to come by, then tries to hustle him out of a quick forty bucks. There's a law against speed traps."

Tory listened with apparent interest. "Are you going to sign the ticket, Mr. Kincaid?"

Phil narrowed his eyes. "No."

"Then you'll be our guest for a while."

"You can't sentence me," Phil began heatedly. "A judge—"

"Justice of the peace," Tory interrupted, then tapped a tinted nail against a small framed certificate. Phil saw the name Victoria L. Ashton.

He gave her a long, dry look. "You?"

"Yes, handy, isn't it?" She cocked her head to the side. "Sixty days, Mr. Kincaid, or two hundred and fifty dollars."

"Two-fifty!"

"Bail's set at five hundred. Would you care to post it?"

"The phone call," he said through clenched teeth.

"The keys," she countered affably.

Swearing under his breath, Phil pulled the keys from

his pocket and tossed them to her. Tory caught them neatly. "You're entitled to one local call, Mr. Kincaid."

"It's long distance," he muttered. "I'll use my credit card."

After indicating the phone on her desk, Tory took the keys to Merle. "Two-fifty!" he said in an avid whisper. "Aren't you being a little rough on him?"

Tory gave a quick, unladylike snort. "Mr. Hollywood Kincaid needs a good kick in the ego," she mumbled. "It'll do him a world of good to stew in a cell for a while. Take the car to Bestler's Garage, Merle."

"Me? *Drive* it?" He looked down at the keys in his hand.

"Lock it up and bring back the keys," Tory added. "And don't play with any of the buttons."

"Aw, Tory."

"Aw, Merle," she responded, then sent him on his way with an affectionate look.

Phil waited impatiently as the phone rang. Someone picked up. "Answering for Sherman, Miller and Stein." He swore.

"Where the hell's Lou?" he demanded.

"Mr. Sherman is out of the office until Monday," the operator told him primly. "Would you care to leave your name?"

"This is Phillip Kincaid. You get Lou now, tell him I'm in—" He turned to cast a dark look at Tory.

"Welcome to Friendly, New Mexico," she said obligingly.

Phil's opinion was a concise four-letter word. "Friendly, New Mexico. In jail, damn it, on some trumped-up charge. Tell him to get his briefcase on a plane, pronto."

"Yes, Mr. Kincaid, I'll try to reach him."

"You reach him," he said tightly and hung up. When he started to dial again, Tory walked over and calmly disconnected him.

"One call," she reminded him.

"I got a damn answering service."

"Tough break." She gave him the dashing smile that both attracted and infuriated him. "Your room's ready, Mr. Kincaid."

Phil hung up the phone to face her squarely. "You're not putting me in that cell."

She looked up with a guileless flutter of lashes. "No?"

"No."

Tory looked confused for a moment. Her sigh was an appealingly feminine sound as she wandered around the desk. "You're making this difficult for me, Mr. Kincaid. You must know I can't manhandle you into a cell. You're bigger than I am."

Her abrupt change of tone caused him to feel more reasonable. "Ms. Ashton…" he began.

"Sheriff Ashton," Tory corrected and drew a .45 out of the desk drawer. Her smile never wavered as Phil gaped at the large gun in her elegant hand. "Now, unless you want another count of resisting arrest on your record, you'll go quietly into that first cell over there. The linen's just been changed."

Phil wavered between astonishment and amusement. "You don't expect me to believe you'd use that thing."

"I told you I don't argue with beliefs." Though she kept the barrel lowered, Tory quite deliberately cocked the gun.

He studied her for one full minute. Her eyes were

too direct and entirely too calm. Phil had no doubt she'd put a hole in him—in some part of his anatomy that she considered unimportant. He had a healthy respect for his body.

"I'll get you for this," he muttered as he headed for the cell.

Her laugh was rich and attractive enough to make him turn in front of the bars. Good God, he thought, he'd like to tangle with her when she didn't have a pistol in her hand. Furious with himself, Phil stalked into the cell.

"Doesn't that line go something like, 'When I break outta this joint, you're gonna get yours'?" Tory pulled the keys from a peg, then locked the cell door with a jingle and snap. Struggling not to smile, Phil paced the cell.

"Would you like a harmonica and a tin cup?"

He grinned, but luckily his back was to her. Dropping onto the bunk, he sent her a fulminating glance. "I'll take the tin cup if it has coffee in it."

"Comes with the service, Kincaid. You've got free room and board in Friendly." He watched her walk back to the desk to replace the pistol. Something in the lazy, leggy gait affected his blood pressure pleasantly. "Cream and sugar?" she asked politely.

"Black."

Tory poured the coffee, aware that his eyes were on her. She was partly amused by him, partly intrigued. She knew exactly who he was. Over her basic disdain for what she considered a spoiled, tinsel-town playboy was a trace of respect. He hadn't attempted to influence her with his name or his reputation. He'd relied on his temper. And it was his temper, she knew, that had landed him in the cell in the first place.

Too rich, she decided, too successful, too attractive. And perhaps, she mused as she poured herself a cup, too talented. His movies were undeniably brilliant. She wondered what made him tick. His movies seemed to state one image, the glossies another. With a quiet laugh she thought she might find out for herself while he was her "guest."

"Black," she stated, carrying both cups across the room. "Made to order."

He was watching the way she moved; fluidly, with just a hint of hip. It was those long legs, he decided, and some innate confidence. Under different circumstances he would have considered her quite a woman. At the moment he considered her an outrageous annoyance. Silently he unfolded himself from the bunk and went to accept the coffee she held between the bars. Their fingers brushed briefly.

"You're a beautiful woman, Victoria L. Ashton," he muttered. "And a pain in the neck."

She smiled. "Yes."

That drew a laugh from him. "What the hell are you doing here, playing sheriff?"

"What the hell are you doing here, playing criminal?"

Merle burst in the door, grinning from ear to ear. "Holy cow, Mr. Kincaid, that's *some* car!" He dropped the keys in Tory's hand, then leaned against the bars. "I swear, I could've just sat in it all day. Bestler's eyes just about popped out when I drove it in."

Making a low sound in his throat, Phil turned away to stare through the small barred window at the rear of the cell. He scowled at his view of the town. Look at this place! he thought in frustration. Dusty little nowhere. Looks like all the color was washed away twenty years ago. Baked away, he corrected himself as sweat ran uncomfortably down his back. There seemed to be nothing but brown—dry, sparse mesa in the distance and parched sand. All the buildings, such as they were, were different dull shades of brown, all stripped bare by the unrelenting sun. Damn place still had wooden sidewalks, he mused, sipping at the strong coffee. There wasn't a coat of paint on a storefront that wasn't cracked and peeling. The whole town looked as though it had drawn one long, tired communal breath and settled down to wait until it was all over.

It was a gritty, hopeless-looking place with a sad sort of character under a film of dust and lethargy. People stayed in a town like this when they had no place else to go or nothing to do. Came back when they'd lost hope for anything better. And here he was, stuck in some steamy little cell….

His mind sharpened.

Staring at the tired storefronts and sagging wood, Phil saw it all through the lens of a camera. His fingers wrapped around a window bar as he began to plot out scene after scene. If he hadn't been furious, he'd have seen it from the first moment.

This was Next Chance.

Chapter 2

For the next twenty minutes Tory paid little attention to her prisoner. He seemed content to stare out of the window with the coffee growing cold in his hand. After dispatching Merle, Tory settled down to work.

She was blessed with a sharp, practical and stubborn mind. These traits had made her education extensive. Academically she'd excelled, but she hadn't always endeared herself to her instructors. *Why?* had always been her favorite question. In addition her temperament, which ranged from placid to explosive, had made her a difficult student. Some of her associates called her a tedious annoyance—usually when they were on the opposing side. At twenty-seven Victoria L. Ashton was a very shrewd, very accomplished attorney.

In Albuquerque she kept a small, unpretentious office in an enormous old house with bad plumbing. She shared it with an accountant, a real-estate broker and a private investigator. For nearly five years she had lived on the third floor in two barnlike rooms while keeping her office below. It was a comfortable arrangement that Tory had had no inclination to alter even when she'd been able to afford to.

Professionally she liked challenges and dealing with finite details. In her personal life she was more lackadaisical. No one would call her lazy, but she saw more virtue in a nap than a brisk jog. Her energies poured out in the office or courtroom—and temporarily in her position as sheriff of Friendly, New Mexico.

She had grown up in Friendly and had been content with its yawning pace. The sense of justice she had inherited from her father had driven her to law school. Still, she had had no desire to join a swank firm on either coast, or in any big city in between. Her independence had caused her to risk starting her own practice. Fat fees were no motivation for Tory. She'd learned early how to stretch a dollar when it suited her—an ability she got from her mother. People, and the way the law could be made to work to their advantage or disadvantage, interested her.

Now Tory settled behind her desk and continued drafting out a partnership agreement for a pair of fledgling songwriters. It wasn't always simple to handle cases long distance, but she'd given her word. Absentmindedly she sipped her coffee. By fall she would be back in Albuquerque, filling her caseload again and trading her badge for a briefcase. In the meantime the weekend was looming. Payday. Tory smiled a little as she wrote. Friendly livened up a bit on Saturday nights. People tended to have an extra beer. And there was a poker

game scheduled at Bestler's Garage that she wasn't supposed to know about. Tory knew when it was advantageous to look the other way. Her father would have said
people need their little entertainments.

Leaning back to study what she had written, Tory
propped one booted foot on the desk and twirled a raven
lock around her finger. Abruptly coming out of his rev-
erie, Phil whirled to the door of the cell.

"I have to make a phone call!" His tone was urgent
and excited. Everything he had seen from the cell window had convinced him that fate had brought him to
Friendly.

Tory finished reading a paragraph, then looked up
languidly. "You've had your phone call, Mr. Kincaid.
Why don't you relax? Take a tip from Dynamite there,"
she suggested, wiggling her fingers toward the mound
of dog. "Take a nap."

Phil curled his hands around the bars and shook
them. "Woman, I have to use the phone. It's important."

"It always is," Tory murmured before she lowered
her eyes to the paper again.

Ready to sacrifice principle for expediency, Phil
growled at her. "Look, I'll sign the ticket. Just let me
out of here."

"You're welcome to sign the ticket," she returned
pleasantly, "but it won't get you out. There's also the
charge of resisting arrest."

"Of all the phony, trumped-up—"

"I could add creating a public nuisance," she considered, then glanced over the top of her papers with a
smile. He was furious. It showed in the rigid stance of
his hard body, in the grim mouth and fiery eyes. Tory
felt a small twinge in the nether regions of her stom-

ach. Oh, yes, she could clearly see why his name was linked with dozens of attractive women. He was easily the most beautiful male animal she'd ever seen. It was that trace of aristocratic aloofness, she mused, coupled with the really extraordinary physique and explosive temper. He was like some sleek, undomesticated cat.

Their eyes warred with each other for a long, silent moment. His were stony; hers were calm.

"All right," he muttered, "how much?"

Tory lifted a brow. "A bribe, Kincaid?"

He knew his quarry too well by this time. "No. How much is my fine…Sheriff?"

"Two hundred and fifty dollars." She sent her hair over her shoulder with a quick toss of her head. "Or you can post bail for five hundred."

Scowling at her, Phil reached for his wallet. *When I get out of here,* he thought dangerously, *I'm going to make that tasty little morsel pay for this.* A glance in his wallet found him more than a hundred dollars short of bond. Phil swore, then looked back at Tory. She still had the gently patient smile on her face. He could cheerfully strangle her. Instead he tried another tack. Charm had always brought him success with women.

"I lost my temper before, Sheriff," he began, sending her the slightly off-center smile for which he was known. "I apologize. I've been on the road for several days and your deputy got under my skin." Tory went on smiling. "If I said anything out of line to you, it was because you just don't fit the image of small-town peace officer." He grinned and became boyishly appealing— Tom Sawyer caught with his hand in the sugar bowl.

Tory lifted one long, slim leg and crossed it over the other on the desk. "A little short, are you, Kincaid?"

Phil clenched his teeth on a furious retort. "I don't like to carry a lot of cash on the road."

"Very wise," she agreed with a nod. "But we don't accept credit cards."

"Damn it, I have to get out of here!"

Tory studied him dispassionately. "I can't buy claustrophobia," she said. "Not when I read you crawled into a two-foot pipe to check camera angles on *Night of Desperation.*"

"It's not—" Phil broke off. His eyes narrowed. "You know who I am?"

"Oh, I make it to the movies a couple of times a year," she said blithely.

The narrowed eyes grew hard. "If this is some kind of shakedown—"

Her throaty laughter cut him off. "Your self-importance is showing." His expression grew so incredulous, she laughed again before she rose. "Kincaid, I don't care who you are or what you do for a living, you're a bad-tempered man who refused to accept the law and got obnoxious." She sauntered over to the cell. Again he caught the hint of a subtle perfume that suited French silk, more than faded denim. "I'm obliged to rehabilitate you."

He forgot his anger in simple appreciation of blatant beauty. "God, you've got a face," he muttered. "I could work a whole damn film around that face."

The words surprised her. Tory was perfectly aware that she was physically attractive. She would have been a fool to think otherwise, and she'd heard men offer countless homages to her looks. This was hardly a homage. But something in his tone, in his eyes, made a tremor skip up her spine. She made no protest when he reached a hand through the bars to touch her hair. He let it fall through his fingers while his eyes stayed on hers.

Tory felt a heat to which she had thought herself immune. It flashed through her as though she had stepped into the sun from out of a cool, dim room. It was the kind of heat that buckled your knees and made you gasp out loud in astonished wonder. She stood straight and absorbed it.

A dangerous man, she concluded, surprised. A very dangerous man. She saw a flicker of desire in his eyes, then a flash of amusement. As she watched, his mouth curved up at the corners.

"Baby," he said, then grinned, "I could make you a star."

The purposely trite words dissolved the tension and made her laugh. "Oh, Mr. Kincaid," she said in a breathy whisper, "can I really have a screen test?" A startled Phil could only watch as she flung herself against the bars of the cell dramatically. "I'll wait for you, Johnny," she said huskily as tears shimmered in her eyes and her soft lips trembled. "No matter how long it takes." Reaching through the bars, she clutched at him. "I'll write you every day," she promised brokenly. "And dream of you every night. Oh, Johnny—" her lashes fluttered down "—kiss me goodbye!"

Fascinated, Phil moved to oblige her, but just before his lips brushed hers, she stepped back, laughing. "How'd I do, Hollywood? Do I get the part?"

Phil studied her in amused annoyance. It was a pity, he thought, that he hadn't at least gotten a taste of that beautiful mouth. "A little overdone," he stated with more asperity than truth. "But not bad for an amateur."

Tory chuckled and leaned companionably against the bars. "You're just mad."

"Mad?" he tossed back in exasperation. "Have you ever spent any time in one of these cages?"

"As a matter of fact I have." She gave him an easy grin. "Under less auspicious circumstances. Relax, Kincaid, your friend will come bail you out."

"The mayor," Phil said on sudden inspiration. "I want to see the mayor. I have a business proposition," he added.

"Oh." Tory mulled this over. "Well, I doubt I can oblige you on a Saturday. The mayor mostly fishes on Saturday. Want to tell me about it?"

"No."

"Okay. By the way, your last film should've taken the Oscar. It was the most beautiful movie I've ever seen."

Her sudden change of attitude disconcerted him. Cautiously, Phil studied her face but saw nothing but simple sincerity. "Thanks."

"You don't look like the type who could make a film with intelligence, integrity and emotion."

With a half laugh he dragged a hand through his hair. "Am I supposed to thank you for that too?"

"Not necessarily. It's just that you really do look like the type who squires all those busty celebrities around. When do you find time to work?"

He shook his head. "I…manage," he said grimly.

"Takes a lot of stamina," Tory agreed.

He grinned. "Which? The work or the busty celebrities?"

"I guess you know the answer to that. By the way," she continued before he could formulate a reasonable response, "don't tell Merle T. you make movies." Tory gave him the swift, dashing grin. "He'll start walking like John Wayne and drive us both crazy."

When he smiled back at her, both of them studied each other in wary silence. There was an attraction on both sides that pleased neither of them.

"Sheriff," Phil said in a friendly tone, "a phone call. Remember the line about the quality of mercy?"

Her lips curved, but before she could agree, the door to the office burst in.

"Sheriff!"

"Right here, Mr. Hollister," she said mildly. Tory glanced from the burly, irate man to the skinny, terrified teenager he pulled in with him. "What's the problem?" Without hurry she crossed back to her desk, stepping over the dog automatically.

"Those punks," he began, puffing with the exertion of running. "I warned you about them!"

"The Kramer twins?" Tory sat on the corner of her desk. Her eyes flickered down to the beefy hand that gripped a skinny arm. "Why don't you sit down, Mr. Hollister. You—" she looked directly at the boy "—it's Tod, isn't it?"

He swallowed rapidly. "Yes, ma'am—Sheriff. Tod Swanson."

"Get Mr. Hollister a glass of water, Tod. Right through there."

"He'll be out the back door before you can spit," Hollister began, then took a plaid handkerchief out of his pocket to wipe at his brow.

"No, he won't," Tory said calmly. She jerked her head at the boy as she pulled up a chair for Hollister. "Sit down, now, you'll make yourself sick."

"Sick!" Hollister dropped into a chair as the boy scrambled off. "I'm already sick. Those—those punks."

"Yes, the Kramer twins."

She waited patiently while he completed a lengthy, sometimes incoherent dissertation on the youth of today. Phil had the opportunity to do what he did best: watch and absorb.

Hollister, he noticed, was a hotheaded old bigot with a trace of fear for the younger generation. He was sweating profusely, dabbing at his brow and the back of his neck with the checkered handkerchief. His shirt was wilted and patched with dark splotches. He was flushed, overweight and tiresome. Tory listened to him with every appearance of respect, but Phil noticed the gentle tap of her forefinger against her knee as she sat on the edge of the desk.

The boy came in with the water, two high spots of color on his cheeks. Phil concluded he'd had a difficult time not slipping out the back door. He judged the boy to be about thirteen and scared right down to the bone. He had a smooth, attractive face, with a mop of dark hair and huge brown eyes that wanted to look everywhere at once. He was too thin; his jeans and grubby shirt were nearly in tatters. He handed Tory the water with a hand that shook. Phil saw that when she took it from him, she gave his hand a quick, reassuring squeeze. Phillip began to like her.

"Here." Tory handed Hollister the glass. "Drink this, then tell me what happened."

Hollister drained the glass in two huge gulps. "Those punks, messing around out back of my store. I've chased 'em off a dozen times. They come in and steal anything they can get their hands on. I've told you."

"Yes, Mr. Hollister. What happened this time?"

"Heaved a rock through the window." He reddened alarmingly again. "This one was with 'em. Didn't run fast enough."

"I see." She glanced at Tod, whose eyes were glued to the toes of his sneakers. "Which one threw the rock?"

"Didn't see which one, but I caught this one." Hollister rose, stuffing his damp handkerchief back in his pocket. "I'm going to press charges."

Phil saw the boy blanch. Though Tory continued to look at Hollister, she laid a hand on Tod's arm. "Go sit down in the back room, Tod." She waited until he was out of earshot. "You did the right thing to bring him in, Mr. Hollister." She smiled. "And to scare the pants off him."

"He should be locked up," the man began.

"Oh, that won't get your window fixed," she said reasonably. "And it would only make the boy look like a hero to the twins."

"In my day—"

"I guess you and my father never broke a window," she mused, smiling at him with wide eyes. Hollister blustered, then snorted.

"Now, look here, Tory..."

"Let me handle it, Mr. Hollister. This kid must be three years younger than the Kramer twins." She lowered her voice so that Phil strained to hear. "He could have gotten away."

Hollister shifted from foot to foot. "He didn't try," he mumbled. "Just stood there. But my window—"

"How much to replace it?"

He lowered his brows and puffed for a minute. "Twenty-five dollars should cover it."

Tory walked around the desk and opened a drawer. After counting out bills, she handed them over. "You have my word, I'll deal with him—and with the twins."

"Just like your old man," he muttered, then awkwardly patted her head. "I don't want those Kramers hanging around my store."

"I'll see to it."

With a nod he left.

Tory sat on her desk again and frowned at her left boot. She wasn't just like her old man, she thought. He'd always been sure and she was guessing. Phil heard her quiet, troubled sigh and wondered at it.

"Tod," she called, then waited for him to come to her. As he walked in his eyes darted in search of Hollister before they focused, terrified, on Tory. When he stood in front of her, she studied his white, strained face. Her heart melted, but her voice was brisk.

"I won't ask you who threw the rock." Tod opened his mouth, closed it resolutely and shook his head. "Why didn't you run?"

"I didn't—I couldn't…." He bit his lip. "I guess I was too scared."

"How old are you, Tod?" She wanted to brush at the hair that tumbled over his forehead. Instead she kept her hands loosely folded in her lap.

"Fourteen, Sheriff. Honest." His eyes darted up to hers, then flew away like a small, frightened bird. "Just last month."

"The Kramer twins are sixteen," she pointed out gently. "Don't you have friends your own age?"

He gave a shrug of his shoulders that could have meant anything.

"I'll have to take you home and talk to your father, Tod."

He'd been frightened before, but now he looked up at her with naked terror in his eyes. It wiped the lecture she had intended to give him out of her mind. "Please." It came out in a whisper, as though he could say nothing more. Even the whisper was hopeless.

"Tod, are you afraid of your father?" He swallowed and said nothing. "Does he hurt you?" He moistened his lips as his breath began to shake. "Tod." Tory's voice became very soft. "You can tell me. I'm here to help you."

"He…" Tod choked, then shook his head swiftly. "No, ma'am."

Frustrated, Tory looked at the plea in his eyes. "Well, then, perhaps since this is a first offense, we can keep it between us."

"M-ma'am?"

"Tod Swanson, you were detained for malicious mischief. Do you understand the charge?"

"Yes, Sheriff." His Adam's apple began to tremble.

"You owe the court twenty-five dollars in damages, which you'll work off after school and on weekends at a rate of two dollars an hour. You're sentenced to six months probation, during which time you're to keep away from loose women, hard liquor and the Kramer twins. Once a week you're to file a report with me, as I'll be serving as your probation officer."

Tod stared at her as he tried to take it in. "You're not…you're not going to tell my father?"

Slowly, Tory rose. He was a few inches shorter, so that he looked up at her with his eyes full of confused hope. "No." She placed her hands on his shoulders. "Don't let me down."

His eyes brimmed with tears, which he blinked back furiously. Tory wanted badly to hold him, but knew better. "Be here tomorrow morning. I'll have some work for you."

"Yes, yes, ma'am—Sheriff." He backed away warily, waiting for her to change her mind. "I'll be here, Sheriff." He was fumbling for the doorknob, still watching her. "Thank you." Like a shot, he was out of the office, leaving Tory staring at the closed door.

"Well, Sheriff," Phil said quietly, "you're quite a lady."

Tory whirled to see Phil eyeing her oddly. For the first time she felt the full impact of the clear blue gaze. Disconcerted, she went back to her desk. "Did you enjoy seeing the wheels of justice turn, Kincaid?" she asked.

"As a matter of fact, I did." His tone was grave enough to cause her to look back at him. "You did the right thing by that boy."

Tory studied him a moment, then let out a long sigh. "Did I? We'll see, won't we? Ever seen an abused kid, Kincaid? I'd bet that fifteen-hundred-dollar watch you're wearing one just walked out of here. There isn't a damn thing I can do about it."

"There are laws," he said, fretting against the bars. Quite suddenly he wanted to touch her.

"And laws," she murmured. When the door swung open, she glanced up. "Merle. Good. Take over here. I have to run out to the Kramer place."

"The twins?"

"Who else?" Tory shot back as she plucked a black flat-brimmed hat from a peg. "I'll grab dinner while

I'm out and pick up something for our guest. How do you feel about stew, Kincaid?"

"Steak, medium rare," he tossed back. "Chef's salad, oil and vinegar and a good Bordeaux."

"Don't let him intimidate you, Merle," Tory warned as she headed for the door. "He's a cream puff."

"Sheriff, the phone call!" Phil shouted after her as she started to close the door.

With a heavy sigh Tory stuck her head back in. "Merle T., let the poor guy use the phone. Once," she added firmly, then shut the door.

Ninety minutes later Tory sauntered back in with a wicker hamper over her arm. Phil was sitting on his bunk, smoking quietly. Merle sat at the desk, his feet propped up, his hat over his face. He was snoring gently.

"Is the party over?" Tory asked. Phil shot her a silent glare. Chuckling, she went to Merle and gave him a jab in the shoulder. He scrambled up like a shot, scraping his boot heels over the desk surface.

"Aw, Tory," he muttered, bending to retrieve his hat from the floor.

"Any trouble with the desperate character?" she wanted to know.

Merle gave her a blank look, then grinned sheepishly. "Come on, Tory."

"Go get something to eat. You can wander down to Hernandez's Bar and the pool hall before you go off duty."

Merle placed his hat back on his head. "Want me to check Bestler's Garage?"

"No," she said, remembering the poker game. Merle would figure it his bound duty to break it up if he happened in on it. "I checked in earlier."

"Well, okay…" He shuffled his feet and cast a side-long glance at Phil. "One of us should stay here tonight."

"I'm staying." Plucking up the keys, she headed for the cell. "I've got some extra clothes in the back room."

"Yeah, but, Tory…" He wanted to point out that she was a woman, after all, and the prisoner had given her a couple of long looks.

"Yes?" Tory paused in front of Phil's cell.

"Nothin'," he muttered, reminded that Tory could handle herself and always had. He blushed before he headed for the door.

"Wasn't that sweet?" she murmured. "He was worried about my virtue." At Phil's snort of laughter she lifted a wry brow.

"Doesn't he know about the large gun in the desk drawer?"

"Of course he does." Tory unlocked the cell. "I told him if he played with it, I'd break all his fingers. Hungry?"

Phil gave the hamper a dubious smile. "Maybe."

"Oh, come on, cheer up," Tory ordered. "Didn't you get to make your phone call?"

She spoke as though appeasing a little boy. It drew a reluctant grin from Phil. "Yes, I made my phone call." Because the discussion with his producer had gone well, Phil was willing to be marginally friendly. Besides, he was starving. "What's in there?"

"T-bone, medium rare, salad, roasted potato—"

"You're kidding!" He was up and dipping into the basket himself.

"I don't kid a man about food, Kincaid, I'm a humanitarian."

"I'll tell you exactly what I think you are—after I've

eaten." Phil pulled foil off a plate and uncovered the steak. The scent went straight to his stomach. Dragging over a shaky wooden chair, he settled down to devour his free meal.

"You didn't specify dessert, so I went for apple pie." Tory drew a thick slice out of the hamper.

"I might just modify my opinion of you," Phil told her over a mouthful of steak.

"Don't do anything hasty," she suggested.

"Tell me something, Sheriff." He swallowed, then indicated the still-sleeping dog with his fork. "Doesn't that thing ever move?"

"Not if he can help it."

"Is it alive?"

"The last time I looked," she muttered. "Sorry about the Bordeaux," she continued. "Against regulations. I got you a Dr Pepper."

"A what?"

Tory pulled out a bottle of soda. "Take it or leave it."

After a moment's consideration Phil held out his hand. "What about the mayor?"

"I left him a message. He'll probably see you tomorrow."

Phil unscrewed the top off the bottle, frowning at her. "You're not actually going to make me sleep in this place."

Cocking her head, Tory met his glance. "You have a strange view of the law, Kincaid. Do you think I should book you a room at the hotel?"

He washed down the steak with the soda, then grimaced. "You're a tough guy, Sheriff."

"Yeah." Grinning, she perched on the edge of the bunk. "How's your dinner?"

"It's good. Want some?"

"No. I've eaten." They studied each other with the same wary speculation. Tory spoke first. "What is Phillip C. Kincaid, boy wonder, doing in Friendly, New Mexico?"

"I was passing through," he said warily. He wasn't going to discuss his plans with her. Something warned him he would meet solid opposition.

"At seventy-two miles per hour," she reminded him.

"Maybe."

With a laugh she leaned back against the brick wall. He watched the way her hair settled lazily over her breasts. A man would be crazy to tangle with that lady, he told himself. Phillip Kincaid was perfectly sane.

"And what is Victoria L. Ashton doing wearing a badge in Friendly, New Mexico?"

She gazed past him for a moment with an odd look in her eyes. "Fulfilling an obligation," she said softly.

"You don't fit the part." Phil contemplated her over another swig from the bottle. "I'm an expert on who fits and who doesn't."

"Why not?" Lifting her knee, Tory laced her fingers around it.

"Your hands are too soft." Thoughtfully, Phil cut another bite of steak. "Not as soft as I expected when I saw that face, but too soft. You don't pamper them, but you don't work with them either."

"A sheriff doesn't work with her hands," Tory pointed out.

"A sheriff doesn't wear perfume that costs a hundred and fifty an ounce that was designed to drive men wild either."

Both brows shot up. Her full bottom lip pushed forward in thought. "Is that what it was designed for?"

"A sheriff," he went on, "doesn't usually look like she just walked off the cover of *Harper's Bazaar,* treat her deputy like he was her kid brother or pay some boy's fine out of her own pocket."

"My, my," Tory said slowly, "you are observant." He shrugged, continuing with his meal. "Well, then, what part would you cast me in?"

"I had several in mind the minute I saw you." Phil shook his head as he finished off his steak. "Now I'm not so sure. You're no fragile desert blossom." When her smile widened, he went on. "You could be if you wanted to, but you don't. You're no glossy sophisticate either. But that's a choice too." Taking the pie, he rose to join her on the bunk. "You know, there are a number of people out in this strange world who would love to have me as a captive audience while they recited their life's story."

"At least three of four," Tory agreed dryly.

"You're rough on my ego, Sheriff." He tasted the pie, approved, then offered her the next bite. Tory opened her mouth, allowing herself to be fed. It was tangy, spicy and still warm.

"What do you want to know?" she asked, then swallowed.

"Why you're tossing men in jail instead of breaking their hearts."

Her laugh was full of appreciation as she leaned her head back against the wall. Still, she wavered a moment. It had been so long, she mused, since she'd been able just to talk to someone—to a man. He was interesting and, she thought, at the moment harmless.

"I grew up here," she said simply.

"But you didn't stay." When she sent him a quizzical look, he fed her another bite of pie. It occurred to him that it had been a long time since he'd been with a woman who didn't want or even expect anything from him. "You've got too much polish, Victoria," he said, finding her name flowed well on his tongue. "You didn't acquire it in Friendly."

"Harvard," she told him, rounding her tones. "Law."

"Ah." Phil sent her an approving nod. "That fits. I can see you with a leather briefcase and a pin-striped suit. Why aren't you practicing?"

"I am. I have an office in Albuquerque." Her brows drew together. "A pin-striped suit?"

"Gray, very discreet. How can you practice law in Albuquerque and uphold it in Friendly?" He pushed the hair from her shoulder in a casual gesture that neither of them noticed.

"I'm not taking any new cases for a while, so my workload's fairly light." She shrugged it off. "I handle what I can on paper and make a quick trip back when I have to."

"Are you a good lawyer?"

Tory grinned. "I'm a terrific lawyer, Kincaid, but I can't represent you—unethical."

He shoved another bite of pie at her. "So what are you doing back in Friendly?"

"You really are nosy, aren't you?"

"Yes."

She laughed. "My father was sheriff here for years and years." A sadness flickered briefly into her eyes and was controlled. "I suppose in his own quiet way he held the town together—such as it is. When he died, nobody knew just what to do. It sounds strange, but in a town this size, one person can make quite a difference, and he was…a special kind of man."

The wound hasn't healed yet, he thought, watching her steadily. He wondered, but didn't ask, how long ago her father had died.

"Anyway, the mayor asked me to fill in until things settled down again, and since I had to stay around to straighten a few things out anyway, I agreed. Nobody wanted the job except Merle, and he's…" She gave a quick, warm laugh. "Well, he's not ready. I know the law, I know the town. In a few months they'll hold an election. My name won't be on the ballot." She shot him a look. "Did I satisfy your curiosity?"

Under the harsh overhead lights, her skin was flawless, her eyes sharply green. Phil found himself reaching for her hair again. "No," he murmured. Though his eyes never left hers, Tory felt as though he looked at all of her—slowly and with great care. Quite unexpectedly her mouth went dry. She rose.

"It should have," she said lightly as she began to pack up the dirty dishes. "Next time we have dinner, I'll expect your life story." When she felt his hand on her arm, she stopped. Tory glanced down at the fingers curled around her arm, then slowly lifted her eyes to his. "Kincaid," she said softly, "you're in enough trouble."

"I'm already in jail," he pointed out as he turned her to face him.

"The term of your stay can easily be lengthened."

Knowing he should resist and that he couldn't, Phil drew her into his arms. "How much time can I get for making love to the sheriff?"

"What you're going to get is a broken rib if you don't

let me go." *Miscalculation,* her mind stated bluntly. This man is never harmless. On the tail of that came the thought of how wonderful it felt to be held against him. His mouth was very close and very tempting. And it simply wasn't possible to forget their positions.

"Tory," he murmured. "I like the way that sounds." Running his fingers up her spine, he caught them in her hair. With her pressed tight against him, he could feel her faint quiver of response. "I think I'm going to have to have you."

A struggle wasn't going to work, she decided, any more than threats. As her own blood began to heat, Tory knew she had to act quickly. Tilting her head back slightly, she lifted a disdainful brow. "Hasn't a woman ever turned you down before, Kincaid?"

She saw his eyes flash in anger, felt the fingers in her hair tighten. Tory forced herself to remain still and relaxed. Excitement shivered through her, and resolutely she ignored it. His thighs were pressed hard against hers; the arms wrapped around her waist were tense with muscle. The firm male feel of him appealed to her, while the temper in his eyes warned her not to miscalculate again. They remained close for one long throbbing moment.

Phil's fingers relaxed before he stepped back to measure her. "There'll be another time," he said quietly. "Another place."

With apparent calm, Tory began gathering the dishes again. Her heart was thudding at the base of her throat. "You'll get the same answer."

"The hell I will."

Annoyed, she turned to see him watching her. With his hands in his pockets he rocked back gently on his heels. His eyes belied the casual stance. "Stick with your bubbleheaded blondes," she advised coolly. "They photograph so well, clinging to your arm."

She was angry, he realized suddenly, and much more moved by him than she had pretended. Seeing his advantage, Phil approached her again. "You ever take off that badge, Sheriff?"

Tory kept her eyes level. "Occasionally."

Phil lowered his gaze, letting it linger on the small star. "When?"

Sensing that she was being outmaneuvered, Tory answered cautiously. "That's irrelevant."

When he lifted his eyes back to hers, he was smiling. "It won't be." He touched a finger to her full bottom lip. "I'm going to spend a lot of time tasting that beautiful mouth of yours."

Disturbed, Tory stepped back. "I'm afraid you won't have the opportunity or the time."

"I'm going to find the opportunity and the time to make love with you several times—" he sent her a mocking grin "—Sheriff."

As he had anticipated, her eyes lit with fury. "You conceited fool," she said in a low voice. "You really think you're irresistible."

"Sure I do." He continued to grin maddeningly. "Don't you?"

"I think you're a spoiled, egotistical ass."

His temper rose, but Phil controlled it. If he lost it, he'd lose his advantage. He stepped closer, keeping a bland smile on his face. "Do you? Is that a legal opinion or a personal one?"

Tory tossed back her head, fuming. "My personal opinion is—"

He cut her off with a hard, bruising kiss.

Taken completely by surprise, Tory didn't struggle. By the time she had gathered her wits, she was too involved to attempt it. His mouth seduced hers expertly, parting her lips so that he could explore deeply and at his leisure. She responded out of pure pleasure. His mouth was hard, then soft—gentle, then demanding. He took her on a brisk roller coaster of sensation. Before she could recover from the first breathtaking plunge, they were climbing again. She held on to him, waiting for the next burst of speed.

He took his tongue lightly over hers, then withdrew it, tempting her to follow. Recklessly, she did, learning the secrets and dark tastes of his mouth. For a moment he allowed her to take the lead; then, cupping the back of her head in his hand, he crushed her lips with one last driving force. He wanted her weak and limp and totally conquered.

When he released her, Tory stood perfectly still, trying to remember what had happened. The confusion in her eyes gave him enormous pleasure. "I plead guilty, Your Honor," he drawled as he dropped back onto the bunk. "And it was worth it."

Hot, raging fury replaced every other emotion. Storming over to him, she grabbed him by the shirt front. Phil didn't resist, but grinned.

"Police brutality," he reminded her. She cursed him fluently, and with such effortless style, he was unable to conceal his admiration. "Did you learn that at Harvard?" he asked when she paused for breath.

Tory released him with a jerk and whirled to scoop up the hamper. The cell door shut behind her with a furious clang. Without pausing, she stormed out of the office.

Still grinning, Phil lay back on the bunk and pulled out a cigarette. She'd won round one, he told himself. But he'd taken round two. Blowing out a lazy stream of smoke, he began to speculate on the rematch.

Chapter 3

When the alarm shrilled, Tory knocked it off the small table impatiently. It clattered to the floor and continued to shrill. She buried her head under the pillow. She wasn't at her best in the morning. The noisy alarm vibrated against the floor until she reached down in disgust and slammed it off. After a good night's sleep she was inclined to be cranky. After a poor one she was dangerous.

Most of the past night had been spent tossing and turning. The scene with Phil had infuriated her, not only because he had won, but because she had fully enjoyed that one moment of mindless pleasure. Rolling onto her back, Tory kept the pillow over her face to block out the sunlight. The worst part was, she mused, he was going to get away with it. She couldn't in all conscience use the law to punish him for something that had been strictly personal. It had been her own fault for lowering her guard and inviting the consequences. And she had enjoyed talking with him, sparring with someone quick with words. She missed matching wits with a man.

But that was no excuse, she reminded herself. He'd made her forget her duty…and he'd enjoyed it. Disgusted, Tory tossed the pillow aside, then winced at the brilliant sunlight. She'd learned how to evade an advance as a teenager. What had caused her to slip up this time? She didn't want to dwell on it. Grumpily she dragged herself from the cot and prepared to dress.

Every muscle in his body ached. Phil stretched out his legs to their full length and gave a low groan. He was willing to swear Tory had put the lumps in the mattress for his benefit. Cautiously opening one eye, he stared at the man in the next cell. The man slept on, as he had from the moment Tory had dumped him on the bunk the night before. He snored outrageously. When she had dragged him in, Phil had been amused. The man was twice her weight and had been blissfully drunk. He'd called her "good old Tory," and she had cursed him halfheartedly as she had maneuvered him into the cell. Thirty minutes after hearing the steady snoring, Phil had lost his sense of humor.

She hadn't spoken a word to him. With a detached interest Phil had watched her struggle with the drunk. It had pleased him to observe that she was still fuming. She'd been in and out of the office several times before midnight, then had locked up in the same frigid silence. He'd enjoyed that, but then had made a fatal error: When she had gone into the back room to bed, he had tortured himself by watching her shadow play on the wall as she had undressed. That, combined with an impossible mattress and a snoring drunk-and-disorderly, had led to an uneasy night. He hadn't awakened in the best of moods.

Sitting up with a wince, he glared at the unconscious man in the next cell. His wide, flushed face was cherubic, ringed with a curling blond circle of hair. Ruefully, Phil rubbed a hand over his own chin and felt the rough stubble. A fastidious man, he was annoyed at not having a razor, a hot shower or a fresh set of clothes. Rising, he determined to gain access to all three immediately.

"Tory!" His voice was curt, one of a man accustomed to being listened to. He received no response. "Damn it, Tory, get out here!" He rattled the bars, wishing belligerently that he'd kept the tin cup. He could have made enough noise with it to wake even the stuporous man in the next cell. "Tory, get out of that bed and come here." He swore, promising himself he'd never allow anyone to lock him in anything again. "When I get out…" he began.

Tory came shuffling in, carrying a pot of water. "Button up, Kincaid."

"You listen to me," he retorted. "I want a shower and a razor and my clothes. And if—"

"If you don't shut up until I've had my coffee, you're going to take your shower where you stand." She lifted the pot of water meaningfully. "You can get cleaned up as soon as Merle gets in." She went to the coffeepot and began to clatter.

"You're an arrogant wretch when you've got a man caged," he said darkly.

"I'm an arrogant wretch anyway. Do yourself a favor, Kincaid, don't start a fight until I've had two cups. I'm not a nice person in the morning."

"I'm warning you." His voice was as low and dangerous as his mood. "You're going to regret locking me in here."

Turning, she looked at him for the first time that morning. His clothes and hair were disheveled. The clean lines of his aristocratic face were shadowed by the night's growth of beard. Fury was in his stance and in the cool water-blue of his eyes. He looked outrageously attractive.

"I think I'm going to regret letting you out," she muttered before she turned back to the coffee. "Do you want some of this, or are you just going to throw it at me?"

The idea was tempting, but so was the scent of the coffee. "Black," he reminded her shortly.

Tory drained half a cup, ignoring her scalded tongue before she went to Phil. "What do you want for breakfast?" she asked as she passed the cup through the bars.

He scowled at her. "A shower, and a sledgehammer for your friend over there."

Tory cast an eye in the next cell. "Silas'll wake up in an hour, fresh as a daisy." She swallowed more coffee. "Keep you up?"

"Him and the feather bed you provided."

She shrugged. "Crime doesn't pay."

"I'm going to strangle you when I get out of here," he promised over the rim of his cup. "Slowly and with great pleasure."

"That isn't the way to get your shower." She turned as the door opened and Tod came in. He stood hesitantly at the door, jamming his hands in his pockets. "Good morning." She smiled and beckoned him in. "You're early."

"You didn't say what time." He came warily, shifting his eyes from Phil to Silas and back to Phil again. "You got prisoners."

"Yes, I do." Catching her tongue between her teeth, she jerked a thumb at Phil. "This one's a nasty character."

"What's he in for?"

"Insufferable arrogance."

"He didn't kill anybody, did he?"

"Not yet," Phil muttered, then added, unable to resist the eager gleam in the boy's eyes, "I was framed."

"They all say that, don't they, Sheriff?"

"Absolutely." She lifted a hand to ruffle the boy's hair. Startled, he jerked and stared at her. Ignoring his reaction, she left her hand on his shoulder. "Well, I'll put you to work, then. There's a broom in the back room. You can start sweeping up. Have you had breakfast?"

"No, but—"

"I'll bring you something when I take care of this guy. Think you can keep an eye on things for me for a few minutes?"

His mouth fell open in astonishment. "Yes, ma'am!"

"Okay, you're in charge." She headed for the door, grabbing her hat on the way. "If Silas wakes up, you can let him out. The other guy stays where he is. Got it?"

"Sure thing, Sheriff." He sent Phil a cool look. "He won't pull nothing on me."

Stifling a laugh, Tory walked outside.

Resigned to the wait, Phil leaned against the bars and drank his coffee while the boy went to work with the broom. He worked industriously, casting furtive glances over his shoulder at Phil from time to time. He's a good-looking boy, Phil mused. He brooded over his reaction to Tory's friendly gesture, wondering how he would react to a man.

"Live in town?" Phil ventured.

Tod paused, eyeing him warily. "Outside."

"On a ranch?"

He began to sweep again, but more slowly. "Yeah."

"Got any horses?"

The boy shrugged. "Couple." He was working his way cautiously over to the cell. "You're not from around here," he said.

"No, I'm from California."

"No, kidding?" Impressed, Tod sized him up again. "You don't look like such a bad guy," he decided.

"Thanks." Phil grinned into his cup.

"How come you're in jail, then?"

Phil pondered over the answer and settled for the unvarnished truth. "I lost my temper."

Tod gave a snort of laughter and continued sweeping. "You can't go to jail for that. My pa loses his all the time."

"Sometimes you can." He studied the boy's profile. "Especially if you hurt someone."

The boy passed the broom over the floor without much regard for dust. "Did you?"

"Just myself," Phil admitted ruefully. "I got the sheriff mad at me."

"Zac Kramer said he don't hold with no woman sheriff."

Phil laughed at that, recalling how easily a woman sheriff had gotten him locked in a cell. "Zac Kramer doesn't sound very smart to me."

Tod sent Phil a swift, appealing grin. "I heard she

went to their place yesterday. The twins have to wash all Old Man Hollister's windows, inside and out. For free."

Tory breezed back in with two covered plates. "Breakfast," she announced. "He give you any trouble?" she asked Tod as she set a plate on her desk.

"No, ma'am." The scent of food made his mouth water, but he bent back to his task.

"Okay, sit down and eat."

He shot her a doubtful look. "Me?"

"Yes, you." Carrying the other plate, she walked over to get the keys. "When you and Mr. Kincaid have finished, run the dishes back to the hotel." Without waiting for a response, she unlocked Phil's cell. But Phil watched the expression on Tod's face as he started at his breakfast.

"Sheriff," Phil murmured, taking her hand, rather than the plate she held out to him, "you're a very classy lady." Lifting her hand, he kissed her fingers lightly.

Unable to resist, she allowed her hand to rest in his a moment. "Phil," she said on a sigh, "don't be disarming— you'll complicate things."

His brow lifted in surprise as he studied her. "You know," he said slowly, "I think it's already too late."

Tory shook her head, denying it. "Eat your breakfast," she ordered briskly. "Merle will be coming by with your clothes soon."

When she turned to leave, he held her hand another moment. "Tory," he said quietly, "you and I aren't finished yet."

Carefully she took her hand from his. "You and I never started," she corrected, then closed the door of the cell with a resolute clang. As she headed back to the coffeepot she glanced at Tod. The boy was making his way through bacon and eggs without any trouble.

"Aren't you eating?" Phil asked her as he settled down to his own breakfast.

"I'll never understand how anyone can eat at this hour," Tory muttered, fortifying herself on coffee. "Tod, the sheriff's car could use a wash. Can you handle it?"

"Sure thing, Sheriff." He was half out of the chair before Tory put a restraining hand on his shoulder.

"Eat first," she told him with a chuckle. "If you finish up the sweeping and the car, that should do it for today." She sat on the corner of the desk, enjoying his appetite. "Your parents know where you are?" she asked casually.

"I finished my chores before I left," he mumbled with a full mouth.

"Hmmm." She said nothing more, sipping instead at her coffee. When the door opened, she glanced over, expecting to see Merle. Instead she was struck dumb.

"Lou!" Phil was up and holding on to the bars. "It's about time."

"Well, Phil, you look very natural."

Lou Sherman, Tory thought, sincerely awed. One of the top attorneys in the country. She'd followed his cases, studied his style, used his precedents. He looked just as commanding in person as in any newspaper or magazine picture she'd ever seen of him. He was a huge man, six foot four, with a stocky frame and a wild thatch of white hair. His voice had resonated in courtrooms for more than forty years. He was tenacious, flamboyant and feared. For the moment Tory could only stare at the figure striding into her office in a magnificent pearl-gray suit and baby-pink shirt.

Phil called him an uncomplimentary name, which

made him laugh loudly. "You'd better have some respect if you want me to get you out of there, son." His eyes slid to Phil's half-eaten breakfast. "Finish eating," he advised, "while I talk to the sheriff." Turning, he gazed solemnly from Tory to Tod. "One of you the sheriff?"

Tory hadn't found her voice yet. Tod jerked his head at her. "She is," he stated with his mouth still full.

Lou let his eyes drift down to her badge. "Well, so she is," he said genially. "Best-looking law person I've seen… No offense," he added with a wide grin.

Remembering herself, Tory rose and extended her hand. "Victoria Ashton, Mr. Sherman. It's a pleasure to meet you."

"My pleasure, Sheriff Ashton," he corrected with a great deal of charm. "Tell me, what's the kid done now?"

"Lou—" Phil began, and got an absent wave of the hand from his attorney.

"Finish your eggs," he ordered. "I gave up a perfectly good golf date to fly over here. Sheriff?" he added with a questioning lift of brow.

"Mr. Kincaid was stopped for speeding on Highway Seventeen," Tory began. "When he refused to sign the ticket, my deputy brought him in." After Lou's heavy sigh she continued. "I'm afraid Mr. Kincaid wasn't co-operative."

"Never is," Lou agreed apologetically.

"Damn it, Lou, would you just get me out of here?"

"All in good time," he promised without looking at him. "Are there any other charges, Sheriff?"

"Resisting arrest," she stated, not quite disguising a grin. "The fine is two hundred and fifty, bail set at five hundred. Mr. Kincaid, when he decided to…cooperate, was a bit short of funds."

Lou rubbed a hand over his chin. The large ruby on his pinky glinted dully. "Wouldn't be the first time," he mused.

Incensed at being ignored and defamed at the same time, Phil interrupted tersely. "She pulled a gun on me."

This information was met with another burst of loud laughter from his attorney. "Damn, I wish I'd been here to see his face."

"It was worth the price of a ticket," Tory admitted.

Phil started to launch into a stream of curses, remembered the boy—who was listening avidly—and ground his teeth instead. "Lou," he said slowly, "are you going to get me out or stand around exchanging small talk all day? I haven't had a shower since yesterday."

"Very fastidious," Lou told Tory. "Gets it from his father. I got him out of a tight squeeze or two as I recall. There was this little town in New Jersey... Ah, well, that's another story. I'd like to consult with my client, Sheriff Ashton."

"Of course." Tory retrieved the keys.

"Ashton," Lou murmured, closing his eyes for a moment. "Victoria Ashton. There's something about that name." He stroked his chin. "Been sheriff here long?"

Tory shook her head as she started to unlock Phil's cell. "No, actually I'm just filling in for a while."

"She's a lawyer," Phil said disgustedly.

"That's it!" Lou gave her a pleased look. "I knew the name was familiar. The Dunbarton case. You did a remarkable job."

"Thank you."

"Had your troubles with Judge Withers," he recalled, flipping through his memory file. "Contempt of court. What was it you called him?"

"A supercilious humbug," Tory said with a wince.

Lou chuckled delightedly. "Wonderful choice of words."

"It cost me a night in jail," she recalled.

"Still, you won the case."

"Luckily the judge didn't hold a grudge."

"Skill and hard work won you that one," Lou disagreed. "Where did you study?"

"Harvard."

"Look," Phil interrupted testily. "You two can discuss this over drinks later."

"Manners, Phil, you've always had a problem with manners." Lou smiled at Tory again. "Excuse me, Sheriff. Well, Phil, give me one of those corn muffins there and tell me your troubles."

Tory left them in privacy just as Merle walked in, carrying Phil's suitcase. Dynamite wandered in behind him, found his spot on the floor and instantly went to sleep. "Just leave that by the desk," Tory told Merle. "After Kincaid's taken care of, I'm going out to the house for a while. You won't be able to reach me for two hours."

"Okay." He glanced at the still-snoring Silas. "Should I kick him out?"

"When he wakes up." She looked over at Tod. "Tod's going to wash my car."

Stuffing in the last bite, Tod scrambled up. "I'll do it now." He dashed out the front door.

Tory frowned after him. "Merle, what do you know about Tod's father?"

He shrugged and scratched at his mustache. "Swanson keeps to himself, raises some cattle couple miles north of town. Been in a couple of brawls, but nothing important."

"His mother?"

"Quiet lady. Does some cleaning work over at the hotel now and again. You remember the older brother, don't you? He lit out a couple years ago. Never heard from him since."

Tory absorbed this with a thoughtful nod. "Keep an eye out for the boy when I'm not around, okay?"

"Sure. He in trouble?"

"I'm not certain." She frowned a moment, then her expression relaxed again. "Just keep your eyes open, Merle T.," she said, smiling at him affectionately. "Why don't you go see if the kid's found a bucket? I don't think it would take much persuasion to get him to wash your car too."

Pleased with the notion, Merle strode out again.

"Sheriff—" Tory turned back to the cell as Lou came out "—my client tells me you also serve as justice of the peace?"

"That's right, Mr. Sherman."

"In that case, I'd like to plead temporary insanity on the part of my client."

"You're cute, Lou," Phil muttered from the cell door. "Can I take that shower now?" he demanded, indicating his suitcase.

"In the back," Tory told him. "You need a shave," she added sweetly.

He picked up the case, giving her a long look. "Sheriff, when this is all over, you and I have some personal business."

Tory lifted her half-finished coffee. "Don't cut your throat, Kincaid."

Lou waited until Phil had disappeared into the back room. "He's a good boy," he said with a paternal sigh. Tory burst out laughing.

"Oh, no," she said definitely, "he's not."

"Well, it was worth a try." He shrugged it off and settled his enormous bulk into a chair. "About the charge of resisting arrest," he began. "I'd really hate for it to go on his record. A night in jail was quite a culture shock for our Phillip, Victoria."

"Agreed." She smiled. "I believe that charge could be dropped if Mr. Kincaid pays the speeding fine."

"I've advised him to do so," Lou told her, pulling out a thick cigar. "He doesn't like it, but I'm…" He studied the cigar like a lover. "Persuasive," he decided. He shot her an admiring look. "So are you. What kind of a gun?"

Tory folded her hands primly. "A .45."

Lou laughed heartily as he lit his cigar. "Now, tell me about the Dunbarton case, Victoria."

The horse kicked up a cloud of brown dust. Responding to Tory's command, he broke into an easy gallop. Air, as dry as the land around them, whipped by them in a warm rush. The hat Tory had worn to shield herself from the sun lay on the back of her neck, forgotten. Her movements were so attuned to the horse, she was barely conscious of his movements beneath her. Tory wanted to think, but first she wanted to clear her mind. Since childhood, riding had been her one sure way of doing so.

Sports had no appeal for her. She saw no sense in hitting or chasing a ball around some court or course. It took too much energy. She might swim a few laps now and again, but found it much more agreeable to float on a raft. Sweating in a gym was laughable. But riding was a different category. Tory didn't consider it exercise or effort. She used it now, as she had over the years, as a way to escape from her thoughts for a short time.

For thirty minutes she rode without any thought of destination. Gradually she slowed the horse to a walk, letting her hands relax on the reins. He would turn, she knew, and head back to the ranch.

Phillip Kincaid. He shot back into her brain. A nuisance, Tory decided. One that should be over. At the moment he should already be back on his way to L.A. Tory dearly hoped so. She didn't like to admit that he had gotten to her. It was unfortunate that despite their clash, despite his undeniable arrogance, she had liked him. He was interesting and funny and sharp. It was difficult to dislike someone who could laugh at himself. There would be no problem if it ended there.

Feeling the insistent beat of the sun on her head, Tory absently replaced her hat. It hadn't ended there because there had been that persistent attraction. That was strictly man to woman, and she hadn't counted on it when she had tossed him in jail. He'd outmaneuvered her once. That was annoying, but the result had been much deeper. When was the last time she had completely forgotten herself in a man's arms? When was the last time she had spent most of the night thinking about a man? Had she ever? Tory let out a deep breath, then frowned at the barren, stone-colored landscape.

No, her reaction had been too strong for comfort— and the fact that she was still thinking about him disturbed her. A woman her age didn't dwell on one kiss that way. Yet, she could still remember exactly how his mouth had molded to hers, how the dark, male taste of him had seeped into her. With no effort at all, she could feel the way his body had fit against hers, strong and hard. It didn't please her.

There were enough problems to be dealt with during her stay in Friendly, Tory reminded herself, without dwelling on a chance encounter with some bad-tempered Hollywood type. She'd promised to ease the town through its transition to a new sheriff; there was the boy, Tod, on her mind. And her mother. Tory closed her eyes for a moment. She had yet to come to terms with her mother.

So many things had been said after her father's death. So many things had been left unsaid. For a woman who was rarely confused, Tory found herself in a turmoil whenever she dealt with her mother. As long as her father had been alive, he'd been the buffer between them. Now, with him gone, they were faced with each other. With a wry laugh Tory decided her mother was just as baffled as she was. The strain between them wasn't lessening, and the distance was growing. With a shake of her head she decided to let it lie. In a few months Tory would be back in Albuquerque and that would be that. She had her life to live, her mother had hers.

The wise thing to do, she mused, was to develop the same attitude toward Phil Kincaid. Their paths weren't likely to cross again. She had purposely absented herself from town for a few hours to avoid him. Tory made a face at the admission. No, she didn't want to see him again. He was trouble. It was entirely too easy for him to be charming when he put his mind to it. And she was wise enough to recognize determination when she saw it. For whatever reason—pique or attraction—he wanted her. He wouldn't be an easy man to handle.

Under most circumstances Tory might have enjoyed pitting her will against his, but something warned her not to press her luck.

"The sooner he's back in Tinsel Town, the better," she muttered, then pressed her heels against the horse's sides. They were off at a full gallop.

Phil pulled his car to a halt beside the corral and glanced around. A short distance to the right was a small white-framed house. It was a very simple structure, two stories high, with a wide wooden porch. On the side was a clothesline with a few things baking dry in the sun. There were a few spots of color from flowers in pottery pots on either side of the steps. The grass was short and parched. One of the window screens was torn. In the background he could see a few outbuildings and what appeared to be the beginnings of a vegetable garden. Tory's sheriff's car was parked in front, freshly washed but already coated with a thin film of dust.

Something about the place appealed to him. It was isolated and quiet. Without the car in front, it might fit into any time frame in the past century. There had been some efforts to keep it neat, but it would never be prosperous. He would consider it more a homestead than a ranch. With the right lighting, he mused, it could be very effective. Climbing out of the car, Phil moved to the right to study it from a different angle. When he heard the low drum of hoofs, he turned and watched Tory approach.

He forgot the house immediately and swore at his lack of a camera. She was perfect. Under the merciless sun she rode a palamino the shade of new gold. Nothing could have been a better contrast for a woman of her coloring. With her hat again at her back, her hair flew freely. She sat straight, her movements in perfect timing with the horse's. Phil narrowed his eyes and saw them in slow motion. That was how he would film it—with her hair lifting, holding for a moment before it fell again. The dust would hang in the air behind them. The horse's strong legs would fold and unfold so that the viewer could see each muscle work. This was strength and beauty and a mastery of rider over horse. He wished he could see her hands holding the reins.

He knew the moment she became aware of him. The rhythm never faltered, but there was a sudden tension in the set of her shoulders. It made him smile. No, we're not through yet, he thought to himself. Not nearly through. Leaning against the corral fence, he waited for her.

Tory brought the palamino to a stop with a quick tug of reins. Remaining in the saddle, she gave Phil a long, silent look. Casually he took sunglasses out of his pocket and slipped them on. The gesture annoyed her. "Kincaid," she said coolly.

"Sheriff," he returned.

"Is there a problem?"

He smiled slowly. "I don't think so."

Tory tossed her hair behind her shoulder, trying to disguise the annoyance she felt at finding him there. "I thought you'd be halfway to L.A. by now."

"Did you?"

With a sound of impatience she dismounted. The saddle creaked with the movement as she brought one slim leg over it, then vaulted lightly to the ground. Keeping the reins in her hand, she studied him a moment. "I assume your fine's been paid. You know the other charges were dropped."

"Yes."

She tilted her head. "Well?"

"Well," he returned amiably, amused at the temper that shot into her eyes. *Yes, I'm getting to you, Victoria,* he thought, *and I haven't even started yet.*

Deliberately she turned away to uncinch the saddle. "Has Mr. Sherman gone?"

"No, he's discussing flies and lures with the mayor." Phil grinned. "Lou found a fishing soulmate."

"I see." Tory hefted the saddle from the palamino, then set it on the fence. "Then you discussed your business with the mayor this morning."

"We came to an amicable agreement," Phil replied, watching as she slipped the bit from the horse's mouth. "He'll give you the details."

Without speaking, Tory gave the horse a slap on the flank, sending him inside the corral. The gate gave a long creak as she shut it. She turned then to face Phil directly. "Why should he?"

"You'll want to know the schedule and so forth before the filming starts."

Her brows drew together. "I beg your pardon."

"I came to New Mexico scouting out a location for my new movie. I needed a tired little town in the middle of nowhere."

Tory studied him for a full ten seconds. "And you found it," she said flatly.

"Thanks to you." He smiled, appreciating the irony. "We'll start next month."

Sticking her hands in her back pockets, Tory turned

to walk a short distance away. "Wouldn't it be simpler to shoot in a studio or in a lot?"

"No."

At his flat answer she turned back again. "I don't like it."

"I didn't think you would." He moved over to join her. "But you're going to live with it for the better part of the summer."

"You're going to bring your cameras and your people and your confusion into town," she began angrily. "Friendly runs at its own pace. Now you want to bring in a lifestyle most of these people can't even imagine."

"We'll give very sedate orgies, Sheriff," he promised with a grin. He laughed at the fury that leaped to her eyes. "Tory, you're not a fool. We're not coming to party, we're coming to work. Keep an actor out in this sun for ten takes, he's not going to be disturbing the peace at night. He's going to be unconscious." He caught a strand of her hair and twisted it around his finger. "Or do you believe everything you read in *Inside Scoop?*"

She swiped his hand away in an irritated gesture. "I know more about Hollywood than you know about Friendly," she retorted. "I've spent some time in L.A., represented a screenwriter in an assault case. Got him off," she added wryly. "A few years ago I dated an actor, went to a few parties when I was on the coast." She shook her head. "The gossip magazines might exaggerate, Phil, but the values and lifestyle come through loud and clear."

He lifted a brow. "Judgmental, Tory?"

"Maybe," she agreed. "But this is my town. I'm responsible for the people and for the peace. If you go ahead with this, I warn you, one of your people gets out of line, he goes to jail."

His eyes narrowed. "We have our own security."

"Your security answers to me in my town," she tossed back. "Remember it."

"Not going to cooperate, are you?"

"Not any more than I have to."

For a moment they stood measuring each other in silence. Behind them the palamino paced restlessly around the corral. A fleeting, precious breeze came up to stir the heat and dust. "All right," Phil said at length, "let's say you stay out of my way, I'll stay out of yours."

"Perfect," Tory agreed, and started to walk away. Phil caught her arm.

"That's professionally," he added.

As she had in his cell, Tory gave the hand on her arm a long look before she raised her eyes to his. This time Phil smiled.

"You're not wearing your badge now, Tory." Reaching up, he drew off his sunglasses, then hooked them over the corral fence. "And we're not finished."

"Kincaid—"

"Phil," he corrected, drawing her deliberately into his arms. "I thought of you last night when I was lying in that damned cell. I promised myself something."

Tory stiffened. Her palms pressed against his chest, but she didn't struggle. Physically he was stronger, she reasoned. She had to rely on her wits. "Your thoughts and your promises aren't my problem," she replied coolly. "Whether I'm wearing my badge or not, I'm still sheriff, and you're annoying me. I can be mean when I'm annoyed."

"I'll just bet you can be," he murmured. Even had he wanted to, he couldn't prevent his eyes from lingering on her mouth. "I'm going to have you, Victoria," he said softly. "Sooner or later." Slowly he brought his eyes back to hers. "I always keep my promises."

"I believe I have something to say about this one."

His smile was confident. "Say no," he whispered before his mouth touched hers. She started to jerk back, but he was quick. His hand cupped the back of her head and kept her still. His mouth was soft and persuasive. Long before the stiffness left her, he felt the pounding of her heart against his. Patiently he rubbed his lips over hers, teasing, nibbling. Tory let out an unsteady breath as her fingers curled into his shirt.

He smelled of soap, a fragrance that was clean and sharp. Unconsciously she breathed it in as he drew her closer. Her arms had found their way around his neck. Her body was straining against his, no longer stiff but eager. The mindless pleasure was back, and she surrendered to it. She heard his quiet moan before his lips left hers, but before she could protest, he pressed them to her throat. He was murmuring something neither of them understood as his mouth began to explore. The desperation came suddenly, as if it had been waiting to take them both unaware. His mouth was back on hers with a quick savageness that she anticipated.

She felt the scrape of his teeth and answered by nipping into his bottom lip. The hands at her hips dragged her closer, tormenting both of them. Passion flowed between them so acutely that avid, seeking lips weren't enough. He ran his hands up her sides, letting his thumbs find their way between their clinging bodies to stroke her breasts. She responded by diving deep into his mouth and demanding more.

Tory felt everything with impossible clarity: the soft, thin material of her shirt rubbing against the straining points of her breasts as his thumbs pressed against her; the heat of his mouth as it roamed wildly over her face, then back to hers; the vibration of two heartbeats.

He hadn't expected to feel this degree of need. Attraction and challenge, but not pain. It wasn't what he had planned—it wasn't what he wanted, and yet, he couldn't stop. She was filling his mind, crowding his senses. Her hair was too soft, her scent too alluring. And her taste…her taste too exotic. Greedily, he devoured her while her passion drove him farther into her.

He knew he had to back away, but he lingered a moment longer. Her body was so sleek and lean, her mouth so incredibly agile. Phil allowed himself to stroke her once more, one last bruising contact of lips before he dragged himself away.

They were both shaken and both equally determined not to admit it. Tory felt her pulse hammering at every point in her body. Because her knees were trembling, she stood very straight. Phil waited a moment, wanting to be certain he could speak. Reaching over, he retrieved his sunglasses and put them back on. They were some defense; a better one was to put some distance between them until he found his control.

"You didn't say no," he commented.

Tory stared at him, warning herself not to think until later. "I didn't say yes," she countered.

He smiled. "Oh, yes," he corrected, "you did. I'll be back," he added before he strode to his car.

Driving away, he glanced in his rearview mirror to

see her standing where he had left her. As he punched in his cigarette lighter he saw his hand was shaking. Round three, he thought on a long breath, was a draw.

Chapter 4

Tory stood exactly where she was until even the dust kicked up by Phil's tires had settled. She had thought she knew the meaning of passion, need, excitement. Suddenly the words had taken on a new meaning. For the first time in her life she had been seized by something that her mind couldn't control. The hunger had been so acute, so unexpected. It throbbed through her still, like an ache, as she stared down the long flat road, which was now deserted. How was it possible to need so badly, so quickly? And how was it, she wondered, that a woman who had always handled men with such casual ease could be completely undone by a kiss?

Tory shook her head and made herself turn away from the road Phil had taken. None of it was characteristic. It was almost as if she had been someone else for a moment—someone whose strength and weakness could be drawn out and manipulated. And yet, even now, when she had herself under control, there was something inside her fighting to be recognized. She was going to have to take some time and think about this carefully.

Hoisting the saddle, Tory carried it toward the barn. *I'll be back.* Phil's last words echoed in her ears and sent an odd thrill over her skin. Scowling, Tory pushed open the barn door. It was cooler inside, permeated with the pungent scent of animals and hay. It was a scent of her childhood, one she barely noticed even when returning after months away from it. It never occurred to her to puzzle over why she was as completely at home there as she was in a tense courtroom or at a sophisticated party. After replacing the tack, she paced the concrete floor a moment and began to dissect the problem.

Phil Kincaid was the problem; the offshoots were her strong attraction to him, his effect on her and the fact that he was coming back. The attraction, Tory decided, was unprecedented but not astonishing. He was appealing, intelligent, fun. Even his faults had a certain charm. If they had met under different circumstances, she could imagine them getting to know each other slowly, dating perhaps, enjoying a congenial relationship. Part of the spark, she mused, was due to the way they had met, and the fact that each was determined not to be outdone by the other. That made sense, she concluded, feeling better.

And if that made sense, she went on, it followed that his effect on her was intensified by circumstances. Logic was comfortable, so Tory pursued it. There was something undeniably attractive about a man who wouldn't take no for an answer. It might be annoying, even infuriating, but it was still exciting. Beneath the sheriff's badge and behind the Harvard diploma, Tory was a woman first and last. It didn't hurt when a man knew how to kiss the way Phil Kincaid knew how to kiss, she added wryly. Unable to resist, Tory ran the tip of her tongue over her lips. Oh, yes, she thought with a quick smile, the man was some terrific kisser.

Vaguely annoyed with herself, Tory wandered from the barn. The sun made her wince in defense as she headed for the house. Unconsciously killing time, she poked inside the henhouse. The hens were sleeping in the heat of the afternoon, their heads tucked under their wings. Tory left them alone, knowing her mother had gathered the eggs that morning.

The problem now was that he was coming back. She was going to have to deal with him—and with his own little slice of Hollywood, she added with a frown. At the moment Tory wasn't certain which disturbed her more. Damn, but she wished she'd known of Phil's plans. If she could have gotten to the mayor first… Tory stopped herself with a self-deprecating laugh. She would have changed absolutely nothing. As mayor, Bud Toomey would eat up the prestige of having a major film shot in his town. And as the owner of the one and only hotel, he must have heard the dollars clinking in his cash register.

Who could blame him? Tory asked herself. Her objections were probably more personal than professional in any case. The actor she had dated had been successful and slick, an experienced womanizer and hedonist. She knew too many of her prejudices lay at his feet. She'd been very young when he'd shown her Hollywood from his vantage point. But even without that, she reasoned, there was the disruption the filming would bring to Friendly, the effect on the townspeople and the very real possibility of property damage. As sheriff, all of it fell to her jurisdiction.

What would her father have done? she wondered as she stepped into the house. As always, the moment she was inside, memories of him assailed her—his big, booming voice, his laughter, his simple, man-of-the-earth logic. To Tory his presence was an intimate part of everything in the house, down to the hassock where he had habitually rested his feet after a long day.

The house was her mother's doing. There were the clean white walls in the living room, the sofa that had been re-covered again and again—this time it wore a tidy floral print. The rugs were straight and clean, the pictures carefully aligned. Even they had been chosen to blend in rather than to accent. Her mother's collection of cacti sat on the windowsill. The fragrance of a potpourri, her mother's mixture, wafted comfortably in the air. The floors and furniture were painstakingly clean, magazines neatly tucked away. A single geranium stood in a slender vase on a crocheted doily. All her mother's doing; yet, it was her father Tory thought of when she entered her childhood home. It always was.

But her father wouldn't come striding down the steps again. He wouldn't catch her to him for one of his bear hugs and noisy kisses. He'd been too young to die, Tory thought as she gazed around the room as though she were a stranger. Strokes were for old men, feeble men, not strapping men in their prime. There was no justice to it, she thought with the same impotent fury that hit her each time she came back. No justice for a man who had dedicated his life to justice. He should have had more time, might have had more time, if... Her thoughts broke off as she heard the quiet sounds coming from the kitchen.

Tory pushed away the pain. It was difficult enough to see her mother without remembering that last night in the hospital. She gave herself an extra moment to settle before she crossed to the kitchen.

Standing in the doorway, she watched as Helen relined the shelves in the kitchen cabinets. Her mother's consistent tidiness had been a sore point between them since Tory had been a girl. The woman she watched was tiny and blond, a youthful-looking fifty, with ladylike hands and a trim pink housedress. Tory knew the dress had been pressed and lightly starched. Her mother would smell faintly of soap and nothing else. Even physically Tory felt remote from her. Her looks, her temperament, had all come from her father. Tory could see nothing of herself in the woman who patiently lined shelves with dainty striped paper. They'd never been more than careful strangers to each other, more careful as the years passed. Tory kept a room at the hotel rather than at home for the same reason she kept her visits with her mother brief. Invariably their encounters ended badly.

"Mother."

Surprised, Helen turned. She didn't gasp or whirl at the intrusion, but simply faced Tory with one brow slightly lifted. "Tory. I thought I heard a car drive away."

"It was someone else."

"I saw you ride out." Helen straightened the paper

meticulously. "There's lemonade in the refrigerator. It's a dry day." Without speaking, Tory fetched two glasses and added ice. "How are you, Tory?"

"Very well." She hated the stiffness but could do nothing about it. So much stood between them. Even as she poured the fresh lemonade from her mother's marigold-trimmed glass pitcher, she could remember the night of her father's death, the ugly words she had spoken, the ugly feelings she had not quite put to rest. They had never understood each other, never been close, but that night had brought a gap between them that neither knew how to bridge. It only seemed to grow wider with time.

Needing to break the silence, Tory spoke as she replaced the pitcher in the refrigerator. "Do you know anything about the Swansons?"

"The Swansons?" The question in Helen's voice was mild. She would never have asked directly. "They've lived outside of town for twenty years. They keep to themselves, though she's come to church a few times. I believe he has a difficult time making his ranch pay. The oldest son was a good-looking boy, about sixteen when he left." Helen replaced her everyday dishes on the shelf in tidy stacks, then closed the cupboard door. "That would have been about four years ago. The younger one seems rather sweet and painfully shy."

"Tod," Tory murmured.

"Yes." Helen read the concern but knew nothing about drawing people out, particularly her daughter. "I heard about Mr. Hollister's window."

Tory lifted her eyes briefly. Her mother's were a calm, deep brown. "The Kramer twins."

A suggestion of a smile flickered on her mother's lips. "Yes, of course."

"Do you know why the older Swanson boy left home?"

Helen picked up the drink Tory had poured her. But she didn't sit. "Rumor is that Mr. Swanson has a temper. Gossip is never reliable," she added before she drank.

"And often based in fact," Tory countered.

They fell into one of the stretches of silence that characteristically occurred during their visits. The refrigerator gave a loud click and began to hum. Helen carefully wiped away the ring of moisture her glass had made on the countertop.

"It seems Friendly is about to be immortalized on film," Tory began. At her mother's puzzled look she continued. "I had Phillip C. Kincaid in a cell overnight. Now it appears he's going to use Friendly as one of the location shoots for his latest film."

"Kincaid," Helen repeated, searching her mind slowly. "Oh, Marshall Kincaid's son."

Tory grinned despite herself. She didn't think Phil would appreciate that sort of recognition; it occurred to her simultaneously that it was a tag he must have fought all of his professional career. "Yes," she agreed thoughtfully. "He's a very successful director," she found herself saying, almost in defense, "with an impressive string of hits. He's been nominated for an Oscar three times."

Though Helen digested this, her thoughts were still on Tory's original statement. "Did you say you had him in jail?"

Tory shook off the mood and smiled a little. "Yes, I

did. Traffic violation," she added with a shrug. "It got a little complicated…." Her voice trailed off as she remembered that stunning moment in his cell when his mouth had taken hers. "He's coming back," she murmured.

"To make a film?" Helen prompted, puzzled by her daughter's bemused expression.

"What? Yes," Tory said quickly. "Yes, he's going to do some filming here, I don't have the details yet. It seems he cleared it with the mayor this morning."

But not with you, Helen thought, but didn't say so. "How interesting."

"We'll see," Tory muttered. Suddenly restless, she rose to pace to the sink. The view from the window was simply a long stretch of barren ground that was somehow fascinating. Her father had loved it for what it was—stark and desolate.

Watching her daughter, Helen could remember her husband standing exactly the same way, looking out with exactly the same expression. She felt an intolerable wave of grief and controlled it. "Friendly will be buzzing about this for quite some time," she said briskly.

"It'll buzz all right," Tory muttered. But no one will think of the complications, she added to herself.

"Do you expect trouble?" her mother asked.

"I'll handle it."

"Always so sure of yourself, Tory."

Tory's shoulders stiffened automatically. "Am I, Mother?" Turning, she found her mother's eyes, calm and direct, on her. They had been just that calm, and just that direct, when she had told Tory she had requested her father's regulator be unplugged. Tory had seen no sorrow, no regret or indecision. There had been only the passive face and the matter-of-fact words. For that, more than anything else, Tory had never forgiven her.

As they watched each other in the sun-washed kitchen, each remembered clearly the garishly lit waiting room that smelled of old cigarettes and sweat. Each remembered the monotonous hum of the air conditioner and the click of feet on tile in the corridor outside....

"No!" Tory had whispered the word, then shouted it. "No, you can't! You can't just let him die!"

"He's already gone, Tory," Helen had said flatly. "You have to accept it."

"No!" After weeks of seeing her father lying motionless with a machine pumping oxygen into his body, Tory had been crazy with grief and fear. She had been a long, long way from acceptance. She'd watched her mother sit calmly while she had paced—watched her sip tea while her own stomach had revolted at the thought of food. *Brain-dead.* The phrase had made her violently ill. It was she who had wept uncontrollably at her father's bedside while Helen had stood dry-eyed.

"You don't care," Tory had accused. "It's easier for you this way. You can go back to your precious routine and not be disturbed."

Helen had looked at her daughter's ravaged face and nodded. "It is easier this way."

"I won't let you." Desperate, Tory had pushed her hands through her hair and tried to think. "There are ways to stop you. I'll get a court order, and—"

"It's already done," Helen had told her quietly.

All the color had drained from Tory's face, just as she had felt all the strength drain from her body. Her father was dead. At the flick of a switch he was dead. Her mother had flicked the switch. "You killed him."

Helen hadn't winced or shrunk from the words. "You know better than that, Tory."

"If you'd loved him—if you'd loved him, you couldn't have done this."

"And your kind of love would have him strapped to that machine, helpless and empty."

"Alive!" Tory had tossed back, letting hate wash over the unbearable grief. "Damn you, he was still alive."

"Gone," Helen had countered, never raising her voice. "He'd been gone for days. For weeks, really. It's time you dealt with it."

"It's so easy for you, isn't it?" Tory had forced back the tears because she had wanted—needed—to meet her mother on her own terms. "Nothing—no one—has ever managed to make you *feel*. Not even him."

"There are different kinds of love, Tory," Helen returned stiffly. "You've never understood anything but your own way."

"Love?" Tory had gripped her hands tightly together to keep from striking out. "I've never seen you show anyone love. Now Dad's gone, but you don't cry. You don't mourn. You'll go home and hang out the wash because nothing—by God, nothing—can interfere with your precious routine."

Helen's shoulders had been very straight as she faced her daughter. "I won't apologize for being what I am," she had said. "Any more than I expect you to defend yourself to me. But I do say you loved your father too much, Victoria. For that I'm sorry."

Tory had wrapped her arms around herself tightly,

unconsciously rocking. "Oh, you're so cold," she had whispered. "So cold. You have no feelings." She had badly needed comfort then, a word, an arm around her. But Helen was unable to offer, Tory unable to ask. "You did this," she had said in a strained, husky voice. "You took him from me. I'll never forgive you for it."

"No." Helen had nodded slightly. "I don't expect you will. You're always so sure of yourself, Tory."

Now the two women watched each other across a new grave: dry-eyed, expressionless. A man who had been husband and father stood between them still. Words threatened to pour out again—harsh, bitter words. Each swallowed them.

"I have to get back to town," Tory told her. She walked from the room and from the house. After standing in the silence a moment, Helen turned back to her shelves.

The pool was shaped like a crescent and its water was deep, deep blue. There were palm trees swaying gently in the night air. The scent of flowers was strong, almost tropical. It was a cool spot, secluded by trees, banked with blossoming bushes. A narrow terrace outlined the pool with mosaic tile that glimmered in the moonlight. Speakers had been craftily camouflaged so that the strains of Debussy seemed to float out of the air. A tall iced drink laced with Jamaican rum sat on a glass-topped patio table beside a telephone.

Still wet from his swim, Phil lounged on a chaise. Once again he tried to discipline his mind. He'd spent the entire day filming two key scenes in the studio. He'd had a little trouble with Sam Dressler, the leading man.

It wasn't surprising. Dressler didn't have a reputation for being congenial or cooperative, just for being good. Phil wasn't looking to make a lifelong friendship, just a film. Still, when the clashes began this early in a production, it wasn't a good omen of things to come. He was going to have to use some strategy in handling Dressler.

At least, Phil mused as he absently picked up his drink, he'd have no trouble with the crew. He'd hand-picked them and had worked with each and every one of them before. Bicks, his cinematographer, was the best in the business—creative enough to be innovative and practical enough not to insist on making a statement with each frame. His assistant director was a workhorse who knew the way Phil's mind worked. Phil knew his crew down to the last gaffer and grip. When they went on location…

Phil's thoughts drifted back to Tory, as they had insisted on doing for days. She was going to be pretty stiff-necked about having her town invaded, he reflected. She'd hang over his shoulder with that tin badge pinned to her shirt. Phil hated to admit that the idea appealed to him. With a little pre-planning, he could find a number of ways to put himself in her path. Oh, yes, he intended to spend quite a bit of time getting under Sheriff Ashton's skin.

Soft, smooth skin, Phil remembered, that smelled faintly of something that a man might find in a harem. Dark, dusky and titillating. He could picture her in silk, something chic and vivid, with nothing underneath but that long, lean body of hers.

The quick flash of desire annoyed him enough to cause him to toss back half his drink. He intended to get under her skin, but he didn't intend for it to work the other way around. He knew women, how to please them, charm them. He also knew how to avoid the complication of *one* woman. There was safety in numbers; using that maxim, Phil had enjoyed his share of women.

He liked them not only sexually but as companions. A great many of the women whose names he had been romantically linked with were simply friends. The number of women he had been credited with conquering amused him. He could hardly have worked the kind of schedule he imposed on himself if he spent all his time in the bedroom. Still, he had enjoyed perhaps a bit more than his share of romances, always careful to keep the tone light and the rules plain. He intended to do exactly the same thing with Tory.

It might be true that she was on his mind a great deal more often than any other woman in his memory. It might be true that he had been affected more deeply by her than anyone else. But...

Phil frowned over the *but* a moment. But, he reaffirmed, it was just because their meeting had been unique. The memory of his night in the steamy little cell caused him to grimace. He hadn't paid her back for that yet, and he was determined to. He hadn't cared for being under someone else's control. He'd grown used to deference in his life, a respect that had come first through his parents and then through his own talent. He never thought much about money. The fact that he hadn't been able to buy himself out of the cell was infuriating. Though more often than not he did for himself, he was accustomed to servants—perhaps more to having his word obeyed. Tory hadn't done what he ordered, and had done what he asked only when it had suited her.

It didn't matter that Phil was annoyed when people fawned over him or catered to him. That was what he was used to. Instead of fawning, Tory had been lightly disdainful, had tossed out a compliment on his work, then laughed at him. And had made him laugh, he remembered.

He wanted to know more about her. For days he had toyed with the notion of having someone check into Victoria L. Ashton, Attorney. What had stopped him had not been a respect for privacy so much as a desire to make the discoveries himself. Who was a woman who had a face like a madonna, a voice like whiskey and honey and handled a .45? Phil was going to find out if it took all of the dry, dusty summer. He'd find the time, he mused, although the shooting schedule was backbreaking.

Leaning back against the cushion of the chaise, Phil looked up at the sky. He'd refused the invitation to a party on the excuse that he had work and a scene to shoot early in the morning. Now he was thinking of Tory instead of the film, and he no longer had any sense of time. He knew he should work her out of his system so that he could give the film his full attention, without distractions. He knew he wouldn't. Since he'd returned from Friendly, he hadn't had the least inclination to pick up the phone and call any of the women he knew. He could pacify friends and acquaintances by using the excuse of his work schedule, but he knew. There was only one companion he wanted at the moment, one woman. One lover.

He wanted to kiss her again to be certain he hadn't imagined the emotions he had felt. And the sense of *rightness*. Oddly, he found he didn't want to dilute the sensation with the taste or feel of another woman. It worried him but he brushed it off, telling himself that the obsession would fade once he had Tory where he wanted her. What worried him more was the fact that he wanted to talk to her. Just talk.

Vaguely disturbed, Phil rose. He was tired, that was all. And there was that new script to read before he went to bed. The house was silent when he entered through the glass terrace doors. Even the music had stopped without his noticing. He stepped down into the sunken living room, the glass still in his hand.

The room smelled very faintly of the lemon oil the maid had used that morning. The maroon floor tiles shone. On the deep, plump cushions of the sofa a dozen pillows were tossed with a carelessness that was both inviting and lush. He himself had chosen the tones of blue and green and ivory that dominated the room, as well as the Impressionist painting on the wall, the only artwork in the room. There were mirrors and large expanses of windows that gave the room openness. It held nothing of the opulence of the houses he had grown up in, yet maintained the same ambience of money and success. Phil was easy with it, as he was with his life, himself and his views on his future.

Crossing the room, he walked toward the curving open staircase that led to the second floor. The treads were uncarpeted. His bare feet slapped the wood gently. He was thinking that he had been pleased with the rushes. He and Huffman had watched them together.

Now that the filming was progressing, his producer was more amiable. There were fewer mutterings about guarantors and cost overruns. And Huffman had been pleased with the idea of shooting the bulk of the film on location. Financially the deal with Friendly had been advantageous. Nothing put a smile on a producer's face quicker, Phil thought wryly. He went to shower.

The bath was enormous. Even more than the secluded location, it had been Phil's main incentive for buying the house high in the hills. The shower ran along one wall, with the spray shooting from both sides. He switched it on, stripping out of his trunks while the bathroom grew steamy. Even as he stepped inside, he remembered the cramped little stall he had showered in that stifling morning in Friendly.

The soap had still been wet, he recalled, from Tory. It had been a curiously intimate feeling to rub the small cake along his own skin and imagine it sliding over hers. Then he had run out of hot water while he was still covered with lather. He'd cursed her fluently and wanted her outrageously. Standing between the hot crisscrossing sprays, Phil knew he still did. On impulse he reached out and grabbed the phone that hung on the wall beside the shower.

"I want to place a call to Friendly, New Mexico," he told the operator. Ignoring the time, he decided to take a chance. "The sheriff's office." Phil waited while steam rose from the shower. The phone clicked and hummed then rang.

"Sheriff's office."

The sound of her voice made him grin. "Sheriff."

Tory frowned, setting down the coffee that was keeping her awake over the brief she was drafting. "Yes?"

"Phil Kincaid."

There was complete silence as Tory's mouth opened and closed. She felt a thrill she considered ridiculously juvenile and straightened at her desk. "Well," she said lightly, "did you forget your toothbrush?"

"No." He was at a loss for a moment, struggling to formulate a reasonable excuse for the call. He wasn't a love-struck teenager who called his girl just to hear her voice. "The shooting's on schedule," he told her, thinking fast. "We'll be in Friendly next week. I wanted to be certain there were no problems."

Tory glanced over at the cell, remembering how he had looked standing there. "Your location manager has been in touch with me and the mayor," she said, deliberately turning her eyes away from the cell. "You have all the necessary permits. The hotel's booked for you. I had to fight to keep my own room. Several people are making arrangements to rent out rooms in their homes to accommodate you." She didn't have to add that the idea didn't appeal to her. Her tone told him everything. Again he found himself grinning.

"Still afraid we're going to corrupt your town, Sheriff?"

"You and your people will stay in line, Kincaid," she returned, "or you'll have your old room back."

"It's comforting to know you have it waiting for me. Are you?"

"Waiting for you?" She gave a quick snort of laughter. "Just like the Egyptians waited for the next plague."

"Ah, Victoria, you've a unique way of putting things."

Tory frowned, listening to the odd hissing on the line. "What's that noise?"

"Noise?"

"It sounds like water running."

"It is," he told her. "I'm in the shower."

For a full ten seconds Tory said nothing, then she burst out laughing. "Phil, why did you call me from the shower?"

Something about her laughter and the way she said his name had him struggling against a fresh torrent of needs. "Because it reminded me of you."

Tory propped her feet on the desk, forgetting her brief. Something in her was softening. "Oh?" was all she said.

"I remembered running out of hot water halfway through my shower in your guest room." He pushed wet hair out of his eyes. "At the time I wasn't in the mood to lodge a formal complaint."

"I'll take it up with the management." She caught her tongue between her teeth for a moment. "I wouldn't expect deluxe accommodations in the hotel, Kincaid. There's no room service or phones in the bathroom."

"We'll survive."

"That's yet to be seen," she said dryly. "Your group may undergo culture shock when they find themselves without a Jacuzzi."

"You really think we're a soft bunch, don't you?" Annoyed, Phil switched the phone to his other hand. It nearly slid out of his wet palm. "You may learn a few things about the people in the business this summer, Victoria. I'm going to enjoy teaching you."

"There's nothing I want to learn from you," she said quietly.

"*Want* and *need* are entirely different words," he pointed out. He could almost see the flash of temper leap into her eyes. It gave him a curious pleasure.

"As long as you play by the rules, there won't be any trouble."

"There'll be a time, Tory," he murmured into the receiver, "that you and I will play by my rules. I still have a promise to keep."

Tory pulled her legs from the desk so that her boots hit the floor with a clatter. "Don't forget to wash behind your ears," she ordered, then hung up with a bang.

Chapter 5

Tory was in her office when they arrived. The rumble of cars outside could mean only one thing. She forced herself to complete the form she was filling out before she rose from her desk. Of course she wasn't in any hurry to see him again, but it was her duty to be certain the town remained orderly during the arrival of the people from Hollywood. Still, she hesitated a moment, absently fingering her badge. She hadn't yet resolved how she was going to handle Phil. She knew the law clearly enough, but the law wouldn't help when she had to deal with him without her badge. Tod burst through the door, his eyes wide, his face flushed.

"Tory, they're here! A whole bunch of them in front of the hotel. There're vans and cars and everything!"

Though she felt more like swearing, she had to smile at him. He only forgot himself and called her Tory when he was desperately excited. And he was such a sweet boy, she mused, so full of dreams. Crossing to him, she dropped an arm over his shoulder. He no longer cringed.

"Let's go see," she said simply.

"Tory—Sheriff," Tod corrected himself, although the words all but tumbled over each other, "do you think that guy'll let me watch him make the movie? You know, the guy you had in jail."

"I know," Tory murmured as they stepped outside. "I imagine so," she answered absentmindedly.

The scene outside was so out of place in Friendly, it almost made Tory laugh. There were several vehicles in front of the hotel, and crowds of people. The mayor stood on the sidewalk, talking to everyone at once. Several of the people from California were looking around the town with expressions of curiosity and astonishment. They were being looked over with the same expressions by people from Friendly.

Different planets, Tory mused with a slight smile. Take me to your leader. When she spotted Phil, the smile faded.

He was dressed casually, as he had been on his first visit to town—no different than the members of his crew. And yet, there was a difference. He held the authority; there was no mistaking it. Even while apparently listening to the mayor, he was giving orders. And, Tory added thoughtfully, being obeyed. There seemed to be a certain friendliness between him and his crew, as well as an underlying respect. There was some laughter and a couple of shouts as equipment was unloaded, but the procedure was meticulously orderly. He watched over every detail.

"Wow," Tod said under his breath. "Look at all that

stuff. I bet they've got cameras in those boxes. Maybe I'll get a chance to look through one."

"Mmm." Tory saw Phil laugh and heard the sound of it drift to her across the street. Then he saw her.

His smile didn't fade but altered subtly. They assessed each other while his people milled and hers whispered. The assessment became a challenge with no words spoken. She stood very straight, her arm still casually draped around the boy's shoulders. Phil noticed the gesture even as he felt a stir that wasn't wholly pleasant. He ached, he discovered, baffled. Just looking at her made him ache. She looked cool, even remote, but her eyes were directed at his. He could see the small badge pinned to the gentle sweep of her breast. On the dry, sweltering day she was wine, potent and irresistible—and perhaps unwise. One of his crew addressed him twice before Phil heard him.

"What?" His eyes never left Tory's.

"Huffman's on the phone."

"I'll get back to him." Phil started across the street.

When Tory's arm stiffened, Tod glanced up at her in question. He saw that her eyes were fixed on the man walking toward them. He frowned, but when Tory's arm relaxed, so did he.

Phil stopped just short of the sidewalk so that their eyes were at the same level. "Sheriff."

"Kincaid," she said coolly.

Briefly he turned to the boy and smiled. "Hello, Tod. How are you?"

"Fine." The boy stared at him from under a thatch of tumbled hair. The fact that Phil had spoken to him, and remembered his name, made something move inside Tory. She pushed it away, reminding herself she couldn't afford too many good feelings toward Phil Kincaid. "Can I…" Tod began. He shifted nervously, then drew up his courage. "Do you think I could see some of that stuff?"

A grin flashed on Phil's face. "Sure. Go over and ask for Bicks. Tell him I said to show you a camera."

"Yeah?" Thrilled, he stared at Phil for a moment, then glanced up at Tory in question. When she smiled down at him, Phil watched the boy's heart leap to his eyes.

Uh-oh, he thought, seeing the slight flush creep into the boy's cheeks. Tory gave him a quick squeeze and the color deepened.

"Go ahead," she told him.

Phil watched the boy dash across the street before he turned his gaze back to Tory. "It seems you have another conquest. I have to admire his taste." When she stared at him blankly, he shook his head. "Good God, Tory, the kid's in love with you."

"Don't be ridiculous," she retorted. "He's a child."

"Not quite," he countered. "And certainly old enough to be infatuated with a beautiful woman." He grinned again, seeing her distress as her eyes darted after Tod. "I was a fourteen-year-old boy once myself."

Annoyed that he had pointed out something she'd been oblivious to, Tory glared at him. "But never as innocent as that one."

"No," he agreed easily, and stepped up on the sidewalk. She had to shift the angle of her chin to keep her eyes in line with his. "It's good to see you, Sheriff."

"Is it?" she returned lazily as she studied his face.

"Yes, I wondered if I'd imagined just how beautiful you were."

"You've brought quite a group with you," she commented, ignoring his statement. "There'll be more, I imagine."

"Some. I need some footage of the town, the countryside. The actors will be here in a couple of days."

Nodding, she leaned against a post. "You'll have to store your vehicles at Bestler's. If you have any plans to use a private residence or a store for filming, you'll have to make the arrangements individually. Hernandez's Bar is open until eleven on weeknights, one on Saturday. Consumption of alcohol on the streets is subject to a fifty-dollar fine. You're liable for any damage to private property. Whatever alterations you make for the filming will again have to be cleared individually. Anyone causing a disturbance in the hotel or on the streets after midnight will be fined and sentenced. As this is your show, Kincaid, I'll hold you personally responsible for keeping your people in line."

He listened to her rundown of the rules with the appearance of careful interest. "Have dinner with me."

She very nearly smiled. "Forget it." When she started to walk by him, he took her arm.

"Neither of us is likely to do that, are we?"

Tory didn't shake off his arm. It felt too good to be touched by him again. She did, however, give him a long, lazy look. "Phil, both of us have a job to do. Let's keep it simple."

"By all means." He wondered what would happen if he kissed her right then and there. It was what he wanted, he discovered, more than anything he had wanted in quite some time. It would also be unwise. "What if we call it a business dinner?"

Tory laughed. "Why don't we call it what it is?"

"Because then you wouldn't come, and I do want to talk to you."

The simplicity of his answer disconcerted her. "About what?"

"Several things." His fingers itched to move to her face, to feel the soft, satiny texture of her skin. He kept them loosely hooked around her arm. "Among them, my show and your town. Wouldn't it simplify matters for both of us if we understood each other and came to a few basic agreements?"

"Maybe."

"Have dinner with me in my room." When her brow arched, he continued lazily. "It's also my office for the time being," he reminded her. "I'd like to clear the air regarding my film. If we're going to argue, Sheriff, let's do it privately."

The *Sheriff* did it. It was both her title and her job. "All right," she agreed. "Seven o'clock."

"Fine." When she started to walk away, he stopped her. "Sheriff," he said with a quick grin, "leave the gun in the desk, okay? It'll kill my appetite."

She gave a snort of laughter. "I can handle you without it, Kincaid."

Tory frowned at the clothes hanging inside her closet. Even while she had been showering, she had considered putting on work clothes—and her badge—for her dinner with Phil. But that would have been petty, and pettiness wasn't her style. She ran a fingertip over an emerald-green silk dress. It was very simply cut, narrow, with a high neck that buttoned to the waist. Serviceable and attractive, she decided, slipping it off the hanger. Laying it across the bed, she shrugged out of her robe.

Outside, the streets were quiet. She hoped they stayed that way, as she'd put Merle in charge for the evening. People would be gathered in their homes, at the drugstore, at the bar, discussing the filming. That had been the main topic of the town for weeks, overriding the heat, the lack of rain and the Kramer twins. Tory smiled as she laced the front of her teddy. Yes, people needed their little entertainments, and this was the biggest thing to happen in Friendly in years. She was going to have to roll with it. To a point.

She slipped the dress over her head, feeling the silk slither on her skin. It had been a long time, she realized, since she had bothered about clothes. In Albuquerque she took a great deal of care about her appearance. A courtroom image was as important as an opening statement, particularly in a jury trial. People judged. Still, she was a woman who knew how to incorporate style with comfort.

The dress flattered her figure while giving her complete freedom of movement. Tory looked in the bureautop mirror to study her appearance. The mirror cut her off at just above the waist. She rose on her toes and turned to the side but was still frustrated with a partial view of herself. Well, she decided, letting her feet go flat again, it would just have to do.

She sprayed on her scent automatically, remembering too late Phil's comment on it. Tory frowned at the delicate bottle as she replaced it on the dresser. She could hardly go and scrub the perfume off now. With a shrug she sat on the bed to put on her shoes. The mattress creaked alarmingly. Handling Phil Kincaid was no problem, she told herself. That was half the reason she had agreed to have dinner with him. It was a matter of principle. She wasn't a woman to be seduced or charmed into submission, particularly by a man of Kincaid's reputation. Spoiled, she thought again, but with a tad too much affection for her liking. He'd grown up privileged, in a world of glitter and glamour. He expected everything to come his way, women included.

Tory had grown up respecting the value of a dollar in a world of ordinary people and day-to-day struggles. She, too, expected everything to come her way—after she'd arranged it. She left the room determined to come out on top in the anticipated encounter. She even began to look forward to it.

Phil's room was right next door. Though she knew he had seen to that small detail himself, Tory planned to make no mention of it. She gave a brisk knock and waited.

When he opened the door, the glib remark Phil had intended to make vanished from his brain. He remembered his own thoughts about seeing her in something silk and vivid and could only stare. *Exquisite.* It was the word that hammered inside his brain, but even that wouldn't come through his lips. He knew at that moment he'd have to have her or go through his life obsessed with the need to.

"Victoria," he managed after a long moment.

Though her pulse had begun to pound at the look in his eyes, at the husky way he had said her name, she gave him a brisk smile. "Phillip," she said very formally. "Shall I come in or eat out here?"

Phil snapped back. Stammering and staring wasn't going to get him very far. He took her hand to draw her inside, then locked the door, uncertain whether he was locking her in or the world out.

Tory glanced around the small, haphazardly furnished room. Phil had already managed to leave his mark on it. The bureau was stacked with papers. There was a notepad, scrawled in from margin to margin, a few stubby pencils and a two-way radio. The shades were drawn and the room was lit with candles. Tory lifted her brows at this, glancing toward the folding card table covered with the hotel's best linen. Two dishes were covered to keep in the heat while a bottle of wine was open. Strolling over, Tory lifted it to study the label.

"Château Haut-Brion Blanc," she murmured with a perfect accent. Still holding the bottle, she sent Phil a look. "You didn't pick this up at Mendleson's Liquors."

"I always take a few...amenities when I go on location."

Tilting her head, Tory set down the bottle. "And the candles?"

"Local drugstore," he told her blandly.

"Wine and candlelight," she mused. "For a business dinner?"

"Humor the director," he suggested, crossing over to pour out two glasses of wine. "We're always setting scenes. It's uncontrollable." Handing her a glass, he touched it with the rim of his own. "Sheriff, to a comfortable relationship."

"Association," she corrected, then drank. "Very nice," she approved. She let her eyes skim over him briefly. He wore casual slacks, impeccably tailored, with an open-collared cream-colored shirt that accented his lean torso. The candlelight picked up the deep tones of red in his hair. "You look more suited to your profession than when I first saw you," she commented.

"And you less to yours," he countered.

"Really?" Turning away, she wandered the tiny room. The small throw rug was worn thin in patches, the headboard of the bed scarred, the nightstand a bit unsteady. "How do you like the accommodations, Kincaid?"

"They'll do."

She laughed into her wine. "Wait until it gets hot."

"Isn't it?"

"Do the immortal words 'You ain't seen nothing yet' mean anything to you?"

He forced himself to keep his eyes from the movements of her body under the silk. "Want to see all the Hollywood riffraff melt away, Tory?"

Turning, she disconcerted him by giving him her dashing smile. "No, I'll wish you luck instead. After all, I invariably admire your finished product."

"If not what goes into making it."

"Perhaps not," she agreed. "What are you feeding me?"

He was silent for a moment, studying the eyes that laughed at him over the rim of a wineglass. "The menu is rather limited."

"Meat loaf?" she asked dubiously, knowing it was the hotel's specialty.

"God forbid. Chicken and dumplings."

Tory walked back to him. "In that case I'll stay." They sat, facing each other across the folding table. "Shall we get business out of the way, Kincaid, or will it interfere with your digestion?"

He laughed, then surprised her by reaching out to take one of her hands in both of his. "You're a hell of a woman, Tory. Why are you afraid to use my first name?"

She faltered a moment, but let her hand lay unresisting in his. Because it's too personal, she thought. "Afraid?" she countered.

"Reluctant?" he suggested, allowing his fingertip to trace the back of her hand.

"Immaterial." Gently she removed her hand from his. "I was told you'd be shooting here for about six weeks." She lifted the cover from her plate and set it aside. "Is that firm?"

"According to the guarantors," Phil muttered, taking another sip of wine.

"Guarantors?"

"Tyco, Inc., completion-bond company."

"Oh, yes." Tory toyed with her chicken. "I'd heard that was a new wave in Hollywood. They guarantee that the movie will be completed on time and within budget—or else they pay the overbudget costs. They can fire you, can't they?"

"Me, the producer, the stars, anyone," Phil agreed.

"Practical."

"Stifling," he returned, and stabbed into his chicken.

"From your viewpoint, I imagine," Tory reflected. "Still, as a business, it makes sense. Creative people often have to be shown certain...boundaries. Such as," she continued, "the ones I outlined this morning."

"And boundaries often have to be flexible. Such as," he said with a smile, "some night scenes we'll be shooting. I'm going to need your cooperation. The townspeople are welcome to watch any phase of the shoot, as long as they don't interfere, interrupt or get in the way. Also, some of the equipment being brought in is very expensive and very sensitive. We have security, but as sheriff, you may want to spread the word that it's off limits."

"Your equipment is your responsibility," she reminded him. "But I will issue a statement. Before you shoot your night scenes, you'll have to clear it through my office."

He gave her a long, hard look. "Why?"

"If you're planning on working in the middle of the night in the middle of town, I'll need prior confirmation. In that way I can keep disorder to a minimum."

"There'll be times I'll need the streets blocked off and cleared."

"Send me a memo," she said. "Dates, times. Friendly can't come to a stop to accommodate you."

"It's nearly there in any case."

"We don't have a fast lane." Irresistibly she sent him a grin. "As you discovered."

He gave her a mild glance. "I'd also like to use some of the locals for extras and walk-ons."

Tory rolled her eyes. "God, you are looking for trouble. Go ahead," she said with a shrug, "send out your casting call, but you'd better use everyone that answers it, one way or another."

As he'd already figured that one out for himself, Phil was unperturbed. "Interested?" he asked casually.

"Hmm?"

"Are you interested?"

Tory laughed as she held out her glass for more wine. "No."

Phil let the bottle hover a moment. "I'm serious, Tory. I'd like to put you on film."

"I haven't got the time or the inclination."

"You've got the looks and, I think, the talent."

She smiled, more amused than flattered. "Phil, I'm a lawyer. That's exactly what I want to be."

"Why?"

He saw immediately that the question had thrown her off balance. She stared at him a moment with the glass to her lips. "Because the law fascinates me," she said after a pause. "Because I respect it. Because I like to think that occasionally I have something to do with the process of justice. I worked hard to get into Harvard, and harder when I got there. It means something to me."

"Yet, you've given it up for six months."

"Not completely." She frowned at the steady flame of the candle. "Regardless, it's necessary. There'll still be cases to try when I go back."

"I'd like to see you in the courtroom," he murmured, watching the quiet light flicker in her eyes. "I bet you're fabulous."

"Outstanding," she agreed, smiling again. "The assistant D.A. hates me." She took another bite of chicken. "What about you? Why directing instead of acting?"

"It never appealed to me." Leaning back, Phil found himself curiously relaxed and stimulated. He felt he could look at her forever. Her fragrance, mixed with the scent of hot wax, was erotic, her voice soothing. "And I suppose I liked the idea of giving orders rather than taking them. With directing you can alter a scene, change a tone, set the pace for an entire story. An actor can only work with one character, no matter how complex it may be."

"You've never directed either of your parents." Tory let the words hang so that he could take them either as a statement or a question. When he smiled, the creases in his cheeks deepened so that she wondered how it would feel to run her fingers along them.

"No." He tipped more wine into his glass. "It might

make quite a splash, don't you think? The three of us together on one film. Even though they've been divorced
for over twenty-five years, they'd send the glossies into
a frenzy."

"You could do two separate films," she pointed out.

"True." He pondered over it a moment. "If the right
scripts came along…" Abruptly he shook his head. "I've
thought of it, even been approached a couple of times,
but I'm not sure it would be a wise move professionally or personally. They're quite a pair," he stated with
a grin. "Temperamental, explosive and probably two
of the best dramatic actors in the last fifty years. Both
of them wring the last drop of blood from a character."

"I've always admired them," Tory agreed. "Especially in the movies they made together. They put a lot
of chemistry on the screen."

"And off it," Phil murmured. "It always amazed me
that they managed to stay together for almost ten years.
Neither of them had that kind of longevity in their other
marriages. The problem was that they never stopped
competing. It gave them the spark on the screen and a
lot of problems at home. It's difficult to live with someone when you're afraid he or she might be just a little
better than you are."

"But you're very fond of them, aren't you?" She
watched his mobile brow lift in question. "It shows,"
she told him. "It's rather nice."

"Fond," he agreed. "Maybe a little wary. They're
formidable people, together or separately. I grew up
listening to lines being cued over breakfast and hearing producers torn to shreds at dinner. My father lived
each role. If he was playing a psychotic, I could expect
to find a crazed man in the bathroom."

"Obsession," Tory recalled, delighted. "1957."

"Very good," Phil approved. "Are you a fan?"

"Naturally. I got my first kiss watching Marshall Kincaid in *Endless Journey.*" She gave a throaty laugh. "The movie was the more memorable of the two."

"You were in diapers when that movie was made," Phil calculated.

"Ever heard of the late show?"

"Young girls," he stated, "should be in bed at that hour."

Tory suppressed a laugh. Resting her elbows on the table, she set her chin on cupped hands. "And young boys?"

"Would stay out of trouble," he finished.

"The hell they would," Tory countered, chuckling. "As I recall, your...exploits started at a tender age. What was the name of that actress you were involved with when you were sixteen? She was in her twenties as I remember, and—"

"More wine?" Phil interrupted, filling her glass before she could answer.

"Then there was the daughter of that comedian."

"We were like cousins."

"Really?" Tory drew out the word with a doubtful look. "And the dancer...ah, Nicki Clark."

"Great moves," Phil remembered, then grinned at her. "You seem to be more up on my...exploits than I am. Did you spend all your free time at Harvard reading movie magazines?"

"My roommate did," Tory confessed. "She was a drama major. I see her on a commercial now and again. And then I knew someone in the business. Your name's dropped quite a bit at parties."

"The actor you dated."

"Total recall," Tory murmured, a bit uncomfortable. "You amaze me."

"Tool of the trade. What was his name?"

Tory picked up her wine, studying it for a moment. "Chad Billings."

"Billings?" Surprised and not altogether pleased, Phil frowned at her. "A second-rate leech, Tory. I wouldn't think him your style."

"No?" She shot him a direct look. "He was diverting and…educational."

"And married."

"Judgmental, Phil?" she countered, then gave a shrug. "He was in between victims at the time."

"Aptly put," Phil murmured. "If you got your view of the industry through him, I'm surprised you didn't put up roadblocks to keep us out."

"It was a thought," she told him, but smiled again. "I'm not a complete fool, you know."

But Phil continued to frown at her, studying her intensely. He was more upset at thinking of her with Billings than he should have been. "Did he hurt you?" he demanded abruptly.

Surprised, Tory stared at him. "No," she said slowly. "Although I suppose he might have if I'd allowed it. We didn't see each other exclusively or for very long. I was in L.A. on a case at the time."

"Why Albuquerque?" Phil wondered aloud. "Lou was impressed with you, and he's not easily impressed. Why aren't you in some glass and leather office in New York?"

"I hate traffic." Tory sat back now, swirling the wine and relaxing. "And I don't rush."

"L.A.?"

"I don't play tennis."

He laughed, appreciating her more each moment. "I love the way you boil things down, Tory. What do you do when you're not upholding the law?"

"As I please, mostly. Sports and hobbies are too demanding." She tossed back her hair. "I like to sleep."

"You forget, I've seen you ride."

"That's different." The wine had mellowed her mood. She didn't notice that the candles were growing low and the hour late. "It relaxes me. Clears my head."

"Why do you live in a room in the hotel when you have a house right outside of town?" Her fingers tightened on the stem of the wineglass only slightly: He was an observant man.

"It's simpler."

Leave this one alone for a while, he warned himself. It's a very tender spot.

"And what do you do when you're not making a major statement on film?" she asked, forcing her hand to relax.

Phil accepted her change of subject without question. "Read scripts…watch movies."

"Go to parties," Tory added sagely.

"That too. It's all part of the game."

"Isn't it difficult sometimes, living in a town where so much is pretense? Even considering the business end of your profession, you have to deal with the lunacy, the make-believe, even the desperation. How do you separate the truth from the fantasy?"

"How do you in your profession?" he countered.

Tory thought for a moment, then nodded. "Touché." Rising, she wandered to the window. She pushed aside the shade, surprised to see that the sun had gone down. A few red streaks hovered over the horizon, but in the east the sky was dark. A few early stars were already out. Phil sat where he was, watched her and wanted her.

"There's Merle making his rounds," Tory said with a smile in her voice. "He's got his official expression on. I imagine he's hoping to be discovered. If he can't be a tough lawman from the nineteenth century, he'd settle for playing one." A car pulled into town, stopping in front of the pool hall with a sharp squeal of brakes. "Oh, God, it's the twins." She sighed, watching Merle turn and stride in their direction. "There's been no peace in town since that pair got their licenses. I suppose I'd better go down and see that they stay in line."

"Can't Merle handle a couple of kids?"

Tory's laugh was full of wicked appreciation. "You don't know the Kramers. There's Merle," she went on, "giving them basic lecture number twenty-two."

"Did they wash all of Hollister's windows?" Phil asked as he rose to join her.

Tory turned her head, surprised. "How did you know about that?"

"Tod told me." He peeked through the window, finding he wanted a look at the infamous twins. They seemed harmless enough from a distance, and disconcertingly alike. "Which one's Zac?"

"Ah…on the right, I think. Maybe," she added with a shake of her head. "Why?"

"'Zac Kramer don't hold with no woman sheriff,'" he quoted.

Tory grinned up at him. "Is that so?"

"Just so." Hardly aware he did so, Phil reached for her hair. "Obviously he's not a very perceptive boy."

"Perceptive enough to wash Mr. Hollister's windows," Tory corrected, amused by the memory. "And to call me a foxy chick only under his breath when he thought I couldn't hear. Of course, that could have been Zeke."

"'Foxy chick'?" Phil repeated.

"Yes," Tory returned with mock hauteur. "'A *very* foxy chick.' It was his ultimate compliment."

"Your head's easily turned," he decided. "What if I told you that you had a face that belongs in a Raphael painting?"

Tory's eyes lit with humor. "I'd say you're reaching."

"And hair," he said with a subtle change in his voice. "Hair that reminds me of night…a hot summer night that keeps you awake, and thinking, and wanting." He plunged both hands into it, letting his fingers tangle. The shade snapped back into place, cutting them off from the outside.

"Phil," Tory began, unprepared for the suddenness of desire that rose in both of them.

"And skin," he murmured, not even hearing her, "that makes me think of satin sheets and tastes like something forbidden." He touched his mouth to her cheek, allowing the tip of his tongue to brush over her. "Tory." She felt her name whisper along her skin and thrilled to it. She had her hands curled tightly around his arms, but not in protest. "Do you know how often I've thought of you these past weeks?"

"No." She didn't want to resist. She wanted to feel that wild sweep of pleasure that came from the press of his mouth on hers. "No," she said again, and slid her arms around his neck.

"Too much," he murmured, then swore. "Too damn much." And his mouth took her waiting one.

The passion was immediate, frenetic. It ruled both of them. Each of them sought the mindless excitement they had known briefly weeks before. Tory had thought she had intensified the sensation in her mind as the days had passed. Now she realized she had lessened it. This sort of fervor couldn't be imagined or described. It had to be experienced. Everything inside her seemed to speed up—her blood, her heart, her brain. And all sensation, all emotion, seemed to be centered in her mouth. The taste of him exploded on her tongue, shooting through her until she was so full of him, she could no longer separate herself. With a moan she tilted her head back, inviting him to plunge deeper into her mouth. But he wanted more.

Her hair fell straight behind her, leaving her neck vulnerable. Surrendering to a desperate hunger, he savaged it with kisses. Tory made a sound that was mixed pain and pleasure. Her scent seemed focused there, heated by the pulse at her throat. It drove him nearer the edge. He dragged at the silk-covered buttons, impatient to find the hidden skin, the secret skin that had preyed on his mind. The groan sounded in his throat as he slipped his hand beneath the thin teddy and found her.

She was firm, and slender enough to fit his palm. Her heartbeat pounded against it. Tory turned her head, but only to urge him to give the neglected side of her neck attention. With her hands in his hair she pulled him back to her. His hands searched everywhere with a sort of wild reverence, exploring, lingering, possessing. She could feel his murmurs as his lips played over her skin, although she could barely hear them and understood them not at all. The room seemed to grow closer and hotter, so that she longed to be rid of her clothes and find relief…and delight.

Then he pulled her close so that their bodies pressed urgently. Their mouths met with fiery demand. It seemed the storm had just begun. Again and again they drew from each other until they were both breathless. Though he had fully intended to end the evening with Tory in his bed, Phil hadn't expected to be desperate. He hadn't known that all control could be so easily lost. The warm curves of a woman should bring easy pleasure, not this trembling pain. A kiss was a prelude, not an all-consuming force. He knew only that all of him, much more than his body, was crying out for her. Whatever was happening to him was beyond his power to stop. And she was the only answer he had.

"God, Tory." He took his mouth on a wild journey of her face, then returned to her lips. "Come to bed. For God's sake, come to bed. I want you."

She felt as though she were standing on the edge of a cliff. The plunge had never seemed more tempting—or more dangerous. It would be so easy, so easy, just to lean forward and fly. But the fall… She fought for sanity through a brain clouded with the knowledge of one man. It was much too soon to take the step.

"Phil." Shaken, she drew away from him to lean against the windowsill. "I… No," she managed, lifting both hands to her temples. He drew her back against him.

"Yes," he corrected, then crushed his lips to hers again. Her mouth yielded irresistibly. "You can't pretend you don't want me as much as I want you."

"No." She let her head rest on his shoulder a moment before she pushed out of his arms. "I can't," she agreed in a voice thickened with passion. "But I don't do everything I want. That's one of the basic differences between us."

His eyes flicked briefly down to the unbuttoned dress. "We also seem to have something important in common. This doesn't happen every time—between every man and woman."

"No." Carefully she began to do up her buttons. "It shouldn't have happened between us. I didn't intend it to."

"I did," he admitted. "But not quite this way."

Her eyes lifted to his. She understood perfectly. This had been more intense than either of them had bargained for. "It's going to be a long summer, Phil," she murmured.

"We're going to be together sooner or later, Tory. We both know it." He needed something to balance him. Going to the table, he poured out another glass of wine. He drank, drank again, then looked at her. "I have no intention of backing off."

She nodded, accepting. But she didn't like the way her hands were shaking. "I'm not ready."

"I can be a patient man when necessary." He wanted nothing more than to pull her to the bed and take what they both needed. Instead he took out a cigarette and reminded himself he was a civilized man.

Tory drew herself up straight. "Let's both concentrate on our jobs, shall we?" she said coolly. She wanted to get out, but she didn't want to retreat. "I'll see you around, Kincaid."

"Damn right you will," he murmured as she headed for the door.

She flicked the lock off, then turned to him with a half smile. "Keep out of trouble," she ordered, closing the door behind her.

Chapter 6

Phil sat beside the cameraman on the Tulip crane. "Boom up." At his order the crane operator took them seventeen feet above the town of Friendly. It was just dawn. He'd arranged to have everyone off the streets, although there was a crowd of onlookers behind the crane and equipment. All entrances to town had been blocked off on the off chance that someone might drive through. He wanted desolation and the tired beginning of a new day.

Glancing down, he saw that Bicks was checking the lighting and angles. Brutes, the big spotlights, were set to give daylight balance. He knew, to an inch, where he wanted the shadows to fall. For this shot Phil would act as assistant cameraman, pulling the focus himself.

Phil turned his attention back to the street. He knew what he wanted, and he wanted to capture it as the sun

rose, with as much natural light as possible. He looked
through the lens and set the shot himself. The crane was
set on tracks. He would have the cameraman begin with
a wide shot of the horizon and the rising sun, then dolly
back to take in the entire main street of Friendly. No
soft focus there, just harsh reality. He wanted to pick
up the dust on the storefront windows. Satisfied with
what he saw through the camera lens, Phil marked the
angle with tape, then nodded to his assistant director.

"Quiet on the set."

"New Chance, scene three, take one."

"Roll it," Phil ordered, then waited. With his eyes
narrowed, he could visualize what his cameraman saw
through the lens. The light was good. Perfect. They'd
have to get it in three takes or less or else they'd have
to beef it up with gels and filters. That wasn't what he
wanted here. He felt the crane roll backward slowly on
cue. A straight shot, no panning right to left. They'd
take in the heart of the town in one long shot. Chipped
paint, sagging wood, torn screens. Later they'd cut in
the scene of the leading man walking in from the train
station. He was coming home, Phil mused, because
there was no place else to go. And he found it, exactly
as he had left it twenty years before.

"Cut." The noise on the ground started immediately.
"I want another take. Same speed."

At the back of the crowd Tory watched. She wasn't
thrilled with being up at dawn. Both her sense of duty
and her curiosity had brought her. Phil had been perfectly clear about anyone peeking through windows
during this shot. He wanted emptiness. She told herself she'd come to keep her people out of mischief, but

when it was all said and done, she had wanted to see Phil at work.

He was very commanding and totally at ease with it, but, she reasoned as she stuck her hands in her back pockets, it didn't seem so hard. Moving a little to the side, she tried to see the scene he was imagining. The town looked tired, she decided, and a little reluctant to face the new day. Though the horizon was touched with golds and pinks, a gray haze lay over the street and buildings.

It was the first time he had shot anything there. For the past week he had been filming landscapes. Tory had stayed in Friendly, sending Merle out occasionally to check on things. It had kept him happy and had given Tory the distance she wanted. As her deputy came back brimming with reports and enthusiasm, she was kept abreast in any case.

But today the urge to see for herself had been too strong to resist. It had been several days—and several long nights—since their evening together. She had managed to keep herself busier than necessary in order to avoid him. But Tory wasn't a woman to avoid a problem for long. Phil Kincaid was still a problem.

Apparently satisfied, Phil ordered the operator to lower the crane. People buzzed around Tory like bees. A few children complained about being sent off to school. Spotting Tod, Tory smiled and waved him over.

"Isn't it neat?" he demanded the moment he was beside her. "I wanted to go up in it," he continued, indicating the crane, "but Mr. Kincaid said something about insurance. Steve let me see his camera though, even let me take some pictures. It's a thirty-five millimeter with all kinds of lenses."

"Steve?"

"The guy who was sitting next to Mr. Kincaid. He's the cameraman." Tod glanced over, watching Phil in a discussion with his cameraman and several members of the crew. "Isn't he something?"

"Steve?" Tory repeated, smiling at Tod's pleasure.

"Well, yeah, but I meant Mr. Kincaid." Shaking his head, he let out a long breath. "He's awful smart. You should hear some of the words he uses. And boy, when he says so, everybody jumps."

"Do they?" Tory murmured, frowning over at the man under discussion.

"You bet," Tod confirmed. "And I heard Mr. Bicks say to Steve that he'd rather work with Mr. Kincaid than anybody. He's a tough sonofa—" Catching himself, Tod broke off and flushed. "I mean, he said he was tough, but the best there was."

As she watched, Phil was pointing, using one hand and then the other as he outlined his needs for the next shot. It was very clear that he knew what he wanted and that he'd get it. She could study him now. He was too involved to notice her or the crowd of people who stared and mumbled behind the barrier of equipment.

He wore jeans and a pale blue T-shirt with scuffed sneakers. Hanging from his belt was a case that held sunglasses and another for a two-way radio. He was very intense, she noted, when working. There was none of the careless humor in his eyes. He talked quickly, punctuating the words with hand gestures. Once or twice he interrupted what he was saying to call out another order to the grips who were setting up light stands.

A perfectionist, she concluded, and realized it shouldn't surprise her. His movies projected the intimate care she was now seeing firsthand. A stocky man in a fielder's cap lumbered up to him, talking over an enormous wad of gum.

"That's Mr. Bicks," Tod murmured reverently. "The cinematographer. He's got two Oscars and owns part of a boxer."

Whatever he was saying, Phil listened carefully, then simply shook his head. Bicks argued another moment, shrugged, then gave Phil what appeared to be a solid punch on the shoulder before he walked away. A tough sonofabitch, Tory mused. Apparently so.

Turning to Tod, she mussed his hair absently. "You'd better get to school."

"Aw, but..."

She lifted her brow, effectively cutting off his excuse. "It's nearly time for summer vacation. They'll still be here."

He mumbled a protest, but she caught the look in his eye as he gazed up at her. Uh-oh, she thought, just as Phil had. Why hadn't she seen this coming? She was going to have to be careful to be gentle while pointing the boy in another direction. A teenage crush was nothing to smile at and brush away.

"I'll come by after school," he said, beaming up at her. Before she could respond, he was dashing off, leaving her gnawing on her bottom lip and worrying about him.

"Sheriff."

Tory whirled sharply and found herself facing Phil. He smiled slowly, setting the sunglasses in front of his eyes. It annoyed her that she had to strain to see his expression through the tinted glass. "Kincaid," she responded. "How's it going?"

"Good. Your people are very cooperative."

"And yours," she said. "So far."

He grinned at that. "We're expecting the cast this afternoon. The location manager's cleared it with you about parking the trailers and so forth?"

"She's very efficient," Tory agreed. "Are you getting what you want?"

He took a moment to answer. "With regard to the film, yes, so far." Casually he reached down to run a finger over her badge. "You've been busy the last few days."

"So have you."

"Not that busy. I've left messages for you."

"I know."

"When are you going to see me?"

She lifted both brows. "I'm seeing you right now." He took a step closer and cupped the back of her neck in his hand. "Phil—"

"Soon," he said quietly.

Though she could feel the texture of each of his fingers on the back of her neck, she gave him a cool look. "Kincaid, create your scenes on the other side of the camera. Accosting a peace officer will land you back in that cell. You'll find it difficult to direct from there."

"Oh, I'm going to accost you," he warned under his breath. "With or without that damn badge, Victoria. Think about it."

She didn't step back or remove his hand, although she knew several pair of curious eyes were on them. "I'll give it a few minutes," she promised dryly.

Only the tensing of his fingers on her neck revealed his annoyance. She thought he was about to release her and relaxed. His mouth was on hers so quickly, she could only stand in shock. Before she could think to push him away, he set her free. Her eyes were sharply green and furious when he grinned down at her.

"See you, Sheriff," he said cheerfully, and sauntered back to his crew.

For the better part of the day Tory stayed in her office and fumed. Now and again Phil's voice carried through her open window as he called out instructions. She knew they were doing pans of the town and stayed away from the window. She had work to do, she reminded herself. And in any case she had no interest in the filming. It was understandable that the townspeople would stand around and gawk, but she had better things to do.

I should have hauled him in, she thought, scowling down at her legal pad. I should have hauled him in then and there. And she would have if it wouldn't have given him too much importance. He'd better watch his step, Tory decided. One wrong move and she was going to come down on him hard. She picked up her coffee and gulped it down with a grimace. It was cold. Swearing, she rose to pour a fresh cup.

Through the screen in the window she could see quite a bit of activity and hear a flood of conversation interrupted when the filming was in progress. It was past noon and hot as the devil. Phil had been working straight through for hours. With a grudging respect she admitted that he didn't take his job lightly. Going back to her desk, Tory concentrated on her own.

She hardly noticed that two hours had passed when Merle came bursting into the office. Hot, tired and annoyed with having her concentration broken, she opened her mouth to snap at him, but he exploded with enthusiasm before she had the chance.

"Tory, they're here!"

"Terrific," she mumbled, turning to her notes again. "Who?"

"The actors. Came from the airport in limousines. Long, black limousines. There are a half dozen of those Winnebagos set up outside of town for dressing rooms and stuff. You should see inside them. They've got telephones and TVs and everything."

She lifted her head. "Been busy, Merle T.?" she asked languidly, but he was too excited to notice.

"Sam Dressler," he went on, pacing back and forth with a clatter of boots. "Sam Dressler, right here in Friendly. I guess I've seen every movie he's ever made. He shook my hand," he added, staring down at his own palm, awed. "Thought I was the sheriff." He sent Tory a quick look. "'Course I told him I was the deputy."

"Of course," she agreed, amused now. It was never possible for her to stay annoyed with Merle. "How'd he look?"

"Just like you'd think," he told her with a puzzled shake of his head. "All tanned and tough, with a diamond on his finger fit to blind you. Signed autographs for everybody who wanted one."

Unable to resist, Tory asked, "Did you get one?"

"Sure I did." He grinned and pulled out his ticket book. "It was the only thing I had handy."

"Very resourceful." She glanced at the bold signature Merle held out for her. At the other end of the page were some elegant looping lines. "Marlie Summers," Tory read. She recalled a film from the year before, and the actress's pouting sexuality.

"She's about the prettiest thing I ever saw," Merle murmured.

Coming from anyone else, Tory would have given

the remark no notice. In this case, however, her eyes shot up and locked on Merle's. What she saw evoked in her a feeling of distress similar to what she had experienced with Tod. "Really?" she said carefully.

"She's just a little thing," Merle continued, gazing down at the autograph. "All pink and blond. Just like something in a store window. She's got big blue eyes and the longest lashes..." He trailed off, tucking the book back in his pocket.

Growing more disturbed, Tory told herself not to be silly. No Hollywood princess was going to look twice at Merle T. Johnson. "Well," she began casually, "I wonder what her part is."

"She's going to tell me all about it tonight," Merle stated, adjusting the brim of his hat.

"What?" It came out in a quick squeak.

Grinning, Merle gave his hat a final pat, then stroked his struggling mustache. "We've got a date." He strode out jauntily, leaving Tory staring with her mouth open.

"A date?" she asked the empty office. Before she could react, the phone beside her shrilled. Picking it up, she barked into it, "What is it?"

A bit flustered by the greeting, the mayor stammered. "Tory—Sheriff Ashton, this is Mayor Toomey."

"Yes, Bud." Her tone was still brusque as she stared at the door Merle had shut behind him.

"I'd like you to come over to the office, Sheriff. I have several members of the cast here." His voice rang with importance again. "Mr. Kincaid thought it might be a good idea for you to meet them."

"Members of the cast," she repeated, thinking of Marlie Summers. "I'd love to," she said dangerously, then hung up on the mayor's reply.

Her thoughts were dark as she crossed the street. No Hollywood tootsie was going to break Merle's heart while she was around. She was going to make that clear as soon as possible. She breezed into the hotel, giving several members of Phil's crew a potent stare as they loitered in the lobby. Bicks doffed his fielder's cap and grinned at her.

"Sheriff."

Tory sent him a mild glance and a nod as she sauntered through to the office. Behind her back he rolled his eyes to the ceiling, placing the cap over his heart. A few remarks were made about the advantages of breaking the law in Friendly while Tory disappeared into a side door.

The tiny office was packed, the window air-conditioning unit spitting hopefully. Eyes turned to her. Tory gave the group a brief scan. Marlie was sitting on the arm of Phil's chair, dressed in pink slacks and a frilled halter. Her enviable curves were displayed to perfection. Her hair was tousled appealingly around a piquant face accented with mink lashes and candy-pink lipstick. She looked younger than Tory had expected, almost like a high school girl ready to be taken out for an ice-cream soda. Tory met the baby-blue eyes directly, and with an expression that made Phil grin. He thought mistakenly that she might be a bit jealous.

"Sheriff." The mayor bustled over to her, prepared to act as host. "This is quite an honor for Friendly," he began, in his best politician's voice. "I'm sure you recognize Mr. Dressler."

Tory extended her hand to the man who approached her. "Sheriff." His voice was rich, the cadence mellow as he clasped her hand in both of his. She was a bit surprised to find them callused. "This is unexpected," he murmured while his eyes roamed her face thoroughly. "And delightful."

"Mr. Dressler, I admire your work." The smile was easy because the words were true.

"Sam, please." His brandy voice had only darkened attractively with age, losing none of its resonance. "We get to be a close little family on location shoots. Victoria, isn't it?"

"Yes." She found herself inclined to like him and gave him another smile.

"Bud, here, is making us all quite comfortable," he went on, clapping the mayor on the shoulder. "Will you join us in a drink?"

"Ginger ale's fine, Bud."

"The sheriff's on duty." Hearing Phil's voice, Tory turned, her head only, and glanced at him. "You'll find she takes her work very seriously." He touched Marlie's creamy bare shoulder. "Victoria Ashton, Marlie Summers."

"Sheriff." Marlie smiled her dazzling smile. The tiniest hint of a dimple peeked at the corner of her mouth. "Phil said you were unusual. It looks like he's right again."

"Really?" Accepting the cold drink Bud handed her, Tory assessed the actress over the rim. Marlie, accustomed to long looks and feminine coolness, met the stare straight on.

"Really," Marlie agreed. "I met your deputy a little while ago."

"So I heard."

So the wind blows in that direction, Marlie mused as she sipped from her own iced sangria. Sensing tension and wanting to keep things smooth, Bud hurried on with the rest of the introductions.

The cast ranged from ingenues to veterans—a girl Tory recognized from a few commercials; an ancient-looking man she remembered from the vague black-and-white movies on late-night television; a glitzy actor in his twenties, suited for heartthrobs and posters. Tory managed to be pleasant, stayed long enough to satisfy the mayor, then slipped away. She'd no more than stepped outside when she felt an arm on her shoulder.

"Don't you like parties, Sheriff?"

Taking her time, she turned to face Phil. "Not when I'm on duty." Though she knew he'd worked in the sun all day, he didn't look tired but exhilarated. His shirt was streaked with sweat, his hair curling damply over his ears, but there was no sign of fatigue on his face. It's the pressure that feeds him, she realized. Again she was drawn to him, no less than when they had been alone in his room. "You've put in a long day," she murmured.

He caught her hair in his hand. "So have you. Why don't we go for a drive?"

Tory shook her head. "No, I have things to do." Wanting to steer away from the subject, she turned to what had been uppermost on her mind. "Your Marlie made quite an impression on Merle."

Phil gave a quick laugh. "Marlie usually does."

"Not on Merle," Tory said so seriously that he sobered.

"He's a big boy, Tory."

"A boy," she agreed significantly. "He's never seen anything like your friend in there. I won't let him get hurt."

Phil let out a deep breath. "Your duties as sheriff

include advice to the lovelorn? Leave him alone," he ordered before she could retort. "You treat him as though he were a silly puppy who doesn't respond to training."

She took a step back at that. "No, I don't," she disagreed, sincerely shaken by the idea. "He's a sweet boy who—"

"Man," Phil corrected quietly. "He's a man, Tory. Cut the apron strings."

"I don't know what you're talking about," she snapped.

"You damn well do," he corrected. "You can't keep him under your wing the way you do with Tod."

"I've known Merle all my life," she said in a low voice. "Just keep Cotton Candy in line, Kincaid."

"Always so sure of yourself, aren't you?"

Her color drained instantly, alarmingly. For a moment Phil stared at her in speechless wonder. He'd never expected to see that kind of pain in her eyes. Instinctively he reached out for her. "Tory?"

"No." She lifted a hand to ward him off. "Just—leave me alone." Turning away, she walked across the street and climbed into her car. With an oath Phil started to go back into the hotel, then swore again and backtracked. Tory was already on her way north.

Her thoughts were in turmoil as she drove. Too much was happening. She squeezed her eyes shut briefly. Why should that throw her now? she wondered. She'd always been able to take things in stride, handle them at her own pace. Now she had a deep-seated urge just to keep driving, just to keep going. So many people wanted things from her, expected things. Including, she admitted, herself. It was all closing in suddenly. She needed someone to talk to. But the only one who had ever fit that job was gone.

God, she wasn't sure of herself. Why did everyone say so? Sometimes it was so hard to be responsible, to *feel* responsible. Tod, Merle, the mayor, the Kramers, Mr. Hollister. Her mother. She just wanted peace—enough time to work out what was happening in her own life. Her feelings for Phil were closing in on her. Pulling the car to a halt, Tory realized it was those feelings that were causing her—a woman who had always considered herself calm—to be tense. Piled on top of it were problems that had to come first. She'd learned that from her father.

Glancing up, she saw she had driven to the cemetery without even being aware of it. She let out a long breath, resting her forehead against the steering wheel. It was time she went there, time she came to terms with what she had closed her mind to since that night in the hospital. Climbing out of the car, Tory walked across the dry grass to her father's grave.

Odd that there'd been a breeze here, she mused, looking at the sky, the distant mountains, the long stretches of nothing. She looked at anything but what was at her feet. There should be some shade, she thought, and cupped her elbows in her palms. Someone should plant some trees. I should have brought some flowers, she thought suddenly, then looked down.

WILLIAM H. ASHTON

She hadn't seen the gravestone before—hadn't been back to the cemetery since the day of the funeral. Now a quiet moan slipped through her lips. "Oh, Dad."

It isn't right, she thought with a furious shake of her head. It just isn't right. How can he be down there in the dark when he always loved the sun? "Oh, no," she murmured again. I don't know what to do, she thought silently, pleading with him. I don't know how to deal with it all. I still need you. Pressing a palm on her forehead, she fought back tears.

Phil pulled up behind her car, then got out quietly. She looked very alone and lost standing among the headstones. His first instinct was to go to her, but he suppressed it. This was private for her. Her father, he thought, looking toward the grave at which Tory stared. He stood by a low wrought-iron gate at the edge of the cemetery and waited.

There was so much she needed to talk about, so much she still needed to say. But there was no more time. He'd been taken too suddenly. Unfair, she thought again on a wave of desolate fury. He had been so young and so good.

"I miss you so much," she whispered. "All those long talks and quiet evenings on the porch. You'd smoke those awful cigars outside so that the smell wouldn't get in the curtains and irritate Mother. I was always so proud of you. This badge doesn't suit me," she continued softly, lifting her hand to it. "It's the law books and the courtroom that I understand. I don't want to make a mistake while I'm wearing it, because it's yours." Her fingers tightened around it. All at once she felt painfully alone, helpless, empty. Even the anger had slipped away unnoticed. And yet the acceptance she tried to feel was blocked behind a grief she refused to release. If she cried, didn't it mean she'd taken the first step away?

Wearily she stared down at the name carved into the granite. "I don't want you to be dead," she whispered. "And I hate it because I can't change it."

When she turned away from the grave, her face was grim. She walked slowly but was halfway across the small cemetery before she saw Phil. Tory stopped and stared at him. Her mind went blank, leaving her with only feelings. He went to her.

For a moment they stood face-to-face. He saw her lips tremble open as if she were about to speak, but she only shook her head helplessly. Without a word he gathered her close. The shock of grief that hit her was stronger than anything that had come before. She trembled first, then clutched at him.

"Oh, Phil, I can't bear it." Burying her face against his shoulder, Tory wept for the first time since her father's death.

In silence he held her, overwhelmed with a tenderness he'd felt for no one before. Her sobbing was raw and passionate. He stroked her hair, offering comfort without words. Her grief poured out in waves that seemed to stagger her and made him hurt for her to a degree that was oddly intimate. He thought he could feel what she felt, and held her tighter, waiting for the first throes to pass.

At length her weeping quieted, lessening to trembles that were somehow more poignant than the passion. She kept her face pressed against his shoulder, relying on his strength when her own evaporated. Light-headed and curiously relieved, she allowed him to lead her to a small stone bench. He kept her close to his side when they sat, his arm protectively around her.

"Can you talk about it?" he asked softly.

Tory let out a long, shuddering sigh. From where they sat she could see the headstone clearly. "I loved him," she murmured. "My mother says too much." Her throat felt dry and abused when she swallowed. "He was everything good. He taught me not just right and wrong but all the shades in between." Closing her eyes, she let her head rest on Phil's shoulder. "He always knew the right thing. It was something innate and effortless. People knew they could depend on him, that he'd make it right. I depended on him, even in college, in Albuquerque—I knew he was there if I needed him."

He kissed her temple in a gesture of simple understanding. "How did he die?"

Feeling a shudder run through her, Phil drew her closer still. "He had a massive stroke. There was no warning. He'd never even been sick that I can remember. When I got here, he was in a coma. Everything…" She faltered, searching for the strength to continue. With his free hand Phil covered hers. "Everything seemed to go wrong at once. His heart just…stopped." She ended in a whisper, lacing her fingers through his. "They put him on a respirator. For weeks there was nothing but that damn machine. Then my mother told them to turn it off."

Phil let the silence grow, following her gaze toward the headstone. "It must have been hard for her."

"No." The word was low and flat. "She never wavered, never cried. My mother's a very decisive woman," she added bitterly. "And she made the decision alone. She told me after it was already done."

"Tory." Phil turned her to face him. She looked pale, bright-eyed and achingly weary. Something seemed to tear inside him. "I can't tell you the right or wrong of it, because there really isn't any. But I do know there comes a time when everyone has to face something that seems impossible to accept."

"If only I could have seen it was done for love and not...expediency." Shutting her eyes, she shook her head. "Hold me again." He drew her gently into his arms. "That last night at the hospital was so ugly between my mother and me. He would have hated that. I couldn't stop it," she said with a sigh. "I still can't."

"Time." He kissed the top of her head. "I know how trite that sounds, but there's nothing else but time."

She remained silent, accepting his comfort, drawing strength from it. If she had been able to think logically, Tory would have found it inconsistent with their relationship thus far that she could share her intimate feelings with him. At the moment she trusted Phil implicitly.

"Once in a while, back there," she murmured, "I panic."

It surprised him enough to draw her back and study her face again. "You?"

"Everyone thinks because I'm Will Ashton's daughter, I'll take care of whatever comes up. There're so many variables to right and wrong."

"You're very good at your job."

"I'm a good lawyer," she began.

"And a good sheriff," he interrupted. Tilting her chin up, he smiled at her. "That's from someone who's been on the wrong side of your bars." Gently he brushed the hair from her cheeks. They were warm and still damp. "And don't expect to hear me say it in public."

Laughing, she pressed her cheek to his. "Phil, you can be a very nice man."

"Surprised?"

"Maybe," she murmured. With a sigh she gave him one last squeeze, then drew away. "I've got work to do."

He stopped her from rising by taking her hands again. "Tory, do you know how little space you give yourself?"

"Yes." She disconcerted him by bringing his hand to her lips. "These six months are for him. It's very important to me."

Standing as she did, Phil cupped her face in his hands. She seemed to him very fragile, very vulnerable, suddenly. His need to look out for her was strong. "Let me drive you back. We can send someone for your car."

"No, I'm all right. Better." She brushed her lips over his. "I appreciate this. There hasn't been anyone I could talk to."

His eyes became very intense. "Would you come to me if you needed me?"

She didn't answer immediately, knowing the question was more complex than the simple words. "I don't know," she said at length.

Phil let her go, then watched her walk away.

Chapter 7

The camera came in tight on Sam and Marlie. Phil wanted the contrast of youth and age, of dissatisfaction and acceptance. It was a key scene, loaded with tension and restrained sexuality. They were using Hernandez's Bar, where the character Marlie portrayed worked as a waitress. Phil had made almost no alterations in the room. The bar was scarred, the mirror behind it cracked near the bottom. It smelled of sweat and stale liquor. He intended to transmit the scent itself onto film.

The windows were covered with neutral-density paper to block off the stream of the sun. It trapped the stale air in the room. The lights were almost unbearably hot, so that he needed no assistance from makeup to add beads of sweat to Sam's face. It was the sixth take, and the mood was growing edgy.

Sam blew his lines and swore ripely.

"Cut." Struggling with his temper, Phil wiped his forearm over his brow. With some actors a few furious words worked wonders. With Dressler, Phil knew, they would only cause more delays.

"Look, Phil—" Sam tore off the battered Stetson he wore and tossed it aside "—this isn't working."

"I know. Cut the lights," he ordered. "Get Mr. Dressler a beer." He addressed this to the man he had hired to see to Sam's needs on the location shoot. The individual attention had been Phil's way of handling Dressler and thus far had had its benefits. "Sit down for a while, Sam," he suggested. "We'll cool off." He waited until Sam was seated at a rear table with a por-table fan and a beer before he plucked a can from the cooler himself.

"Hot work," Marlie commented, leaning against the bar.

Glancing over, Phil noted the line of sweat that ran down the front of her snug blouse. He passed her the can of beer. "You're doing fine."

"It's a hell of a part," she said before she took a deep drink. "I've been waiting for one like this for a long time."

"The next take," Phil began, narrowing his eyes, "when you say the bit about sweat and dust, I want you to grab his shirt and pull him to you."

Marlie thought it over, then set the can on the bar. "Like this...? *There's nothing,*" she spat out, grabbing Phil's damp shirt, *"nothing in this town but sweat and dust."* She put her other hand to his shirt and pulled him closer. *"Even the dreams have dust on them."*

"Good."

Marlie flashed a smile before she picked up the beer

again. "Better warn Sam," she suggested, offering Phil the can. "He doesn't like improvising."

"Hey, Phil." Phil glanced over to see Steve with his hand on the doorknob. "That kid's outside with the sheriff. Wants to know if they can watch."

Phil took a long, slow drink. "They can sit in the back of the room." His eyes met Tory's as she entered. It had been two days since their meeting in the cemetery. Since then there had been no opportunity—or she'd seen to it that there'd been none—for any private conversation. She met the look, nodded to him, then urged Tod back to a rear table.

"The law of the land," Marlie murmured, causing Phil to look at her in question. "She's quite a woman, isn't she?"

"Yes."

Marlie grinned before she commandeered the beer again. "Merle thinks she's the greatest thing to come along since sliced bread."

Phil pulled out a cigarette. "You're seeing quite a bit of the deputy, aren't you? Doesn't seem your style."

"He's a nice guy," she said simply, then laughed. "His boss would like me run out of town on a rail."

"She's protective."

With an unintelligible murmur that could have meant anything, Marlie ran her fingers through her disordered cap of curls. "At first I thought she had something going with him." In response to Phil's quick laugh she lifted a thin, penciled brow. "Of course, that was before I saw the way you looked at her." It was her turn to laugh when Phil's expression became aloof. "Damn, Phil, you can look like your father sometimes." After handing him the empty can of beer, she turned away. "Makeup!" she demanded.

"Those are 4Ks," Tod was telling Tory, pointing to lights. "They have to put that stuff over the windows so the sun doesn't screw things up. On an inside shoot like this, they have to have something like 175-foot candles."

"You're getting pretty technical, aren't you?"

Tod shifted a bit in his chair, but his eyes were excited when they met Tory's. "Mr. Kincaid had them develop the film I shot in the portable lab. He said it was good. He said there were schools I could go to to learn about cinematography."

She cast a look in Phil's direction, watching him discuss something in undertones with Steve. "You're spending quite a lot of time with him," she commented.

"Well, when he's not busy... He doesn't mind."

"No, I'm sure he doesn't." She gave his hand a squeeze.

Tod returned the pressure boldly. "I'd rather spend time with you," he murmured.

Tory glanced down at their joined hands, wishing she knew how to begin. "Tod..."

"Quiet on the set!"

With a sigh Tory turned her attention to the scene in front of the bar. She'd come because Tod had been so pitifully eager that she share his enthusiasm. And she felt it was good for him to take such an avid interest in the technical aspects of the production. Unobtrusively she had kept her eye on him over the past days, watching him with members of the film crew. Thus far, no one appeared to object to his presence or his questions. In fact, Tory mused, he was becoming a kind of mascot. More and more his conversations were accented with the jargon of the industry. His mind seemed to soak up the terms, and his understanding was almost intuitive. He didn't appear to be interested in the glamorous end of it.

And what was so glamorous about it? she asked herself. The room was airless and steaming. It smelled, none too pleasantly, of old beer. The lights had the already unmerciful temperature rising. The two people in position by the bar were circled by equipment. How could they be so intense with each other, she wondered, when lights and cameras were all but on top of them? Yet, despite herself, Tory became engrossed with the drama of the scene.

Marlie's character was tormenting Sam's, ridiculing him for coming back a loser, taunting him. But somehow a rather abrasive strength came through in her character. She seemed a woman trapped by circumstances who was determined to fight her way out. Somehow she made the differences in their ages inconsequential. As the scene unfolded, an objective viewer would develop a respect for her, perhaps a cautious sympathy. Before long the viewer would be rooting for her. Tory wondered if Dressler realized, for all his reputation and skill, who would be the real star of this scene.

She's very good, Tory admitted silently. Marlie Summers wasn't the pampered, glittery Tinsel Town cutie Tory had been ready to believe her to be. Tory recognized strength when she saw it. Marlie infused both a grit and a vulnerability into the character that was instantly admirable. And the sweat, Tory continued, was her own.

"Cut!" Phil's voice jolted her in her chair. "That's it." Tory saw Marlie exhale a long breath. She wondered if there was some similarity in finishing a tense scene such as that one and winding up a difficult cross-examination. She decided that the emotion might be very much the same.

"Let's get some reaction shots, Marlie." Painstakingly he arranged for the change in angles and lighting. When the camera was in position, he checked through the lens himself, repositioned Marlie, then checked again. "Roll it…. Cue."

They worked for another thirty minutes, perfecting the shot. It was more than creativity, more than talent. The nuts and bolts end of the filming were tough, technical and wearily repetitious. No one complained, no one questioned, when told to change or to do over. There was an unspoken bond: the film. Perhaps, she reflected, it was because they knew it would outlast all of them. Their small slice of immortality. Tory found herself developing a respect for these people who took such an intense pride in their work.

"Cut. That's a wrap." Tory could almost feel the communal sigh of relief. "Set up for scene fifty-three in…" Phil checked his watch. "Two hours." The moment the lights shut down, the temperature dropped.

"I'm going to see what Mr. Bicks is doing," Tod announced, scrambling up. Tory remained sitting where she was a moment, watching Phil answer questions and give instructions. He never stops, she realized. One might be an actor, another a lighting expert or a cinematographer, but he touches every aspect. Rich and privileged, yes, she reflected, but not afraid of hard work.

"Sheriff."

Tory turned her head to see Marlie standing beside her. "Ms. Summers. You were very impressive."

"Thanks." Without waiting for an invitation, Marlie took a chair. "What I need now is a three-hour shower." She took a long pull from the glass of ice water she held in her hand as the two women studied each other in silence. "You've got an incredible face," Marlie said at length. "If I'd had one like that, I wouldn't have had to fight for a part with some meat on it. Mine's like a sugarplum."

Tory found herself laughing. Leaning back, she hooked her arm over the back of her chair. "Ms. Summers, as sheriff, I should warn you that stealing's a crime. You stole that scene from Sam very smoothly."

Tilting her head, Marlie studied her from a new angle. "You're very sharp."

"On occasion."

"I can see why Merle thinks you hold the answer to the mysteries of the universe."

Tory sent her a long, cool look. "Merle is a very naive, very vulnerable young man."

"Yes." Marlie set down her glass. "I like him." They gave each other another measuring look. "Look, let me ask you something, from one attractive woman to another. Did you ever find it pleasant to be with a man who liked to talk to you, to listen to you?"

"Yes, of course." Tory frowned. "Perhaps it's that I can't imagine what Merle would say to interest you."

Marlie gave a quick laugh, then cupped her chin on her palm. "You're too used to him. I've been scrambling my way up the ladder since I was eighteen. There's nothing I want more than to be on top. Along the way, I've met a lot of men. Merle's different."

"If he falls in love with you, he'll be hurt," Tory

pointed out. "I've looked out for him on and off since we were kids."

Marlie paused a moment. Idly she drew patterns through the condensation on the outside of her water glass. "He's not going to fall in love with me," she said slowly. "Not really. We're just giving each other a bit of the other's world for a few weeks. When it's over, we'll both have something nice to remember." She glanced over her shoulder and spotted Phil. "We all need someone now and again, don't we, Sheriff?"

Tory followed the direction of Marlie's gaze. At that moment Phil's eyes lifted to hers. "Yes," she murmured, watching him steadily. "I suppose we do."

"I'm going to get that shower now." Marlie rose. "He's a good man," she added. Tory looked back at her, knowing who she referred to now.

"Yes, I think you're right." Deep in thought, Tory sat a moment longer. Then, standing, she glanced around for Tod.

"Tory." Phil laid a hand on her arm. "How are you?"

"Fine." She smiled, letting him know she hadn't forgotten the last time they had been together. "You're tougher than I thought, Kincaid, working in this oven all day."

He grinned. "That, assuredly, is a compliment."

"Don't let it go to your head. You're sweating like a pig."

"Really," he said dryly. "I hadn't noticed."

She spotted a towel hung over the back of a chair and plucked it up. "You know," she said as she wiped off his face, "I imagined directors would do more delegating than you do."

"My film," he said simply, stirred by the way she

brushed the cloth over his face. "Tory." He captured her free hand. "I want to see you—alone."

She dropped the towel back on the table. "Your film," she reminded him. "And there's something I have to do." Her eyes darted past him, again in search of Tod.

"Tonight," he insisted. He'd gone beyond the point of patience. "Take the evening off, Tory."

She brought her eyes back to his. She'd gone beyond the point of excuses. "If I can," she agreed. "There's a place I know," she added with a slow smile. "South of town, about a mile. We used it as a swimming hole when I was a kid. You can't miss it—it's the only water around."

"Sunset?" He would have lifted her hand to his lips, but she drew it away.

"I can't promise." Before he could say anything else, she stepped past him, then called for Tod.

Even as she drew the boy back outside, he was expounding. "Tory, it's great, isn't it? About the greatest thing to happen in town in forever! If I could, I'd go with them when they leave." He sent her a look from under his tumbled hair. "Wouldn't you like to go, Tory?"

"To Hollywood?" she replied lightly. "Oh, I don't think it's my style. Besides, I'll be going back to Albuquerque soon."

"I want to come with you," he blurted out.

They were just outside her office door. Tory turned and looked down at him. Unable to resist, she placed her hand on his cheek. "Tod," she said softly.

"I love you, Tory," he began quickly. "I could—"

"Tod, come inside." For days she had been working out what she would say to him and how to say it. Now, as they walked together into her office, she felt completely inadequate. Carefully she sat on the edge of her desk and faced him. "Tod—" She broke off and shook her head. "Oh, I wish I were smarter."

"You're the smartest person I know," he said swiftly. "And so beautiful, and I love you, Tory, more than anything."

Her heart reached out for him even as she took his hands. "I love you, too, Tod." As he started to speak she shook her head again. "But there are different kinds of love, different ways of feeling."

"I only know how I feel about you." His eyes were very intense and just above hers as she sat on the desk. Phil had been right, she realized. He wasn't quite a child.

"Tod, I know this won't be easy for you to understand. Sometimes people aren't right for each other."

"Just because I'm younger," he began heatedly.

"That's part of it," Tory agreed, keeping her voice quiet. "It's hard to accept, when you feel like a man, that you're still a boy. There's so much you have to experience yet, and to learn."

"But when I do…" he began.

"When you do," she interrupted, "you won't feel the same way about me."

"Yes, I will!" he insisted. He surprised both of them by grabbing her arms. "It won't change because I don't want it to. And I'll wait if I have to. I love you, Tory."

"I know you do. I know it's very real." She lifted her hands to cover his. "Age doesn't mean anything to the heart, Tod. You're very special to me, a very important part of my life."

"But you don't love me." The words trembled out with anger and frustration.

"Not in the way you mean." She kept her hands firm on his when he would have jerked away.

"You think it's funny."

"No," she said sharply, rising. "No, I think it's lovely. And I wish things could be different because I know the kind of man you'll be. It hurts—for me too."

He was breathing quickly, struggling with tears and a sharp sense of betrayal. "You don't understand," he accused, pulling away from her. "You don't care."

"I do. Tod, please—"

"No." He stopped her with one ravaged look. "You don't." With a dignity that tore at Tory's heart, he walked out of the office.

She leaned back against the desk, overcome by a sense of failure.

The sun was just setting when Tory dropped down on the short, prickly grass by the water. Pulling her knees to her chest, she watched the flaming globe sink toward the horizon. There was an intensity of color against the darkening blue of the sky. Nothing soft or mellow. It was a vivid and demanding prelude to night.

Tory watched the sky with mixed emotions. The day as a whole was the kind she would have liked to wrap up and ship off to oblivion. The situation with Tod had left her emotionally wrung out and edgy. As a result she had handled a couple of routine calls with less finesse than was her habit. She'd even managed to snarl at Merle before she had gone off duty. Glancing down at the badge on her breast, she considered tossing it into the water.

A beautiful mess you've made of things, Sheriff, she told herself. Ah, the hell with it, she decided, resting her chin on her knees. She was taking the night off. Tomorrow she would straighten everything out, one disaster at a time.

The trouble was, she thought with a half smile, she'd forgotten the art of relaxation over the past few weeks. It was time to reacquaint herself with laziness. Lying back, Tory shut her eyes and went instantly to sleep.

Drifting slowly awake with the feather-light touch of fingers on her cheek, Tory gave a sleepy sigh and debated whether she should open her eyes. There was another touch—a tracing of her lips this time. Enjoying the sensation, she made a quiet sound of pleasure and let her lashes flutter up.

The light was dim, deep, deep dusk. Her eyes focused gradually on the sky above her. No clouds, no stars, just a mellow expanse of blue. Taking a deep breath, she lifted her arms to stretch. Her hand was captured and kissed. Tory turned her head and saw Phil sitting beside her.

"Hello."

"Watching you wake up is enough to drive a man crazy," he murmured, keeping her hand in his. "You're sexier sleeping than most women are wide awake."

She gave a lazy laugh. "Sleeping's always been one of my best things. Have you been here long?"

"Not long. The filming ran a bit over schedule." He flexed his back muscles, then smiled down at her. "How was your day?"

"Rotten." Tory blew out a breath and struggled to sit up. "I talked with Tod this afternoon. I didn't handle it well. Damn." Tory rested her forehead on her knees again. "I didn't want to hurt that boy."

"Tory—" Phil stroked a hand down her hair "—there

was no way he wouldn't be hurt some. Kids are resilient. He'll bounce back."

"I know." She turned her head to look at him, keeping her cheeks on her knees. "But he's so fragile. Love's fragile, isn't it? So easily shattered. I suppose it's best that he hate me for a while."

"He won't," Phil disagreed. "You mean too much to him. After a while his feelings will slip into perspective. I imagine he'll always think of you as his first real love."

"It makes me feel very special, but I don't think I made him believe that. Anyway," she continued, "after I'd made a mess out of that, I snarled at one of the town fathers, bit off the head of a rancher and took a few swipes at Merle." She swore with the expertise he had admired before. "Sitting here, I knew I was in danger of having a major pity party, so I went to sleep instead."

"Wise choice. I came near to choking my overseer."

"Overseer? Oh, the guarantor." Tory laughed, shaking back her hair. "So we both had a lovely day."

"Let's drink to it." Phil picked up a bottle of champagne from beside him.

"Well, how about that." Tory glanced at the label and pursed her lips. "You always go first-class, Kincaid."

"Absolutely," he agreed, opening the bottle with a pop and fizz. He poured the brimming wine into a glass. Tory took it, watching the bubbles explode as he filled his own. "To the end of the day."

"To the end of the day!" she agreed, clinking her glass against his. The ice-cold champagne ran excitedly over her tongue. "Nice," she murmured, shutting her eyes and savoring. "Very nice."

They drank in companionable silence as the darkness deepened. Overhead a few stars flickered hesitantly while the moon started its slow rise. The night was as hot and dry as the afternoon and completely still. There wasn't even a whisper of breeze to ripple the water. Phil leaned back on an elbow, studying Tory's profile.

"What are you thinking?"

"That I'm glad I took the night off." Smiling, she turned her head so she faced him fully. The pale light of the moon fell over her features, accenting them.

"Good God, Tory," he breathed. "I've got to get that face on film."

She threw back her head and laughed with a freedom she hadn't felt in days. "So take a home movie, Kincaid."

"Would you let me?" he countered immediately.

She merely filled both glasses again. "You're obsessed," she told him.

"More than's comfortable, yes," he murmured. He sipped, enjoying the taste, but thinking of her. "I wasn't sure you'd come."

"Neither was I." She studied the wine in her glass with apparent concentration. "Another glass of this and I might admit I enjoy being with you."

"We've half a bottle left."

Tory lifted one shoulder in a shrug before she drank again. "One step at a time," she told him. "But then," she murmured, "I suppose we've come a few steps already, haven't we?"

"A few." His fingers ran over the back of her hand. "Does it worry you?"

She gave a quick, rueful laugh. "More than's comfortable, yes."

Sitting up, he draped a casual arm around her shoulders. "I like the night best. I have the chance to think."

He sensed her complete relaxation, feeling a pleasant stir as she let her head rest on his shoulder. "During the day, with all the pressure, the demands, when I think, I think on my feet."

"That's funny." She lifted a hand across her body to lace her fingers with his. "In Albuquerque I did some of my best planning in bed the night before a court date. It's easier to let things come and go in your head at night." Tilting her face, Tory brushed his lips with hers. "I do enjoy being with you."

He returned the kiss, but with equal lightness. "I didn't need the champagne?"

"Well…it didn't hurt." When he chuckled, she settled her head in the crook of his shoulder again. It felt right there, as if it belonged. "I've always loved this spot," Tory said quietly. "Water's precious around here, and this has always been like a little mirage. It's not very big, but it's pretty deep in places. The townspeople enjoy calling it a lake." She laughed suddenly. "When we were kids, we'd troop out here sometimes on an unbearably hot day. We'd strip and jump in. Of course, it was frowned on when we were teenagers, but we still managed."

"Our decadent youth."

"Good, clean fun, Kincaid," she disagreed.

"Oh, yeah? Why don't you show me?"

Tory turned to him with a half smile. When he only lifted a brow in challenge, she grinned. A small pulse of excitement beat deep inside her. "You're on." Pushing him away, she tugged off her shoes. "The name of the game is to get in first."

As he stripped off his shirt it occurred to him that he'd never seen her move quickly before. He was still pulling off his shoes when she was naked and racing for the water. The moonlight danced over her skin, over the hair that streamed behind her back, causing him to stop and stare after her. She was even more exquisite than he had imagined. Then she was splashing up to her waist and diving under. Shaking himself out of the trance, Phil stripped and followed her.

The water was beautifully cool. It shocked his heated skin on contact, then caressed it. Phil gave a moan of pure pleasure as he sank to his shoulders. The small swimming hole in the middle of nowhere gave him just as much relief as his custom-made pool. More, he realized, glancing around for Tory. She surfaced, face lifted, hair slicked back. The moonlight caught the glisten of water on her face. A naiad, he thought. She opened her eyes. They glimmered green, like a cat's.

"You're slow, Kincaid."

He struggled against an almost painful flood of desire. This wasn't the moment to rush. They both knew this was their time, and there were hours yet to fill. "I've never seen you move fast before," he commented, treading water.

"I save it up." The bottom was just below her toes. Tory kicked lazily to keep afloat. "Conserving energy is one of my personal campaigns."

"I guess that means you don't want to race."

She gave him a long look. "You've got to be kidding."

"Guess you wouldn't be too hard to beat," he considered. "Skinny," he added.

"I am not." Tory put the heel of her hand into the water, sending a spray into his face.

"Couple of months in a good gym might build you

up a bit." He smiled, calmly wiping the water from his eyes.

"I'm built up just fine," she returned. "Is this amateur psychology, Kincaid?"

"Did it work?" he countered.

In answer she twisted and struck out, kicking up a curtain of water into his face as she headed for the far side of the pool. Phil grinned, observing that she could move like lightning when she put her mind to it, then started after her.

She beat him by two full strokes, then waited, laughing, while she shook back her hair. "Better keep up your membership to that gym, Kincaid."

"You cheated," he pointed out.

"I won. That's what counts."

He lifted a brow, amused and intrigued that she wasn't even winded. Apparently her statement about strong energy was perfectly true. "And that from an officer of the law."

"I'm not wearing my badge."

"I noticed."

Tory laughed again, moving out in a gentle sidestroke toward the middle of the pool. "I guess you're in pretty good shape...for a Hollywood director."

"Is that so?" He swam alongside of her, matching her languid movements.

"You don't have a paunch—yet," she added, grinning. Gently but firmly, Phil pushed her head under. "So you want to play dirty," she murmured when she surfaced. In a quick move she had his legs scissored between hers, then gave his chest a firm shove. Off guard, Phil went over backward and submerged. He came up, giving his head a toss to free his eyes of dripping hair. Tory was already a few yards away, treading water and chuckling.

"Basic Self-Defense 101," she informed him. "Though you have to make allowances for buoyancy in the water."

This time Phil put more effort into his strokes. Before Tory had reached the other side, he had a firm grip on her ankle. With a tug he took her under the water and back to him. Sputtering, she found herself caught in his arms.

"Want to try a few free throws?" he invited.

A cautious woman, Tory measured her opponent and the odds. "I'll pass. Water isn't my element."

Her arms were trapped between their bodies, but when she tried to free them, he only brought her closer. His smile faded into a look of understanding. She felt her heart begin a slow, dull thud.

He took her mouth with infinite care, wanting to savor the moment. Her lips were wet and cool. With no hesitation her tongue sought his. The kiss deepened slowly, luxuriously while he supported her, keeping her feet just above the sandy bottom. The feeling of weightlessness aroused her and she allowed herself to float, holding on to him as though he were an anchor. Their lips warmed from an intimate heat before they began to search for new tastes.

Without hurry they roamed each other's faces, running moist kisses over moist skin. With quiet whispers the water lapped around them as they shifted and searched.

Finding her arms free at last, Tory wrapped them about his neck, pressing her body against his. She heard Phil suck in his breath at the contact, felt the shudder race through him before his mouth crushed down

on hers. The time had passed for slow loving. Passion
too long suppressed exploded as mouth sought eager
mouth. Keeping one arm firm at her waist, he began
to explore her as he had longed to do. His fingers slid
over her wet skin.

Tory moved against him, weakening them both so
that they submerged, locked together. Streaming wet,
they surfaced with their lips still fused, then gasped for
air. Her hands ran over him, drawing him closer, then
away, to seek more of him. Unable to bear the hunger,
she thrust her fingers into his hair and pulled his lips
back to hers. With a sudden violence he bent her back
until her hair streamed behind her on the surface of
the water. His mouth rushed over her face, refusing her
efforts to halt it with hers while he found her breast
with his palm.

The throaty moan that wrenched from her evoked a
new wave of passion. Phil lifted her so he could draw
her hot, wet nipple into his mouth. His tongue tormented
them both until her hands fell into the pool in a submission he hadn't expected. Drunk on power, he took
his mouth over her trembling skin, down to where the
water separated him from her. Frustrated with the barrier, he let his mouth race up again to her breast until
Tory clutched at his shoulders, shuddering.

Her head fell back as he lowered her so that her
neck was vulnerable and glistening in the moonlight.
He kissed it hungrily, hearing her cry with anguished
delight.

Cool, cool water, but she was so hot that his legs
nearly buckled at the feel of her. Tory was beyond all
but dark, vivid sensations. To her the water felt steamy,
heated by her own body. Her breathing seemed to echo

in the empty night, then shudder back to her. She would have shouted for him to take her, but his name would only come as a gasp through her lips. She couldn't bear it; the need was unreasonable. With a strength conceived in passion she locked her legs tightly around his waist and lowered herself to him.

They swayed for a moment, equally stunned. Then he gripped her legs, letting her take him on a wild, impossible journey. There was a rushing, like the sound of the wind inside her head. Trembling, they slid down into the water.

With some vague recollection of where they were, Phil caught Tory against him again. "We'd better get out of here," he managed. "We'll drown."

Tory let her head fall on his shoulder. "I don't mind."

With a low, shaky laugh, Phil lifted her into his arms and carried her from the pond.

Chapter 8

He laid her down, then dropped on his back on the grass beside her. For some time the only sound in the night was their mixed breathing. The stars were brilliant now, the moon nearly full. Both of them stared up.

"You were saying something," Phil began in a voice that still wasn't steady, "about water not being your element."

Tory gave a choke of laughter that turned into a bubble, then a burst of pure appreciation. "I guess I could be wrong."

Phil closed his eyes, the better to enjoy the heavy weakness that flowed through his system.

Tory sighed and stretched. "That was wonderful."

He drew her closer against his side. "Cold?"

"No."

"This grass—"

"Terrible, isn't it?" With another laugh Tory twisted so that she lay over his chest. Her wet skin slid over his. Lazily he ran a hand down the length of her back as she smiled back at him. Her hair was slicked close to her head, her skin as pale and exquisite as marble in the moonlight. A few small drops of water clung to her lashes.

"You're beautiful when you're wet," he told her, drawing her down for a slow, lingering kiss.

"So are you." When he grinned, she ran both thumbs from his jaw to his cheekbones. "I like your face," she decided, tilting her head as she studied it. "That aristocratic bone structure you get from your father. It's no wonder he was so effective playing those swashbuckling roles early in his career." She narrowed her eyes as if seeking a different perspective. "Of course," she continued thoughtfully, "I rather like it when yours takes on that aloof expression."

"Aloof?" He shifted a bit as the grass scratched his bare skin.

"You do it very well. Your eyes have a terrific way of saying 'I beg your pardon' and meaning 'Go to hell.' I've noticed it, especially when you talk to that short man with the little glasses."

"Tremaine," Phil muttered. "Associate producer and general pain in the neck."

Tory chuckled and kissed his chin. "Don't like anyone else's hands on your movie, do you?"

"I'm very selfish with what belongs to me." He took her mouth again with more fervor than he had intended. As the kiss lengthened and deepened he gave a quick sound of pleasure and pressed her closer. When their lips parted, their eyes met. Both of them knew they were heading for dangerous ground. Both of them treaded carefully. Tory lowered her head to his chest, trying to think logically.

"I suppose we knew this was going to happen sooner or later."

"I suppose we did."

She caught her bottom lip between her teeth a moment. "The important thing is not to let it get complicated."

"No." He frowned up at the stars. "We both want to avoid complications."

"In a few weeks we'll both be leaving town." They were unaware that they had tightened their holds on the other. "I have to pick up my caseload again."

"I have to finish the studio scenes," he murmured.

"It's a good thing we understand each other right from the beginning." She closed her eyes, drawing in his scent as though she were afraid she might forget it. "We can be together like this, knowing no one will be hurt when it's over."

"Yeah."

They lay in silence, dealing with a mutual and unstated sense of depression and loss. We're adults, Tory thought, struggling against the mood. Attracted to each other. It isn't any more than that. Can't be any more than that. But she wasn't as sure of herself as she wanted to be.

"Well," she said brightly, lifting her head again. "So tell me how the filming's going? That scene today seemed to click perfectly."

Phil forced himself to match her mood, ignoring the doubts forming in his own head. "You came in on the last take," he said dryly. "It was like pulling teeth."

Tory reached across him for the bottle of champagne. The glass was covered with beads of sweat. "It looked to me like Marlie Summers came out on top," she commented as she poured.

"She's very good."

Resting her arm on his chest, Tory drank. The wine still fizzled cold. "Yes, I thought so, too, but I wish she'd steer away from Merle."

"Worried about his virtue, Tory?" he asked dryly.

She shot him an annoyed look. "He's going to get hurt."

"Why?" he countered. "Because a beautiful woman's interested enough to spend some time with him? Now, look," he continued before she could retort, "you have your own view of him. It's possible someone else might have another."

Frowning, she drank again. "How's he going to feel when she leaves?"

"That's something he'll have to deal with," Phil said quietly. "He already knows she's going to."

Again their eyes met in quick, almost frightened recognition. Tory looked away to study the remaining wine in her glass. It was different, she told herself. She and Phil both had certain priorities. When they parted, it would be without regret or pain. It had to be.

"It might not be easy to accept," she murmured, wanting to believe she still spoke of Merle.

"On either side," he replied after a long pause.

Tory turned her head to find his eyes on hers, light and clear and very intense. The ground was getting shaky again. "I suppose it'll work out for the best... for everyone." Determined to lighten the mood, she smiled down at him. "You know, the whole town's excited about those scenes you're shooting with them as extras. The Kramer twins haven't gotten out of line for an entire week."

"One of them asked me if he could have a close-up."

"Which one?"

"Who the hell can tell?" Phil demanded. "This one tried to hustle a date with Marlie."

Tory laughed, pressing the back of her wrist to her mouth to hold in a swallow of champagne. "Had to be Zac. He's impossible. Are you going to give him his close-up?"

"I'll give him a swift kick in the pants if he messes around the crane again," Phil returned.

"Uh-oh, I didn't hear about that."

Phil shrugged. "It didn't seem necessary to call the law on him."

"Tempting as it might be," she returned. "I wouldn't have thrown him in the penitentiary. Handling the Kramers has become an art."

"I had one of my security guards put the fear of God into him," Phil told her easily. "It seemed to do the trick."

"Listen, Phil, if any of my people need restraining, I expect to be informed."

With a sigh, he plucked the glass from her hand, tossed it aside, then rolled on top of her. "You've got the night off, Sheriff. We're not going to talk about it."

"Really." Her arms were already linked around his neck. "Just what are we going to talk about, then?"

"Not a damn thing," he muttered and pressed his mouth to hers.

Her response was a muffled sound of agreement. He could taste the champagne on her tongue and lingered over it. The heat of the night had already dried their skin, but he ran his hands through the cool dampness of her hair. He could feel her nipples harden against the pressure of his chest. This time, he thought, there would be no desperation. He could enjoy her slowly— the long, lean lines of her body, the silken texture of her skin, the varied, heady tastes of her.

From the wine-flavored lips he took an unhurried journey to the warmer taste of her throat. But his hands were already roaming demandingly. Tory moved under him with uncontrollable urgency as his thumb found the peak of her breast, intensifying her pleasure. To his amazement Phil found he could have taken her immediately. He banked the need. There was still so much of her to learn of, so much to experience. Allowing the tip of his tongue to skim along her skin, he moved down to her breast.

Tory arched, pressing him down. His slow, teasing kisses made her moan in delighted frustration. Beneath the swell of her breast, his mouth lingered to send shivers and more shivers of pleasure through her. His tongue flicked lazily over her nipple, then retreated to soft flesh. She moaned his name, urging him back. He circled slowly, mouth on one breast, palm on the other, thrilling to her mindless murmurs and convulsive movements beneath him. Taking exquisite care, he captured a straining peak between his teeth. Leaving it moist and wanting, he journeyed to her other breast to savor, to linger, then to devour.

His hands had moved lower, so that desire throbbed over her at so many points, she was delirious for fulfillment. Anxious to discover all she could about his body, Tory ran her fingertips over the taut muscles of his shoulders, down the strong back. Through a haze of sensation she felt him shudder at her touch. With delicious slowness she skimmed her fingers up his rib cage. She heard him groan before his teeth nipped into her tender flesh. Open and hungry, his mouth came swiftly back to hers.

When she reached for him, he drew in a sharp breath at the contact. Burying his face in her neck, Phil felt himself drowning in pleasure. The need grew huge, but again he refused it.

"Not yet," he murmured to himself and to her. "Not yet."

He passed down the valley between her breasts, wallowing in the hot scent that clung to her skin. Her stomach quivered under his lips. Tory no longer felt the rough carpet of grass under her back, only Phil's seeking mouth and caressing hands. His mouth slipped lower and she moaned, arching—willing, wanting. His tongue was quick and greedy, shooting pleasure from the core of her out even to her fingertips. Her body was heavy with it, her head light. He brought her to a shuddering crest, but relentlessly allowed no time for recovery. His fingers sought her even as his mouth found fresh delight in the taste of her thigh.

She shook her head, unable to believe she could be so helpless. Her fingers clutched at the dry grass while her lips responded to the dizzying pace he set. Her skin was damp again, quivering in the hot night air. Again and again he drove her up, never letting her settle, never allowing her complete release.

"Phil," she moaned between harsh, shallow breaths. "I need…"

He'd driven himself to the verge of madness. His

body throbbed in one solid ache for her. Wildly he took his mouth on a frantic journey up her body. "What?" he demanded. "What do you need?"

"You," she breathed, no longer aware of words or meanings. "You."

With a groan of triumph he thrust into her, catapulting them both closer to what they insisted on denying.

She'd warned him about the heat. Still, Phil found himself cursing the unrelenting sun as he set up for another outdoor shot. The grips had set up stands with butterflies—long black pieces of cloth—to give shade between takes. The cameraman stood under a huge orange-and-white umbrella and sweated profusely. The actors at least could spend a few moments in the shade provided while Phil worked almost exclusively in the streaming sun, checking angles, lighting, shadows. Reflectors were used to bounce the sunlight and carbon arcs balanced the back lighting. A gaffer, stripped to the waist, adjusted a final piece of blue gel over a bulb. The harsh, glaring day was precisely what Phil wanted, but it didn't make the work any more pleasant.

Forcing down more salt tablets, he ordered the next take. Oddly, Dressler seemed to have adjusted to the heat more easily than the younger members of the cast and crew. Or, Phil mused as he watched him come slowly down the street with the fledgling actor who played his alter ego, he's determined not to be outdone. As time went on, he became more competitive—and the more competitive he became, particularly with Marlie, the more Phil was able to draw out of him.

Yeah, Phil thought as Dressler turned to the younger actor with a look of world-weariness. He ran through his dialogue slowly, keeping the pace just short of dragging. He was a man giving advice reluctantly, without any confidence that it was viable or would be listened to in any case. He talked almost to himself. For a moment Phil forgot his own discomfort in simple admiration for a pro who had found the heart of his character. He was growing old and didn't give a damn—wanted to be left alone, but had no hope that his wishes would be respected. Once he had found his moment of glory, then had lost it. He saw himself in the younger man and felt a bitter pity. Ultimately he turned and walked slowly away. The camera stayed on him for a silent thirty seconds.

"Cut. Perfect," Phil announced in a rare show of unconditional approval. "Lunch," he said dropping a hand on the younger actor's shoulder. "Get out of the sun for a while. I'll need you for reaction shots in thirty minutes." He walked over to meet Sam. "That was a hell of a job."

Grinning, Sam swiped at his brow. "Somebody's got to show these kids how it's done. That love scene with Marlie's going to be interesting," he added a bit ruefully. "I keep remembering she's my daughter's age."

"That should keep you in character."

Sam laughed, running his fingers through his thick salt-and-pepper hair. "Well, the girl's a pro," he said after a moment. "This movie's going to shoot her into the fast lane quick." He sent Phil a long, steady look. "And you and I," he added, "are going to win each other an Oscar." When Phil only lifted a brow, Sam slapped him on the back. "Don't give me that look, boy," he said, amused. "You're talking to one who's been passed over a few times himself. You can be lofty and say awards don't mean a damn…but they do." Again his eyes met

Phil's. "I want this one just as much as you do." He ran a hand over his stomach. "Now I'm going to get myself a beer and put my feet up."

He sauntered off, leaving Phil looking after him. He didn't want to admit, even to himself, that he desired his profession's ultimate accolade. In a few short words Dressler had boiled it all down. Yes, he wanted to direct outstanding films—critically and financially successful, lasting, important. But he wanted that little gold statue. With a wry grin Phil swiped at his brow with his forearm. It seemed that the need to win, and to be acknowledged, didn't fade with years. Dressler had been in the business longer than Phil had been alive; yet, he was still waiting for the pot at the end of the rainbow. Phil adjusted his sunglasses, admitting he wasn't willing to wait thirty-five years.

"Hey, Phil." Bicks lumbered over to him, mopping his face. "Look, you've got to do something about that woman."

Phil pulled out a cigarette. "Which?"

"That sheriff." Bicks popped another piece of gum into his mouth. "Great looker," he added. "Got a way of walking that makes a man home right in on her…" He trailed off, observing the look in Phil's eyes. "Just an observation," he muttered.

"What do you expect me to do about the way Sheriff Ashton walks, Bicks?"

Catching the amusement in Phil's tone, Bicks grinned. "Nothing, please. A man's got to have something pleasant to look at in this place. But damn it, Phil, she gave me a ticket and slapped a two-hundred-and-fifty-dollar fine on me."

Phil pushed his glasses up on his head with a weary

sigh. He'd wanted to catch a quick shower before resuming the shoot. "What for?"

"Littering."

"Littering?" Phil repeated over a snort of laughter.

"Two hundred and fifty bucks for dropping gum wrappers in the street," Bicks returned, not seeing the humor. "Wouldn't listen to reason either. I'd have picked 'em up and apologized. Two hundred and fifty bucks for a gum wrapper, Phil. Jeez."

"All right, all right, I'll talk to her." After checking his watch, Phil started up the street. "Set up for the next scene in twenty minutes."

Tory sat with her feet propped up on the desk as she struggled to decipher Merle's report on a feud between two neighboring ranches. It seemed that a dispute over a line of fence was becoming more heated. It was going to require her attention. So was the letter she had just received from one of her clients in Albuquerque. When Phil walked in, she glanced up from the scrawled pad and smiled.

"You look hot," she commented.

"Am hot," he countered, giving the squeaking fan above their heads a glance. "Why don't you get that thing fixed?"

"And spoil the atmosphere?"

Phil stepped over the sleeping dog, taking a seat on the corner of her desk. "We're going to be shooting one of the scenes with the townspeople milling around later. Are you going to watch?"

"Sure."

"Want to do a cameo?" he asked with a grin.

"No, thanks."

Leaning over, he pressed his lips to hers. "Dinner in my room tonight?"

Tory smiled. "You still have those candles?"

"All you want," he agreed.

"You talked me into it," she murmured, drawing his face back for a second kiss.

"Tory, if I brought a camera out to your ranch one day, would you let me film you riding that palomino?"

"Phil, for heaven's sake—"

"Home movies?" he interrupted, twirling her hair around his finger.

She gave a capitulating sigh. "If it's important to you."

"It is." He straightened, checked his watch, then pulled out a cigarette. "Listen, Tory, Bicks tells me you fined him for littering."

"That's right." The phone rang, and Phil waited while she took the call. After a moment he realized her tone was slightly different. With interest he listened to the legal jargon roll off her tongue. It must be Albuquerque, he realized. He watched her carefully, discovering this was a part of her life he knew nothing of. She'd be tough in court, he mused. There was an intensity under that languid exterior that slipped out at unexpected moments. And what did she do after a day in court or a day in the office?

There'd be men, he thought, instantly disliking the image. A woman like Tory would only spend evenings alone, nights alone, if she chose to. He looked away, taking a deep drag on his cigarette. He couldn't start thinking along those lines, he reminded himself. They were both free agents. That was the first rule.

"Phil?"

He turned back to see that she had replaced the receiver. "What?"

"You were saying?"

"Ah…" He struggled to remember the point of his visit. "Bicks," he continued.

"Yes, what about him?"

"A two-hundred-and-fifty-dollar fine for littering," Phil stated, not quite erasing the frown that had formed between his brows.

"Yes, that's the amount of the fine."

"Tory, be reasonable."

Her brow lifted. "Reasonable, Kincaid?"

Her use of his surname told him what level they were dealing on. "It's certainly extreme for a gum wrapper."

"We don't vary the fine according to the style of trash," she replied with an easy shrug. "A tin of caviar would have cost him the same amount."

Goaded, Phil rose. "Listen, Sheriff—"

"And while we're on the subject," she interrupted, "you can tell your people that if they don't start picking up after themselves more carefully, they're all going to be slapped with fines." She gave him a mild smile. "Let's keep Friendly clean, Kincaid."

He took a slow drag. "You're not going to hassle my people."

"You're not going to litter my town."

He swore, coming around the desk when the door opened. Pleased to see Tod, Tory swung her legs to the floor and started to stand. It was then that she saw the dull bruise on the side of his face. Fury swept through her so quickly, she was forced to clench her hands into fists to control it. Slowly she walked to him and took his face in her hands.

"How did you get this?"

He shrugged, avoiding her eyes. "It's nothing."

Fighting for calm, Tory lifted his hands, examining the knuckles carefully. There was no sign that he'd been fighting. "Your father?"

He shook his head briskly. "I came to do the sweeping up," he told her, and tried to move away.

Tory took him firmly by the shoulders. "Tod, look at me."

Reluctantly he lifted his eyes. "I've still got five dollars to work off," he said tightly.

"Did your father put this bruise on your face?" she demanded. When he started to drop his eyes again, she gave him a quick shake. "You answer me."

"He was just mad because—" He broke off, observing the rage that lit her face. Instinctively he cringed away from it. Tory set him aside and started for the door.

"Where are you going?" Moving quickly, Phil was at the door with her, his hand over hers on the knob.

"To see Swanson."

"No!" They both turned to see Tod standing rigid in the center of the room. "No, you can't. He won't like it. He'll get awful mad at you."

"I'm going to talk to your father, Tod," Tory said in a careful voice, "to explain to him why it's wrong for him to hurt you this way."

"Only when he loses his temper." Tod dashed across the room to grab her free hand. "He's not a bad man. I don't want you to put him in jail."

Though her anger was lethal, Tory gave Tod's hand a reassuring squeeze. "I'm just going to talk to him, Tod."

"He'll be crazy mad if you do, Tory. I don't want him to hurt you either."

"He won't, don't worry." She smiled, seeing by the expression in Tod's eyes that she'd already been forgiven. "Go get the broom now. I'll be back soon."

"Tory, please…"

"Go on," she said firmly.

Phil waited until the boy had disappeared into the back room. "You're not going."

Tory sent him a long look, then pulled open the door. Phil spun her around as she stepped outside. "I said you're not going."

"You're interfering with the law, Kincaid."

"The hell with that!" Infuriated, Phil pushed her back against the wall. "You're crazy if you think I'm going to let you go out there."

"You don't *let* me do anything," she reminded him. "I'm sworn to protect the people under my jurisdiction. Tod Swanson is one of my people."

"A man who punches a kid isn't going to hesitate to take a swing at you just because you've got that little piece of tin on your shirt."

Because her anger was racing, Tory forced herself to speak calmly. "What do you suggest I do? Ignore what I just saw?"

Frustrated by the image of Tod's thin face, Phil swore. "I'll go."

"You have no right." She met his eyes squarely. "You're not the law, and what's more, you're an outsider."

"Send Merle."

"Don't you hold with no woman sheriff, Kincaid?"

"Damn it, Tory." He shook her, half in fear, half in frustration. "This isn't a joke."

"No, it's not," she said seriously. "It's my job. Now, let go of me, Phil."

Furious, Phil complied, then watched her stride to her car. "Tory," he called after her, "if he puts a hand on you, I'll kill him."

She slipped into the car, driving off without looking back.

Tory took the short drive slowly, wanting to get her emotions under control before she confronted Swanson. She had to be objective, she thought, as her knuckles whitened on the steering wheel. But first she had to be calm. It wasn't possible to do what she needed to do in anger, or to let Phil's feelings upset her. To live up to the badge on her shirt, she had to set all that aside.

She wasn't physically afraid, not because she was foolishly brave, but because when she saw a blatant injustice, Tory forgot everything but the necessity of making it right. As she took the left fork toward the Swanson ranch, however, she had her first stirring of self-doubt.

What if she mishandled the situation? she thought in sudden panic. What if her meeting with Swanson only made more trouble for the boy? The memory of Tod's terrified face brought on a quick queasiness that she fought down. No, she wasn't going to mishandle it, she told herself firmly as the house came into view. She was going to confront Swanson and at the very least set the wheels in motion for making things right. Tory's belief that all things could be set right with patience, through the law, had been indoctrinated in childhood. She knew and accepted no other way.

She pulled up behind Swanson's battered pickup, then climbed out of the sheriff's car. Instantly a dog who had been sleeping on the porch sent out angry, warning barks. Tory eyed him a moment, wary, then saw that he came no farther than the edge of the sagging porch. He looked as old and unkempt as the house itself.

Taking a quick look around, Tory felt a stir of pity for Tod. This was borderline poverty. She, too, had grown up where a tightened belt was often a rule, but between her mother's penchant for neatness and the hard work of both her parents, their small ranch had always had a homey charm. This place, on the other hand, looked desolate and hopeless. The grass grew wild, long overdue for trimming. There were no brightening spots of color from flowers or potted plants. The house itself was frame, the paint faded down to the wood in places. There was no chair on the porch, no sign that anyone had the time or inclination to sit and appreciate the view.

No one came to the door in response to the dog's barking. Tory debated calling out from where she stood or taking a chance with the mangy mutt. A shout came from the rear of the house with a curse and an order to shut up. The dog obeyed, satisfying himself with low growls as Tory headed in the direction of the voice.

She spotted Swanson working on the fence of an empty corral. The back of his shirt was wet with sweat, while his hat was pulled low to shade his face. He was a short, stocky man with the strong shoulders of a laborer. Thinking of Tod's build, Tory decided he had inherited it, and perhaps his temperament, from his mother.

"Mr. Swanson?"

His head jerked up. He had been replacing a board

on the fence; the hand that swung the hammer paused on the downswing. Seeing his face, Tory decided he had the rough, lined face of a man constantly fighting the odds of the elements. He narrowed his eyes; they passed briefly over her badge.

"Sheriff," he said briefly, then gave the nail a final whack. He cared little for women who interfered in a man's work.

"I'd like to talk to you, Mr. Swanson."

"Yeah?" He pulled another nail out of an old coffee can. "What about?"

"Tod." Tory waited until he had hammered the nail into the warped board.

"That boy in trouble?"

"Apparently," she said mildly. She told herself to overlook his rudeness as he turned his back to take out another nail.

"I handle my own," he said briefly. "What's he done?"

"He hasn't done anything, Mr. Swanson."

"Either he's in trouble or he's not." Swanson placed another nail in position and beat it into the wood. The sound echoed in the still air. From somewhere to the right, Tory heard the lazy moo of a cow. "I ain't got time for conversation, Sheriff."

"He's in trouble, Mr. Swanson," she returned levelly. "And you'll talk to me here or in my office."

The tone had him taking another look and measuring her again. "What do you want?"

"I want to talk to you about the bruise on your son's face." She glanced down at the meaty hands, noting that the knuckles around the hammer whitened.

"You've got no business with my boy."

"Tod's a minor," she countered. "He's very much my business."

"I'm his father."

"And as such, you are not entitled to physically or emotionally abuse your child."

"I don't know what the hell you're talking about." The color in his sun-reddened face deepened angrily. Tory's eyes remained calm and direct.

"I'm well aware that you've beaten the boy before," she said coolly. "There are very strict laws to protect a child against this kind of treatment. If they're unknown to you, you might want to consult an attorney."

"I don't need no damn lawyer," he began, gesturing at Tory with the hammer as his voice rose.

"You will if you point that thing at me again," she told him quietly. "Attempted assault on a peace officer is a very serious crime."

Swanson looked down at the hammer, then dropped it disgustedly to the ground. "I don't assault women," he muttered.

"Just children?"

He sent her a furious glance from eyes that watered against the sun. "I got a right to discipline my own. I got a ranch to run here." A gesture with his muscular arm took in his pitiful plot of land. "Every time I turn around, that boy's off somewheres."

"Your reasons don't concern me. The results do."

With rage burning on his face, he took a step toward her. Tory held her ground. "You just get back in your car and get out. I don't need nobody coming out here telling me how to raise my boy."

Tory kept her eyes on his, although she was well

aware his hands had clenched into fists. "I can start proceedings to make Tod a ward of the court."

"You can't take my boy from me."

Tory lifted a brow. "Can't I?"

"I got rights," he blustered.

"So does Tod."

He swallowed, then turned back to pick up his hammer and nails. "You ain't taking my boy."

Something in his eyes before he had turned made Tory pause. Justice, she reminded herself, was individual. "He wouldn't want me to," she said in a quieter tone. "He told me you were a good man and asked me not to put you in jail. You bruise his face, but he doesn't stop loving you."

She watched Swanson's back muscles tighten. Abruptly he flung the hammer and the can away. Nails scattered in the wild grass. "I didn't mean to hit him like that," he said with a wrench in his voice that kept Tory silent. "Damn boy should've fixed this fence like I told him." He ran his hands over his face. "I didn't mean to hit him like that. Look at this place," he muttered, gripping the top rail of the fence. "Takes every minute just to keep it up and scrape by, never amount to anything. But it's all I got. All I hear from Tod is how he wants to go off to school, how he wants this and that, just like—"

"His brother?" Tory ventured.

Swanson turned his head slowly, and his face was set. "I ain't going to talk about that."

"Mr. Swanson, I know something about what it takes to keep up a place like this. But your frustrations and your anger are no excuse for misusing your boy."

He turned away again, the muscles in his jaw tightening. "He's gotta learn."

"And your way of teaching him is to use your fists?"

"I tell you I didn't mean to hit him." Furious, he whirled back to her. "I don't mean to take a fist to him the way my father done to me. I know it ain't right, but when he pushes me—" He broke off again, angry with himself for telling his business to an outsider. "I ain't going to hit him anymore," he muttered.

"But you've told yourself that before, haven't you?" Tory countered. "And meant it, I'm sure." She took a deep breath, as he only stared at her. "Mr. Swanson, you're not the only parent who has a problem with control. There are groups and organizations designed to help you and your family."

"I'm not talking to any psychiatrists and do-gooders."

"There are ordinary people, exactly like yourself, who talk and help each other."

"I ain't telling strangers my business. I can handle my own."

"No, Mr. Swanson, you can't." For a moment Tory wished helplessly that there was an easy answer. "You don't have too many choices. You can drive Tod away, like you did your first boy." Tory stood firm as he whirled like a bull. "Or," she continued calmly, "you can seek help, the kind of help that will justify your son's love for you. Perhaps your first decision is what comes first, your pride or your boy."

Swanson stared out over the empty corral. "It would kill his mother if he took off too."

"I have a number you can call, Mr. Swanson. Someone who'll talk to you, who'll listen. I'll give it to Tod."

His only acknowledgment was a shrug. She waited a

moment, praying her judgment was right. "I don't like ultimatums," she continued. "But I'll expect to see Tod daily. If he doesn't come to town, I'll come here. Mr. Swanson, if there's a mark on that boy, I'll slap a warrant on you and take Tod into custody."

He twisted his head to look at her again. Slowly, measuringly, he nodded. "You've got a lot of your father in you, Sheriff."

Automatically Tory's hand rose to her badge. She smiled for the first time. "Thanks." Turning, she walked away. Not until she was out of sight did she allow herself the luxury of wiping her sweaty palms on the thighs of her jeans.

Chapter 9

Tory was stopped at the edge of town by a barricade. Killing the engine, she stepped out of the car as one of Phil's security men approached her.

"Sorry, Sheriff, you can't use the main street. They're filming."

With a shrug Tory leaned back on the hood of her car. "It's all right. I'll wait."

The anger that had driven her out to the Swanson ranch was gone. Now Tory appreciated the time to rest and think. From her vantage point she could see the film crew and the townspeople who were making their debut as extras. She watched Hollister walk across the street in back of two actors exchanging lines in the scene. It made Tory smile, thinking how Hollister would brag about this moment of glory for years to come. There were a dozen people she knew, milling on the streets or waiting for their opportunity to mill. Phil cut the filming, running through take after take. Even with the distance Tory could sense he was frustrated. She frowned, wondering if their next encounter would turn into a battle. She couldn't back down, knowing that she had done the right thing—essentially the only thing.

Their time together was to be very brief, she mused. She didn't want it plagued by arguments and tension. But until he accepted the demands and responsibilities of her job, tension was inevitable. It had already become very important to Tory that the weeks ahead be unmarred. Perhaps, she admitted thoughtfully, too important. It was becoming more difficult for her to be perfectly logical when she thought of Phil. And since the night before, the future had become blurred and distant. There seemed to be only the overwhelming present.

She couldn't afford that, Tory reminded herself. That wasn't what either one of them had bargained for. She shifted her shoulders as her shirt grew hot and damp against her back. There was the summer, and just the summer, before they both went their separate ways. It was, of course, what each of them wanted.

"Sheriff...ah, Sheriff Ashton?"

Disoriented, Tory shook her head and stared at the man beside her. "What—? Yes?"

The security guard held out a chilled can of soda. "Thought you could use this."

"Oh, yeah, thanks." She pulled the tab, letting the air out in a hiss. "Do you think they'll be much longer?"

"Nah." He lifted his own can to drink half of it down without a breath. "They've been working on this one scene over an hour now."

Gratefully, Tory let the icy drink slide down her dry throat. "Tell me, Mr.—"

"Benson, Chuck Benson, ma'am."

"Mr. Benson," Tory continued, giving him an easy smile. "Have you had any trouble with any of the townspeople?"

"Nothing to speak of," he said as he settled beside her against the hood. "Couple of kids—those twins."

"Oh, yes," Tory murmured knowingly.

"Only tried to con me into letting them on the crane." He gave an indulgent laugh, rubbing the cold can over his forehead to cool it. "I've got a couple teenagers of my own," he explained.

"I'm sure you handled them, Mr. Benson." Tory flashed him a dashing smile that lifted his blood pressure a few degrees. "Still, I'd appreciate hearing about it if anyone in town gets out of line—particularly the Kramer twins."

Benson chuckled. "I guess those two keep you busy."

"Sometimes they're a full-time job all by themselves." Tory rested a foot on the bumper and settled herself more comfortably. "So tell me, how old are your kids?"

By the time Phil had finished shooting the scene, he'd had his fill of amateurs for the day. He'd managed, with a good deal of self-control, to hold on to his patience and speak to each one of his extras before he dismissed them. He wanted to shoot one more scene before they wrapped up for the day, so he issued instructions immediately. It would take an hour to set up, and with luck they'd have the film in the can before they lost the light.

The beeper at his hip sounded, distracting him. Impatiently, Phil drew out the walkie-talkie. "Yeah, Kincaid."

"Benson. I've got the sheriff here. All right to let her through now?"

Automatically, Phil looked toward the edge of town. He spotted Tory leaning lazily against the hood, drinking from a can. He felt twin surges of relief and annoyance. "Let her in," he ordered briefly, then shoved the radio back in place. Now that he knew she was perfectly safe, Phil had a perverse desire to strangle her. He waited until she had parked in front of the sheriff's office and walked up the street to meet her. Before he was halfway there, Tod burst out of the door.

"Sheriff!" He teetered at the edge of the sidewalk, as if unsure of whether to advance any farther.

Tory stepped up and ran a fingertip down the bruise on his cheek. "Everything's fine, Tod."

"You didn't…" He moistened his lips. "You didn't arrest him?"

She rested her arms on his shoulders. "No." Tory felt his shuddering sigh.

"He didn't get mad at you or…" He trailed off again and looked at her helplessly.

"No, we just talked. He knows he's wrong to hurt you, Tod. He wants to stop."

"I was scared when you went, but Mr. Kincaid said you knew what you were doing and that everything would be all right."

"Did he?" Tory turned her head as Phil stepped beside her. The look held a long and not quite comfortable moment. "Well, he was right." Turning back to Tod, she gave his shoulders a quick squeeze. "Come inside a minute. There's a number I want you to give to your father. Want a cup of coffee, Kincaid?"

"All right."

Together, they walked into Tory's office. She went directly to her desk, pulling out a smart leather-bound address book that looked absurdly out of place. After flipping through it, she wrote a name and phone number on a pad, then ripped off the sheet. "This number is for your whole family," she said as she handed Tod the paper. "Go home and talk to your father, Tod. He needs to understand that you love him."

He folded the sheet before slipping it into his back pocket. Shifting from foot to foot, he stared down at the cluttered surface of her desk. "Thanks. Ah…I'm sorry about the things I said before." Coloring a bit, he glanced at Phil. "You know," he murmured, lowering his gaze to the desk again.

"Don't be sorry, Tod." She laid a hand over his until he met her eyes. "Okay?" she said, and smiled.

"Yeah, okay." He blushed again, but drew up his courage. Giving Tory a swift kiss on the cheek, he darted for the door.

With a low laugh she touched the spot where his lips had brushed. "I swear," she murmured, "if he were fifteen years older…" Phil grabbed both her arms.

"Are you really all right?"

"Don't I look all right?" she countered.

"Damn it, Tory!"

"Phil." Taking his face in her hands, she gave him a hard, brief kiss. "You had no reason to worry. Didn't you tell Tod that I knew what I was doing?"

"The kid was terrified." And so was I, he thought

as he pulled her into his arms. "What happened out there?" he demanded.

"We talked," Tory said simply. "He's a very troubled man. I wanted to hate him and couldn't. I'm counting on him calling that number."

"What would you have done if he'd gotten violent?"

"I would have handled it," she told him, drawing away a bit. "It's my job."

"You can't—"

"Phil—" Tory cut him off quickly and firmly "—I don't tell you how to set a scene. Don't tell me how to run my town."

"It's not the same thing and you know it." He gave her an angry shake. "Nobody takes a swing at me when I do a retake."

"How about a frustrated actor?"

His eyes darkened. "Tory, you can't make a joke out of this."

"Better a joke than an argument," she countered. "I don't want to fight with you. Phil, don't focus on something like this. It isn't good for us."

He bit off a furious retort, then strode away to stare out the window. Nothing seemed as simple as it had been since the first time he'd walked into that cramped little room. "It's hard," he murmured. "I care."

Tory stared at his back while a range of emotions swept through her. Her heart wasn't listening to the strict common sense she had imposed on it. No longer sure what she wanted, she suppressed the urge to go to him and be held again. "I know," she said at length. "I care too."

He turned slowly. They looked at each other as they had once before, when there were bars between them—

a bit warily. For a long moment there was only the sound
of the whining fan and the mumble of conversation outside. "I have to get back," he told her, carefully slipping
his hands in his pockets. The need to touch her was too
strong. "Dinner?"

"Sure." She smiled, but found it wasn't as easy to
tilt her lips up as it should have been. "It'll have to be
a little later—around eight?"

"That's fine. I'll see you then."

"Okay." She waited until the door had closed behind
him before she sat at her desk. Her legs were weak.
Leaning her head on her hand, she let out a long breath.

Oh, boy, she thought. Oh, boy. The ground was a lot
shakier than she had anticipated. But she couldn't be
falling in love with him, she reassured herself. Not that.
Everything was intensified because of the emotional
whirlwind of the past couple of days. She wasn't ready
for the commitments and obligations of being in love,
and that was all there was to it. Rising, she plugged in
the coffeepot. She'd feel more like herself if she had a
cup of coffee and got down to work.

Phil spent more time than he should have in the
shower. It had been a very long, very rough twelve-
hour day. He was accustomed to impossible hours and
impossible demands in his job. Characteristically he
took them in stride. Not this time.

The hot water and steam weren't drawing out the
tension in his body. It had been there from the moment
when Tory had driven off to the Swanson ranch, then
had inexplicably increased during their brief conversation in her office. Because he was a man who always

dealt well with tension, he was annoyed that he wasn't doing so this time.

He shut his eyes, letting the water flood over his head. She'd been perfectly right, he mused, about his having no say in her work. For that matter he had no say in any aspect of her life. There were no strings on their relationship. And he didn't want them any more than Tory did. He'd never had this problem in a relationship before. Problem? he mused, pushing wet hair out of his eyes. A perspective problem, he decided. What was necessary was to put his relationship with Tory back in perspective.

And who better to do that than a director? he thought wryly, then switched off the shower with a jerk of the wrist. He was simply letting too much emotion leak into the scene. Take two, he decided, grabbing a towel. Somehow he'd forgotten a very few basic, very vital rules. Keep it simple, keep it light, he reminded himself. Certainly someone with his background and experience was too smart to look for complications. What was between him and Tory was completely elemental and without strain, because they both wanted to keep it that way.

That was one of the things that had attracted him to her in the first place, Phil remembered. Hooking a towel loosely around his waist, he grabbed another to rub his hair dry. She wasn't a woman who expected a commitment, who looked for a permanent bond like love or marriage. Those were two things they were both definitely too smart to get mixed up with. In the steam-hazed mirror Phil caught the flicker of doubt in his own eyes.

Oh, no, he told himself, absolutely not. He wasn't in

love with her. It was out of the question. He cared, naturally: She was a very special woman—strong, beautiful, intelligent, independent. And she had a great deal of simple sweetness that surfaced unexpectedly. It was that one quality that kept a man constantly off-balance. So he cared about her, Phil mused, letting the second towel fall to the floor. He could even admit that he felt closer to her than to many people he'd known for years. There was nothing unusual about that. They had something in common that clicked—an odd sort of friendship, he decided. That was safe enough. It was only because he'd been worried about her that he'd allowed things to get out of proportion for a time.

But he was frowning abstractedly at his reflection when he heard the knock on the door.

"Who is it?"

"Room service."

The frown turned into a grin instantly as he recognized Tory's voice.

"Well, hi." Tory gave him a look that was both encompassing and lazy when he opened the door. "You're a little late for your reservation, Kincaid."

He stepped aside to allow her to enter with a large tray. "I lost track of time in the shower. Is that our dinner?"

"Bud phoned me." Tory set the tray on the card table they'd used before. "He said you'd ordered dinner for eight but didn't answer your phone. Since I was starving, I decided to expedite matters." Slipping her arms around his waist, she ran her hands up his warm, damp back. "Ummm, you're tense," she murmured, enjoying the way his hair curled chaotically around his face. "Rough day?"

"And then some," he agreed before he kissed her.

He smelled clean—of soap and shampoo—yet, Tory found the scent as arousing as the darker musky fragrance she associated with him. Her hunger for food faded as quickly as her hunger for him rose. Pressing closer, she demanded more. His arms tightened; his muscles grew taut. He was losing himself in her again, and found no power to control it.

"You really are tense," Tory said against his mouth. "Lie down."

He gave a half chuckle, nibbling on her bottom lip. "You work fast."

"I'll rub your back," she informed him as she drew away. "You can tell me all the frustrating things those nasty actors did today while you were striving to be brilliant."

"Let me show you how we deal with smart alecks on the coast," Phil suggested.

"On the bed, Kincaid."

"Well…" He grinned. "If you insist."

"On your stomach," she stated when he started to pull her with him.

Deciding that being pampered might have its advantages, he complied. "I've got a bottle of wine in the cooler." He sighed as he stretched out full length. "It's a hell of a place to keep a fifty-year-old Burgundy."

"Don't be a snob," Tory warned, sitting beside him. "You must have worked ten or twelve hours today," she began. "Did you get much accomplished?"

"Not as much as we should have." He gave a quiet groan of pleasure as she began to knead the muscles in his shoulders. "That's wonderful."

"The guys in the massage parlor always asked for Tory."

His head came up. "What?"

"Just wanted to see if you were paying attention. Down, Kincaid." She chuckled softly, working down his arms. "Were there technical problems or temperament ones?"

"Both," he answered, settling again. He found closing his eyes was a sensuous luxury. "Had some damaged dichroics. With luck the new ones'll get here tomorrow. Most of the foul-ups came during the crowd scene. Your people like to grin into the camera," he said dryly. "I expected one of them to wave any minute."

"That's show biz," Tory concluded as she shifted to her knees. She hiked her dress up a bit for more freedom. Opening his eyes, Phil was treated to a view of thigh. "I wouldn't be surprised if the town council elected to build a theater in Friendly just to show your movie. Think of the boon to the industry."

"Merle walked across the street like he's sat on a horse for three weeks." Because her fingers were working miracles over his back muscles, Phil shut his eyes again.

"Merle's still seeing Marlie Summers."

"Tory."

"Just making conversation," she said lightly, but dug a bit harder than necessary into his shoulder blades.

"Ouch!"

"Toughen up, Kincaid." With a laugh she placed a loud, smacking kiss in the center of his back. "You're not behind schedule, are you?"

"No. With all the hazards of shooting on location,

we're doing very well. Another four weeks should wrap it up."

They were both silent for a moment, unexpectedly depressed. "Well, then," Tory said briskly, "you shouldn't have to worry about the guarantor."

"He'll be hanging over my shoulder until the film's in the can," Phil muttered. "There's a spot just to the right…oh, yeah," he murmured as her fingers zeroed in on it.

"Too bad you don't have any of those nifty oils and lotions," she commented. In a fluid movement Tory straddled him, the better to apply pressure. "You're a disappointment, Kincaid. I'd have thought all you Hollywood types would carry a supply of that kind of thing."

"Mmmm." He would have retorted in kind, but his mind was beginning to float. Her fingers were cool and sure as they pressed on the small of his back just above the line of the towel. Her legs, clad in thin stockings, brushed his sides, arousing him with each time she flexed. The scent of her shampoo tickled his nostrils as she leaned up to knead his shoulders again. Though the sheet was warm—almost too warm—beneath him, he couldn't summon the energy to move. As the sun was setting, the light shifted, dimming. The room was filled with a golden haze that suited his mood. He could hear the rumble of a car on the street below, then only the sound of Tory's light, even breathing above him. His muscles were relaxed and limber, but he didn't consider telling her to stop. He'd forgotten completely about the dinner growing cold on the table behind them.

Tory continued to run her hands along his back, thinking him asleep. He had a beautiful body, she mused, hard and tanned and disciplined. The muscles in his back were supple and strong. For a moment she simply enjoyed exploring him. When she shifted lower, the skirt of her dress rode up high on her thighs. With a little sound of annoyance she unzipped the dress and pulled it over her head. She could move with more freedom in her sheer teddy.

His waist was trim. She allowed her hands to slide over it, approving its firmness. Before their lovemaking had been so urgent, and she had been completely under his command. Now she enjoyed learning the lines and planes of his body. Down the narrow hips, over the brief swatch of towel, to his thighs. There were muscles there, too, she discovered, hardened by hours of standing, tennis, swimming. The light mat of hair over his skin made her feel intensely feminine. She massaged his calves, then couldn't resist the urge to place a light kiss on the back of his knee. Phil's blood began to heat in a body too drugged with pleasure to move. It gave her a curiously warm feeling to rub his feet.

He worked much harder than she'd initially given him credit for, she mused as she roamed slowly back up his legs. He spent hours in the sun, on his feet, going over and over the same shot until he'd reached the perfection he strove for. And she had come to know that the film was never far from his thoughts, even during his free hours. Phillip Kincaid, she thought with a gentle smile, was a very impressive man—with much more depth than the glossy playboy the press loved to tattle on. He'd earned her respect during the time he'd been in Friendly, and she was growing uncomfortably certain he'd earned something more complex. She wouldn't think of it now. Perhaps she would have no choice but to think of it after he'd gone. But for now, he was here. That was enough.

With a sigh she bent low over his back to lay her cheek on his shoulder. The need for him had crept into her while she was unaware. Her pulse was pounding, and a thick warmth, like heated honey, seemed to flow through her veins.

"Phil." She moved her mouth to his ear. Her tongue traced it, slipping inside to arouse him to wakefulness. She heard his quiet groan as her heart began to beat jerkily. With her teeth she pulled and tugged on the lobe, then moved to experiment with the sensitive area just below. "I want you," she murmured. Quickly she began to take her lips over him with the same thorough care as her fingers.

He seemed so pliant as she roamed over him that when a strong arm reached out to pull her down, it took her breath away. Before she could recover it, his mouth was on hers. His lips were soft and warm, but the kiss was bruisingly potent. His tongue went deep to make an avid search of moist recesses as his weight pressed her into the mattress. He took a quick, hungry journey across her face before he looked down at her. There was nothing sleepy in his expression. The look alone had her breath trembling.

"My turn," he whispered.

With nimble fingers he loosened the range of tiny buttons down the front of her teddy. His lips followed, to send a trail of fire along the newly exposed skin. The plunge of the V stopped just below her navel. He lingered there, savoring the soft, honey-hued flesh. Tory felt herself swept through a hurricane of sensation to the heavy, waiting air of the storm's eye. Phil's hands cupped her upper thighs, his thumbs pressing insistently where the thin silk rose high. Expertly he unhooked her stockings, drawing them off slowly, his mouth hurrying to taste. Tory moaned, bending her leg to help him as torment and pleasure tangled.

For one heady moment his tongue lingered at the top of her thigh. With his tongue he gently slipped beneath the silk, making her arch in anticipation. His breath shot through the material into the core of her. But he left her moist and aching to come greedily back to her mouth. Tory met the kiss ardently, dragging him closer. She felt his body pound and pulse against hers with a need no greater than her own. He found her full bottom lip irresistible and nibbled and sucked gently. Tory knew a passion so concentrated and volatile, she struggled under him to find the ultimate release.

"Here," he whispered, moving down to the spot on her neck that always drew him. "You taste like no one else," he murmured. Her flavor seemed to tremble on the tip of his tongue. With a groan he let his voracious appetite take over.

Her breasts were hard, waiting for him. Slowly he moistened the tips with his tongue, listening to her shuddering breathing as he journeyed from one to the other—teasing, circling, nibbling, until her movements beneath him were abandoned and desperate. Passion built to a delicious peak until he drew her, hot and moist, into his mouth to suckle ravenously. She wasn't aware when he slipped the teddy down her shoulders, down her body, until she was naked to the waist. The last lights of the sun poured into the room like a dark red mist. It gave her skin an exotic cast that aroused him further. He drew the silk lower and still lower, until it was lost in the tangle of sheets.

Desperate, Tory reached for him. She heard Phil's sharp intake of breath as she touched him, felt the sudden, convulsive shudder. She wanted him now with an intensity too strong to deny.

"More," he breathed, but was unable to resist as she drew him closer.

"Now," she murmured, arching her hips to receive him.

Exhausted, they lay in silence as the first fingers of moonlight flickered into the room. He knew he should move—his full weight pushed Tory deep into the mattress. But they felt so right, flesh to flesh, his mouth nestled comfortably against her breast. Her fingers were in his hair, tangling and stroking with a sleepy gentleness. Time crept by easily—seconds to minutes without words or the need for them. He could hear her heartbeat gradually slow and level. Lazily he flicked his tongue over a still-erect nipple and felt it harden even more.

"Phil," she moaned in weak protest.

He laughed quietly, enormously pleased that he could move her so effortlessly. "Tired?" he asked, nibbling a moment longer.

"Yes." She gave a low groan as he began to toy with her other breast. "Phil, I can't."

Ignoring her, he brought his mouth to hers for long, slow kisses while his hands continued to stroke. He had intended only to kiss her before taking his weight from her. Her lips were unbearably soft and giving. Her breath shuddered into him, rebuilding his passion with dizzying speed. Tory told herself it wasn't possible as sleepy desire became a torrent of fresh need.

Phil found new delight in the lines of her body, in the heady, just-loved flavor of her skin. A softly glowing spark rekindled a flame. "I want a retake," he murmured.

He took her swiftly, leaving them both staggered and damp and clinging in a room speckled with moonlight.

"How do you feel?" Phil murmured later. She was close to his side, one arm flung over his chest.

"Astonished."

He laughed, kissing her temple. "So do I. I guess our dinner got cold."

"Mmm. What was it?"

"I don't remember."

Tory yawned and snuggled against him. "That's always better cold anyway." She knew with very little effort she could sleep for a week.

"Not hungry?"

She considered a moment. "Is it something you have to chew?"

He grinned into the darkness. "Probably."

"Uh-uh." She arched like a contented cat when he ran a hand down her back. "Do you have to get up early?"

"Six."

Groaning, she shut her eyes firmly. "You're ruining your mystique," she told him. "Hollywood Casanovas don't get up at six."

He gave a snort of laughter. "They do if they've got a film to direct."

"I suppose when you leave, you'll still have a lot of work to do before the film's finished."

His frown mirrored hers, although neither was aware of it. "There's still a lot to be shot in the studio, then the editing... I wish there was more time."

She knew what he meant, and schooled her voice carefully. "We both knew. I'll only be in town a few weeks longer than you," she added. "I've got a lot of work to catch up on in Albuquerque."

"It's lucky we're both comfortable with the way things are." Phil stared up at the ceiling while his fingers continued to tangle in her hair. "If we'd fallen in love, it would be an impossible situation."

"Yes," Tory murmured, opening her eyes to the darkness. "Neither of us has the time for impossible situations."

Chapter 10

Tory pulled up in front of the ranch house. Her mother's geraniums were doing beautifully. White-and-pink plants had been systematically placed between the more common red. The result was an organized, well-tended blanket of color. Tory noted that the tear in the window screen had been mended. As always, a few articles of clothing hung on the line at the side of the house. She dreaded going in.

It was an obligation she never shirked but never did easily. At least once a week she drove out to spend a strained half hour with her mother. Only twice since the film crew had come to Friendly had her mother made the trip into town. Both times she had dropped into Tory's office, but the visits had been brief and uncomfortable for both women. Time was not bridging the gap, only widening it.

Normally, Tory confined her trips to the ranch to

Sunday afternoons. This time, however, she had driven out a day early in order to placate Phil. The thought caused her to smile. He'd finally pressured her into agreeing to his "home movies." When he had wound up the morning's shoot in town, he would bring out one of the backup video cameras. Though she could hardly see why it was so vital to him to put her on film, Tory decided it wouldn't do any harm. And, she thought wryly, he wasn't going to stop bringing it up until she agreed. So let him have his fun, she concluded as she slipped from the car. She'd enjoy the ride.

From the corral the palomino whinnied fussily. He pawed the ground and pranced as Tory watched him. He knew, seeing Tory, that there was a carrot or apple in it for him, as well as a bracing ride. They were both aware that he could jump the fence easily if he grew impatient enough. As he reared, showing off for her, Tory laughed.

"Simmer down, Justice. You're going to be in the movies." She hesitated a moment. It would be so easy to go to the horse, pamper him a bit in return for his unflagging affection. There were no complications or undercurrents there. Her eyes drifted back to the house. With a sigh she started up the walk.

Upon entering, Tory caught the faint whiff of bee's wax and lemon and knew her mother had recently polished the floors. She remembered the electric buffer her father had brought home one day. Helen had been as thrilled as if he'd brought her diamonds. The windows glittered in the sun without a streak or speck.

How does she do it? Tory wondered, gazing around the spick-and-span room. How does she stand spending each and every day chasing dust? Could it really be all she wants out of life?

As far back as she could remember, she could recall her mother wanting nothing more than to change slipcovers or curtains. It was difficult for a woman who always looked for angles and alternatives to understand such placid acceptance. Perhaps it would have been easier if the daughter had understood the mother, or the mother the daughter. With a frustrated shake of her head she wandered to the kitchen, expecting to find Helen fussing at the stove.

The room was empty. The appliances winked, white and gleaming, in the strong sunlight. The scent of fresh-baked bread hovered enticingly in the air. Whom did she bake it for? Tory demanded of herself, angry without knowing why. There was no one there to appreciate it now—no one to break off a hunk and grin as he was scolded. Damn it, didn't she know that everything was different now? Whirling away, Tory strode out of the room.

The house was too quiet, she realized. Helen was certainly there. The tired little compact was in its habitual place at the side of the house. It occurred to Tory that her mother might be in one of the outbuildings. But then, why hadn't she come out when she heard the car drive up? Vaguely disturbed, Tory glanced up the stairs. She opened her mouth to call, then stopped. Something impelled her to move quietly up the steps.

At the landing she paused, catching some faint sound coming from the end of the hall. Still moving softly, Tory walked down to the doorway of her parents' bedroom. The door was only half closed. Pushing it open, Tory stepped inside.

Helen sat on the bed in a crisp yellow housedress.
Her blond hair was caught back in a matching kerchief.
Held tight in her hands was one of Tory's father's work
shirts. It was a faded blue, frayed at the cuffs. Tory remembered it as his favorite, one that Helen had claimed
was fit only for a dust rag. Now she clutched it to her
breast, rocking gently and weeping with such quiet despair that Tory could only stare.

She'd never seen her mother cry. It had been her father whose eyes had misted during her high school and
college graduations. It had been he who had wept with
her when the dog she had raised from a puppy had died.
Her mother had faced joy and sadness with equal restraint. But there was no restraint in the woman Tory
saw now. This was a woman in the depths of grief, blind
and deaf to all but her own mourning.

All anger, all resentment, all sense of distance, vanished in one illuminating moment. Tory felt her heart
fill with sympathy, her throat burn from her own grief.

"Mother."

Helen's head jerked up. Her eyes were glazed and
confused as they focused on Tory. She shook her head
as if in denial, then struggled to choke back the sobs.

"No, don't." Tory rushed to her, gathering her close.
"Don't shut me out."

Helen went rigid in an attempt at composure, but
Tory only held her tighter. Abruptly, Helen collapsed,
dropping her head on her daughter's shoulder and weeping without restraint. "Oh, Tory, Tory, why couldn't it
have been me?" With the shirt caught between them,
Helen accepted the comfort of her daughter's strong
arms. "Not Will, never Will. It should have been me."

"No, don't say that." Hot tears coursed down her

face. "You mustn't think that way. Dad wouldn't want you to."

"All those weeks, those horrible weeks, in the hospital I prayed and prayed for a miracle." She gripped Tory tighter, as if she needed something solid to hang on to. "They said no hope. No hope. Oh, God, I wanted to scream. He couldn't die without me...not without me. That last night in the hospital before...I went into his room. I begged him to show them they were wrong, to come back. He was gone." She moaned and would have slid down if Tory hadn't held her close. "He'd already left me. I couldn't leave him lying there with that machine. I couldn't do that, not to Will. Not to my Will."

"Oh, Mother." They rocked together, heads on each other's shoulders. "I'm so sorry. I didn't know—I didn't think...I'm so sorry."

Helen breathed a long, shuddering sigh as her sobs quieted. "I didn't know how to tell you or how to explain. I'm not good at letting my feelings out. I knew how much you loved your father," she continued. "But I was too angry to reach out. I suppose I wanted you to lash out at me. It made it easier to be strong, even though I knew I hurt you more."

"That doesn't matter now."

"Tory—"

"No, it doesn't." Tory drew her mother back, looking into her tear-ravaged eyes. "Neither of us tried to understand the other that night. We were both wrong. I think we've both paid for it enough now."

"I loved him so much." Helen swallowed the tremor in her voice and stared down at the crumpled shirt still in her hand. "It doesn't seem possible that he won't walk through the door again."

"I know. Every time I come in the house, I still look for him."

"You're so like him." Hesitantly, Helen reached up to touch her cheek. "There's been times it's been hard for me even to look at you. You were always his more than mine when you were growing up. My fault," she added before Tory could speak. "I was always a little awed by you."

"Awed?" Tory managed to smile.

"You were so smart, so quick, so demanding. I always wondered how much I had to do with the forming of you. Tory—" she took her hands, staring down at them a moment "—I never tried very hard to get close to you. It's not my way."

"I know."

"It didn't mean that I didn't love you."

She squeezed Helen's hands. "I know that too. But it was always him we looked at first."

"Yes." Helen ran a palm over the crumpled shirt. "I thought I was coping very well," she said softly. "I was going to clean out the closet. I found this, and... He loved it so. You can still see the little holes where he'd pin his badge."

"Mother, it's time you got out of the house a bit, starting seeing people again." When Helen started to shake her head, Tory gripped her hands tighter. "Living again."

Helen glanced around the tidy room with a baffled smile. "This is all I know how to do. All these years…"

"When I go back to Albuquerque, why don't you come stay with me awhile? You've never been over."

"Oh, Tory, I don't know."

"Think about it," she suggested, not wanting to push.

"You might enjoy watching your daughter rip a witness apart in cross-examination."

Helen laughed, brushing the lingering tears briskly away. "I might at that. Would you be offended if I said sometimes I worry about you being alone—not having someone like your father to come home to?"

"No." The sudden flash of loneliness disturbed her far more than the words. "Everyone needs something different."

"Everyone needs someone, Tory," Helen corrected gently. "Even you."

Tory's eyes locked on her mother's a moment, then dropped away. "Yes, I know. But sometimes the someone—" She broke off, distressed by the way her thoughts had centered on Phil. "There's time for that," she said briskly. "I still have a lot of obligations, a lot of things I want to do, before I commit myself...to anyone."

There was enough anxiety in Tory's voice to tell Helen that "anyone" had a name. Feeling it was too soon to offer advice, she merely patted Tory's hand. "Don't wait too long," she said simply. "Life has a habit of moving quickly." Rising, she went to the closet again. The need to be busy was too ingrained to allow her to sit for long. "I didn't expect you today. Are you going to ride?"

"Yes." Tory pressed a hand down on her father's shirt before she stood. "Actually I'm humoring the director of the film being shot in town." Wandering to the window, she looked down to see Justice pacing the corral restlessly. "He has this obsession with getting me on film. I flatly refused to be an extra in his production, but I finally agreed to let him shoot some while I rode Justice."

"He must be very persuasive," Helen commented.

Tory gave a quick laugh. "Oh, he's that all right."

"That's Marshall Kincaid's son," Helen stated, remembering. "Does he favor his father?"

With a smile Tory thought that her mother would be more interested in the actor than the director. "Yes, actually he does. The same rather aristocratic bone structure and cool blue eyes." Tory saw the car kicking up dust on the road leading to the ranch. "He's coming now, if you'd like to meet him."

"Oh, I…" Helen pressed her fingers under her eyes. "I don't think I'm really presentable right now, Tory."

"All right," she said as she started toward the door. In the doorway she hesitated a moment. "Will you be all right now?"

"Yes, yes, I'm fine. Tory…" She crossed the room to give her daughter's cheek a brief kiss. Tory's eyes widened in surprise at the uncharacteristic gesture. "I'm glad we talked. Really very glad."

Phil again stopped his car beside the corral. The horse pranced over to hang his head over the fence, waiting for attention. Leaving the camera in the backseat, Phil walked over to pat the strong golden neck. He found the palomino avidly nuzzling at his pockets.

"Hey!" With a half laugh he stepped out of range.

"He's looking for this." Holding a carrot in her hand, Tory came down the steps.

"Your friend should be arrested for pickpocketing," Phil commented as Tory drew closer. His smile of greeting faded instantly. "Tory…" He took her shoulders, studying her face. "You've been crying," he said in an odd voice.

"I'm fine." Turning, she held out the carrot, letting the horse pluck in from her hand.

"What's wrong?" he insisted, pulling her back to him again. "What happened?"

"It was my mother."

"Is she ill?" he demanded quickly.

"No." Touched by the concern in his voice, Tory smiled. "We talked," she told him, then let out a long sigh. "We really talked, probably for the first time in twenty-seven years."

There was something fragile in the look as she lifted her eyes to his. He felt much as he had the day in the cemetery—protective and strong. Wordlessly he drew her into the circle of his arms. "Are you okay?"

"Yes, I'm fine." She closed her eyes as her head rested against his shoulder. "Really fine. It's going to be so much easier now."

"I'm glad." Tilting her face to his, he kissed her softly. "If you don't feel like doing this today—"

"No you don't, Kincaid," she said with a quick grin. "You claimed you were going to immortalize me, so get on with it."

"Go fix your face first, then." He pinched her chin. "I'll set things up."

She turned away to comply, but called back over her shoulder. "There's not going to be any of that 'Take two' business. You'll have to get it right the first time."

He enjoyed her hoot of laughter before he reached into the car for the camera and recorder.

Later, Tory scowled at the apparatus. "You said film," she reminded him. "You didn't say anything about sound."

"It's tape," he corrected, expertly framing her. "Just saddle the horse."

"You're arrogant as hell when you play movies, Kincaid." Without fuss Tory slipped the bit into the palomino's mouth. Her movements were competent as she hefted the saddle onto the horse's back. She was a natural, he decided. No nerves, no exaggerated gestures for the benefit of the camera. He wanted her to talk again. Slowly he circled around for a new angle. "Going to have dinner with me tonight?"

"I don't know," Tory considered as she tightened the cinches. "That cold steak you fed me last night wasn't very appetizing."

"Tonight I'll order cold cuts and beer," he suggested. "That way it won't matter when we get to it."

Tory sent him a grin over her shoulder. "It's a deal."

"You're a cheap date, Sheriff."

"Uh-uh," she disagreed, turning to him while she wrapped a companionable arm around the horse's neck. "I'm expecting another bottle of that French champagne very soon. Why don't you let me play with the camera now and you can stand next to the horse?"

"Mount up."

Tory lifted a brow. "You're one tough cookie, Kincaid." Grasping the saddle horn, Tory swung into the saddle in one lazy movement. "And now?"

"Head out, the direction you took the first time I saw you ride. Not too far," he added. "When you come back, keep it at a gallop. Don't pay any attention to the camera. Just ride."

"You're the boss," she said agreeably. "For the moment." With a kick of her heels Tory sent the palomino west at a run.

She felt the exhilaration instantly. The horse wanted speed, so Tory let him have his head as the hot air whipped at her face and hair. As before, she headed toward the mountains. There was no need to escape this time, but only a pleasure in moving fast. The power and strength below her tested her skill.

Zooming in on her, Phil thought she rode with understated flair. No flash, just confidence. Her body hardly seemed to move as the horse pounded up dust. It almost seemed as though the horse led her, but something in the way she sat, in the way her face was lifted, showed her complete control.

When she turned, the horse danced in place a moment, still anxious to run. He tossed his head, lifting his front feet off the ground in challenge. Over the still, silent air, Phil heard Tory laugh. The sound of it sent shivers down his spine.

Magnificent, he thought, zooming in on her as close as the lens would allow. She was absolutely magnificent. She wasn't looking toward him. Obviously she had no thoughts about the camera focused on her. Her face was lifted to the sun and the sky as she controlled the feisty horse with apparent ease. When she headed back, she started at a loping gallop that built in speed.

The palomino's legs gathered and stretched, sending up a plume of dirt in their wake. Behind them was a barren land of little more than rock and earth with the mountains harsh in the distance. She was Eve, Phil thought. The only woman. And if this Eve's paradise was hard and desolate, she ruled it in her own style.

Once, as if remembering he was there, Tory looked over, full into the camera. With her face nearly filling the lens, she smiled. Phil felt his palms go damp.

If a man had a woman like that, he realized abruptly, he'd need nothing and no one else. The only woman, he thought again, then shook his head as if to clear it.

With a quick command and a tug on the reins, Tory brought the horse to a stop. Automatically she leaned forward to pat his neck. "Well, Hollywood?" she said lazily.

Knowing he wasn't yet in complete control, Phil kept the camera trained on her. "Is that the best you can do?"

She tossed her hair behind her head. "What did you have in mind?"

"No fancy tricks?" he asked, moving around the horse to vary the angle.

Tory looked down on him with tolerant amusement. "If you want to see someone stand on one foot in the saddle, go to the circus."

"We could set up a couple of small jumps—if you can handle it."

As she ruffled the palomino's blond mane, she gave a snort of laughter. "I thought you wanted me to ride, not win a blue ribbon." Grinning, she turned the horse around. "But okay," she said obligingly. At an easy lope she went for the corral fence. The horse took the four feet in a long, powerful glide. "Will that do?" she asked as she doubled back and rode past.

"Again," Phil demanded, going down on one knee. With a shrug Tory took the horse over the fence again. Lowering his camera for the first time, Phil shaded his eyes and looked up at her. "If he can do that, how do you keep him in?"

"He knows a good thing when he's got it," Tory stated, letting the palomino prance a bit while she rubbed his neck. "He's just showing off for the camera. Is that a wrap, Kincaid?"

Lifting the camera again, he aimed it at her. "Is that all you can do?"

"Well…" Tory considered a moment, then sent him a slow smile. "How about this?" Keeping one hand loosely on the reins, she started to unbutton her blouse.

"I like it."

After three buttons she paused, catching her tongue between her teeth. "I don't want you to lose your G rating," she decided. Swinging a leg over the saddle, she slid to the ground.

"This is a private film," he reminded her. "The censors'll never see it."

She laughed, but shook her head. "Fade out," she suggested, loosening the horse's girth. "Put your toy away, Kincaid," she told him as he circled around the horse, still taping.

"Look at me a minute." With a half smile Tory complied. "God, that face," he muttered. "One way or the other, I'm going to get it on the screen."

"Forget it." Tory lifted the saddle to balance it on the fence. "Unless you start videotaping court cases."

"I can be persistent."

"I can be stubborn," she countered. At her command the palomino trotted back into the corral.

After loading the equipment back in the car, Phil turned to gather Tory in his arms. Without a word their mouths met in long, mutual pleasure. "If there was a way," he murmured as he buried his face in her hair, "to have a few days away from here, alone…"

Tory shut her eyes, feeling the stir…and the ache.

"Obligations, Phil," she said quietly. "We both have a job to do."

He wanted to say the hell with it, but knew he couldn't. Along with the obligations was the agreement they had made at the outset. "If I called you in Albuquerque, would you see me?"

She hesitated. It was something she wanted and feared. "Yes." She realized abruptly that she was suffering. For a moment she stood still, absorbing the unexpected sensation. "Phil, kiss me again."

She found his mouth quickly to let the heat and pleasure of the kiss dull the pain. There were still a few precious weeks left, she told herself as she wrapped her arms tighter around him. There was still time before... with a moan she pressed urgently against him, willing her mind to go blank. There was a sigh, then a tremble, before she rested her head against his shoulder. "I have to put the tack away," she murmured. It was tempting to stay just as she was, held close, with her blood just beginning to swim. Taking a long breath, she drew away from him and smiled. "Why don't you be macho and carry the saddle?"

"Directors don't haul equipment," he told her as he tried to pull her back to him.

"Heave it up, Kincaid." Tory swung the reins over her shoulder. "You've got some great muscles."

"Yeah?" Grinning, he lifted the saddle and followed her toward the barn. Bicks was right, Phil mused, watching her walk. She had a way of moving that drove men mad.

The barn door creaked in protest when Tory pulled it open. "Over here." She moved across the concrete floor to hang the reins on a peg.

Phil set down the saddle, then turned. The place was large, high-ceilinged and refreshingly cool. "No animals?" he asked, wandering to an empty stall.

"My mother keeps a few head of cattle," Tory explained as she joined him. "They're grazing. We had more horses, but she doesn't ride much." Tory lifted a shoulder. "Justice has the place mostly to himself."

"I've never been in a barn."

"A deprived child."

He sent her a mild glance over his shoulder as he roamed. "I don't think I expected it to be so clean."

Tory's laugh echoed. "My mother has a vendetta against dirt," she told him. Oddly, she felt amusement now rather than resentment. It was a clean feeling. "I think she'd have put curtains on the windows in the loft if my father had let her."

Phil found the ladder and tested its sturdiness. "What's up there?"

"Hay," Tory said dryly. "Ever seen hay?"

"Don't be smug," he warned before he started to climb. Finding his fascination rather sweet, Tory exerted the energy to go up with him. "The view's incredible." Standing beside the side opening, he could see for miles. The town of Friendly looked almost neat and tidy with the distance.

"I used to come up here a lot." Tucking her hands in her back pockets, Tory looked over his shoulder.

"What did you do?"

"Watch the world go by," she said, nodding toward Friendly. "Or sleep."

He laughed, turning back to her. "You're the only person I know who can turn sleeping into an art."

"I've dedicated quite a bit of my life to it." She took his hand to draw him away.

Instead he pulled her into a dim corner. "There's something I've always wanted to do in a hayloft."

With a laugh Tory stepped away. "Phil, my mother's in the house."

"She's not here," he pointed out. He hooked a hand in the low V where she had loosened her blouse. A hard tug had her stumbling against him.

"Phil—"

"It must have been carrying that saddle," he mused, giving her a gentle push that had her falling backward into a pile of hay.

"Now, wait a minute…" she began, and struggled up on her elbows.

"And the primitive surroundings," he added as he pressed her body back with his own. "If I were directing this scene, it would start like this." He took her mouth in a hot, urgent kiss that turned her protest into a moan. "The lighting would be set so that it seemed one shaft of sunlight was slanting down across here." With a fingertip he traced from her right ear, across her throat, to the hollow between her breasts. "Everything else would be a dull gold, like your skin."

She had her hands pressed against his shoulders, holding him off, although her heart was beating thickly. "Phil, this isn't the time."

He placed two light kisses at either corner of her mouth. He found it curiously exciting to have to persuade her. Light as a breeze, his hand slipped under her blouse until his fingers found her breast. The peak was already taut. At his touch her eyes lost focus and darkened. The hands at his shoulders lost their resistance and clutched at him. "You're so sensitive," he murmured, watching the change in her face. "It drives me crazy to know when I touch you like this your bones turn to water and you're completely mine."

Letting his fingers fondle and stroke, he lowered his mouth to nibble gently at her yielding lips. *Strong, self-sufficient, decisive.* Those were words he would have used to describe her. Yet, he knew, when they were together like this, he had the power to mold her. Even now, as she lifted them to his face to urge him closer, he felt the weakness come over him in thick waves. It was both frightening and irresistible.

She could have asked anything of him, and he would have been unable to deny her. Even his thoughts could no longer be considered his own when she was so intimately entwined in them. The fingers that loosened the rest of her buttons weren't steady. He should have been used to her by now, he told himself as he sought the tender skin of her neck almost savagely. It shouldn't be so intense every time he began to make love to her. Each time he told himself the desperation would fade; yet, it only returned—doubled, tripled, until he was completely lost in her.

There was only her now, over the clean, country smell of hay. Her subtly alluring fragrance was a contrast too exciting to bear. She was murmuring to him as she drew his shirt over his head. The sound of her voice seemed to pulse through his system. The sun shot through the window to beat on his bare back, but he only felt the cool stroking of her fingers as she urged him down until they were flesh to flesh.

His mouth devoured hers as he tugged the jeans over her hips. Greedily he moved to her throat, her shoulders, her breasts, ravenous for each separate taste. His mouth ranged over her, his tongue moistening, savoring, as her skin heated. She was naked but for the brief swatch riding low on her hips. He hooked his fingers beneath it, tormenting them both by lowering it fraction by fraction while his lips followed the progress.

The pleasure grew unmanageable. He began the wild journey back up her body, his fingers fumbling with the snap of his jeans until Tory's brushed them impatiently away.

She undressed him swiftly, while her own mouth streaked over his skin. The sudden change from pliancy to command left him stunned. Then she was on top of him, straddling him while her lips and teeth performed dark magic at the pulse in his throat. Beyond reason, he grasped her hips, lifting her. Tory gave a quick cry as they joined. In delight her head flung back as she let this new exhilaration rule her. Her skin was shiny with dampness when she crested. Delirious, she started to slide toward him, but he rolled her over, crushing her beneath him as he took her to a second peak, higher than the first.

As they lay, damp flesh to damp flesh, their breaths shuddering, she knew a contentment so fulfilling, it brought the sting of tears to her eyes. Hurriedly blinking them away, Tory kissed the curve of his shoulder.

"I guess there's more to do in a hayloft than sleep."

Phil chuckled. Rolling onto his back, he drew her against his side to steal a few more moments alone with her.

Chapter 11

One of the final scenes to be filmed was a tense night sequence outside Hernandez's Bar. Phil had opted to shoot at night with a low light level rather than film during the day with filters. It would give the actors more of a sense of the ambience and keep the gritty realism in the finished product. It was a scene fraught with emotion that would lose everything if overplayed. From the beginning nothing seemed to go right.

Twice the sound equipment broke down, causing lengthy delays. A seasoned supporting actress blew her lines repeatedly and strode off the set, cursing herself. A defective bulb exploded, scattering shards of glass that had to be painstakingly picked up. For the first time since the shooting began, Phil had to deal with a keyed-up, uncooperative Marlie.

"Okay," he said, taking her by the arm to draw her away. "What the hell's wrong with you?"

"I can't get it right," she said furiously. With her hands on her hips she strode a few paces away and kicked at the dirt. "Damn it, Phil, it just doesn't *feel* right."

"Look, we've been at this over two hours. Everybody's a little fed up." His own patience was hanging on by a thread. In two days at the most, he'd have no choice but to head back to California. He should have been pleased that the bulk of the filming was done— that the rushes were excellent. Instead he was tense, irritable and looking for someone to vent his temper on. "Just pull yourself together," he told Marlie curtly. "And get it done."

"Now, just a damn minute!" Firing up instantly, Marlie let her own frustration pour out in temper. "I've put up with your countless retakes, with that stinking, sweaty bar and this godforsaken town because this script is gold. I've let you work me like a horse because I need you. This part is my ticket into the big leagues and I know it right down to the gut."

"You want the ticket," Phil tossed back, "you pay the price."

"I've paid my dues," she told him furiously. A couple of heads turned idly in their direction, but no one ventured over. "I don't have to take your lousy temper on the set because you've got personal problems."

He measured her with narrowed eyes. "You have to take exactly what I give you."

"I'll tell you something, Kincaid—" she poked a small finger into his chest "—I don't have to take anything, because I'm every bit as important to this movie as you are, and we both know it. It doesn't mean a damn who's getting top billing. Kate Lohman's the key to this picture, and I'm Kate Lohman. Don't you forget it, and don't throw your weight around with me."

When she turned to stride off, Phil grabbed her arm, jerking her back. His eyes had iced. The fingers on her arm were hard. Looking down at her set face, he felt temper fade into admiration. "Damn you, Marlie," he said quietly, "you know how to stay in character, don't you?"

"I know this one inside out," she returned. The stiffness went out of her stance.

"Okay, what doesn't feel right?"

The corners of her mouth curved up. "I wanted to work with you," she began, "because you're the best out there these days. I didn't expect to like you. All right," she continued, abruptly professional, "when Sam follows me out of the bar, grabs me, finally losing control, he's furious. Everything he's held in comes pouring out. His dialogue's hard."

"You haven't been off his back since he came into town," Phil reminded her, running over the scene in his mind. "Now he's had enough. After the scene he's going to take you back to your room and make love. You win."

"Do I?" Marlie countered. "My character is a tough lady. She's got reason to be. She's got enough vulnerabilities to keep the audience from despising her, but she's no pushover."

"So?"

"So he comes after me, he calls me a tramp—a cold, money-grabbing whore, among other things—and my response is to take it—damp-eyed and shocked."

Phil considered, a small smile growing. "What would you do?"

"I'd punch the jerk in the mouth."

His laugh echoed down the street. "Yeah, I guess you would at that."

"Tears, maybe," Marlie went on, tasting victory, "but anger too. She's becoming very close to what he's accusing her of. And she hates it—and him, for making it matter."

Phil nodded, his mind already plotting the changes and the angles. Frowning, he called Sam over and outlined the change.

"Can you pull this off without busting my caps?" Sam demanded of Marlie.

She grinned. "Maybe."

"After she hits you," Phil interrupted, "I want dead silence for a good ten seconds. You wipe your mouth with the back of your hand, slow, but don't break the eye contact. Let's set it up from where Marlie walks out of the bar. Bicks!" He left the actors to give his cinematographer a rundown.

"Quiet.... Places.... Roll...." Standing by the cameraman's shoulder, Phil watched the scene unfold. The adrenaline was pumping now. He could see it in Marlie's eyes, in the set of her body, as she burst out the door of the bar onto the sidewalk. When Sam grabbed her, instead of merely being whirled around, she turned on him. The mood seemed to fire into him as well, as his lines became harsher, more emotional. Before there had been nothing in the scene but the man's anger; now there was the woman's too. Now the underlying sexuality was there. When she hit him, it seemed everyone on the set held their breath. The gesture was completely unexpected and, Phil mused as the silence trembled, completely in character. He could almost feel Sam's desire to strike her back, and his inability to do so. She

challenged him to, while her throat moved gently with a nervous swallow. He wiped his mouth, never taking his eyes from hers.

"Cut!" Phil swore jubilantly as he walked over and grabbed Marlie by the shoulders. He kissed her, hard. "Fantastic," he said, then kissed her again. "Fantastic." Looking up, he grinned at Sam.

"Don't try that on me," Sam warned, nursing his lower lip. "She packs a hell of a punch." He gave her a rueful glance. "Ever heard about pulling right before you make contact?" he asked. "Show biz, you know."

"I got carried away."

"I nearly slugged you."

"I know." Laughing, she pushed her hair back with both hands.

"Okay, let's take it from there." Phil moved back to the cameraman. "Places."

"Can't we take it from right before the punch?" Marlie asked with a grin for Sam. "It would sort of give me a roll into the rest of the scene."

"Stand-in!" Sam called.

In her office Tory read over with care a long, detailed letter from an opposing attorney. The tone was very clear through the legal terms and flowery style. The case was going through litigation, she thought with a frown. It might take two months or more, she mused, but this suit wasn't going to be settled out of court. Though normally she would have wanted to come to terms without a trial, she began to feel a tiny flutter of excitement. She'd been away from her own work for too long. She would be back in Albuquerque in a month.

Tory discovered she wanted—needed—something complicated and time-consuming on her return.

Adjustments, she decided as she tried to concentrate on the words in the letter. There were going to be adjustments to be made when she left Friendly this time. When she left Phil. No, she corrected, catching the bridge of her nose between her thumb and forefinger. He was leaving first—tomorrow, the day after. It was uncomfortably easy to see the hole that was already taking shape in her life. Tory reminded herself that she wasn't allowed to think of it. The rules had been made plain at the outset—by both of them. If things had begun to change for her, she simply had to backpedal a bit and reaffirm her priorities. *Her* work, *her* career, *her* life. At that moment the singular possessive pronoun never sounded more empty. Shaking her head, Tory began to read the letter from the beginning a second time.

Merle paced the office, casting quick glances at Tory from time to time. He'd made arrangements for Marlie to meet him there after her work was finished. What he hadn't expected was for Tory to be glued to her desk all evening. No expert with subtleties, Merle had no idea how to move his boss along and have the office to himself. He peeked out the window, noting that the floodlights up the street were being shut off. Shuffling his feet and clearing his throat, he turned back to Tory.

"Guess you must be getting tired," he ventured.

"Hmmm."

"Things are pretty quiet tonight," he tried again, fussing with the buttons on his shirt.

"Um-hmm." Tory began to make notations on her yellow pad.

Merle lifted his eyes to the ceiling. Maybe the direct approach would do it, he decided. "Why don't you knock off and go home."

Tory continued to write. "Trying to get rid of me, Merle T.?"

"Well, no, ah..." He looked down at the dusty tips of his shoes. Women never got any easier to handle.

"Got a date?" she asked mildly as she continued to draft out her answer to the letter.

"Sort of...well, yeah," he said with more confidence.

"Go ahead, then."

"But—" He broke off, stuffing his hands in his pockets.

Tory looked up and studied him. The mustache, she noted, had grown in respectability. It wasn't exactly a prizewinner, but it added maturity to a face she'd always thought resembled a teddy bear's. He still slouched, and even as she studied him, color seeped into his cheeks. But he didn't look away as he once would have done. His eyes stayed on hers so that she could easily read both frustration and embarrassment. The old affection stirred in her.

"Marlie?" she asked gently.

"Yeah." He straightened his shoulders a bit.

"How are you going to feel when she leaves?"

With a shrug Merle glanced toward the window again. "I guess I'll miss her. She's a terrific lady."

The tone caused Tory to give his profile a puzzled look. There was no misery in it, just casual acceptance. With a light laugh she stared back at her notes. Odd, she thought, it seemed their reactions had gotten reversed somewhere along the line. "You don't have to stay, Merle," she said lightly. "If you'd planned to have a late supper or—"

"We did," he interrupted. "Here."

Tory looked up again. "Oh, I see." She couldn't quite control the smile. "Looks like I'm in the way."

Uncomfortable, he shuffled again. "Aw, Tory."

"It's okay." Rising, she exaggerated her accommodating tone. "I know when I'm not wanted. I'll just go back to my room and work on this all by myself."

Merle struggled with loyalty and selfishness while Tory gathered her papers. "You could have supper with us," he suggested gallantly.

Letting the papers drop, Tory skirted the desk. With her hands on his shoulders, she kissed both of his cheeks. "Merle T.," she said softly, "you're a jewel."

Pleased, he grinned as the door opened behind them. "Just like I told you, Phil," Marlie stated as they entered. "Beautiful woman can't keep away from him. You'll have to stand in line, Sheriff," she continued, walking over to hook her arm through Merle's. "I've got first dibs tonight."

"Why don't I get her out of your way?" Phil suggested. "It's the least I can do after that last scene."

"The man is totally unselfish," Marlie confided to Tory. "No sacrifice is too great for his people."

With a snort Tory turned back to her desk. "I might let him buy me a drink," she considered while slipping her papers into a small leather case. When he sat on the corner of her desk, she cast him a look. "And dinner," she added.

"I might be able to come up with some cold cuts," he murmured.

Tory's low, appreciative laugh was interrupted by the phone. "Sheriff's office." Her sigh was automatic as she listened to the excited voice on the other end.

"Yes, Mr. Potts." Merle groaned, but she ignored him. "I see. What kind of noise?" Tory waited while the old man jabbered in her ear. "Are your doors and windows locked? No, Mr. Potts, I don't want you going outside with your shotgun. Yes, I realize a man has to protect his property." A sarcastic sound from Merle earned him a mild glare. "Let me handle it. I'll be there in ten minutes. No, I'll be quiet, just sit tight."

"Sheep thieves," Merle muttered as Tory hung up.

"Burglars," she corrected, opening the top drawer of her desk.

"Just what do you think you're going to do with that?" Phil demanded as he saw Tory pull out the gun.

"Absolutely nothing, I hope." Coolly she began to load it.

"Then why are you—? Wait a minute," he interrupted himself, rising. "Do you mean that damn thing wasn't loaded?"

"Of course not." Tory slipped in the last bullet. "Nobody with sense keeps a loaded gun in an unlocked drawer."

"You got me into that cell with an empty gun?"

She sent him a lazy smile as she strapped on a holster. "You were so cute, Kincaid."

Ignoring amusement, he took a step toward her. "What would you have done if I hadn't backed down?"

"The odds were in my favor," she reminded him. "But I'd have thought of something. Merle, keep an eye on things until I get back."

"Wasting your time."

"Just part of the job."

"If you're wasting your time," Phil began as he stopped her at the door, "why are you taking that gun?"

"It looks so impressive," Tory told him as she walked outside.

"Tory, you're not going out to some sheep ranch with a gun at your hip like some modern-day Belle Starr."

"She was on the wrong side," she reminded him.

"Tory, I mean it!" Infuriated, Phil stepped in front of the car to block her way.

"Look, I said I'd be there in ten minutes. I'm going to have to drive like a maniac as it is."

He didn't budge. "What if there is someone out there?"

"That's exactly why I'm going."

When she reached for the door handle, he put his hand firmly over hers. "I'm going with you."

"Phil, I don't have time."

"I'm going."

Narrowing her eyes, she studied his face. There was no arguing with that expression, she concluded. "Okay, you're temporarily deputized. Get in and do what you're told."

Phil lifted a brow at her tone. The thought of her going out to some secluded ranch with only a gun for company had him swallowing his pride. He slid across to the passenger seat. "Don't I get a badge?" he asked as Tory started the engine.

"Use your imagination," she advised.

Tory's speed was sedate until they reached the town limits. Once the buildings were left behind, Phil watched the climbing speedometer with growing trepidation. Her hands were relaxed and competent on the wheel. The open window caused her hair to fly wildly, but her expression was calm.

She doesn't think there's anything to this, he decided

as he watched the scenery whiz by. But if she did, his thoughts continued, she'd be doing exactly the same thing. The knowledge gave him a small thrill of fear. The neat black holster at her side hid an ugly, very real weapon. She had no business chasing burglars or carrying guns. She had no business taking the remotest chance with her own well-being. He cursed the phone call that had made it all too clear just how potentially dangerous her position in Friendly was. It had been simpler to think of her as a kind of figurehead, a referee for small-town squabbles. The late-night call and the gun changed everything.

"What will you do if you have to use that thing?" he demanded suddenly.

Without turning, Tory knew where his thoughts centered. "I'll deal with that when the time comes."

"When's your term up here?"

Tory took her eyes from the road for a brief two seconds. Phil was looking straight ahead. "Three weeks."

"You're better off in Albuquerque," he muttered. *Safer* was the word heard but not said. Tory recalled the time a client had nearly strangled her in his cell before the guards had pulled him off. She decided it was best unmentioned. Hardly slackening the car's speed, she took a right turn onto a narrow, rut-filled dirt road. Phil swore as the jolting threw him against the door.

"You should have strapped in," she told him carelessly.

His response was rude and brief.

The tiny ranch house had every light blazing. Tory pulled up in front of it with a quick squeal of brakes.

"Think you missed any?" Phil asked her mildly as he rubbed the shoulder that had collided with the door.

"I'll catch them on the way back." Before he could retort, Tory was out of the car and striding up the porch steps. She knocked briskly, calling out to identify herself. When Phil joined her on the porch, the door opened a crack. "Mr. Potts," she began.

"Who's he?" the old man demanded through the crack in the door.

"New deputy," Tory said glibly. "We'll check the grounds and the outside of the house now."

Potts opened the door a bit more, revealing an ancient, craggy face and a shiny black shotgun. "I heard them in the bushes."

"We'll take care of it, Mr. Potts." She put her hands on the butt of his gun. "Why don't you let me have this for now?"

Unwilling, Potts held firm. "I gotta have protection."

"Yes, but they're not in the house," she reminded him gently. "I could really use this out here."

He hesitated, then slackened his grip. "Both barrels," he told her, then slammed the door. Tory heard the triple locks click into place.

"That is not your average jolly old man," Phil commented.

Tory took the two shells out of the shotgun. "Alone too long," she said simply. "Let's take a look around."

"Go get 'em, big guy."

Tory barely controlled a laugh. "Just keep out of the way, Kincaid."

Whether she considered it a false alarm or not, Phil noted that Tory was very thorough. With the empty shotgun in one hand and a flashlight in the other, she checked every door and window on the dilapidated ranch house. Watching her, he walked into a pile of empty paint cans, sending them clattering. When he swore, Tory turned her head to look at him.

"You move like a cat, Kincaid," she said admiringly.

"The man's got junk piled everywhere," he retorted. "A burglar doesn't have a chance."

Tory smothered a chuckle and moved on. They circled the house, making their way through Potts's obstacle course of old car parts, warped lumber and rusted tools. Satisfied that no one had attempted to break into the house for at least twenty-five years, Tory widened her circle to check the ground.

"Waste of time," Phil muttered, echoing Merle.

"Then let's waste it properly." Tory shone her light on the uneven grass as they continued to walk. Resigned, Phil kept to her side. There were better ways, he was thinking, to spend a warm summer night. And the moon was full. Pure white, he observed as he gazed up at it. Cool and full and promising. He wanted to make love to her under it, in the still, hot air with nothing and no one around for miles. The desire came suddenly, intensely, washing over him with a wave of possession that left him baffled.

"Tory," he murmured, placing a hand on her shoulder.

"Ssh!"

The order was sharp. He felt her stiffen under his hand. Her eyes were trained on a dry, dying bush directly in front of them. Even as he opened his mouth to say something impatient, Phil saw the movement. His fingers tightened on Tory's shoulder as he automatically stepped forward. The protective gesture was instinctive, and so natural neither of them noticed it. He never thought: This is my woman, and I'll do anything to keep her from harm; he simply reacted. With his body as a shield for hers, they watched the bush in silence.

There was a slight sound, hardly a whisper on the air, but Tory felt the back of her neck prickle. The dry leaves of the bush cracked quietly with some movement. She reached in her pocket for the two shells, then reloaded the shotgun. The moonlight bounced off the oiled metal. Her hands were rock steady. Phil was poised, ready to lunge as Tory aimed the gun at the moon and fired both barrels. The sound split the silence like an axe.

With a terrified bleat, the sheep that had been grazing lazily behind the bush scrambled for safety. Without a word Phil and Tory watched the dirty white blob run wildly into the night.

"Another desperate criminal on the run from the law," Tory said dryly.

Phil burst into relieved laughter. He felt each separate muscle in his body relax. "I'd say 'on the lamb.'"

"I was hoping you wouldn't." Because the hand holding the gun was shaking, Tory lowered it to her side. She swallowed; her throat was dry. "Well, let's go tell Potts his home and hearth are safe. Then we can go have that drink."

Phil laid his hands on her shoulders, looking down on her face in the moonlight. "Are you all right?"

"Sure."

"You're trembling."

"That's you," she countered, smiling at him.

Phil slid his hand down to her wrist to feel the race of her pulse. "Scared the hell out of you," he said softly.

Tory's eyes didn't waver. "Yeah." She was able to smile again, this time with more feeling. "How about you?"

"Me too." Laughing, he gave her a light kiss. "I'm not going to need that badge after all." And I'm not going to feel safe, he added silently, until you take yours off for the last time.

"Oh, I don't know, Kincaid." Tory led the way back with the beam of her flashlight. "First night on the job and you flushed out a sheep."

"Just give the crazy old man his gun and let's get out of here."

It took ten minutes of Tory's diplomacy to convince Potts that everything was under control. Mollified more by the fact that Tory had used his gun than the information that his intruder was one of his own flock, he locked himself in again. After contacting Merle on the radio, she headed back to town at an easy speed.

"I guess I could consider this a fitting climax to my sojourn to Friendly," Phil commented. "Danger and excitement on the last night in town."

Tory's fingers tightened on the wheel, but she managed to keep the speed steady. "You're leaving tomorrow."

He listened for regret in the statement but heard none. Striving to match her tone, he continued to stare out the window. "We finished up tonight, a day ahead of schedule. I'll head out with the film crew tomorrow. I want to be there when Huffman sees the film."

"Of course." The pain rammed into her, dazzlingly physical. It took concentrated control to keep from moaning with it. "You've still quite a lot of work to do before it's finished, I suppose."

"The studio scenes," he agreed, struggling to ignore twin feelings of panic and desolation. "The editing, the mixing… I guess your schedule's going to be pretty tight when you get back to Albuquerque."

"It looks that way." Tory stared at the beams of the headlights. A long straight road, no curves, no hills. No end. She bit the inside of her lip hard before she trusted herself to continue. "I'm thinking about hiring a new law clerk."

"That's probably a good idea." He told himself that the crawling emptiness in his stomach was due to a lack of food. "I don't imagine your caseload's going to get any smaller."

"No, it should take me six months of concentrated work to get it under control again. You'll probably start on a new film the minute this one's finished."

"It's being cast now," he murmured. "I'm going to produce it too."

Tory smiled. "No guarantors?"

Phil answered the smile. "We'll see."

They drove for another half mile in silence. Slowing down, Tory pulled off onto a small dirt road and stopped. Phil took a quick glance around at nothing in particular, then turned to her. "What are we doing?"

"Parking." She scooted from under the steering wheel, winding her arms around his neck.

"Isn't there some legality about using an official car for illicit purposes?" His mouth was already seeking hers, craving.

"I'll pay the fine in the morning." She silenced his chuckle with a deep, desperate kiss.

As if by mutual consent, they went slowly. All pleasure, all desire, was concentrated in tastes. Lips, teeth and tongues brought shuddering arousal, urging them to hurry. But they would satisfy needs with mouths only first. Her lips were silkily yielding even as they met and increased his demand. Wild, crazy desires whipped through him, but her mouth held him prisoner. He touched her nowhere else. This taste—spiced honey, this texture—heated satin—would live with him always.

Tory let her lips roam his face. She knew each crease, each angle, each slope, more intimately than she knew her own features. With her eyes closed she could see him perfectly, and knew she had only to close her eyes again, in a year, in ten years, to have the same vivid picture. The skin on his neck was damp, making the flavor intensify as her tongue glided over it. Without thinking, she ran her fingers down his shirt, nimbly loosening buttons. When his chest was vulnerable, she spread both palms over it to feel his quick shudder. Then she brought her mouth, lazily, invitingly, back to his.

Her fingertips sent a path of ice, a path of fire, over his naked skin. Her mouth was drawing him in until his head swam. His labored breathing whispered on the night air. Wanting her closer, he shifted, cursed the cramped confines of the car, then dragged her across his lap. Lifting her to him, he buried his face against the side of her neck. He fed there, starving for her until she moaned and brought his hand to rest on her breast. With torturous slowness he undid the series of buttons, allowing his fingertips to trail along her skin as it was painstakingly exposed. He let the tips of his fingers bring her to desperation.

The insistent brush of his thumb over the point of her breast released a shaft of exquisite pain so sharp, she cried out with it, dragging him closer. Open and hungry, her mouth fixed on his while she fretted to touch more of him. Their position made it impossible, but her body was his. He ran his hands over it, feeling her skin jump as he roamed to the waistband of her jeans. Loosening them, he slid his hand down to warm, moist secrets. His mouth crushed hers as he drank in her moan.

Tory struggled, maddened by the restrictions, wild with desire, as his fingers aroused her beyond belief. He kept her trapped against him, knowing once she touched him that his control would shatter. This night, he thought, this final night, would last until there was no tomorrow.

When she crested, he rose with her, half delirious. No woman was so soft, no woman was so responsive. His heart pounded, one separate pain after another, as he drove her up again.

Her struggles ceased. Compliance replaced them. Tory lay shuddering in a cocoon of unrivaled sensations. She was his. Though her mind was unaware of the total gift of self, her body knew. She'd been his, perhaps from the first, perhaps only for that moment, but there would never be any turning back. Love swamped her; desire sated her. There was nothing left but the need to possess, to be possessed, by one man. In that instant she conceded her privacy.

The change in her had something racing through him. Phil couldn't question, couldn't analyze. He knew only that they must come together now—now, while there was something magic shimmering. It had nothing to do with the moonlight beaming into the car or the eerie silence surrounding them. It concerned only them and the secret that had grown despite protests. He didn't think, he didn't deny. With a sudden madness he tugged on her clothes and his own. Speed was foremost in his mind. He had to hurry before whatever trembled in the tiny confines was lost. Then her body was beneath his, fused to his, eager, asking.

He took her on the seat of the car like a passionate teenager. He felt like a man who had been given something precious, and as yet unrecognizable.

Chapter 12

A long sleepy time. Moonlight on the back of closed lids…night air over naked skin. The deep, deep silence of solitude by the whispering breathing of intimacy.

Tory floated in that luxurious plane between sleep and wakefulness—on her side, on the narrow front seat, with her body fitted closely against Phil's. Their legs were tangled, their arms around each other, as much for support as need. With his mouth near her ear, his warm breath skipped along her skin.

There were two marginally comfortable beds back at the hotel. They could have chosen either of them for their last night together, but they had stayed where they were, on a rough vinyl seat, on a dark road, as the night grew older. There they were alone completely. Morning still seemed very far away.

A hawk cried out as it drove toward earth. Some

small animal screamed in the brush. Tory's lids fluttered up to find Phil's eyes open and on hers. In the moonlight his irises were very pale. Needing no words, perhaps wanting none, Tory lifted her mouth to his. They made love again, quietly, slowly, with more tenderness than either was accustomed to.

So they dozed again, unwilling to admit that the night was slipping away from them. When Tory awoke, there was a faint lessening in the darkness—not light, but the texture that meant morning was close.

A few more hours, she thought, gazing at the sky through the far window as she lay beside him. When the sun came up, it would be over. Now his body was warm against hers. He slept lightly, she knew. She had only to shift or murmur his name and he would awaken. She remained still. For a few more precious moments she wanted the simple unity that came from having him sleep at her side. There would be no stopping the sun from rising in the east—or stopping her lover from going west. It was up to her to accept the second as easily as she accepted the first. Closing her eyes, she willed herself to be strong. Phil stirred, dreaming.

He walked through his house in the hills, purposely, from room to room, looking, searching, for what was vague to him; but time after time he turned away, frustrated. Room after room after room. Everything was familiar: the colors, the furniture, even small personal objects that identified his home, his belongings. Something was missing. Stolen, lost? The house echoed emptily around him as he continued to search for something vital and unknown. The emotions of the man in the dream communicated themselves to the man dreaming. He felt the helplessness, the anger and the panic.

Hearing him murmur her name, Tory shifted yet closer. Phil shot awake, disoriented. The dream slipped into some corner of his mind that he couldn't reach.

"It's nearly morning," she said quietly.

A bit dazed, struggling to remember what he had dreamed that had left him feeling so empty, Phil looked at the sky. It was lightening. The first pale pinks bloomed at the horizon. For a moment they watched in silence as the day crept closer, stealing their night.

"Make love to me again," Tory whispered. "Once more, before morning."

He could see the quiet need in her eyes, the dark smudges beneath that told of patchy sleep, the soft glow that spoke clearly of a night of loving. He held the picture in his mind a moment, wanting to be certain he wouldn't lose it when time had dimmed other memories. He lowered his mouth to hers in bittersweet goodbye.

The sky paled to blue. The horizon erupted with color. The gold grew molten and scarlet bled into it as dawn came up. They loved intensely one final time. As morning came they lost themselves in each other, pretending it was still night. Where he touched, she trembled. Where she kissed, his skin hummed until they could no longer deny the need. The sun had full claim when they came together, so that the light streamed without mercy. Saying little, they dressed, then drove back to town.

When Tory stopped in front of the hotel, she felt she was in complete control again. No regrets, she reminded herself, as she turned off the ignition. We've just come to the fork in the road. We knew it was there when we started. Turning, she smiled at Phil.

"We're liable to be a bit stiff today."

Grinning, he leaned over and kissed her chin. "It was worth it."

"Remember that when you're moaning for a hot bath on your way back to L.A." Tory slid from the car. When she stepped up on the sidewalk, Phil took her hand. The contact threatened her control before she snapped it back into place.

"I'm going to be thinking of you," he murmured as they stepped into the tiny lobby.

"You'll be busy." She let her hand slide on the banister as they mounted the stairs.

"Not that busy." Phil turned her to him when they reached the top landing. "Not that busy, Tory," he said again.

Her courtroom experience came to her aid. Trembling inside, Tory managed an easy smile. "I'm glad. I'll think of you too." *Too often, too much. Too painful.*

"If I call you—"

"I'm in the book," she interrupted. Play it light, she ordered herself. The way it was supposed to be, before… "Keep out of trouble, Kincaid," she told him as she slipped her room key into its lock.

"Tory."

He stepped closer, but she barred the way into the room. "I'll say goodbye now." With another smile she rested a hand on his cheek. "It'll be simpler, and I think I'd better catch a couple hours' sleep before I go into the office."

Phil took a long, thorough study of her face. Her eyes were direct, her smile easy. Apparently there was nothing left to say. "If that's what you want."

Tory nodded, not fully trusting herself. "Be happy,

Phil," she managed before she disappeared into her room. Very carefully Tory turned the lock before she walked to the bed. Lying down, she curled into a ball and wept, and wept, and wept.

It was past noon when Tory awoke. Her head was pounding. Dragging herself to the bathroom, she studied herself objectively in the mirror over the sink. Terrible, she decided without emotion. The headache had taken the color from her cheeks, and her eyes were swollen and red from tears. Dispassionately, Tory ran the water until it was icy cold, then splashed her face with it. When her skin was numb, she stripped and stepped under the shower.

She decided against aspirin. The pills would dull the pain, and the pain made it difficult to think. Thinking was the last thing she felt she needed to do at the moment. Phil was gone, back to his own life. She would go on with hers. The fact that she had fallen in love with him over her own better judgment was simply her hard luck. In a few days she would be able to cope with it easily enough. Like hell you will, she berated herself as she dried her skin with a rough towel. You fell hard, and some bruises take years to heal…if ever.

Wasn't it ironic, she mused as she went back into the bedroom to dress. Victoria L. Ashton, Attorney at Law, dedicated to straightening out other people's lives, had just made a beautiful mess of her own. And yet, there hadn't been any options. A deal was a deal.

Phil, she said silently, I've decided to change our contract. Circumstances have altered, and I'm in love with you. I propose we include certain things like commitment and reciprocal affection into our arrangement, with options for additions such as marriage and children, should both parties find it agreeable.

She gave a short laugh and pulled on a fresh shirt. Of course, she could merely have clung to him, tearfully begging him not to leave her. What man wouldn't love to find himself confronted with a hysterical woman who won't let go?

Better this way, she reminded herself, tugging on jeans. Much better to have a clean, civilized break. Aloud, she said something potent about being civilized as she pinned on her badge. The one thing she had firmly decided during her crying jag was that it was time for her to leave Friendly. Merle could handle the responsibilities of the office for the next few weeks without too much trouble. She had come to terms with her father's death, with her mother. She felt confident that she'd helped in Tod's family situation. Merle had grown up a bit. All in all, Tory felt she wasn't needed any longer. In Albuquerque she could put her own life in motion again. She needed that if she wasn't going to spend three weeks wallowing in self-pity and despair. At least, she decided, it was something she could start on. Naturally she would have to talk to the mayor and officially resign. There would be a visit to her mother. If she spent a day briefing Merle, she should be able to leave before the end of the week.

Her own rooms, Tory thought, trying to work up some excitement. The work she was trained for—a meaty court case that would take weeks of preparation and a furnace of energy. She felt suddenly that she had a surplus of it and nowhere to go. Back in the bath, she applied a careful layer of makeup to disguise the effects of tears, then brushed her hair dry. The first step was the mayor. There was no point putting it off.

It took thirty minutes for Tory to convince the mayor she was serious and another fifteen to assure him that Merle was capable of handling the job of acting sheriff until the election.

"You know, Tory," Bud said when he saw her mind was made up, "we're going to be sorry to lose you. I guess we all kept hoping you'd change your mind and run. You've been a good sheriff, I guess you come by it naturally."

"I appreciate that—really." Touched, Tory took the hand he offered her. "Pat Rowe and Nick Merriweather are both fair men. Whoever wins, the town's in good hands. In a few years Merle will make you a fine sheriff."

"If you ever change your mind…" Bud trailed off wanting to leave the door open.

"Thanks, but my niche in the law isn't in enforcement. I have to get back to my practice."

"I know, I know." He sighed, capitulating. "You've done more than we had a right to expect."

"I did what I wanted to do," she corrected.

"I guess things will be quiet for a while, especially with the movie people gone." He gave a regretful glance toward the window. Excitement, he mused, wasn't meant for Friendly. "Come by and see me before you leave town."

Outside, the first thing Tory noticed was the absence of the movie crew. There were no vans, no sets, no lights or packets of people. Friendly had settled back into its yawning pace as though there had never been a ripple. Someone had written some graffiti in the dust on the window of the post office. A car puttered into town and stopped in front of the hardware store. Tory started to cross the street, but stopped in the center when she was hailed. Shielding her eyes, she watched Tod race toward her.

"Sheriff, I've been looking for you."

"Is something wrong?"

"No." He grinned the quick-spreading grin that transformed his thin face. "It's real good, I wanted you to know. My dad…well, we've been talking, you know, and we even drove out to see those people you told us about."

"How'd it go?"

"We're going to go back—my mom too."

"I'm happy for you." Tory brushed her knuckles over his cheek. "It's going to take time, Tod. You'll all have to work together."

"I know, but…" He looked up at her, his eyes wide and thrilled. "He really loves me. I never thought he did. And my mom, she wondered if you could come out to the house sometime. She wants to thank you."

"There isn't any need for that."

"She wants to."

"I'll try." Tory hesitated, finding that this goodbye would be more difficult than most. "I'm going away in a couple of days."

His elated expression faded. "For good?"

"My mother lives here," she reminded him. "My father's buried here. I'll come back from time to time."

"But not to stay."

"No," Tory said softly. "Not to stay."

Tod lowered his gaze to the ground. "I knew you'd leave. I guess I was pretty stupid that day in your office when I..." He trailed off with a shrug and continued to stare at the ground.

"I didn't think you were stupid. It meant a lot to me." Tory put out a hand to lift his face. "*Means* a lot to me."

Tod moistened his lips. "I guess I still love you—if you don't mind."

"Oh." Tory felt the tears spring to her eyes and pulled him into her arms. "I'm going to miss you like crazy. Would you think I was stupid if I said I wish I were a fourteen-year-old girl?"

Grinning, he drew away. Nothing she could have said could have pleased him more. "I guess if you were I could kiss you goodbye."

With a laugh Tory brushed a light kiss on his lips. "Go on, get out of here," she ordered unsteadily. "Nothing undermines the confidence of a town more than having its sheriff crying in the middle of the street."

Feeling incredibly mature, Tod dashed away. Turning, he ran backward for a moment. "Will you write sometime?"

"Yes, yes, I'll write." Tory watched him streak off at top speed. Her smile lost some of its sparkle. She was losing, she discovered, quite a bit in one day. Briskly shaking off the mood, she turned in the direction of her office. She was still a yard away when Merle strolled out.

"Hey," he said foolishly, glancing from her, then back at the door he'd just closed.

"Hey yourself," she returned. "You just got yourself a promotion, Merle T."

"Tory, there's— Huh?"

"Incredibly articulate," she replied with a fresh

smile. "I'm resigning. You'll be acting sheriff until the election."

"Resigning?" He gave her a completely baffled look. "But you—" He broke off, shaking his head at the door again. "How come?"

"I need to get back to my practice. Anyway—" she stepped up on the sidewalk "—it shouldn't take long for me to fill you in on the procedure. You already know just about everything. Come on inside and we'll get started."

"Tory." In an uncharacteristic gesture he took her arm and stopped her. Shrewdly direct, his eyes locked on hers. "Are you upset about something?"

Merle was definitely growing up, Tory concluded. "I just saw Tod." It was part of the truth, and all she would discuss. "That kid gets to me."

His answer was a slow nod, but he didn't release her arm. "I guess you know the movie people left late this morning."

"Yes, I know." Hearing her own clipped response, Tory took a mental step back. "I don't suppose it was easy for you to say goodbye to Marlie," she said more gently.

"I'll miss her some," he admitted, still watching Tory critically. "We had fun together."

His words were so calm that Tory tilted her head as she studied him. "I was afraid you'd fallen in love with her."

"In love with her?" He let out a hoot of laughter. "Shoot, I ain't ready for that. No way."

"Sometimes being ready doesn't make any difference," Tory muttered. "Well," she said more briskly, "since you're not crying in your beer, why don't we go over some things? I'd like to be in Albuquerque before the end of the week."

"Ah...yeah, sure." Merle glanced around the empty street. "I gotta talk to somebody first over at, um...the hotel," he announced. "Be right back."

Tory shot him an exasperated glance as he loped across the street. "Well," she murmured, "some things never change." Deciding she could spend the time packing her books and papers, Tory walked into the office.

Seated at her desk, casually examining the .45, was Phil Kincaid. She stopped dead, gaping at him. "Sheriff," he said mildly, giving the barrel an idle spin.

"Phil." She found her voice, barely. "What are you doing here?"

He didn't rise, but propped his feet up on the desk instead. "I forgot something. Did you know you didn't unload this thing last night?"

She didn't even glance at the gun, but stood rooted to the spot. "I thought you'd left hours ago."

"Did you?" He gave her a long, steady look. The cold water and makeup had helped, but he knew her face intimately. "I did," he agreed after a moment. "I came back."

"Oh." So now she would have to deal with the good-bye a second time. Tory ignored the ache in her stomach and smiled. "What did you forget?"

"I owe you something," he said softly. The gesture with the gun was very subtle, but clear enough.

Only partially amused, Tory lifted a brow. "Let's call it even," she suggested. Wanting to busy her hands, she went to the shelf near the desk to draw out her books.

"No," he said mildly. "I don't think so. Turn around, Sheriff."

Annoyance was the least painful of her emotions, so Tory let it out. "Look, Phil—"

"In the cell," he interrupted. "I can recommend the first one."

"You're out of your mind." With a thud she dropped the books. "If that thing's loaded, you could hurt someone."

"I have some things to say to you," he continued calmly. "In there." Again he gestured toward the cell.

Her hands went to her hips. "All right, Kincaid, I'm still sheriff here. The penalty for armed assault on a peace officer—"

"Shut up and get in," Phil ordered.

"You can take that gun," Tory began dangerously, "and—"

Her suggestion was cut off when Phil grabbed her arm and hauled her into a cell. Stepping in with her, he pulled the door shut with a shattering clang.

"You *idiot!*" Impotently, Tory gave the locked door a furious jerk. "Now just how the hell are we supposed to get out?"

Phil settled comfortably on the bunk, propped on one elbow, with the gun lowered toward the floor. It was just as empty as it had been when Tory had bluffed him. "I haven't anyplace better to go."

Fists on hips, Tory whirled. "Just what is this all about, Kincaid?" she demanded. "You're supposed to be halfway to L.A. Instead you're propped up at my desk. Instead of a reasonable explanation, you throw that gun around like some two-bit hood—"

"I thought I did it with such finesse," he complained, frowning at the object under discussion. "Of course, I'd rather have a piece with a bit more style." He grinned up at her. "Pearl handle, maybe."

"Do you have to behave like such a fool?"

"I suppose."

"When this is over, you're going to find yourself locked up for months. Years, if I can manage it," she added, turning to tug uselessly on the bars again.

"That won't work," he told her amiably. "I shook them like crazy a few months ago."

Ignoring him, Tory stalked to the window. Not a soul on the street. She debated swallowing her pride and calling out. It would look terrific, she thought grimly, to have the sheriff shouting to be let out of one of her own cells. If she waited for Merle, at least she could make him swear to secrecy.

"All right, Kincaid," she said between her teeth. "Let's have it. Why are you here and why the devil are we locked in the cell?"

He glanced down at the gun again, then set it on the edge of the bunk. Automatically, Tory judged the distance. "Because—" and his voice had altered enough to lure her eyes to his "—I found myself in an impossible situation."

At those words Tory felt her heart come to a stop, then begin again at a furious rate. Cautiously she warned herself not to read anything into the statement. True, she remembered his use of the phrase when talking about love, but it didn't follow that he meant the same thing now.

"Oh?" she managed, and praised herself for a brilliant response.

"*'Oh?'*" Phil pushed himself off the bunk in a quick move. "Is that all you can say? I got twenty miles out of town," he went on in sudden fury. "I told myself that was it. You wanted—I wanted—a simple transient relationship. No complications. We'd enjoyed each other— it was over."

Tory swallowed. "Yes, we'd agreed—"

"The hell with what we agreed." Phil grabbed her shoulders, shaking her until her mouth dropped open in shock. "It got complicated. It got very, very complicated." Releasing her abruptly, he began to pace the cell he had locked them both into.

"Twenty miles out of town," he repeated, "and I couldn't make it. Even last night I told myself it was all for the best. You'd go your way, I'd go mine. We'd both have some great memories." He turned to her then; although his voice lowered, it was no calmer. "Damn it, Tory, I want more than memories of you. I need more. You didn't want this to happen, I know that." Agitated, he ran a hand through his hair, while she said nothing. "I didn't want it, either, or thought I didn't. I'm not sure anymore. It might have been the first minute I walked in here, or that day at the cemetery. It might have been that night at the lake or a hundred other times. I don't know when it happened, why it happened." He shook his head as though it was a problem he'd struggled with and ultimately given up on. "I only know I love you. And God knows I can't leave you. I tried—I can't."

With a shuddering sigh Tory walked back to the bars and rested her head against them. The headache she had awoken with was now a whirling dizziness. A minute, she told herself. I just need a minute to take it in.

"I know you've got a life in Albuquerque," Phil continued, fighting against the fluttering panic in his stomach. "I know you've got a career that's important to

you. It isn't something I'm asking you to choose between. There are ways to balance things if people want
to badly enough. I broke the rules. I'm willing to make
the adjustments."

"Adjustments…" Tory managed before she turned
back to him.

"I can live in Albuquerque," he told her as he crossed
the cell. "That won't stop me from making movies."

"The studio—"

"I'll buy a plane and commute," he said quickly. "It's
been done before."

"A plane." With a little laugh she walked away, dragging a hand through her hair. "A plane."

"Yes, damn it, a plane." Her reaction was nothing
that he had expected. The panic grew. "You didn't want
me to go," he began in defense, in fury. "You've been
crying. I can tell."

A bit steadier, Tory faced him again. "Yes, I cried.
No, I didn't want you to go. Still, I thought it was best
for both of us."

"Why?"

"It wouldn't be easy, juggling two careers and one
relationship."

"Marriage," he corrected firmly. "Marriage, Tory.
The whole ball of wax. Kids too. I want you to have
my children." He saw the change in her eyes—shock,
fear? Unable to identify it, Phil went to her again. "I
said I love you." Again he took her by the shoulders.
This time he didn't shake her but held her almost ten-
tatively. "I have to know what you feel for me."

She spent a moment simply looking into his eyes.
Loved her? Yes, she realized with something like a jolt.
She could see it. It was real. And more, he was hurt-

ing because he wasn't sure. Doubts melted away. "I've been in an impossible situation, I think, from the first moment Merle hauled you in here."

She felt his fingers tense, then relax again. "Are you sure?" he asked, fighting the need to drag her against him.

"That I'm in love with you?" For the first time a ghost of a smile hovered around her mouth. "Sure enough that I nearly died when I thought you were leaving me. Sure enough that I was going to let you go because I'm just as stupid as you are."

His hands dove into her hair. "Stupid?" he repeated, drawing her closer.

"'He needs his own life. We agreed not to complicate things. He'd hate it if I begged him to stay.'" She smiled more fully. "Sound familiar?"

"With a slight change in the personal pronoun." Phil pulled her close just to hold her. *Mine,* they thought simultaneously, then clung. "Ah, Tory, last night was so wonderful—and so terrible."

"I know, thinking it was the last time." She drew back only enough so their mouths could meet. "I've been giving some thought to it for a while," she murmured, then lost the trend of thought as they kissed again.

"To what?"

"To...oh, to moving to the coast."

Framing her face with his hands, Phil tilted it to his. "You don't have to do that. I told you, I can—"

"Buy a plane," she finished on a laugh. "And I'm sure you can. But I have given some thought lately to moving on. Why not California?"

"We'll work that out."

"Eventually," she agreed, drawing his mouth back to hers.

"Tory." He held her off a moment, his eyes serious again. "Are you going to marry me?"

She considered a moment, letting her fingers twine in his hair. "It might be wise," she decided, "since we're going to have those kids."

"When?"

"It takes nine months," she reminded him.

"Marriage," he corrected, nipping her bottom lip.

"Well, after you've served your sentence…about three months."

"Sentence?"

"Illegal use of a handgun, accosting a peace officer, improper use of a correctional facility…" She shrugged, giving him her dashing grin. "Time off for good behavior, you should be out in no time. Remember, I'm still sheriff here, Kincaid."

"The hell you are." Pulling the badge from her blouse, he tossed it through the bars of the window. "Besides, you'll never make it stick."

* * * * *

OPPOSITES ATTRACT

For Joan Schulhafer,
leader of tours, handler of details and good friend.

Chapter 1

"Advantage, Starbuck."

Isn't it always? Asher mused. For a moment the large arena held that humming silence peculiar to indoor sports events. There was an aroma of roasted peanuts and sweat. The overhead lights heated the scent somewhat pleasantly while the crush of bodies added enforced camaraderie. A small child sent up a babbling complaint and was hushed.

Seated several rows back at mid-court, Asher Wolfe watched Ty Starbuck—tennis master, Gypsy, eternal boy of summer and former lover. She thought again, as she had several times during more than two hours of play, that he'd changed. Just how wasn't yet completely clear. More than three years had passed since she'd seen him in the flesh. But he hadn't aged, or thickened, or lost any of his characteristic verve.

Rarely over the years had she watched a televised match—it was too painful. Too many faces were familiar, with his the most strictly avoided. If Asher had chanced to come across a write-up or picture of him in the sports pages or in a gossip column, she had immediately put it aside. Ty Starbuck was out of her life. Her decision. Asher was a very decisive woman.

Even her decision to come to the U.S. Indoor Tennis Championship had been a cool-headed one. Before making this trip, she had carefully weighed the pros and cons. In the end logic had won. She was getting back into the game herself. On the circuit, meetings with Ty would be unavoidable. She would see him now, letting the press, her colleagues and fans see clearly that there was nothing left of what had been three years before. Ty would see too, and, she hoped fervently, so would she.

Ty stood behind the baseline, preparing to serve. His stance was the same, she mused, as was his sizzling concentration. He tossed the ball up, coming back and over with the wicked left-handed serve that had become synonymous with his name, a Starbuck.

Asher heard the explosion of his breath that forced the power into it. She held her own. A lesser player than the Frenchman, Grimalier, would never have gotten a racket on the ball. His return was quick—force meeting force—and the rally began.

The crowd grew noisier as the ball smashed and thudded. Echoes bounced crazily. There were cries of encouragement, shouts of appreciation for the prowess of the two players. Ty's basic entertainment value hadn't decreased since Asher had been out of the game. Fans adored or detested him, but they never, never ignored him. Nor could she, though she was no longer certain which category she fell into. Every muscle of his body was familiar to her, every move, every expression. Her feelings were a confused jumble of respect, admiration and longing, which swirled to reach a vortex of pain, sharply remembered. Still, she was caught up in him again. Ty Starbuck demanded every last emotion and didn't really give a damn if it was love or hate.

Both men moved quickly, their eyes riveted on the small white sphere. Backhand, forehand, drop shot. Sweat poured down unheeded. Both the game and the fans demanded it. A tennis buff wanted to see the effort, the strain, wanted to hear the grunts and whistling breaths, wanted to smell the sweat. Despite her determination to remain dispassionate, Asher found herself watching Ty with the undiluted admiration she'd held for him for more than ten years.

He played with nonchalant flash—contradictory terms, but there it was. Strength, agility, form—he had them all. He had a long, limber body, seemingly elastic until the muscles flowed and bunched. His six-two height gave him an advantage of reach, and he could twist and turn on a dime. He played like a fencer— Asher had always thought a swashbuckler. Graceful sweeps, lunges, parries, with an almost demonic glint in his dusk-gray eyes. His face was that of the adventurer—narrow, rakish, with a hint of strong bone vying with an oddly tender mouth. As always, his hair was a bit too long, flowing wild and black around a white sweatband.

He was a set up, and held advantage, but he played as though his life depended on this one point. That hadn't changed, Asher thought, as her heart pounded at double time. She was as involved in the match as if she were the one with the racket in her hand and the sweat rolling over her skin. Her palms were slick, her own muscles tight. Tennis involved its onlookers. Starbuck absorbed them. That hadn't changed either.

Ty smashed the ball crosscourt at the sideline. It careened away even as the Frenchman dove toward it. Asher sucked in her breath at the speed and placement of the ball.

"Wide," the line judge said dispassionately. A loud complaint poured out of the crowd. Asher fixed her eyes on Ty and waited for the explosion.

He stood, breathing hard from the punishing rally, his eyes fixed on the judge. The crowd continued to roar disapproval as deuce was called. Slowly, his eyes still on the judge, Ty swiped his wristband over his brow. His face was inscrutable but for his eyes, and his eyes spoke volumes. The crowd quieted to a murmur of speculation. Asher bit hard on her bottom lip. Ty walked back to the baseline without having uttered a sound.

This was the change, Asher realized with a jolt. Control. Her breath came out slowly as the tension in her shoulders diminished. In years past, Ty Starbuck would have hurled abuse—and an occasional racket—snarled, implored the crowd for support or berated them. Now he walked silently across the service court with temper smoldering in his eyes. But he held it in check. This was something new.

Behind the baseline Ty took his time, took his stance, then cracked an ace, like a bullet from a gun. The crowd screamed for him. With a quiet, insolent patience he waited while the scoring was announced. Again, he held advantage. Knowing him, and others like him, Asher was aware that his mind was occupied with his next move. The ace was already a memory, to be taken out and savored later. He still had a game to win.

The Frenchman connected with the next serve with a blazing forehand smash. The volley was sweating, furious and blatantly male. It was all speed and fire, two pirates blasting at each other across a sea of hardwood. There was the sound of the ball hitting the heart of the racket, the skid of rubber soles on wood, the grunts of the competitors as they drew out more force, all drowned beneath the echoes of cheers. The crowd was on its feet. Asher was on hers without even being aware of it. Neither man gave quarter as the seconds jumped to a minute, and a minute to more.

With a swing of the wrist the Frenchman returned a nearly impossible lob that drove him behind the baseline. The ball landed deep in the right court. With a forceful backhand Ty sent the ball low and away from his opponent, ending the two-and-a-half-hour match, three sets to one.

Starbuck was the U.S. Indoor Tennis champion, and the crowd's hero.

Asher let the enthusiasm pour around her as Ty walked to the net for the traditional handshake. The match had affected her more than she'd anticipated, but she passed this off as professional admiration. Now she allowed herself to wonder what his reaction would be when he saw her again.

Had she hurt him? His heart? His pride? The pride, she mused. That she could believe. The heart was a different matter. He would be angry, she concluded. She would be cool. Asher knew how to maintain a cool exterior as well as she knew how to smash an overhead lob. She'd learned it all as a child. When they met, she would

simply deploy his temper. She had been preparing for
the first encounter almost as religiously as she had been
preparing to pick up her profession again. Asher was
going to win at both. After he had finished with the
showers and the press, she would make it a point to seek
him out. To congratulate him—and to present the next
test. It was much wiser for her to make the first move,
for her to be the one prepared. Confident, she watched
Ty exchange words with Grimalier at the net.

Then Ty turned his head very slowly, very deliberately. With no searching through the crowd, no hesitation, his eyes locked on hers. The strength of the
contact had her drawing in a sharp, unwilling breath.
His eyes held, no wavering. Her mouth went dry. Then
he smiled, an unpleasant, direct challenge. Asher met it,
more from shock than temerity as the crowd bellowed
his name. *Starbuck* echoed from the walls like a litany.
Ten seconds—fifteen—he neither blinked nor moved.
For a man of action he had an uncanny ability for stillness. Boring into hers, his eyes made the distance between them vanish. The smile remained fixed. Just as
Asher's palms began to sweat, he turned a full circle
for the crowd, his racket above his head like a lance.
They adored him.

He'd known, Asher thought furiously as people
swarmed around her. He had known all along that she
was there. Her anger wasn't the hot, logical result of
being outmaneuvered, but small, silver slices of cold
fury. Ty had let her know in ten seconds, without words,
that the game was still on. And he always won.

Not this time though, she told herself. She had
changed too. But she stood where she was, rooted,
staring out at the now empty court. Her thoughts were

whirling with memories, emotions, remembered sensations. People brushed by her, already debating the match.

She was a tall, reed-slim figure tanned gold from hours in the sun. Her hair was short, sculptured and misty-blond. The style flattered, while remaining practical for her profession. Over three years of retirement, Asher hadn't altered it. Her face seemed more suited to the glossy pages of a fashion magazine than the heat and frenzy of a tennis court. A weekender, one might think, looking at her elegant cheekbones in an oval face. Not a pro. The nose was small and straight above a delicately molded mouth she rarely thought to tint. Makeup on the courts was a waste of time, as sweat would wash it away. Her eyes were large and round, a shade of blue that hinted at violet. One of her few concessions to vanity was to darken the thick pale lashes that surrounded them. While other women competitors added jewelry or ribbons and bows to the court dress, Asher had never thought of it. Even off the court her attire leaned toward the simple and muted.

An enterprising reporter had dubbed her "The Face" when she had been eighteen. She'd been nearly twenty-three when she had retired from professional play, but the name had stuck. Hers was a face of great beauty and rigid control. On court, not a flicker of expression gave her opponent or the crowd a hint of what she was thinking or feeling. One of her greatest defenses in the game was her ability to remain unruffled under stress. The standard seeped into her personal life.

Asher had lived and breathed tennis for so long that the line of demarcation between woman and athlete was smudged. The hard, unbendable rule, imposed by her father, was ingrained into her—privacy, first and last. Only one person had ever been able to cross the boundary. Asher was determined he would not do so again.

As she stood staring down at the empty court, her face told nothing of her anger or turmoil—or the pain she hadn't been prepared for. It was calm and aloof. Her concentration was so deep that the leader of the small packet of people that approached her had to speak her name twice to get her attention.

She'd been recognized, she discovered. Though Asher had known it was inevitable, it still gave her a twist of pleasure to sign the papers and programs thrust at her. She hadn't been forgotten.

The questions were easy to parry, even when they skirted close to her relationship with Ty. A smile and double-talk worked well with fans. Asher wasn't naïve enough to think it would work with reporters. That, she hoped, was for another day.

As she signed, and edged her way back, Asher spotted a few colleagues—an old foe, a former doubles partner, a smattering of faces from the past. Her eyes met Chuck Prince's. Ty's closest friend was an affable player with a wrist of steel and beautiful footwork. Though the silent exchange was brief, even friendly, Asher saw the question in his eyes before she gave her attention to the next fan.

The word's out, she thought almost grimly as she smiled at a teenage tennis buff. Asher Wolfe's picking up her racket again. And they'd wonder, and eventually ask, if she was picking up Ty Starbuck too.

"Asher!" Chuck moved to her with the same bouncy stride he used to cross a court. In his typical outgoing style he seized her by the shoulders and kissed her full on the mouth. "Hey, you look terrific!"

With a laugh Asher drew back the breath his greeting had stolen from her. "So do you." It was inevitably true. Chuck was average in almost every way—height, build, coloring. But his inner spark added appeal and a puckish sort of sexuality. He'd never hesitated to exploit it—good-naturedly.

"No one knew you were coming," Chuck complained, easing her gently through the thinning crowd. "I didn't know you were here until..." His voice trailed off so that Asher knew he referred to the ten seconds of potent contact with Ty. "Until after the match," he finished. He gave her shoulder a quick squeeze. "Why didn't you give someone a call?"

"I wasn't entirely sure I'd make it." Asher allowed herself to be negotiated to a clear spot in a rear hallway. "Then I thought I'd just melt into the crowd. It didn't seem fair to disrupt the match with any the-prodigal-returns business."

"It was a hell of a match." The flash of teeth gleamed with enthusiasm. "I don't know if I've ever seen Ty play better than he did in the last set. Three aces."

"He always had a deadly serve," Asher murmured.

"Have you seen him?"

From anyone else the blunt question would have earned a cold stare. Chuck earned a quick grimace. "No. I will, of course, but I didn't want to distract him before the match." Asher linked her fingers—an old nervous habit. "I didn't realize he knew I was here."

Distract Starbuck, she thought with an inner laugh. No one and nothing distracted him once he picked up his game racket.

"He went crazy when you left."

Chuck's quiet statement brought her back. Deliberately she unlaced her fingers. "I'm sure he recovered quickly." Because the retort was sharper than she had intended, Asher shook her head as if to take back the words. "How have you been? I saw an ad with you touting the virtues of a new line of tennis shoes."

"How'd I look?"

"Sincere," she told him with a quick grin. "I nearly went out and bought a pair."

He sighed. "I was shooting for macho."

As the tension seeped out of her, Asher laughed. "With that face?" She cupped his chin with her hand and moved it from side to side. "It's a face a mother could trust—foolishly," she added.

"Shh!" He glanced around in mock alarm. "Not so loud, my reputation."

"Your reputation suffered a few dents in Sydney," she recalled. "What was that—three seasons ago? The stripper."

"Exotic dancer," Chuck corrected righteously. "It was merely an exchange of cultures."

"You did look kind of cute wearing those feathers." With another laugh she kissed his cheek. "Fuchsia becomes you."

"We all missed you, Asher." He patted her slim, strong shoulder.

The humor fled from her eyes. "Oh, Chuck, I missed you. Everyone, all of it. I don't think I realized just how much until I walked in here today." Asher looked into space at her own thoughts, her own memories. "Three years," she said softly.

"Now you're back."

Her eyes drifted to his. "Now I'm back," she agreed. "Or will be in two weeks."

"The Foro Italico."

Asher gave him a brief smile that was more determination than joy. "I've never won on that damn Italian clay. I'm going to this time."

"It was your pacing."

The voice from behind her had Asher's shoulders stiffening. As she faced Chuck her eyes showed only the merest flicker of some secret emotion before they calmed. When she turned to Ty he saw first that his memory of her beauty hadn't been exaggerated with time, and second that her layer of control was as tough as ever.

"So you always told me," she said calmly. The jolt was over, she reasoned, with the shock of eye contact in the auditorium. But her stomach muscles tightened. "You played beautifully, Ty...after the first set."

They were no more than a foot apart now. Neither could find any changes in the other. Three years, it seemed, was barely any time at all. It occurred to Asher abruptly that twenty years wouldn't have mattered. Her heart would still thud, her blood would still swim. For him. It had always, would always be for him. Quickly she pushed those thoughts aside. If she were to remain calm under his gaze, she couldn't afford to remember.

The press were still tossing questions at him, and now at her as well. They began to crowd in, nudging Asher closer to Ty. Without a word he took her arm and drew her through the door at his side. That it happened to be a woman's rest room didn't faze him as he turned the lock. He faced her, leaning lazily back against the door while Asher stood straight and tense.

As he had thirty minutes before, Ty took his time studying her. His eyes weren't calm, they rarely were, but the emotion in them was impossible to decipher. Even in his relaxed stance there was a sense of force, a storm brewing. Asher met his gaze levelly, as he expected. And she moved him. Her power of serenity always moved him. He could have strangled her for it.

"You haven't changed, Asher."

"You're wrong." Why could she no longer breathe easily or control the furious pace of her heart?

"Am I?" His brows disappeared under his tousled hair for a moment. "We'll see."

He was a very physical man. When he spoke, he gestured. When he held a conversation, he touched. Asher could remember the brush of his hand—on her arm, her hair, her shoulder. It had been his casualness that had drawn her to him. And had driven her away. Now, as they stood close, she was surprised that Ty did not touch her in any way. He simply watched and studied her.

"I noticed a change," she countered. "You didn't argue with the referees or shout at the line judge. Not once." Her lips curved slightly. "Not even after a bad call."

He gave her a lightly quizzical smile. "I turned over that leaf some time ago."

"Really?" She was uncomfortable now, but merely moved her shoulders. "I haven't been keeping up."

"Total amputation, Asher?" he asked softly.

"Yes." She would have turned away, but there was nowhere to go. Over the line of sinks to her left the mirrors tossed back her reflection...and his. Deliberately she shifted so that her back was to them. "Yes," she repeated, "it's the cleanest way."

"And now?"

"I'm going to play again," Asher responded simply. His scent was reaching out for her, that familiar, somehow heady fragrance that was sweat and victory and sex all tangled together. Beneath the placid expression her thoughts shot off in a tangent.

Nights, afternoons, rainy mornings. He'd shown her everything a man and woman could be together, opened doors she had never realized existed. He had knocked down every guard until he had found her.

Oh God, dear God, she thought frantically. Don't let him touch me now. Asher linked her fingers together. Though his eyes never left hers, Ty noted the gesture. And recognized it. He smiled.

"In Rome?"

Asher controlled the urge to swallow. "In Rome," she agreed. "To start. I'll go in unseeded. It has been three years."

"How's your backhand?"

"Good." Automatically she lifted her chin. "Better than ever."

Very deliberately Ty circled her arm with his fingers. Asher's palms became damp. "It was always a surprise," he commented, "the power in that slender arm. Still lifting weights?"

"Yes."

His fingers slid down until they circled the inside of her elbow. It gave him bitter pleasure to feel the tiny pulse jump erratically. "So," he murmured softly, "Lady Wickerton graces the courts again."

"Ms. Wolfe," Asher corrected him stiffly. "I've taken my maiden name back."

His glance touched on her ringless hands. "The divorce is final?"

"Quite final. Three months ago."

"Pity." His eyes had darkened with anger when he lifted them back to hers. "A title suits you so well. I imagine you fit into an English manor as easily as a piece of Wedgwood. Drawing rooms and butlers," he murmured, then scanned her face as if he would memorize it all over again. "You have the looks for them."

"The reporters are waiting for you." Asher made a move to her left in an attempt to brush by him. Ty's fingers clamped down.

"Why, Asher?" He'd promised himself if he ever saw her again, he wouldn't ask. It was a matter of pride. But pride was overwhelmed by temper as the question whipped out, stinging them both. "Why did you leave that way? Why did you run off and marry that damn English jerk without a word to me?"

She didn't wince at the pressure of his fingers, nor did she make any attempt to pull away. "That's my business."

"*Your* business?" The words were hardly out of her mouth before he grabbed both her arms. "*Your* business? We'd been together for months, the whole damn circuit that year. One night you're in my bed, and the next thing I know you've run off with some English lord." His control slipped another notch as he shook her. "I had to find out from my sister. You didn't even have the decency to dump me in person."

"Decency?" she tossed back. "I won't discuss decency with you, Ty." She swallowed the words, the accusations she'd promised herself never to utter. "I made my choice," she said levelly, "I don't have to justify it to you."

"We were lovers," he reminded her tightly. "We lived together for nearly six months."

"I wasn't the first woman in your bed."

"You knew that right from the start."

"Yes, I knew." She fought the urge to beat at him with the hopeless rage that was building inside her. "I made my choice then, just as I made one later. Now, let me go."

Her cool, cultured control had always fascinated and infuriated him. Ty knew her, better than anyone, even her own father—certainly better than her ex-husband. Inside, she was jelly, shuddering convulsively, but outwardly she was composed and lightly disdainful. Ty wanted to shake her until she rattled. More, much more, he wanted to taste her again—obliterate three years with one long greedy kiss. Desire and fury hammered at him. He knew that if he gave in to either, he'd never be able to stop. The wound was still raw.

"We're not finished, Asher." But his grip relaxed. "You still owe me."

"No." Defensive, outraged, she jerked free. "No, I don't owe you anything."

"Three years," he answered, and smiled. The smile was the same biting challenge as before. "You owe me three years, and by God, you're going to pay."

He unlocked the door and opened it, stepping back so that Asher had no choice but to meet the huddle of reporters head-on.

"Asher, how does it feel to be back in the States?"

"It's good to be home."

"What about the rumors that you're going to play professionally again?"

"I intend to play professionally beginning with the opening of the European circuit in Rome."

More questions, more answers. The harsh glare of a flash causing light to dance in front of her eyes. The press always terrified her. She could remember her father's constant instructions: Don't say any more than absolutely necessary. Don't let them see what you're feeling. They'll devour you.

Churning inside, Asher faced the pack of avid reporters with apparent ease. Her voice was quiet and assured. Her fingers were locked tightly together. With a smile she glanced quickly down the hall, searching for an escape route. Ty leaned negligently against the wall and gave her no assistance.

"Will your father be in Rome to watch you play?"

"Possibly." An ache, a sadness, carefully concealed.

"Did you divorce Lord Wickerton so you could play again?"

"My divorce has nothing to do with my profession." A half-truth, a lingering anger, smoothly disguised.

"Are you nervous about facing young rackets like Kingston and old foes like Martinelli?"

"I'm looking forward to it." A terror, a well of doubt, easily masked.

"Will you and Starbuck pair up again?"

Fury, briefly exposed.

"Starbuck's a singles player," she managed after a moment.

"You guys'll have to keep your eyes open to see if that changes." With his own brand of nonchalance, Ty slipped an arm around Asher's rigid shoulders. "There's no telling what might happen, is there, Asher?"

Her answer was an icy smile. "You've always been more unpredictable than I have, Ty."

He met the smile with one of his own. "Have I?" Leaning down, he brushed her lips lightly. Flashbulbs popped in a blaze of excitement. Even as their lips met, so did their eyes. Hers were twin slits of fury, his grimly laughing and ripe with purpose. Lazily he straightened. "The Face and I have some catching up to do."

"In Rome?" a reporter cracked.

Ty grinned and quite deliberately drew Asher closer. "That's where it started."

Chapter 2

Rome. The Colosseum. The Trevi fountain. The Vatican. Ancient history, tragedy and triumphs. Gladiators and competition. In the Foro Italico the steaming Italian sun beat down on the modern-day competitors just as it had on those of the Empire. To play in this arena was a theatrical experience. It was sun and space. There were lush umbrella pines and massive statues to set the forum apart from any other on the circuit. Beyond the stadium, wooded hills rose from the Tiber. Within its hedge trimmings, ten thousand people could chant, shout and whistle. Italian tennis fans were an emotional, enthusiastic and blatantly patriotic lot. Asher hadn't forgotten.

Nor had she forgotten that the Foro Italico had been the setting for the two biggest revelations in her life: her consuming love for tennis, her overwhelming love for Ty Starbuck.

She had been seven the first time she had watched her father win the Italian championship in the famed *campo central*. Of course she had seen him play before. One of her earliest memories was of watching her tall, tanned father dash around a court in blazing white. Jim Wolfe had been a champion before Asher had been born, and a force to be reckoned with long after.

Her own lessons had begun at the age of three. With her shortened racket she had hit balls to some of the greatest players of her father's generation. Her looks and her poise had made her a pet among the athletes. She grew up finding nothing unusual about seeing her picture in the paper or bouncing on the knee of a Davis Cup champion. Tennis and travel ruled her world. She had napped in the rear of limousines and walked across the pampered grass of Wimbledon. She had curtsied to heads of state and had her cheek pinched by a president. Before she began attending school she had already crossed the Atlantic a half dozen times.

But it had been in Rome, a year after the death of her mother, that Asher Wolfe had found a life's love and ambition.

Her father had still been wet and glowing from his victory, his white shorts splattered with the red dust of the court, when she had told him she would play in the *campo central* one day. And win.

Perhaps it had been a father's indulgence for his only child, or his ambition. Or perhaps it had been the quietly firm determination he saw in seven-year-old eyes. But Asher's journey had begun that day, with her father as her guide and her mentor.

Fourteen years later, after her own defeat in the semifinals, Asher had watched Starbuck's victory. There had been nothing similar in the style of her father and the style of the new champion. Jim Wolfe had played a meticulous game—cold control with the accent on form. Starbuck played like a fireball—all emotion and muscle. Often, Asher had speculated on what the results would be if the two men were to meet across a net. Where her father brought her pride, Ty brought her excitement. Watching him, she could understand the sense of sexuality onlookers experienced during a bullfight. Indeed, there was a thirst for blood in his style that both alarmed and fascinated.

Ty had pursued her doggedly for months, but she had held him off. His reputation with women, his temper, his flamboyance and nonconformity had both attracted and repulsed her. Though the attraction was strong, and her heart was already lost, Asher had sensibly listened to her head. Until that day in May.

He'd been like a god, a powerful, mythological warrior with a strength and power that even the biased Italian crowd couldn't resist. Some cheered him, some cheerfully cursed him. He'd given them the sweat they had come to see. And the show.

Ty had taken the championship in seven frenzied sets. That night Asher had given him both her innocence and her love. For the first time in her life she had allowed her heart complete freedom. Like a blossom kept in the sheltered, controlled climate of a hothouse, she took to the sun and storm wildly. Days were steamier and more passionate—nights both turbulent and tender. Then the season had ended.

Now, as Asher practiced in the early morning lull on court five, the memories stirred, sweet and bitter as old wine. Fast rides on back roads, hot beaches, dim hotel rooms, foolish laughter, crazy loving. Betrayal.

"If you dream like that this afternoon, Kingston's going to wipe you out of the quarter-finals."

At the admonishment, Asher snapped back. "Sorry."

"You should be, when an old lady drags herself out of bed at six to hit to you."

Asher laughed. At thirty-three, Madge Haverbeck was still a force to be reckoned with across a net. Small and stocky, with flyaway brown hair and comfortably attractive features, she looked like an ad for home-baked cookies. She was, in fact, a world-class player with two Wimbledon championships, a decade of other victories that included the Wightman Cup and a wicked forehand smash. For two years Asher had been her doubles partner to their mutual satisfaction and success. Her husband was a sociology professor at Yale whom Madge affectionately termed "The Dean."

"Maybe you should sit down and have a nice cup of tea," Asher suggested while tucking her tongue in her cheek. "This game's rough on middle-aged matrons."

After saying something short and rude, Madge sent a bullet over the net. Light and agile, Asher sprang after it. Her concentration focused. Her muscles went to work. In the drowsy morning hum the ball thudded on clay and twanged off strings. Madge wasn't a woman to consider a practice workout incidental. She hustled over the court, driving Asher back to the baseline, luring her to the net, hammering at her by mixing her shots while Asher concentrated on adjusting her pace to the slow, frustrating clay.

For a fast, aggressive player, the surface could be deadly. It took strength and endurance rather than speed. Asher thanked the endless hours of weight lifting as she swung the racket again and again. The muscles in the slender arm were firm.

After watching one of Asher's returns scream past, Madge shifted her racket to her left hand. "You're pretty sharp for three years off, Face."

Asher filled her lungs with air. "I've kept my hand in."

Though Madge wondered avidly about Asher's marriage and years of self-imposed retirement, she knew her former partner too well to question. "Kingston hates to play the net. It's her biggest weakness."

"I know." Asher slipped the spare ball in her pocket. "I've studied her. Today she's going to play my game."

"She's better on clay than grass."

It was a roundabout way of reminding Asher of her own weakness. She gave Madge one of her rare, open smiles. "It won't matter. Next week I'm playing center court."

Slipping on a warm-up jacket, Madge gave a hoot of laughter. "Haven't changed much, have you?"

"Bits and pieces." Asher dabbed at sweat with her wristband. "What about you? How're you going to play Fortini?"

"My dear." Madge fluffed at her hair. "I'll simply overpower her."

Asher snorted as they strolled off the court. "You haven't changed either."

"If you'd told me you were coming back," Madge put in, "we'd be playing doubles. Fisher's good, and I like her, but…"

"I couldn't make the decision until I was sure I wouldn't make a fool of myself." Slowly Asher flexed her racket arm. "Three years, Madge. I ache." She sighed with the admission. "I don't remember if I ached like this before."

"We can trade legs any time you say, Face."

Remembering, Asher turned with a look of concern. "How's the knee?"

"Better since the surgery last year." Madge shrugged. "I can still forecast rain though. Here's to a sunny season."

"I'm sorry I wasn't there for you."

Madge hooked her arm through Asher's in easy comradeship. "Naturally I expected you to travel six thousand miles to hold my hand."

"I would have if…" Asher trailed off, remembering the state of her marriage at the time of Madge's surgery.

Recognizing guilt, Madge gave Asher a friendly nudge with her elbow. "It wasn't as big a deal as the press made out. Of course," she added with a grin, "I milked it for a lot of sympathy. The Dean brought me breakfast in bed for two months. Bless his heart."

"Then you came back and demolished Rayski in New York."

"Yeah." Madge laughed with pleasure. "I enjoyed that."

Asher let her gaze wander over the serene arena, quiet but for the thud of balls and hum of bees. "I have to win this one, Madge. I need it. There's so much to prove."

"To whom?"

"Myself first." Asher moved her shoulders restlessly, shifting her bag to her left hand. "And a few others."

"Starbuck? No, don't answer," Madge continued,

seeing Asher's expression out of the corner of her eye. "It just sort of slipped out."

"What was between Ty and me was finished three years ago," Asher stated, deliberately relaxing her muscles.

"Too bad." Madge weathered Asher's glare easily. "I like him."

"Why?"

Stopping, Madge met the direct look. "He's one of the most alive people I know. Ever since he learned to control his temper, he brings so such emotion to the courts. It's good for the game. You don't have a stale tournament when Starbuck's around. He also brings that same emotion into his friendships."

"Yes," Asher agreed. "It can be overwhelming."

"I didn't say he was easy," Madge countered. "I said I liked him. He is exactly who he is. There isn't a lot of phony business to cut through to get to Starbuck." Madge squinted up at the sun. "I suppose some of it comes from the fact that we turned pro the same year, did our first circuit together. Anyway, I've watched him grow from a cocky kid with a smart mouth to a cocky man who manages to keep that wicked temper just under the surface."

"You like him for his temper?"

"Partly." The mild, homey-looking woman smiled. "Starbuck's just plain strung right, Asher. He's not a man you can be ambivalent about. You're either for him or against him."

It was as much inquiry as statement. Saying nothing, Asher began to walk again. Ambivalence had never entered into her feeling for Ty.

On his way home from his own practice court Ty

watched them. More accurately he watched Asher. While she remained unaware of him, he could take in every detail. The morning sun glinted down on her hair. Her shoulders were strong and slender, her gait long, leggy and confident. He was grateful he could study her now with some dispassion.

When he had looked out and had seen her in the stands two weeks before, it had been like catching a fast ball with his stomach. Shimmering waves of pain, shock, anger, one sensation had raced after the other. He had blown the first set.

Then he had done more than pull himself together. He had used the emotions against his opponent. The Frenchman hadn't had a chance against Ty's skill combined with three years of pent-up fury. Always, he played his best under pressure and stress. It fed him. With Asher in the audience the match had become a matter of life and death. When she had left him she'd stolen something from him. Somehow, the victory had helped him regain a portion of it.

Damn her that she could still get to him. Ty's thoughts darkened as the distance between them decreased. Just looking at her made him want.

He had wanted her when she had been seventeen. The sharp, sudden desire for a teenager had astonished the then twenty-three-year-old Ty. He had kept a careful distance from her all that season. But he hadn't stopped wanting her. He had done his best to burn the desire out by romancing women he considered more his style— flamboyant, reckless, knowledgeable.

When Asher had turned twenty-one Ty had abandoned common sense and had begun a determined, almost obsessive pursuit. The more she had evaded him, the firmer she refused, the stronger his desire had grown. Even the victory, tasted first in Rome, hadn't lessened his need.

His life, which previously had had one focus, then had realigned with two dominating forces. Tennis and Asher. At the time he wouldn't have said he loved tennis, but simply that it was what and who he was. He wouldn't have said he loved Asher, but merely that he couldn't live without her.

Yet he had had to—when she'd left him to take another man's name. A title and a feather bed, Ty thought grimly. He was determined to make Asher Wolfe pay for bringing him a pain he had never expected to feel.

By turning left and altering his pace Ty cut across her path, apparently by chance. "Hi, Madge." He gave the brunette a quick grin, flicking his finger down her arm before turning his attention fully to Asher.

"Hiya, Starbuck." Madge glanced from the man to the woman and decided she wasn't needed. "Hey, I'm late," she said by way of explanation, then trotted off. Neither Asher nor Ty commented.

From somewhere in the surrounding trees Asher heard the high clear call of a bird. Nearer at hand was the slumberous buzz of bees and dull thud of balls. On court three, someone cursed fluently. But Asher was conscious only of Ty beside her.

"Just like old times," he murmured, then grinned at her expression. "You and Madge," he added.

Asher struggled not to be affected. The setting had too many memories. "She hit to me this morning. I hope I don't have to face her in the tournament."

"You go against Kingston today."

"Yes."

He took a step closer. In her mind's eye Asher saw the hedge beside her. With Ty directly in her path, dignified retreat was impossible. For all her delicacy of looks, Asher didn't run from a battle. She linked her fingers, then dragged them apart, annoyed.

"And you play Devereux."

His acknowledgment was a nod. "Is your father coming?"

"No." The answer was flat and brief. Ty had never been one to be put off by a subtle warning.

"Why?"

"He's busy." She started to move by him, but succeeded only in closing the rest of the distance between them. Maneuvering was one of the best aspects of Ty's game.

"I've never known him to miss one of your major tournaments." In an old habit he couldn't resist nor she prevent, he reached for her hair. "You were always his first order of business."

"Things change," she responded stiffly. "People change."

"So it seems." His grin was sharp and cocky. "Will your husband be here?"

"Ex-husband." Asher tossed her head to dislodge his hand. "And no."

"Funny, as I recall he was very fond of tennis." Casually he set down his bag. "Has that changed too?"

"I need to shower." Asher had drawn nearly alongside of him before Ty stopped her. His hand slipped to her waist too quickly and too easily.

"How about a quick set for old times' sake?"

His eyes were intense—that oddly compelling color that was half night and half day. Asher remembered how they seemed to darken from the pupils out when he was aroused. The hand at her waist was wide-palmed and long-fingered—a concert pianist's hand, but it was rough and worked. The strength in it would have satisfied a prizefighter.

"I don't have time." Asher pushed to free herself and connected with the rock-hard muscles of his forearm. She pulled her fingers back as though she'd been burned.

"Afraid?" There was mockery and a light threat with the overtones of sex. Her blood heated to the force she had never been able to fully resist.

"I've never been afraid of you." And it was true enough. She had been fascinated.

"No?" He spread his fingers, drawing her an inch closer. "Fear's one of the popular reasons for running away."

"I didn't run," she corrected him. "I left." *Before you did,* she added silently. For once, she had outmaneuvered him.

"You still have some questions to answer, Asher." His arm slid around her before she could step back. "I've waited a long time for the answers."

"You'll go on waiting."

"For some," he murmured in agreement. "But I'll have the answer to one now."

She saw it coming and did nothing. Later she would curse herself for her passivity. But when he lowered his mouth to hers, she met it without resistance. Time melted away.

He had kissed her like this the first time—slowly, thoroughly, gently. It was another part of the enigma that a man so full of energy and turbulence could show such sensitivity. His mouth was exactly as Asher remembered. Warm, soft, full. Perhaps she had been lost the first time he had kissed her—drawn to the fury—captured by the tenderness. Even when he brought her closer, deepening the kiss with a low-throated groan, the sweetness never diminished.

As a lover he excelled because beneath the brash exterior was an underlying and deep-rooted respect for femininity. He enjoyed the softness, tastes and textures of women, and instinctively sought to bring them pleasure in lovemaking. As an inherent loner, it was another contradiction that Ty saw a lover as a partner, never a means to an end. Asher had sensed this from the first touch so many years ago. Now she let herself drown in the kiss with one final coherent thought. It had been so long.

Her arm, which should have pushed him away, curved up his back instead until her hand reached his shoulders. Her fingers grasped at him. Unhesitatingly she pressed her body to his. He was the one man who could touch off the passion she had so carefully locked inside. The only man who had ever reached her core and gained true intimacy—the meeting of minds as well as of bodies. Starved for the glimpses of joy she remembered, Asher clung while her mouth moved avidly on his. Her greed for more drove away all her reserve, and all her promises.

Oh, to be loved again, truly loved, with none of the emptiness that had haunted her life for too long! To give herself, to take, to know the pure, searing joy of belonging! The thoughts danced in her mind like dreams suddenly remembered. With a moan, a sigh, she pressed against him, hungry for what had been.

The purpose of the kiss had been to punish, but he'd forgotten. The hot-blooded passion that could spring from the cool, contained woman had forced all else from his mind but need. He needed her, still needed her, and was infuriated. If they had been alone, he would have taken her and then faced the consequences. His impulses were still difficult to control. But they weren't alone. Some small part of his mind clung to reality even while his body pulsed. She was soft and eager. Everything he had ever wanted. All he had done without. Ty discovered he had gotten more answers than he'd bargained for.

Drawing her away, he took his time studying her face. Who could resist the dangerous power of a hurricane? The wicked, primitive rumblings of a volcano? She stared at him, teetering between sanity and desire.

Her eyes were huge and aware, her lips parted breathlessly. It was a look he remembered. Long nights in her bed, hurried afternoons or lazy mornings, she would look at him so just before loving. Hot and insistent, desire spread, then closed like a fist in his stomach. He stepped back so that they were no longer touching.

"Some things change," he remarked. "And some things don't," he added before turning to walk away.

There was time for deep breathing before Asher took her position for the first serve. It wasn't the thousand pairs of eyes watching around the court that had her nerves jumping. It was one pair, dark brown and intense, seventy-eight feet away. Stacie Kingston, age twenty, hottest newcomer to the game in two years. She had energy, force and drive, along with a fierce will to win. Asher recognized her very well. The red clay spread out before her, waiting.

Because she knew the importance of mastering the skittish nerves and flood of doubts, she continued to take long, deep breaths. Squeezing the small white ball, Asher discovered the true meaning of trial by fire. If she won, here where she had never won before, three years after she had last lifted a racket professionally, she would have passed the test. Rome, it seemed, would always be her turning point.

Because it was the only way, she blocked out the past, blocked out tomorrow and focused wholly on the contest. Tossing the ball up, she watched the ascent, then struck home. Her breath came out in a hiss of effort.

Kingston played a strong, offensive game. A studied, meticulous player, she understood and used the personality of clay to her advantage, forcing Asher to the baseline again and again. Asher found the dirt frustrating. It cut down on her speed. She was hurrying, defending herself. The awareness of this only made her rush more. The ball eluded her, bouncing high over her head when she raced to the net, dropping lazily into the forecourt when she hugged the baseline. Unnerved by her own demons, she double-faulted. Kingston won the first game, breaking Asher's serve and allowing her only one point.

The crowd was vocal, the sun ferocious. The air was thick with humidity. From the other side of the hedge Asher could hear the games and laughter of schoolchildren. She wanted to throw aside her racket and walk off the court. It was a mistake, a mistake, her mind repeated, to have come back. Why had she subjected herself to this again? To the effort and pain and humiliation?

Her face was utterly passive, showing none of the turmoil. Gripping the racket tightly, she fought off the weakness. She had played badly, she knew, because she had permitted Kingston to set the pace. It had taken Asher less than six minutes from first service to defeat. Her skin wasn't even damp. She hadn't come back to give up after one game, nor had she come back to be humiliated. The stands were thick with people watching, waiting. She had only herself.

Flicking a hand at the short skirt of her tennis dress, she walked back to the baseline. Crouched, she shifted her weight to the balls of her feet. Anger with herself was forced back. Fear was conquered. A cool head was one of her greatest weapons, and one she hadn't used in the first game. This time, she was determined. This time, the game would be played her way.

She returned the serve with a drop shot over the net that caught Kingston off balance. The crowd roared its approval as the ball boy scurried across the court to scoop up the dead ball.

Love-fifteen. Asher translated the scoring in her head with grim satisfaction. Fear had cost her the first game. Now, in her own precise way, she was out for blood. Kingston became more symbol than opponent.

Asher continued to draw her opponent into the net, inciting fierce volleys that brought the crowd to its feet. The roar and babble of languages did not register with her. She saw only the ball, heard only the effortful breathing that was hers. She ended that volley with a neatly placed ball that smacked clean at the edge of the baseline.

Something stirred in her—the hot, bubbling juice of victory. Asher tasted it, reveled in it as she walked coolly back to position. Her face was wet now, so she brushed her wristband over her brow before she cupped the two service balls in her hand. Only the beginning, she told herself. Each game was its own beginning.

By the end of the first set the court surface was zigzagged with skid marks. Red dust streaked the snowy material of her dress and marked her shoes. Sweat rolled down her sides after thirty-two minutes of ferocious play. But she'd taken the first set six-three.

Adrenaline was pumping madly, though Asher looked no more flustered than a woman about to hostess a dinner party. The competitive drives she had buried were in complete control. Part of her sensed Starbuck was watching. She no longer cared. At that moment Asher felt that if she had faced him across the net, she could have beaten him handily. When Kingston returned her serve deep, Asher met it with a topspin backhand that brushed the top of the net. Charging after the ball, she met the next return with a powerful lob.

The sportswriters would say that it was at that moment, when the two women were eye to eye, that Asher won the match. They remained that way for seconds only, without words, but communication had been made. From then Asher dominated, forcing Kingston into a defensive game. She set a merciless pace. When she lost a point she came back to take two. The aggressiveness was back, the cold-blooded warfare the sportswriters remembered with pleasure from her early years on the court.

Where Starbuck was fire and flash, she was ice and control. Never once during a professional match had Asher lost her iron grip on her temper. It had once been a game among the sportswriters—waiting for The Face to cut loose.

Only twice during the match did she come close to giving them satisfaction, once on a bad call and once on her own poor judgment of a shot. Both times she stared down at her racket until the urge to stomp and swear had passed. When she had again taken her position, there had been nothing but cool determination in her eyes.

She took the match six-three, six-one, six-two in an hour and forty-nine minutes. Twice she had held Kingston's service to love. Three times she had served aces— something Kingston with her touted superserve had been unable to accomplish. Asher Wolfe would go on to the semi-finals. She had made her comeback.

Madge dropped a towel over Asher's shoulders as she collapsed on her chair. "Good God, you were terrific! You destroyed her." Asher said nothing, covering her face with the towel a moment to absorb sweat. "I swear, you're better than you were before."

"She wanted to win," Asher murmured, letting the towel drop limply again. "I *had* to win."

"It showed," Madge agreed, giving her shoulder a quick rub. "Nobody'd believe you haven't played pro in three years. I hardly believe it myself."

Slowly Asher lifted her face to her old partner. "I'm not in shape yet, Madge," she said beneath the din of the still-cheering crowd. "My calves are knotted. I don't even know if I can stand up again."

Madge skimmed a critical glance over Asher's features. She couldn't detect a flicker of pain. Bending, she scooped up Asher's warm-up jacket, then draped it over Asher's shoulders. "I'll help you to the showers. I don't play for a half hour. You just need a few minutes on the massage table."

Exhausted, hurting, Asher started to agree, then spotted Ty watching her. His grin might have been acknowledgment of her victory. But he knew her, Asher reflected, knew her inside as no one else did.

"No thanks, I'll manage." Effortfully she rose to zip the cover around her racket. "I'll see you after you beat Fortini."

"Asher—"

"No, really, I'm fine now." Head high, muscles screaming, she walked toward the tunnel that led to the locker rooms.

Alone in the steam of the showers, Asher let herself empty, weeping bitterly for no reason she could name.

Chapter 3

It was the night after her victory in the semi-finals that Asher confronted Ty again. She had kept herself to a rigorous schedule of practice, exercise, press, and play. Her pacing purposely left her little time for recreation. Practice was a religion. Morning hours were spent in the peaceful tree-shaded court five, grooving in, polishing her footwork, honing her reflexes.

Exercise was a law. Push-ups and weight lifting, stretching and hardening the muscles. Good press was more than a balm for the ego. Press was important to the game as a whole as well as the individual player. And the press loved a winner.

Play was what the athlete lived for. Pure competition—the testing of the skills of the body, the use of the skills of the mind. The best played as the best dancers danced—for the love of it. During the days of her second debut, Asher rediscovered love.

In her one brief morning meeting with Ty she had rediscovered passion. Only her fierce concentration on her profession kept her from dwelling on a need that had never died. Rome was a city for lovers—it had been once for her. Asher knew that this time she must think of it only as a city for competition if she was to survive the first hurdle of regaining her identity. Lady Wickerton was a woman she hardly recognized. She had nearly lost Asher Wolfe trying to fit an image. How could she recapture herself if she once again became Starbuck's lady?

In a small club in the Via Sistina where the music was loud and the wine was abundant, Asher sat at a table crowded with bodies. Elbows nudged as glasses were reached for. Liquor spilled and was cheerfully cursed. In the second and final week of the Italian Open, the tension grew, but the pace mercifully slowed.

Rome was noise, fruit stands, traffic, outdoor cafés. Rome was serenity, cathedrals, antiquity. For the athletes it was days of grueling competition and nights of celebration or commiseration. The next match was a persistent shadow over the thoughts of the winners and the losers. As the music blared and the drinks were poured, they discussed every serve, every smash and error and every bad call. Rome was blissfully indolent over its reputation for bad calls.

"Long!" A dark, lanky Australian brooded into his wine. "That ball was inside by two inches. Two bloody inches."

"You won the game, Michael," Madge reminded him philosophically. "And in the second game of the fifth set, you had a wide ball that wasn't called."

The Australian grinned and shrugged. "It was only a

little wide." He brought his thumb and forefinger close together at the good-natured razzing of his peers. "What about this one?" His gesture was necessarily shortened by the close quarters as he lifted a drink toward Asher. "She beats an Italian in the Foro Italico, and the crowd still cheers her."

"Breeding," Asher returned with a mild smile. "The fans always recognize good breeding."

Michael snorted before he swallowed the heavy red wine. "Since when does a bloody steamroller need breeding?" he countered. "You flattened her." To emphasize his point he slammed a palm down on the table and ground it in.

"Yeah." Her smile widened in reminiscent pleasure. "I did, didn't I?" She sipped her dry, cool wine. The match had been longer and more demanding than her first with Kingston, but her body had rebelled a bit less afterward. Asher considered it a double victory.

"Tia Conway will go for your jugular," he said pleasantly, then called to his countrywoman at a nearby table. "Hey, Tia, you gonna beat this nasty American?"

A dark, compact woman with striking black eyes glanced over. The two women measured each other slowly before Tia lifted her glass in salute. Asher responded in kind before the group fell back to its individual conversations. With the music at high volume, they shouted to be heard, but words carried only a foot.

"A nice woman," Michael began, "off the court. On it, she's a devil. Off, she grows petunias and rosemary. Her husband sells swimming pools."

Madge chuckled. "You make that sound like a misdemeanor."

"I bought one," he said ruefully, then looked back

at Asher. She was listening with half an ear to the differing opinions on either side of her of a match by two players. "Still, if I played mixed doubles, I'd want Face for a partner." Asher acknowledged this with a curious lift of a brow. "Tia plays like a demon, but you have better court sense. And," he added as he downed more wine, "better legs."

For this Madge punched him in the shoulder. "What about me?"

"You have perhaps the best court sense of any female world-class player," Michael decided slowly. "But," he continued as Madge accepted her due with a regal nod, "you have legs like a shotputter."

A roar of laughter rose up over Madge's indignation. Asher leaned back in her chair, enjoying the loosening freedom of mirth as Madge challenged Michael to show his own and be judged. At that moment Asher's eyes locked with Ty's. Her laughter died unnoticed by her companions.

He'd come in late and alone. His hair was unruly, as though he had ridden in a fast car with the top down. Even completely relaxed, dressed in jeans, his hands in his pockets, some aura of excitement swirled around him. In the dim light his face was shadowed, all hollows and planes, with his eyes dark and knowing. No woman could be immune to him. A former lover was helpless not to remember what magic his mouth could perform.

Asher sat still as a stone—marble, pale and elegant in the rowdy, smoke-curtained bar. She couldn't forget any more than she could stop wanting. All she could do was refuse, as she had three years before.

Without taking his eyes from hers Ty crossed the room, skirted crowded tables. He had Asher by the arm, drawing her to her feet before the rest of the group had greeted him.

"We'll dance." It was a command formed in the most casual tones. As on court, Asher's decision had to be made in a tenth of a second. To refuse would have incited speculative gossip. To agree meant she had her own demons to deal with.

"I'd love to," she said coolly, and went with him.

The band played a slow ballad at ear-splitting volume. The vocalist was flat, and tried to make up for it by being loud. Someone knocked a glass off a table with a splintering crash. There was a pungent scent of spilled wine. A bricklayer argued with a Mexican tennis champion on the proper way to handle a topspin lob. Someone was smoking a pipe filled with richly sweet cherry tobacco. The floorboards were slightly warped.

Ty gathered her into his arms as though she had never been away. "The last time we were here," he murmured in her ear, "we sat at that corner table and drank a bottle of Valpolicella."

"I remember."

"You wore the same perfume you're wearing now." His lips grazed her temple as he drew her closer. Asher felt the bones in her legs liquefy, the muscles in her thighs loosen. "Like sun-warmed petals." Her heartbeat was a light, uncertain flutter against his. "Do you remember what we did afterward?"

"We walked."

The two hoarsely spoken words seemed to shiver along his skin. It was impossible to keep his mouth from seeking small tastes of her. "Until sunrise." His breath feathered intimately at her ear. "The city was all rose and gold, and I wanted you so badly, I nearly exploded. You wouldn't let me love you then."

"I don't want to go back." Asher tried to push away, but his arms kept her pressed tight against him. It seemed every line of his body knew every curve of hers.

"Why? Because you might remember how good we were together?"

"Ty, stop it." She jerked her head back—a mistake as his lips cruised lazily over hers.

"We'll be together again, Asher." He spoke quietly. The words seemed to sear into the tender flesh of her lips. "Even if it's only once…for old times' sake."

"It's over, Ty." The claim was a whisper, the whisper unsteady.

"Is it?" His eyes darkened as he pressed her against him almost painfully. "Remember, Asher, I know you, inside out. Did your husband ever find out who you really are? Did he know how to make you laugh? How," he added in a low murmur, "to make you moan?"

She stiffened. The music whirled around them, fast now with an insistent bass beat. Ty held her firmly against him, barely swaying at all. "I won't discuss my marriage with you."

"I damn well don't want to know about your *marriage*." He said the word as if it were an obscenity as his fingers dug into the small of her back. Fury was taking over though he'd sworn he wouldn't let it. He could still get to her. Yes, yes, that was a fact, he knew, but no more than she could still get to him. "Why did you come back?" he demanded. "Why the hell did you come back?"

"To play tennis." Her fingers tightened on his shoulder. "To win." Anger was growing in her as well. It appeared he was the only man who could make her forget herself enough to relinquish control. "I have every right to be here, every right to do what I was trained to do. I don't owe you explanations."

"You owe me a hell of a lot more." It gave him a certain grim satisfaction to see the fury in her eyes. He wanted to push. Wanted to see her anger. "You're going to pay for the three years you played lady of the manor."

"You don't know anything about it." Her breath came short and fast. Her eyes were nearly cobalt. "I paid, Starbuck, I paid more than you can imagine. Now I've finished, do you understand?" To his surprise, her voice broke on a sob. Quickly she shook her head and fought back tears. "I've finished paying for my mistakes."

"What mistakes?" he demanded. Frustrated, he took her by the shoulders. "What mistakes, Asher?"

"You." She drew in her breath sharply, as if stepping back from a steep edge. "Oh, God, you."

Turning, she fought her way through the swarm of enthusiastic dancers. Even as she sprang out into the sultry night Ty whirled her around. "Let me go!" She struck out blindly, but he grabbed her wrist.

"You're not going to walk out on me again." His voice was dangerously low. "Not ever again."

"Did it hurt your pride, Ty?" Emotion erupted from her, blazing as it could only from one who constantly denied it. "Did it hurt your ego that a woman could turn her back on you and choose someone else?"

Pain ripped through him and took over. "I never had your kind of pride, Asher." He dragged her against him, needing to prove he had some kind of power over her, even if it was only physical. "The kind you wear so that no one can see you're human. Did you run because I knew you? Because in bed I could make you forget to be the perfect lady?"

"I left because I didn't want you!" Completely unstrung, she shouted, pounding with her free hand. "I didn't want—"

He cut her off with a furious kiss. Their tempers soared with vivid passion. Anger sizzled in two pairs of lips that clung because they were helpless to do otherwise. There was never any choice when they were together. It had been so almost from the first, and the years had changed nothing. She could resist him, resist herself, for only so long. The outcome was inevitable.

Suddenly greedy, Asher pressed against him. Here was the sound and the speed. Here was the storm. Here was home. His hair was thick and soft between her questing fingers, his body rock-hard against the firmness of hers. His scent was his "off-court" fragrance—something sharp and bracing that she'd always liked.

The first taste was never enough to satisfy her, so she probed deeper into his mouth, tongue demanding, teeth nipping in the way he himself had taught her. A loud crash of brass from the band rattled the windows behind them. Asher heard only Ty's moan of quiet desperation. Between the shadows and the moonlight they clung, passion building, old needs merging with new.

Her breath trembled into the night as he took a crazed journey of her face. His hands slid up until his thumbs hooked gently under her chin. It was a familiar habit, one of his more disarming. Asher whispered his name half in plea, half in acceptance before his mouth found hers again. He drew her into him, slowly, inevitably, while his fingers skimmed along her cheekbones. The more tempestuous the kiss, the more tender his touch.

Asher fretted for the strong, sure stroke of his hands on her body.

Full circle, she thought dizzily. She had come full circle. But if once before in Rome she had been frightened when his kisses had drained and exhilarated her, now she was terrified.

"Please, Ty." Asher turned her head until her brow rested on his shoulder. "Please, don't do this."

"I didn't do it alone," he muttered.

Slowly she lifted her head. "I know."

It was the vulnerability in her eyes that kept him from dragging her back to him. Just as it had been her vulnerability all those years before that had prevented him taking her. He had waited for her to come to him. The same would hold true this time, he realized. Cursing potently under his breath, Ty released her.

"You've always known how to hold me off, haven't you, Asher?"

Knowing the danger had passed, she let out an unsteady breath. "Self-preservation."

Ty gave an unexpected laugh as his hands dove for his pockets. "It might have been easier if you'd managed to get fat and ugly over the last three years. I wanted to think you had."

A hint of a smile played on her mouth. So his moods could change, she thought, just as quickly as ever. "Should I apologize for not accommodating you?"

"Probably wouldn't have made any difference if you had." His eyes met hers again, then roamed her face. "Just looking at you—it still takes my breath away." His hands itched to touch. He balled them into fists inside his pockets. "You haven't even changed your hair."

This time the smile bloomed. "Neither have you. You still need a trim."

He grinned. "You were always conservative."

"You were always unconventional."

He gave a low appreciative laugh, one she hadn't heard in much too long. "You've mellowed," he decided. "You used to say radical."

"*You've* mellowed," Asher corrected him. "It used to be true."

With a shrug he glanced off into the night. "I used to be twenty."

"Age, Starbuck?" Sensing a disturbance, Asher automatically sought to soothe it.

"Inevitably." He brought his eyes back to hers. "It's a young game."

"Ready for your rocking chair?" Asher laughed, forgetting caution as she reached up to touch his cheek. Though she snatched her hand away instantly, his eyes had darkened. "I—" She searched for a way to ease the fresh tension. "You didn't seem to have any problem smashing Bigelow in the semi-finals. He's what, twenty-four?"

"It went to seven sets." His hand came out of his pocket. Casually he ran the back of it up her throat.

"You like it best that way."

He felt her swallow quickly, nervously, though her eyes remained level. "Come back with me, Asher," he murmured. "Come with me now." It cost him to ask, but only he was aware of how much.

"I can't."

"Won't," he countered.

From down the street came a high-pitched stream of Italian followed by a bellow of laughter. Inside the club the band murdered a popular American tune. She could smell the heat-soaked fragrance of the window-box geraniums above their heads. And she could remember, remember too well, the sweetness that could be hers if she crossed the line. And the pain.

"Ty." Asher hesitated, then reached up to grasp the hand that lingered at her throat. "A truce, please. For our mutual benefit," she added when his fingers interlaced possessively with hers. "With us both going into the finals, we don't need this kind of tension right now."

"Save it for later?" He brought her reluctant hand to his lips, watching her over it. "Then we pick this up in Paris."

"I didn't mean—"

"We deal now or later, Face, but we deal." He grinned again, tasting challenge, tasting victory. "Take it or leave it."

"You're just as infuriating as ever."

"Yeah." The grin only widened. "That's what keeps me number one."

On an exasperated laugh, Asher let her hand relax in his. "Truce, Starbuck?"

He let his thumb glide back and forth over her knuckles. "Agreed, on one condition." Sensing her withdrawal, he continued. "One question, Asher. Answer one question."

She tried to wrest her hand away and failed. "What question?" she demanded impatiently.

"Were you happy?"

She became very still as quick flashes of the past raced through her head. "You have no right—"

"I have every right," he interrupted. "I'm going to know that, Asher. The truth."

She stared at him, wanting to pit her will against his. Abruptly she found she had no energy for it. "No," she said wearily. "No."

He should have felt triumph, and instead felt misery. Releasing her hand, he stared out at the street. "I'll get you a cab."

"No. No, I'll walk. I want to walk."

Ty watched her move into the flood of a streetlight and back into the dark. Then she was a shadow, disappearing.

The streets were far from empty. Traffic whizzed by at the pace that seemed the pride of European cities. Small, fast cars and daredevil taxis. People scattered on the sidewalks, rushing toward some oasis of nightlife. Still, Ty thought he could hear the echo of his own footsteps.

Perhaps it was because so many feet had walked the Roman streets for so many centuries. Ty didn't care much for history or tradition. Tennis history perhaps— Gonzales, Gibson, Perry, these names meant more to him than Caesar, Cicero or Caligula. He rarely thought of his own past, much less of antiquity. Ty was a man who focused on the present. Until Asher had come back into his life, he had thought little about tomorrow.

In his youth he had concentrated fiercely on the future, and what he would do if… Now that he had done it, Ty had come to savor each day at a time. Still, the future was closing in on him, and the past was never far behind.

At ten he had been a hustler. Skinny and streetwise, he had talked his way out of trouble when it was possible, and slugged his way out when it wasn't. Growing up in the tough South Side of Chicago, Ty had been introduced to the seamier side of life early. He'd tasted his first beer when he should have been studying rudimentary math. What had saved him from succumbing to the streets was his dislike and distrust of organized groups. Gangs had held no appeal for Ty. He had no desire to lead or to follow. Still, he might have chosen a less honorable road had it not been for his unquestioning love for his family.

His mother, a quiet, determined woman who worked nights cleaning office buildings, was precious to him. His sister, four years his junior, was his pride and self-assumed responsibility. There was no father, and even the memory of him had faded before Ty reached midchildhood. Always, he had considered himself the head of the family, with all the duties and rights that it entailed. No one corrected him. It was for his family that he studied and kept on the right side of the law—though he brushed the line occasionally. It was for them that he promised himself, when he was still too young to realize the full extent of his vow, to succeed. One day he would move them out, buy them a house, bring his mother up off her knees. The picture of how hadn't been clear, only the final result. The answer had been a ball and racket.

Ada Starbuck had given her son a cheap, nylon-stringed racket for his tenth birthday. The gift had been an impulse. She had been determined to give the boy something other than the necessary socks and underwear. The racket, such as it was, had been a gesture of hope. She could see too many of her neighbors' children fall into packs. Ty, she knew, was different. A loner. With the racket he could entertain himself. A baseball or football required someone to catch or pass.

Now Ty could use a concrete wall as his partner. And so he did—at first for lack of something better to do. In the alley between apartment buildings he would smash the ball against a wall scrawled with spray paint. DIDI LOVES FRANK and other less romantic statements littered his playing field.

He enjoyed setting his own rhythm, enjoyed the steady thud, thump, smash he could make. When he became bored with the wall, he began haunting the neighborhood playground courts. There, he could watch teenagers or middle-aged weekenders scramble around the courts. He hustled pennies retrieving balls. Deciding he could do better than the people he watched, Ty badgered an older boy into a game.

His first experience on a court was a revelation. A human forced you to run, sent balls over your head or lined them at you with a speed a stationary wall couldn't match. Though he lost handily, Ty had discovered the challenge of competition. And the thirst to win.

He continued to haunt the courts, paying more attention to details. He began to select the players who took the game seriously. Possessing quite a bit of charm even at that age, Ty talked himself into more games. If someone took the time to teach, he listened and adjusted the advice to suit his own style. And he was developing a style. It was rough and untutored, with the flash the sportwriters would later rave about just a spark. His serve was a far cry from a grown Starbuck's, but it was strong and uncannily accurate. He was still awkward, as growing boys are, but his speed was excellent. More than anything else, his fierce desire to win had his game progressing.

When the cheap racket simply disintegrated under

constant use, Ada raided the household budget and
bought Ty another. Of the hundreds of rackets he had
used in his career, some costing more than his mother
had made in a week, Ty had never forgotten that first
one. He had kept it, initially from childhood sentiment,
then as a symbol.

He carved out a name for himself in the neighborhood. By the time he was thirteen it was a rare thing
for anyone, child or adult, to beat Ty Starbuck on the
courts. He knew his game. He had read everything he
could get his hands on—tennis as a sport, its history,
its great players. When his contemporaries were im-
mersed in the progress of the White Sox or the Cubs,
Ty watched the Wimbledon matches on the flickering
black-and-white TV in his apartment. He had already
made up his mind to be there one day. And to win.
Again, it was Ada who helped the hand of fate.

One of the offices she cleaned belonged to Martin
Derick, a lawyer and tennis enthusiast who patronized
a local country club. He was an offhandedly friendly
man whose late hours brought him in contact with
the woman who scrubbed the hall outside his door.
He called her Mrs. Starbuck because her dignity demanded it, and would exchange a word of greeting on
his way in or out. Ada was careful to mention her son
and his tennis abilities often enough to intrigue and
not often enough to bore. Ty had come by his shrewd-
ness naturally.

When Martin casually mentioned he would be interested in seeing the boy play, Ada told him there was
an informal tournament set for that Saturday. Then she
hurriedly arranged one. Whether curiosity or interest

prompted Martin to drive to the battered South Side court, the results were exactly as Ada hoped.

Ty's style was still rough, but it was aggressive. His temper added to the spark, and his speed was phenomenal. At the end of a set, Martin was leaning against the chain-link fence. At the end of the match, he was openly cheering. Two hours on the manicured courts of his club had never brought him quite this degree of excitement. Ideas humming in his brain, he walked over to the sweaty, gangly teenager.

"You want to play tennis, kid?"

Ty spun the racket as he eyed the lawyer's pricey suit. "You ain't dressed for it." He gave the smooth leather shoes a mild sneer.

Martin caught the insolent grin, but focused on the intensity of the boy's eyes. Some instinct told him they were champion's eyes. The ideas solidified into a goal. "You want to play for pay?"

Ty kept spinning the racket, wary of a hustle, but the question had his pulse leaping. "Yeah. So?"

This time Martin smiled at the deliberate rudeness. He was going to like this kid, God knew why. "So, you need lessons and a decent court." He glanced at Ty's worn racket. "And equipment. What kind of power can you get out of plastic strings?"

Defensive, Ty tossed up a ball and smashed it into the opposing service court.

"Not bad," Martin decided mildly. "You'd do better with sheep gut."

"Tell me something I don't know."

Martin drew out a pack of cigarettes and offered one to Ty. He refused with a shake of his head. Taking his time, Martin lit one, then took a long drag.

"Those things'll mess up your lungs," Ty stated idly.

"Tell me something I don't know," the lawyer countered. "Think you can play on grass?"

Ty answered with a quick, crude expletive, then sliced another ball over the net.

"Pretty sure of yourself."

"I'm going to play Wimbledon," Ty told him matter-of-factly. "And I'm going to win."

Martin didn't smile, but reached into his pocket. He held out a discreet, expensively printed business card. "Call me Monday," he said simply, and walked away.

Ty had a patron.

The marriage wasn't made in heaven. Over the next seven years there were bitter arguments, bursts of temper and dashes of love. Ty worked hard because he understood that work and discipline were the means to the end. He remained in school and studied only because his mother and Martin had a conspiracy against him. Unless he completed high school with decent grades, the patronage would be removed. As to the patronage itself, Ty accepted it only because his needs demanded it. But he was never comfortable with it. The lessons polished his craft. Good equipment tightened his game. He played on manicured grass, well-tended clay and wood, learning the idiosyncrasies of each surface.

Every morning before school he practiced. Afternoons and weekends were dedicated to tennis. Summers, he worked part-time in the pro shop at Martin's club, then used the courts to hone his skill. By the time he was sixteen the club's tennis pro could beat him only if Ty had an off day.

His temper was accepted. It was a game of histrionics. Women found a certain appeal in his lawlessness.

Ty learned of female pleasures young, and molded his talent there as carefully as he did his game.

The only break in his routine came when he injured his hand coming to the defense of his sister. Ty considered the two-week enforced vacation worth it, as the boy Jess had been struggling with had a broken nose.

He traveled to his first tournament unknown and unseeded. In a lengthy, gritty match heralded in the sports pages, he found his first professional victory. When he lost, Ty was rude, argumentative and brooding. When he won, he was precisely the same. The press tolerated him because he was young, brilliant and colorful. His rise from obscurity was appreciated in a world where champions were bred in the affluent, select atmosphere of country clubs.

Before his nineteenth birthday Ty put a down payment on a three-bedroom house in a Chicago suburb. He moved his family out. When he was twenty he won his first Wimbledon title. The dream was realized, but his intensity never slackened.

Now, walking along the dark streets of Rome, he thought of his roots. Asher made him think of them, perhaps because hers were so markedly different. There had been no back alleys or street gangs in her life. Her childhood had been sheltered, privileged and rich. With James Wolfe as a father, her introduction to tennis had come much earlier and much easier than Ty's. At four she had a custom-made racket and had hit balls on her father's private courts. Her mother had hired maids to scrub floors, not been hired out to scrub them.

At times Ty wondered if it was that very difference that had attracted him to her. Then he would remember the way she felt in his arms. Backgrounds were blown to hell. Yet there was something about her reserve that had drawn him. That and the passion he had sensed lay beneath.

The challenge. Yes, Ty admitted with a frown, he was a man who couldn't resist a challenge. Something about the cool, distant Asher Wolfe had stirred his blood even when she had been little more than a child. He'd waited for her to grow up. And to thaw out, he reminded himself ruefully. Turning a corner without direction, Ty found himself approaching one of Rome's many fountains. The water twinkled with light gaiety while he watched, wishing his blood were as cool.

God, how he wanted her still. The need grated against pride, infuriating and arousing him. He would have taken her back that night even knowing she had been another man's wife, shared another man's bed. It would have been less difficult to have thought about her with many lovers than with one husband—that damn titled Englishman whose arms she had run to straight from his own. *Why?* The question pounded at him.

How many times in those first few months had he relived their last few days together, looking for the key? Then he'd layered over the hurt and the fury. The wound had healed jaggedly, then callused. Ty had gone on because he was a survivor. He'd survived poverty, and the streets, and the odds. With an unsteady laugh he raked a hand through his thick mop of hair. But had he really survived Asher?

He knew he had taken more than one woman to bed because her hair was nearly the same shade, her voice nearly the same tone. Nearly, always nearly. Now, when he had all but convinced himself that what he remembered was an illusion, she was back. And free. Again,

Ty laughed. Her divorce meant nothing to him. If she had still been legally tied to another man, it would have made no difference. He would still have taken her.

This time, he determined, he'd call the shots. He was out of patience. He would have her again, until he decided to walk away. Challenge, strategy, action. It was a course he had followed for half his life. Taking out a coin, he flipped it insolently into the rippling waters of a fountain, as if daring luck to evade him. It drifted down slowly until it nestled with a hundred other wishes.

His eyes skimmed the streets until he found the neon lights of a tiny bar. He wanted a drink.

Chapter 4

Asher had time to savor her title as Italian Women's Champion on the flight between Rome and Paris. After the match she had been too exhausted from nearly two hours of unrelenting competition to react. She could remember Madge hugging her, the crowd cheering for her. She could remember the glare of flashbulbs in her face and the barrage of questions she had forced herself to answer before she all but collapsed on the massage table. Then the celebrations had run together in a blur of color and sound, interviews and champagne. Too many faces and handshakes and hugs. Too many reporters. Now, as the plane leveled, reaction set in. She'd done it.

For all of her professional career, the Italian clay had beaten her. Now—now her comeback was viable. She had proven herself. Every hour of strain, every moment of physical pain during the last six months of training had been worth it. At last Asher could rid herself of all the lingering doubts that she had made the right decision.

Though there had been no doubts about her choice to leave Eric, she mused, feeling little emotion at the dissolution of her marriage—a marriage, Asher remembered, that had been no more than a polite play after the first two months. If she had ever made a truly unforgivable mistake, it had been in marrying Lord Eric Wickerton.

All the wrong reasons, Asher reflected as she leaned back in her seat with her eyes closed. Even with her bitter thoughts of Eric, she could never remove the feeling of responsibility for taking the step that had legally bound them. He had known she hadn't loved him. It hadn't mattered to him. She had known he wanted her to fit the title of Lady. She hadn't cared. At the time the need to escape had been too overpowering. Asher had given Eric what he had wanted—a groomed, attractive wife and hostess. She had thought he would give her what she needed in return. Love and understanding. The reality had been much, much different, and almost as painful as what she had sought to escape. Arguments were more difficult, she had discovered, when two people had no mutual ground. And when one felt the other had sinned…

She wouldn't think of it, wouldn't think of the time in her life that had brought such pain and disillusionment. Instead, she would think of victory.

Michael had been right in his assessment of Tia on the court. She was a small, vibrant demon who played hard and never seemed to tire. Her skill was in picking holes in her opponent's game, then ruthlessly exploiting them. On court she wore gold—a thin chain around her neck, swinging hoops at her ears and a thick clip to tame her raven hair. Her dress was pastel and frilled. She played like an enraged tigress. Both women had run miles during the match, taking it to a full five sets. The last one had consisted of ten long, volatile games with the lead shooting back and forth as quickly as the ball. Never had it been more true that the match wasn't over until it was over.

And when it was over, both women had limped off the court, sweaty, aching and exhausted. But Asher had limped off with a title. Nothing else mattered.

Looking back at it, Asher found herself pleased that the match had been hard won. She wanted something the press would chatter about, something they would remember for more than a day or two. It was always news when an unseeded player won a world title—even considering Asher's record. As it was, her past only made her hotter copy. She needed that now to help keep the momentum going.

With Italy behind her, Paris was next. The first leg of the Grand Slam. She had won there before, on clay, the year she had been Starbuck's lady. As she had with Eric, Asher tried to block Ty out of her mind. Characteristically he wasn't cooperative.

We pick this up in Paris.

The words echoed softly in her head, part threat, part promise. Asher knew him too well to believe either was idle. She would have to deal with him when the time came. But she wasn't naïve or innocent any longer. Life had taught her there weren't any easy answers or fairy-tale endings. She'd lost too much to believe happy-ever-after waited at the end of every love affair—as she had once believed it had waited for her and Ty. They were no longer the prince and princess of the courts, but older, and, Asher fervently hoped, wiser.

She was certain he would seek to soothe his ego by trying to win her again—her body if not her heart. Remembering the verve and depth of his lovemaking, Asher knew it wouldn't be easy to resist him. If she could have done so without risking her emotions, Asher would have given Ty what he wanted. For three color-less years she had endured without the passion he had brought to her life. For three empty years she had won-dered and wanted and denied.

But her emotions weren't safe. On a sigh, Asher al-lowed herself to feel. She still cared. Not a woman to lie to herself, Asher admitted she loved Ty, had never once stopped loving him. It had never been over for her, and deep within she carried the memory of that love. It brought guilt.

What if he had known? she thought with the famil-iar stir of panic. How could she have told him? Asher opened her eyes and stared blindly through the sunlight. It was as harsh and unforgiving as the emotions that raged through her. Would he have believed? Would he have accepted? Before the questions were fully formed, Asher shook her head in denial. He could never know that she had unwittingly married another man while she carried Ty's child. Or that through her own grief and despair she had lost that precious reminder of her love for him.

Closing her eyes, Asher willed herself to sleep. Paris was much too close.

"Ty! Ty!"

Pausing in the act of zipping the cover on his racket,

Ty turned. Pleasure shot into his eyes. In a quick move he dropped his racket and grabbed the woman who had run to him. Holding her up, he whirled her in three dizzying circles before he crushed her against him. Her laughter bounced off the air in breathless gasps.

"You're breaking me!" she cried, but hugged him tighter.

Ty cut off her protest with a resounding kiss, then held her at arm's length. She was a small woman, nearly a foot shorter than he, nicely rounded without being plump. Her gray-green eyes were sparkling, her generous mouth curved in a dazzling smile. She was a beauty, he thought—had always been a beauty. Love surrounded him. He tousled her hair, dark as his own, but cut in a loose swinging style that brushed her shoulders. "Jess, what are you doing here?"

Grinning, she gave his ear a sisterly tug. "Being mauled by the world's top tennis player."

Ty slipped an arm around her shoulders, only then noticing the man who stood back watching them. "Mac." Keeping his arm around Jess, Ty extended a hand.

"Ty, how are you?"

"Fine. Just fine."

Mac accepted the handshake and careful greeting with light amusement. He knew how Ty felt about his little sister—the little sister who was now twenty-seven and the mother of his child. When he had married Jess, over two years before, Mac had understood that there was a bond between brother and sister that would not be severed. An only child, he both respected and envied it. Two years of being in-laws had lessened Ty's caution with him but hadn't alleviated it. Of course, Mac mused ruefully, it hadn't helped that he was fifteen years Jess's senior, or that he had moved her across the country to California, where he headed a successful research and development firm. And then, he preferred chess to tennis. He'd never have gotten within ten yards of Jessica Starbuck if he hadn't been Martin Derick's nephew.

Bless Uncle Martin, Mac thought with a glance at his lovely, adored wife. Ty caught the look and relaxed his grip on his sister. "Where's Pete?" he asked, making the overture by addressing Mac rather than his sister.

Mac acknowledged the gesture with a smile. "With Grandma. They're both pretty pleased with themselves."

Jess gave the bubbling laugh that both men loved. "Hardly more than a year old and he can move like lightning. Mom's thrilled to chase him around for a few weeks. She sends her love," she told Ty. "You know how she feels about long plane flights."

"Yeah." He released his sister to retrieve his bag and racket. "I talked to her just last night; she didn't say anything about your coming."

"We wanted to surprise you." Smug, Jess hooked her hand into Mac's. "Mac thought Paris was the perfect place for a second honeymoon." She sent her husband a brief but intimate look. Their fingers tightened.

"The trick was getting her away from Pete for two weeks." He gave Ty a grin. "You were a bigger incentive than Paris." Bending, he kissed the top of his wife's head. "She dotes on Pete."

"No, I don't," Jess disagreed, then grinned. "Well, I wouldn't if Pete weren't such a smart baby."

Mac began to unpack an old, favored pipe. "She's ready to enroll him in Harvard."

"Next year," Jess responded dryly. "So, you're going

in as top seed," she continued, giving her full attention to her brother. Was there some strain around his eyes? she wondered, then quickly discounted it. "Martin's proud enough to bust."

"I was hoping he might make it out for the tournament." Ty glanced toward the empty stands. "Funny, I still have a habit of looking for him before a match."

"He wanted to be here. If there had been any way for him to postpone this trial, but…" Jess trailed off and smiled. "Mac and I will have to represent the family."

Ty slung the bag over his shoulder. "You'll do fine. Where are you staying?"

"At the—" Jess's words came to a stop as she spotted a slender blonde crossing an empty court a short distance away. Reaching up, she brushed at her brow as if pushing aside an errant strand of hair. "Asher," she murmured.

Ty twisted his head. Asher wasn't aware of them, as Chuck was keeping her involved in what appeared to be a long, detailed description of a match. "Yes," Ty said softly. "Asher." He kept his eyes on her, watching the movements of her body beneath the loosely fitting jogging suit. "Didn't you know she was here?"

"Yes, I—" Jess broke off helplessly. How could she explain the flurry of feelings that she experienced in seeing Asher Wolfe again. The years were winked away in an instant. Jess could see the cool blue eyes, hear the firmly controlled voice. At the time there'd been no doubt in her mind about right and wrong. Even the chain reaction that had begun on a hazy September afternoon had only served to cement Jess's certainty. Now there'd been a divorce, and Asher was back. She felt her husband's warm palm against hers. Right and wrong weren't so clearly defined any longer.

A bubble of nausea rose as she turned to her brother. He was still watching Asher. Had he loved her? Did he still? What would he do if he ever learned of his sister's part in what had happened three years before? Jess found the questions trembling on her tongue and was afraid of the answers. "Ty…"

His eyes were dark and stormy, a barometer of emotion. Something in them warned Jess to keep her questions to herself. Surely there would be a better time to bring up the past. She had both a sense of reprieve and a feeling of guilt.

"Beautiful, isn't she?" he asked lightly. "Where did you say you were staying?"

"And because he's eighteen and played like a rocket in the qualifying rounds, they're muttering about an upset." Chuck tossed a tennis ball idly, squeezing it when it returned to his palm. "I wouldn't mind if he weren't such a little twerp."

Asher laughed and snatched the ball as Chuck tossed it again. "And eighteen," she added.

He gave a snort. "He wears designer underwear, for God's sake. His mother has them dry cleaned."

"Down boy," Asher warned good-naturedly. "You'll feel better once you wipe him out in the quarter-finals. Youth versus experience," she added because she couldn't resist. Chuck twisted a lock of her hair around his finger and pulled.

"You meet Rayski," he commented. "I guess we could call that two old pros."

Asher winced. "Your point," she conceded. "So, what's your strategy for this afternoon?"

"To beat the tar out of him," Chuck responded instantly, then grinned as he flexed his racket arm. "But if he gets lucky, I'll leave it up to Ty to smash him in the semis or the finals."

Asher bounced the ball on the clay. Her fingers closed over it, then released it again. "You're so sure Ty will get to the finals?"

"Money in the bank," he claimed. "This is his year. I swear, I've never seen him play better." Pleasure for his friend with the light lacing of envy gave the statement more impact. "He's going to be piling up titles like dominoes."

Asher said nothing, not even nodding in agreement as Chuck sought to prove his point by giving her a replay of Ty's qualifying match. A breeze stirred, sending blossoms drifting to the court at her feet. It was early morning, and the Stade Roland Garros was still drowsily charming and quiet. The thump of balls was hardy noticeable. In a few hours the fourteen thousand seats around the single center court would be jammed with enthusiasts. The noise would be human and emotional, accented by the sounds of traffic and squealing brakes on the highway that separated the stadium from the Bois de Boulogne.

Asher watched the breeze tickle a weeping willow as Chuck continued his rundown. In this first week of the games, tennis would be played for perhaps eleven hours a day so that even the first-round losers used the courts enough to make the trip worthwhile. It was considered by most pros the toughest championship to win. Like Ty, Asher was after her second victory.

Paris. Ty. Was there nowhere she could go that wasn't so firmly tied in with memories of him? In Paris they'd sat in the back of a darkened theater, necking like teenagers while an Ingmar Bergman film had flickered on the screen unnoticed. In Paris he had doctored a strained muscle in her calf, pampering and bullying so that she had won despite the pain. In Paris they had made love, and made love, and made love until they were both weak and exhausted. In Paris Asher had still believed in happy endings.

Fighting off memories, Asher glanced around the stadium. Her eyes locked with Jess's. Separated by a hundred yards, both women endured a jolt of shock and distress. They stared, unable to communicate, unable to look away.

"Hey, it's Jess!" Chuck interrupted himself to make the announcement. He waved, then grabbed Asher's hand to drag her with him. "Let's go say hi."

Panicked, Asher dug in her heels. "No, I—I have to meet…" Her mind was devoid of excuses, but she snatched her hand from Chuck's. "You go ahead, I'll see you later." Over Chuck's protest, she dashed in the opposite direction.

Breathless, Asher found herself in the Jardin des Plantes with its sweet, mingling scents, little plaques and poetry. It seemed an odd setting for jangled nerves. Making an effort to calm herself, she slowed her pace.

Silly to run, she told herself. No, she corrected herself, stupid. But she hadn't been prepared to see Ty's sister, the one person who knew all the reasons. To have confronted Jess then, when her mind was already so crowded with Ty, would have been disastrous. Steadying, Asher told herself she just needed a little time to prepare. And it had been obvious Jess had been just as stunned as she. At the moment, Asher was too busy calming herself to wonder why.

She wouldn't, couldn't, think about the last time she'd seen Jessica Starbuck—that hot, close Indian summer afternoon. It would be too easy to remember each word spoken in the careless disorder of the hotel room Asher had shared with Ty. She would remember the hurt, the frantic packing, then her irrevocable decision to go to Eric.

Oh, Ty had been right, she had run away—but she hadn't escaped. So little had changed in three years, and so much. Her heart had remained constant. With a sigh Asher admitted it had been foolish to believe she could take back what she had given so long ago. Ty Starbuck was her first lover, and the only man she had ever loved.

A child had been conceived, then lost before it could be born. She'd never forgiven herself for the accident that had taken that precious, fragile life from her. Perhaps more than a lack of love and understanding, it had been the loss of Ty's child that had destroyed any hope for her marriage.

And if the child had lived? she asked herself wearily. What then? Could she have kept it from him? Could she have remained the wife of one man while bearing the child of another? Asher shook her head. No, she would no longer dwell on possibilities. She'd lost Ty, his child, and the support of her own father. There could be no greater punishments to face. She would make her own future.

The touch of a hand on her shoulder had her whirling around. Asher stared up at Ty, her mind a blank, her emotions in turmoil. A hush seemed to spread over the garden, so she could hear the whisper of air over leaves and blossoms. The scent that reached her was sweet and heady—like a first kiss. He said nothing, nor did she until his hand slid down her arm to link with hers.

"Worried about the match?"

Almost afraid he would sense them, Asher struggled to push all thoughts of the past aside. "Concerned," she amended, nearly managing a smile. "Rayski's top seed."

"You've beaten her before."

"And she's beaten me." It didn't occur to her to remove her hand from his or to mask her doubts. Slowly the tension seeped out of her. Through the link of hands Ty felt it. They had stood here before, and the memory was sweet.

"Play her like you played Conway," he advised. "Their styles are basically the same."

With a laugh Asher ran her free hand through her hair. "That's supposed to be a comfort?"

"You're better than she is," he said simply, and earned an astonished stare. Smiling, he brushed his fingers carelessly over her cheek. "More consistent," he explained. "She's faster, but you're stronger. That gives you an advantage on clay even though it isn't your best surface."

At a loss, Asher managed a surprised, "Well."

"You've improved," Ty stated as they began to walk. "Your backhand doesn't have the power it should have, but—"

"It worked pretty well on Conway," Asher interrupted testily.

"Could be better."

"It's perfect," she disagreed, rising to the bait before she caught his grin. Her lips curved before she could stop them. "You always knew how to get a rise out of me. You're playing Kilroy," she went on, "I've never heard of him."

"He's been around only two years. Surprised everyone in Melbourne last season." He slipped an arm around her shoulders in a gesture so familiar, neither of them noticed. "What's that flower?"

Asher glanced down. "Lady's slipper."

"Silly name."

"Cynic."

He shrugged. "I like roses."

"That's because it's the only flower you can identify." Without thinking, she leaned her head on his shoulder. "I remember going in to take a bath one night and finding you'd filled the tub with roses. Dozens of them."

The scent of her hair reminded him of much more. "By the time we got around to clearing them out, it took over an hour."

Her sigh was wistful. "It was wonderful. You could always surprise me by doing something absurd."

"A tub of lady's slippers is absurd," he corrected. "A tub of roses is classy."

Her laughter was quick and appreciative. Her head still rested on his shoulders. "We filled everything in the room that could pass for a vase, including a bottle of ginger ale. Sometimes when I—" She cut herself off, abruptly realizing she would say too much.

"When you what?" Ty demanded as he turned her to face him. When she only shook her head, he tightened his grip. "Would you remember sometimes, in the middle of the night? Would you wake up and hurt because you couldn't forget?"

Truth brought tension to the base of her neck. In

defense, Asher pressed her palms against his chest. "Ty, please."

"I did." He gave her a frustrated shake that knocked her head back. "Oh, God, I did. I've never stopped wanting you. Even hating you I wanted you. Do you know what it's like to be awake at three o'clock in the morning and need someone, and know she's in another man's bed."

"No, no, don't." She was clinging to him, her cheek pressed against his, her eyes tightly shut. "Ty, don't."

"Don't what?" he demanded as he drew her head back. "Don't hate you? Don't want you? Hell, I can't do anything else."

His eyes blazed into her, dark with fury, hot with passion. She could feel the race of his heart compete with hers. Abandoning pride, she pressed her lips to his.

At the instant of contact he stood still, neither giving nor taking. On a moan she drew him closer, letting her lips have their way. A shudder coursed through him, an oath ripped out, then he was responding, demanding, exciting. Why had he tried to resist? Nothing was clear to him as her lips raced crazily over his face. Wasn't this what he wanted? To have her again, to prove he could, to purge his system of her once and for all. Motives dimmed in desire. There was only Asher—the sweet taste of her, her scent more heady, more seductive than the garden of flowers. He couldn't breathe and not fill himself on her. So he surrendered to the persuading lips and soft body that had haunted his dreams.

Dragging his lips from hers only a moment, Ty pulled her through the fragile branches of a willow. The sun filtered through the curtain of leaves, giving intermittent light. In the cool dimness his mouth sought hers again and found it yielding. The blood pounded in his veins.

He had to know if her body was the same, unchanged during the years he'd been denied her. As his hand took her breast he groaned. She was small and firm and familiar. Through the material of her jacket he felt the nipple harden in quick response. Impatient, he tugged the zipper down, then dove under her shirt until he found the smooth tender flesh that had always made him feel his hands were too rough. Yet she didn't draw away as his calluses met her. She pressed against him. Her moan was not one of discomfort, but of unmistakable pleasure.

Trembling, her fingers reached for his hair. He could feel the urgency in them just as he could taste it on her heated lips. He broke his kiss only to change angles, then deepened it, allowing his tongue to drink up all the dark flavors of her mouth. Against his palm her heart thudded wildly, but only his fingers moved to arouse her.

Slowly his other hand journeyed to her hip to mold the long, slender bone. He was lost somewhere between yesterday and today. The heavy fragrance of flowers still wet with morning dew was more seductive than perfume. Half dreaming, Ty took his mouth to her throat. He heard her sigh float off on the scented air. Was she dreaming too? Was the past overlapping this moment for her as well as for him? The thoughts drifted into his mind, then out again before they could be answered. Nothing mattered but that he was holding her again.

From far off came a ripple of laughter. Ty brought his mouth back to Asher's. A rapid smattering of French drifted to him. Ty drew her closer until their bodies seemed fused. Footsteps and a giggle. Like a dreamer, he sensed the intrusion and swore against it. For another moment he clung, drawing on her lingering passion.

When he released her, Asher was breathless and swaying. Wordlessly he stared down at her with eyes nearly black with emotion. Her lips were parted, swollen from his, and he gave in to need and kissed her one long last time. Gently now, slowly, to store up every dram of sweetness. This time she trembled, her breath coming harsh and fast like a diver's who breaks surface after a long submersion. Disoriented, she gripped his arms.

How long had they been there? she wondered. It could have been seconds or days. All she was sure of was that the longing had intensified almost beyond control. Her blood was racing in her veins, her heart pounding desperately. She was alive. So alive. And no longer certain which path she would take.

"Tonight," Ty murmured, bringing her palm to his lips.

The vibration shot up her arm and into her core. "Ty..." Asher shook her head as she tried to draw her hand away. His fingers tightened.

"Tonight," he repeated.

"I can't." Seeing the temper shoot into his eyes, Asher covered their joined hands with her free one. "Ty, I'm frightened."

The quiet admission killed his anger. He let out a weary sigh. "Damn you, Asher."

Saying nothing, she wrapped her arms around his waist, pressing her cheek to his chest. Automatically Ty reached to smooth her hair. His eyes closed. "I'm sorry," she whispered. "I was frightened of you once before.

It seems to be happening again." And I love you, she told him silently. As much as ever. More, she realized. More, because of the years of famine.

"Asher." He held her away from him. She felt the passion swirling around him. "I won't promise to wait for you to come to me this time. I won't promise to be gentle and patient. Things aren't the same."

She shook her head, but in agreement. "No, things aren't the same. It might be better, much better for both of us if we just stayed away from each other."

Ty laughed shortly. "We won't."

"If we tried," Asher began.

"*I* won't."

She let out a breath of exasperation. "You're pressuring me."

"Damn right." Before she could decide whether to laugh or to scream, she was in his arms again. "Do you think I don't feel pressured too?" he demanded with a sudden intensity that kept Asher from answering. "Every time I look at you I remember the way things were for us and drive myself crazy trying to figure out why you left me. Do you know what that does to me?"

She gripped his upper arms with strong hands. "You have to understand, I won't go back. Whatever happens to us now begins now. No questions, no whys." She saw the anger boiling in his eyes, but kept hers level. "I mean that, Ty. I can't give you explanations. I won't dig up the past."

"You expect me to live with that?"

"I expect nothing," she said quietly. The tone caused him to look deeper for the answers she refused to give. "And I've agreed to nothing. Not yet."

"You ask for too much," he bit off as he released her. "Too damn much."

She wanted to go to him, go back to his arms and beg him to forget the past. Perhaps it was possible to live for the moment if one wanted to badly enough. It might have been pride that stopped her, or the deeply ingrained survival instinct she had developed since that long-ago September afternoon when she had fled from him and the prospect of pain. Asher laced her fingers together and stared down at them. "Yes, I know. I'm sorry, Ty, we'll only hurt each other."

Tense and tormented, he turned back. "I've never wanted to hurt you, Asher. Not even when I thought I did."

The ache spread so quickly, she almost gasped from it. Isn't that what Jess had said that day? *He'd never want to hurt you...never want to hurt you.* Asher could hear the words echoing inside her head. "Neither of us wanted to," she murmured. "Both of us did. Isn't it foolish to do it again?"

"Look at me." The command was quiet and firm. Bracing herself, Asher obeyed. His eyes were locked on hers—those dark, penetrating eyes that conveyed such raw feeling. Gently he touched her cheek. Without hesitation her hand rose to cover his. "Now," he whispered, "ask me again."

A long, shuddering breath escaped. "Oh, Ty, I was so sure I could prevent this. So sure I could resist you this time."

"And now?"

"Now I'm not sure of anything." She shook her head before he could speak again. "Don't ask now. Give us both some time."

He started to protest, then managed to restrain it. He'd waited three years, a bit longer wouldn't matter. "Some time," he agreed, lowering his hand. But as she started to relax, he took her wrist. The grip was neither gentle nor patient. "The next time, Asher, I won't ask."

She nodded, accepting. "Then we understand each other."

His smile was a trifle grim. "That we do. I'll walk you back." He drew her through the curtain of leaves.

Chapter 5

Fifth set. Seventh game. At the baseline Ty crouched, ready to spring for Michael's serve. The air was heavy, the sky thick with rain-threatening clouds so that the light was dreary. Ty didn't notice. He didn't notice the stadium full of people, some dangling through the railing, some hanging from the scoreboard. He didn't notice the shouts and whistles that were either for or against him.

Tennis was a game of the individual. That was what had drawn him to it. There was no one to blame for a loss, no one to praise for a win but yourself. It was a game of motion and emotion, both of which he excelled in.

He had looked forward to meeting Michael in the semis. The Australian played a hot, passionate game full of dramatic gestures, furious mutters and pizzazz.

There were perhaps five competitors Ty fully respected, Michael being one of them. Wanting to win was only a step below wanting a challenge. A fight. He'd grown up scrapping. Now the racket was merely an extension of his arm. The match was a bout. The bout was one on one. It had never—would never—be only a game.

The Australian was a set up, with his momentum still flowing. Ty's only thought at the moment was to break his serve and even the match. Thus far he had spotted no weaknesses in his opponent's game. Like a boxer, he watched for the opening.

He heard the sound of the ball hitting the sweet spot of the racket before it rocketed toward him. It landed deep in the corner of the service court, beautifully placed. Ty's mind and body moved as one as he sprang for the return. Defense, offense, strategy all had to be formulated in a fraction of a second. Strength had to be balanced with form. Both men sprinted over the court for the rally, faces glowing with concentration and sweat. The roar of the crowd rose to meet the distant thunder.

Thus far, the ratio had been nearly ten to one in favor of ground strokes. Ty decided to alter the pace and go with power. Using a vicious left-to-right slice, he shook Michael's balance. Ty blasted away at the attempted passing shot, barely shortening his backswing. Michael couldn't reach the backhand volley, let alone return it. Love-fifteen.

Shaking the damp hair back from his face, Ty returned to the baseline. A woman in the crowd called out what could have been a congratulations or a proposition. Ty's French wasn't strong enough to decipher the phrase. Michael's serve sent up a puff of smoke.

Before his return was over the net, Ty was at mid-court and waiting. A testing ground stroke, a sharp return. A tricky topspin, a slice. Michael's decision to try to lob over Ty was a mistake. The smoking smash careened off the court and into the grandstands. Love-thirty.

Michael walked a complete circle, cursing himself before he took his position again. Casting off impatience, Ty waited. Crouched, swaying side to side, unblinking, he was ready. Both players exploited angles and depths with ground strokes. There was a long, patient rally as each watched for the chance to smash a winner. It might have been pure showmanship if it hadn't been for the sounds of exertion coming from the two players.

A UPI photographer had his motor drive humming as he recorded the game. He framed Ty, arms extended for balance, legs spread for the stretch, face fierce. It crossed his mind as he continued to snap that he wouldn't want to face that American on any playing field.

Gracefully, with an elegance belied by his expression, Ty executed a backhand with a touch of underspin. Michael's return thudded against the net. Love-forty.

Angry and shaken, Michael punched his first serve into the net. Having no choice at game point, he placed his next serve carefully. Ty went straight for the volley and took the net. The exchange was fast and furious, the players moving on instinct, the crowd screaming in a mixture of languages. Ty's wrist was locked. The ball whipped from racket to racket at terrifying speed. There were bare seconds between contact, making both men anticipate flight rather than see it. Changing tactics in the wink of an instant, Ty brought the racket face under at the moment of impact. With a flick of a wrist he dropped a dump shot over the net. Risky, experts would say. Gutsy, fans would claim. Ty would ignore both. Game and set.

"Oh, Mac!" Jess leaned back and expelled a long breath. "I'd nearly forgotten what it was like to watch Ty play."

"You watched him just a few weeks ago," he pointed out, using a damp handkerchief to wipe his neck. The wish for his air-conditioned office flitted only briefly into his mind.

"On television," Jess returned. "That's different. Being here...can't you feel it?"

"I thought it was the humidity."

Laughing, Jess shook her head. "Always down to earth, Mac. That's why I love you."

Her smile seemed to open just for him. It could still make his blood sing. "Then I intend to stay there," he murmured, kissing her knuckles. Feeling her hand tense, he looked up, puzzled. Her eyes were aimed over his shoulder. Curious, he turned, spotting a few tennis faces he recognized. Among them was Asher Wolfe. It was on her that his wife's gaze was locked.

"That's the former Lady Wickerton, isn't it?" he asked casually. "She's stunning."

"Yes." Jess tore her eyes away, but the tension in her fingers remained. "Yes, she is."

"She won her match this morning. We'll have an American going into the women's finals." Jess said nothing as Mac stuffed the handkerchief back into his pocket. "She was away from the game for a while, wasn't she?"

"Yes."

Intrigued by his wife's flat answer, Mac probed. "Didn't she and Ty have something going a few years back?"

"It was nothing." With a nervous swallow Jess prayed she spoke the truth. "Just a passing thing. She's not Ty's type. Asher's very cool, much more suited to Wickerton than to Ty. He was attracted to that for a while, that's all." She moistened her lips. "And it was obvious she wasn't serious about him, otherwise she'd never have married Wickerton so quickly. She was making Ty unhappy, very unhappy."

"I see," Mac murmured after a moment. Jess had spoken too quickly and too defensively. Studying his wife's profile, he wondered. "I suppose Ty's too involved in his career to be serious about a woman?"

"Yes." The look Jess gave him was almost pleading. "Yes, he'd never have let her go if he'd been in love with her. Ty's too possessive."

"And proud," he reminded her quietly. "I don't think he'd run after any woman, no matter how he felt about her."

Feeling her stomach roll, Jess said nothing. She turned to watch her brother take the position for his first serve.

Instead of the hazy afternoon she saw a brilliant morning. Instead of the clay of Roland Garros she saw the newly empty grass courts of Forest Hills. Ty was leaning over the rail, staring out at center court. She had a fanciful thought that he looked like the captain of a ship with his eyes on the open, endless sea. In her world she loved no one more than him, could conceive of loving no one more. He was brother and father and hero. He'd provided her with a home, clothes and an education, asking nothing in return. As a result, she would have given him anything.

Crossing to him, she slipped her arm around him, nestling her head in the crook of his shoulder.

"Thinking about this afternoon?" she murmured. He was slated to face Chuck Prince in the finals of the U.S. Open.

"Hmm?" Distracted, Ty shrugged. "No, not really."

"It must feel odd to compete against your closest friend."

"You must forget you're friends for a couple hours," Ty returned.

He was brooding; she sensed it. And unhappy. There was no one, including her mother, Jess felt more loyalty to. Her grip around him tightened. "Ty, what is it?"

"Just restless."

"Have you fought with Asher?"

Absently he tousled her hair. "No, I haven't fought with Asher."

He lapsed into silence for so long that Jess began to suspect he wasn't telling the entire truth. She was already worried about him and Asher. The relationship had lasted longer than was habitual for Ty. Jess saw Asher's reserve as coldness, her independence as indifference. She didn't hang on Ty as other women did. She didn't listen raptly to every word he spoke. She didn't adore him.

"Do you ever think back, Jess?" he asked suddenly.

"Think back?"

"To when we were kids." His eyes skimmed over the manicured courts, but didn't see them. "That crummy apartment with the paper walls. The DeMarcos next door screaming at each other in the middle of the night.

The stairwell always smelled of old garbage and stale sweat."

The tone of his voice disturbed her. Seeking comfort as much as to comfort, she turned her face into his chest. "Not often. I guess I don't remember it as well as you. I hadn't turned fifteen when you got us out."

"I wonder sometimes if you can ever escape that, if you can ever really turn your back on it." His eyes were focused on something Jess couldn't see. She strained to share the vision. "Old garbage and stale sweat," he repeated quietly. "I can't forget that. I asked Asher once what smell she remembered most from her childhood. She said the wisteria that hung over her bedroom window."

"Ty, I don't understand."

He swore softly. "Neither do I."

"You left all that behind," she began.

"I left it," he corrected her. "That doesn't mean I left it behind. We were having dinner last night. Wickerton stopped by the table and started a conversation about French Impressionists. After five minutes I didn't know what the hell they were talking about."

Jess bristled. She knew because Ty had sent her to college. She knew because he had provided the opportunity. "You should have told him to get lost."

With a laugh Ty kissed her cheek. "That was my first thought." Abruptly he sobered. "Then I watched them. They understand each other, speak the same language. It made me realize there are some fences you just can't climb."

"You could if you wanted to."

"Maybe. I don't." He let out a long breath. "I don't really give a damn about French Impressionists. I don't give a damn about the mutual friends they have that are distant cousins of the Queen of England, or who won at Ascot last month." Storm warnings were in his eyes, but he shrugged. "Even if I did, I wouldn't fit into that kind of life because I'd always remember the garbage and sweat."

"Asher has no business encouraging that man," Jess stated heatedly. "He's been following her around since Paris."

Ty gave a grim laugh. "She doesn't encourage or discourage. Drawing room conversation," he murmured. "Ingrained manners. She's different from us, Jess, I've known that all along."

"If *she'd* tell him to get lost—"

"She couldn't tell anyone to get lost any more than she could sprout wings and fly."

"She's cold."

"She's different," Ty returned immediately but without heart. He cupped his sister's chin in his hand. "You and me, we're the same. Everything's up front. If we want to shout, we shout. If we want to throw something, we throw it. Some people can't."

"Then they're stupid."

This time his laugh was warm and genuine. "I love you, Jess."

Throwing her arms around him, she hugged him fiercely. "I can't bear to see you unhappy. Why do you let her do this to you?"

Frowning, Ty stroked her hair. "I've been trying to figure that out. Maybe…maybe I just need a shove in the right direction."

Jess held him tighter, searching her mind for the answer.

* * *

Seventh set. Tenth game. The crowd was as vocal, as enthusiastic and as hungry as it had been an hour before. Leaning forward in his seat, his eyes glued to the ball, Chuck sat between Asher and Madge.

"You've got something riding on this one, don't you, cowboy?" Madge commented dryly though her own heart was pumping. Chuck would face the winner in the finals.

"It's the best match I've seen in two years." His own face was damp, his own muscles tense. The ball traveled at such speeds, it was often only a white blur.

Asher spoke to neither of them. Her objectivity had been long since destroyed. Ty enthralled her. Both men possessed the raw athletic ability competitors admired and envied. Both were draining the other's resources without mercy. But it was Ty, always Ty, who ripped the emotion from her.

She could admire Michael, admit his brilliance, but he didn't cause that slow, churning ache in her stomach. Had she not once been Ty's lover, had she not even known him, would she still be so drawn? Controlled rage. How was it a woman raised in such an ordered, sheltered existence would be pulled irresistibly to a man with such turbulent passion? Opposites attract? she wondered. No, that was much too simple.

Sitting in the crowded stadium, Asher felt the thrill of desire as clearly as though she had been naked in his arms. She felt no shame. It was natural. She felt no fear. It was inevitable. Years made up of long, unending days vanished. What a waste of time, she thought suddenly. No, a loss, she corrected herself. A loss of time—nothing's ever wasted. *Tonight.* The decision came to her as effortlessly as it had the first time. To-night they would be together. And if it was only once—if once was all he wanted—it would have to be enough. The long wait was over. She laughed out loud in relief and joy. Chuck sent her an odd look.

"He's going to win," Asher said on a second laugh. Leaning on the rail, she rested her chin on her folded hands. "Oh, yes, he's going to win."

There was a dull ache in his racket arm that Ty ignored. The muscles in his legs promised to cramp the moment he stopped moving. He wouldn't give in to them any more than he would give in to the man across the net. One thing hadn't changed in twenty years. He still hated to lose.

A point away from the match, he played no less tigerishly than he had in the first game. The rallies had been long and punishing. The ball whistled. Sweat dripped. For the last twenty minutes Ty had forsaken artistry for cunning. It was working.

Power for power, they were in a dead heat, so that Ty chose to outmaneuver the Australian. He worked him over the court, pacing him, some might say stalking him. The game went to deuce three times while the crowd grew frantic. An ace gave him advantage—a screeching bullet that brought Ty the final impetus he needed. Then Ty played him hot-bloodedly. The men drove from side to side, their faces masks of effort and fury. The shot came that he'd been waiting for. Michael's awesome backhand drove crosscourt to his southpaw forehand. The ball came to Ty at waist level. Michael didn't even have to see the return to know it was over.

Game, set and match.

The heat hit him then, and the fatigue. It took an effort not to stagger. Simply to have fallen to his knees would have been a relief. He walked to the net.

Michael took his hand, then draped his free arm around Ty's shoulder. "Damn you, Starbuck," he managed breathlessly. "You nearly killed me."

Ty laughed, using his opponent for balance a moment. "You too."

"I need a bloody drink." Michael straightened, giving Ty a glazed grin. "Let's go get drunk."

"You're on."

Turning, they separated, victor and vanquished, to face the press, the showers and the massage tables. Ty grabbed the towel someone handed him, nodding at the questions and congratulations being hurled at him. Behind the cloth he could hear the click and whir of cameras. He was too weary to curse them. Someone was gathering his rackets. He could hear the clatter of wood on wood. The strength that had flowed freely through him only moments before drained. Exhausted, he let the drenched towel fall. His eyes met Asher's.

So blue, he thought. Her eyes are so blue. And cool, and deep. He could drown in them blissfully. The unbearable heat vanished, as though someone had opened a window to a fresh spring breeze.

"Congratulations." When she smiled, his fatigue slid away. Strangely it wasn't desire that replaced it, but comfort, sweet simple comfort.

"Thanks." He took the racket bag from her. Their hands barely brushed.

"I suppose the press is waiting for you inside."

The short retort Ty made was both agreement and opinion. On a low laugh she stepped closer.

"Can I buy you dinner?"

The quirk of his brow was the only indication of surprise. "Sure."

"I'll meet you at seven in the lobby of the hotel."

"All right."

"Starbuck, what do you feel was the turning point of the match?"

"What strategy will you use playing Prince in the finals?"

Ty didn't answer the reporters, didn't even hear them as he watched Asher weave her way through the crowd. From overhead Jess watched with a small, fluttering sensation of déjà vu.

Ty got under the stream of the shower fully dressed. He let the cool water sluice over him while he stripped. A reporter from *World of Sports* leaned against a tiled wall, scribbling notes and tossing questions. Naked, with his clothes in a soggy heap at his feet, Ty answered. Always, he handled the press naturally because he didn't give a damn what they printed. He knew his mother kept a scrapbook, but he never read the articles or interviews. Lathering the soap over his face with both hands, he washed the sticky sweat away. Someone passed him a plastic jug of fruit juice. With the water streaming over him, he guzzled it down, replacing lost fluid. The weakness was seeping back, and with it the pain. He made his way to the massage table by instinct, then collapsed onto it.

Strong fingers began to work on him. Questions still hammered in his ear, but now he ignored them. Ty simply closed his eyes and shut them out. A line of pain ran up his calf as the muscles were kneaded. He winced and held on, knowing relief would follow. For ten agonizing minutes he lay still while his body was rubbed and pounded. He began to drift. Like a mother's memory of the pain of childbirth, his memory of the pain began to dim. He could remember winning. And he could remember dark blue eyes. With those two visions tangling in his mind, he slept.

The floor of the lobby was marble. White marble veined with pink. Madge had commented that it would be the devil to keep clean. Her husband had dryly commented that she wouldn't know one end of the mop from the other. Asher sat, listening to their comfortable banter while she told herself she wasn't nervous. It was six-fifty.

She'd dressed carefully, choosing a simple crêpe de Chine as pale as the inside of a peach. Her hair fluffed back from her face, exposing the tiny pearl and coral drops at her ears. Her ringless fingers were interlaced.

"Where are you eating?"

Asher brought her attention back to Madge. "A little place on the Left Bank." There was an enthusiastic violinist, she remembered. Ty had once passed him twenty American dollars and cheerfully told him to get lost.

At the bellow of thunder Madge glanced toward the lobby doors. "You're going to play hell getting a cab tonight." She leaned back. "Have you seen Ty since the match?"

"No."

"Chuck said both he and Michael were sleeping on the tables like babies." A chuckle escaped as she crossed strong, short legs. "Some industrious stringer for a French paper got a couple of classic shots."

"Athletes in repose," her husband mused.

"It kind of blows the tough-guy image."

Asher smiled, thinking how young and vulnerable Ty looked in sleep. When the lids closed over those dramatic eyes, he reminded her of an exhausted little boy. It was the only time the frenetic energy stilled. Something stirred in her. If the child had lived… Hurriedly she censored the thought.

"Hey, isn't that Ty's sister?"

Asher turned her head to see Jess and Mac crossing the lobby. "Yes." Their eyes met, leaving no choice. Gripping her husband's hand, Jess walked across the white marble.

"Hello, Asher."

"Jess."

A quick moistening of lips betrayed nerves. "I don't think you know my husband. Mackenzie Derick, Lady Wickerton."

"Asher Wolfe," she replied smoothly, taking Mac's hand. "Are you related to Martin?"

"My uncle," Mac informed her. "Do you know him?"

The smile brought warmth to her eyes. "Very well." She made the rest of the introductions with a natural poise Mac approved of. Cool, yes, he mused, remembering his wife's description. But with an underlying vibrancy perhaps a man would discern more quickly than another woman. He began to wonder if Jess's opinion of Ty's feelings was accurate.

"Are you a tennis fan, Mr. Derick?" Asher asked him.

"Mac," he supplied. "Only by marriage. And no, I don't play, much to Uncle Martin's disgust."

Asher laughed, appreciating the humor in his eyes. A strong man, she thought instantly. His own man.

He wouldn't take second place to Ty in his wife's life. "Martin should be satisfied having cultivated one champion." Her eyes drifted to Jess, who was sitting straight and tense beside Madge. "Is your mother well?"

"Yes, yes, Mom's fine." Though she met the cool, clear gaze, her fingers began to pleat the material of her skirt. "She's at home with Pete."

"Pete?"

"Our son."

Asher's throat constricted. Mac noticed with some surprise that her knuckles whitened briefly on the arm of her chair. "I didn't know you'd had a baby. Ada must be thrilled to have a grandchild." The pressure on her heart was unbearable. Her smile was casual. "How old is he?" she made herself ask.

"Fourteen months." As the tension built in one woman, it flowed out of the other. Jess was already reaching into her purse for her wallet. "I swear he never walked, he started out running. Mom says he's like Ty. He has his coloring too." She was offering a picture. Asher had no choice but to accept it.

There was some of his father in him—the shape of the face. But the Starbuck genes were strong. The baby's hair was dark and thick, like his mother's. Like Ty's. The eyes were large and gray. Asher wondered if she could actually feel the air of perpetual motion around the child, or if she imagined it. Another baby would have had dark hair and gray eyes. Hadn't she pictured the face countless times?

"He's beautiful," she heard herself say in a calm voice. "You must be very proud of him." When she handed the snapshot back her hands were perfectly steady.

"Jess thinks he should wait until he's twelve before he runs for president."

Asher smiled, but this time Mac didn't find the reflected warmth in her eyes. "Has Ty bought him a racket yet?"

"You know him very well," Mac observed.

"Yes." She looked back at Jess steadily. "Tennis and his family come first, always."

"I hate to admit it," Madge put in with a sigh, "but I can remember a dozen years ago when this one was a skinny teenager, chewing her fingernails at every one of Ty's matches. Now you're a mother."

Jess grinned, holding out her hands for inspection. "And I still bite my nails at Ty's matches."

It was Asher who saw him first. But then, her senses were tuned for him. Ty stepped off the elevator dressed in slim black slacks and a smoke-gray shirt. He wouldn't have chosen the shirt because it matched his eyes so perfectly. Asher knew he wore it because it would have been the first thing his hand had grabbed from the closet. He wore clothes with the casual style of one who gave no thought to them and still looked marvelous. A disciplined body and trained grace made it inevitable. His hair had been combed, but defied order. He paused briefly, even in stillness communicating motion. Asher's heartbeat was a dull, quick thud.

"Oh, there's Ty!" Jess sprang up, hurrying across the lobby to meet him. "I didn't get to congratulate you. You were absolutely wonderful."

Though his arm slipped around her, Jess saw that his eyes had drifted over her head. Without turning, she knew who they focused on.

Asher didn't see, nor did she speak.

"Well, Starbuck, you earned your pay today," Madge commented. "The Dean and I are going to the Lido to hold Michael's hand."

"Tell him I lost three pounds on the court today." He spoke to her, lightly enough, but his eyes never left Asher's.

"I don't think that's going to make him feel a hell of a lot better," she returned, giving her husband a nudge as she rose. "Well, we're off to fight for a taxi. Anyone going our way?"

"As a matter of fact," Mac began, picking up the hint easily, "Jess and I were on our way out too."

"Want a lift, Ty?" Madge's husband gave her an offended look as she ground her heel into his foot. But he shut his mouth firmly when Madge shot him a deadly glance.

Even to a man who rarely comprehended subtleties, it became obvious there were things being said without words. The little group had simply ceased to exist for Ty and Asher. After a hard look at the silent couple The Dean straightened his glasses and grinned at his wife.

"I guess not, huh?"

"You're so quick, babe." Madge began shepherding the rest toward the doors. "Anyone know some French obscenities? It's the best way to get a cab in the rain."

Asher rose slowly. From behind her she could hear the ding of a bell on the desk and the whoosh of the storm as the doors were opened then quickly closed. For a moment Ty thought she looked like something that should be enclosed in glass. Not to be touched, not to be soiled. She reached out her hand.

When he took it, it was warm. Flesh and blood.

In unspoken agreement they turned away from the doors and walked to the elevator.

Chapter 6

They didn't speak, but then they didn't need to. With one hand still holding hers, Ty pushed the button for his floor. The elevator began its silent rise. Once, the hand in his trembled lightly. He found it unbearably exciting. The numbers above their heads flashed ponderously until at last the car stopped. When the doors slid open they stepped into the carpeted hall together.

Asher heard the key jingle against loose change as Ty reached into his pocket. She heard the click of the lock before he released her hand. The choice was still hers. She stepped out of the light into the dimness of the room.

It smelled of him. That was her first thought. The air carried Ty's lingering fragrance. Something sharp, something vital. Something she had never forgotten. All at once her nerves began to jump. The poise that had

carried her this far fell away. Searching for something
to say, she wandered the room. It was untidy, with a
shirt thrown here, shoes tossed there. She knew if she
opened the closet, she would find a neat stack of rackets, the only semblance of order. Instead, she moved to
the window. Rain ran like tears down the glass.

"It's going to storm all night."

As if to accent her words, lightning split the sky.
Asher counted to five, then heard the thunder answer.
Hundreds of lights spread through the darkness. The
city was there, crowded, moving—distant. Staring
through the wet glass, she waited for Ty to speak.

Silence. The patter of rain on the window. The distant hum of traffic. Another moan of thunder. Unable
to bear it, Asher turned.

He was watching her. The small bedside lamp threw
both light and shadow into the room. His stance was
neither relaxed nor threatening, and she understood.
He had given her a choice before she entered. Now he
wouldn't let her go. A bridge had been burned. Asher
felt nothing but relief that the decision was already
made. But her fingers were numb as she reached to
loosen the thin belt at her waist.

Crossing to her, Ty laid his hands over hers, stopping the movement. Asher stared up at him, unsure, as
nervous as the first time. Without speaking he took her
face in his hands to study her. He wanted to remember her this way—in shadowed light with the fury of
a storm at her back. Her eyes were dark with traces
of fear, traces of desire. In a gesture of surrender her
arms had dropped to her sides. But he didn't want surrender—perhaps she had forgotten.

As he lowered his head Ty watched her lids shut, her

lips part in anticipation. Gently he kissed her temple, then the other, then the delicate curve of an eyebrow. Without haste, his eyes closed. He reacquainted himself with her face through taste and touch. Her lips beckoned, but he nibbled along the line of her jaw, on the hollow of her cheek.

His thumb brushed her bottom lip as he whispered kisses over her face. He remembered every curve. Her breath shuddered out as he kissed the corners of her mouth. He brushed his over it, retreating when Asher sought more pressure. There was only the fleeting promise of more. With a moan she gripped his forearms. He'd waited for the strength. He'd waited for the demands. Again he touched his lips to hers, allowing his tongue a brief taste. Now her arms wrapped possessively around him. Now passion exploded, mouth against mouth. Lightning flashed, illuminating them as one form in the ageless wonder of lovers.

"Undress me," she whispered breathlessly, hardly able to speak as her lips fused again and again with his. "I want you to undress me."

In answer, he lowered the zipper slowly, allowing his fingers to trail along her bare skin. He found more silk, something thin and fragile. The dress slithered down her body to lie at her feet. Growing impatient, Asher worked her hands between them to deal with the buttons of his shirt while her mouth continued to cling to his. She felt the hard muscle, the line of ribs, the mat of hair. A moan wrenched from her out of deep, desperate need.

The thigh-length chemise was too much of a barrier. Longing for the intimacy of flesh against flesh, Asher reached to draw down the strap. Again Ty stopped her.

"Don't rush," he murmured, then tore at her control with a deep, lingering kiss. The pressure was hard and demanding, the lips soft and heated. "Come to bed."

In a haze she let him lead her, felt the mattress give under her weight, then his. Anticipation shivered along her skin. "The light," she whispered.

As he circled her throat with his hand, Ty's eyes met hers. "I need to see you." Thunder exploded as his mouth crushed down on hers.

When she would have hurried, he set the pace. Languorous, sleepy, enervating. It seemed her lips alone would pleasure him enough for a lifetime. She was so soft, so moist. Far from pliant, Asher moved against him, inviting, insisting. Her urgency excited him, but Ty chose to savor. Over the silk his hands roamed to trace her shape from thigh to breast. The peaks strained against the sheer material.

He took his mouth to her shoulder, catching the narrow strap of the silk with his teeth. Inch by inch he lowered it until her flesh was exposed to him. She was firm and creamy-white in contrast to the tan of her arms and shoulders.

"So lovely," he whispered while his fingertip brought down the second strap.

When she was naked to the waist, his mouth ranged down slowly, though with her hands in his hair she urged him down. With lips parted, Ty sought the peak of her breast. Asher arched, pressing him down. She wanted him to be greedy, wanted to feel the rough scrape of his tongue. When she did she could no longer be still. Her body vibrated with the beat of a hundred tiny pulses. Desire, raw and primitive, tore through her with the power to obliterate all but one thought. She was woman; he was man. Seeking pleasure, Asher moved under him, letting her hands roam.

He abandoned gentleness because she wanted none. It had always driven him wild when her passion was unleashed. She had no inhibitions, no shame. When they came together like this she was all fire, and as dangerous as the lightning in the night sky. Ty wasn't even aware of his control slipping away. Hard-palmed hands ran bruisingly over tender skin. Short, manicured nails dug into strong shoulders.

His breathing was ragged when he tore the garment from her. She gave him no time to view her nakedness. Her fingers were busy, struggling to remove the last barrier of his clothing. Their frantic movements took them over the bed, tangling in the sheets. Her skin was damp and trembling, but her hands were so strong, and so certain. There could be no more waiting.

A pain stabbed into him as he entered her. It was sharp, then sweet. He thought he heard her cry out as she had that first night when he had taken her innocence. Then she was wrapped around him—legs, arms. Her mouth fastened on his. The storm crashed directly overhead. They rose with it.

His hand lay lightly on her breast. Asher sighed. Had she ever known such pure contentment? she wondered. No, not even when they had been together before. Then she hadn't known what it would be like to do without him. She shuddered, then moved closer.

"Cold?" Ty drew her to him until her head rested on the curve of his shoulder.

"A little. Where's my chemise?"

"Devoured."

She laughed, flinging her arms around him as though she would never let go. Free, she thought. How wonderful to be free—to love, to laugh. Supporting herself on his chest, she stared down into his face. For once his eyes were calm. A faint smile curved his lips. Beneath her his breathing was even and slow, to match hers. To match, her mind repeated. They had always been like two halves of the same whole.

"Oh, God, I missed you, Ty." On those words she buried her face against his throat. Empty, empty, she thought. It seemed like a lifetime of emptiness had been wiped away with an hour of fulfillment.

"Asher—"

"No, no questions. No questions." Wildly she rained kisses over his face. "Just feel, just be with me. I need to laugh tonight, the way we used to."

He stopped her hurried movements by taking her head in his hands. There was a plea in her eyes and a light trace of desperation. No, he didn't want to see that now. Pushing away the questions that drummed in his head, he smiled at her.

"I thought you were going to buy me dinner."

Relief washed over her before she grinned. "I have no idea what you're talking about."

"You asked me for a date."

Tossing her head back, she arched an elegant brow. "*I* asked you? You've been out in the heat too long, Starbuck."

"Dinner," he repeated, rolling her over until he loomed above her.

"As far as I can tell, you've already eaten a sixty-dollar silk chemise. Are you still hungry?"

For an answer, he lowered his mouth to her neck and

bit, none too gently. Laughing, she tried to twist away. "Food," he muttered. "I have to eat."

Remembering a weakness, she found the spot on his ribs and squeezed. His body jerked, giving her the opportunity to slither away. She was giggling like a girl when he grabbed her and pulled her back. "How many people know the indomitable Starbuck is ticklish?" she demanded when he pinned her arms over her head. "What would the press pay to find out?"

"About the same as they'd pay to find out elegant Asher Wolfe has a heart-shaped birthmark on her very attractive bottom."

Asher considered this a moment. "Even," she decided. Her smile slanted seductively. "Do you really want to go out to eat?"

Desire fluttered lightly in the pit of his stomach as he looked down at her. The light angled across her face, accenting the smooth, glowing skin and darkened eyes. The thunder was a distant rumble now, but he felt it vibrate in his head.

"There's always room service," he murmured, tasting her lips. He kept her arms pinned as he dropped light, teasing kisses over her face. Nestling in the vulnerable curve of her neck, he used his tongue to stir and arouse.

"Ty," she moaned, unable to struggle against the captivity. "Make love to me."

His chuckle was low and he was pleased. "Oh, I am. This time," he whispered into her ear, "we won't hurry. Hours, love." His tongue darted to her ear, making her squirm in agonized delight. "Hours and hours." Then he shifted, bringing her close to his side. Cradling her, he felt her heart pounding against him. When he reached for the phone, Asher glanced up, puzzled. "Food," he reminded her.

She gave a weak laugh. "I should have remembered your stomach comes first."

His hand grazed over her breast. "Not necessarily." Her nipple was already taut. He flicked his thumb over it lazily.

"Ty—" With a kiss he silenced her.

"Champagne," he said into the phone while driving Asher mad with careless strokes and fondling. "Dom Pérignon. Caviar," he went on, sending her a questioning look that she was powerless to answer. "Beluga." He gave her a light kiss, running his hand down to the flat of her stomach. She quivered, turning into him. Legs tangled as he brushed his lips over her shoulder. "Cold shrimp." He bit her tender bottom lip. "Mmm, that'll do. Yes, for two." As he dropped the phone back on its cradle, Asher found his mouth in a desperate, yearning kiss. "Food excites you?" he mumbled against the hungry lips. Struggling not to take her instantly, he ran his hand to her hip, kneading warm flesh.

"I want you." Her voice was low and throaty, her hands questing. "I want you now."

"Shh." Slow, patient, his stroking aroused rather than subdued. "Relax. There's time. I want to see you again." He drew away from her. "Really see you."

She was burning for him. Now she lay naked and vulnerable under his gaze. As she watched, his eyes darkened, grew stormy. Her breathing quickened. When she reached out he took her hand, burying his lips in the palm.

"You're more beautiful than ever," he said huskily.

"It shouldn't be possible. I've looked at you so many times and have been afraid to touch."

"No." Asher pulled him to her until they were heart to heart. "I'm never more alive than when you touch me." With a sigh Ty nestled down until his head rested between her breasts. Asher combed her fingers through his hair as contentment layered over desire. "Today, when I watched you playing Michael, I wanted you. Sitting there, surrounded by thousands of people in the middle of the afternoon, all I could think about was being with you like this." She gave a gurgle of laughter. "Wicked thoughts, such wonderfully wicked thoughts."

"So your invitation to dinner carried an ulterior motive."

"In your weakened condition I knew you'd be a push-over, though I had thought I'd have to take you out and ply you with food and wine first."

"And if I'd refused?"

"I'd have come up with something else."

Grinning, he lifted his head. "What?"

Asher shrugged. "I could have come up here and seduced you before you'd gotten your strength back."

"Hmm…I almost wish I'd said no."

"Too late. I have you now."

"I could get stubborn."

Slowly she smiled. "I know your weaknesses," she whispered, running a fingertip up the nape of his neck. His shudder was quick and uncontrollable. Leaning up, she took his face in her hands. Lazily she rubbed her lips over his, then deepened the touch into a kiss— a long, draining taste that left him weak. Her tongue glided over his, then retreated.

"Asher." On an oath he crushed her beneath him, savaging her mouth with a need that had risen so quickly, it left him dazed. He didn't hear the discreet knock on the door, nor did he understand her murmurs.

"The door," she managed. "Ty, it's room service."

"What?"

"The door."

Laying his forehead on hers, he struggled to recapture his control. "They're awful damn quick," he muttered. He found he was trembling. How could he have forgotten that she could make him tremble? After letting out a long breath, he rose. Asher pulled the sheets up to her chin and watched him cross to the closet.

A beautiful body, she thought, both proud and admiring. Long and lean, with a network of muscle. She looked her fill as he rummaged through his closet for a robe. Strong shoulders, trim waist, narrow hips and long legs. An athlete's body, or a dancer's. He was made to compete.

He shrugged into the robe, belting it carelessly. Grinning, he turned to her. Asher's heart lodged in her throat. "Ty, you're so beautiful."

His eyes widened in astonishment. Torn between amusement and masculine discomfort, he headed for the door. "Good God," he said, making Asher smother a giggle. She brought her knees up to her chest as he signed the check at the door. In some ways, she mused, he was a little boy. To his way of thinking, the word *beautiful* applied only to a woman—or to an ace. He'd be more insulted than complimented having it applied to himself. Yet she saw him that way—not only physically. He was a man capable of lovely gestures, a man unashamed of his deep love for his mother, unafraid to show tenderness. He had no cruelty in him, though on the court he was unmerciful. His temper was explosive, but he was incapable of holding a grudge. Asher realized that it was his basic capacity for feeling that she had missed most of all. And still he had never, in all their closeness, in all the months of intimacy, told her that he loved her. If he had once said the words, she would never have left him.

"Where have you gone?"

Asher turned her head to see him standing beside a tray, a bottle of champagne in his hands. Quickly she shook her head and smiled again. "Nowhere." She cocked her head at the bottle. "All that just for us?"

He walked to the bed and sat on the edge. "Did you want some too?" The cork came off with a resounding pop as she cuffed his shoulder. With an easy stretch he rolled the tray toward them. "Here, hold the glasses." Without ceremony he poured champagne until it nearly ran over the rims.

"Ty, it'll spill on the bed."

"Better be careful then," he advised as he set the bottle back in the ice. He grinned as she sat cross-legged, balancing two glasses in her hands. The sheet was held in place over her breasts by arms pressed tightly to her sides.

She returned the grin with a glance of exasperation. "Aren't you going to take one?"

"Oh, I don't know." Hooking a finger under the sheet, he nudged it downward, exposing creamy flesh.

"Ty, cut it out, I'll spill it!"

"Better not, we have to sleep here." He urged the sheet a trifle lower. Frustrated, Asher looked from glass to glass. Wine swayed dangerously.

"This is a dirty trick, Starbuck."

"Yeah, I like it."

Asher narrowed her eyes. "I'm going to pour both glasses into your lap."

"Terrible waste," he decided, kissing her. "It's good stuff. I always found it strange," he began, lazily kissing her face as he spoke, "that I was bred for beer and you were bred for champagne, but you haven't any head for it."

"I have a perfectly good head for champagne."

Chuckling, he brushed his lips over her throat. "I remember one very memorable night when we shared a bottle. Three glasses make you crazy. I like you crazy."

"That's absurd." The lift of brow challenged him. Without hesitation Asher brought a glass to her lips, losing the sheet as she drank it. Ty watched the linen pool into her lap before she drained the last drop. "That's one," Asher announced, lifting the second glass. Ty plucked it from her fingers.

"Let's spread it out a little," he advised, amused. He drank, more conservatively, then reached for the tray of caviar. "You like this stuff."

"Mmm." Suddenly hungry, Asher spread a generous amount on a toast point. Ty settled down to the bowl of cold shrimp and spicy sauce. "Here, it's good." Though he allowed her to feed him a bite, he wrinkled his nose.

"Overrated," he stated. "This is better." He popped a shrimp into Asher's mouth.

"'S wonderful," she agreed with a full mouth, then chose another. "I didn't know I was so hungry."

Ty filled her glass again. Could anyone else imagine her, he wondered, sitting naked in bed, licking sauce from her finger? Did anyone else know how totally open she could be? She was talking now, in fits and starts as she ate, replaying her match. Ty let her ramble, pleased just to hear her voice, to see her animation. She was satisfied with her serve, worried about her backhand volley.

Publicly she chose her words with care, and made certain there were few of them. If a reporter could see her now, Ty mused, he'd wear a pencil down to the nub. She was full of joy and doubt, fear and self-congratulation. Words tumbled out without discretion. Her face was animated, her hands gestured. By the time she had slowed down, her second glass was empty. Perhaps she was completely happy, because she wasn't even aware of the sensation. She was simply at ease, completely herself. Comfortably full, she toyed with the last of the caviar.

"Are you worried about playing Chuck in the finals?"

Ty bit into a shrimp. "Why?"

"He was always good," Asher began, frowning a bit. "But he's developed over the past few years."

Grinning, Ty tilted more wine into her glass. "Don't you think I can beat him?"

She sent him a long, considering look. "You were always good too."

"Thanks." After setting the caviar on the tray, he stretched lengthwise on the bed.

"Chuck plays a bit like my father did," Asher mused. "Very clean, very precise. His talent's polished rather than raw."

"Like mine."

"Yes. That raw athletic ability is something every competitor envies. My father used to say that you had more natural talent than any player he'd seen in his career." Over the rim of her glass she smiled down at him.

"Yet he always wanted to smooth out your form. Then there were your...antics on the court."

Ty laughed, kissing her knee through the sheet. "It used to drive him crazy."

"I imagine he'd be more pleased if he saw you play now."

"And you?" Ty countered. "How would he feel if he saw you play now?"

Asher shifted her eyes from his to stare into her glass. "He won't."

"Why?"

As if to erase the question, she lifted her hand. "Ty, please."

"Asher," he said quietly, grasping her fingers. "You're hurting."

If she could have held it back, she would have. But the words tumbled out. "I let him down. He won't forgive me."

"He's your father."

"And he was my coach."

Unable to comprehend, Ty shook his head. "What difference does that make?"

"All the difference." The pain slipped out. As if to numb it, she swallowed more wine. "Please, not tonight. I don't want anything to spoil tonight."

Her fingers had tightened on his. One by one Ty kissed them until he felt the tension relax. "Nothing could." Over their joined hands, dark, intense eyes met hers. Spontaneously her pulse began to race. "I never got you completely out of my mind," he confessed. "Too many things reminded me—a phrase, a song. Silence. There were times alone at night I would have sworn I heard you breathing in the quiet beside me."

The words moved her...hurt her. "Ty, those were yesterdays. We can start now."

"Now," he agreed. "But we'll have to deal with yesterday sooner or later."

Though she opened her mouth to disagree, she knew. "Later then. Right now I don't want to think about anything but being with you."

He grinned, brushing a stray curl from her cheek. "It's difficult to argue with that."

"Don't get cocky," she told him, then tossed off the rest of her champagne. "That was three," Asher said haughtily. "And I'm not the least affected."

Ty had no trouble recognizing the signs—the flushed cheeks, the glowing eyes and misty smile. Whatever she might say, he knew the champagne was swimming in her head. And when they loved again, she would be soft and strong and passionate. He found himself wanting to simply look at her for a few minutes more. Once they touched, the fire would take them.

"Want another?" he offered.

"Sure."

Wisely he filled her glass only halfway before he replaced the bottle. "I caught your interview today," Ty commented. "It was on while I was changing."

"Oh?" Asher shifted to lie on her stomach, propping herself on her elbows. "How'd I do?"

"Hard to say. It was all in French."

She laughed, adjusting her position so that she could take another sip. "I'd forgotten."

"How about a translation?"

"He asked things like—Mademoiselle Wolfe, do you find any changes in your style after your temporary retirement? And I said something like I feel I've tightened my serve." She chuckled into her wine. "I didn't mention that my muscles beg for me to give them a break after two sets. He asked how I felt about playing the *young* Miss Kingston in the finals and I refrained from punching him in the mouth."

"That was diplomatic," Ty answered, slipping the glass from her fingers.

"I'm a hell of a diplomat," Asher agreed. Rolling over on her back, she looked up at him. He lounged just behind her so that she had to tilt her head at an odd angle to make eye contact. "You stole my glass."

"Yes, I did." After setting it on the tray, Ty gave the wheeled table a slight shove.

"Did we finish dinner?" Reaching up and back, she locked her arms around his neck.

"We've definitely finished dinner." He allowed her to urge him down until his mouth hovered above hers.

"Got any suggestions about what we should do now?" She liked the strangeness of having his face upside down over hers. Playfully she nipped at his lip.

"No. Do you?"

"Got a deck of cards?"

"Uh-uh."

"Then I guess we'll have to make love." She gave a rich, low laugh before she kissed him again. "All night—just to pass the time."

"It's something to do. Rainy nights are so boring."

Eyes dancing, she nodded. "Mmm, yes. Let's make the best of it."

Her lips were curved in a smile as his met them, but they parted eagerly. She found it strangely seductive to have his tongue meet hers this way. On a gurgle of laughter, she closed her teeth gently, capturing him. In response, he trailed his fingers over her breast until her moan freed him.

"I get dizzy kissing you upside down," Asher murmured.

"I like you dizzy." Leaning forward, he trailed moist kisses over her throat. The tip of his tongue picked up her flavor, then lingered over it. He could feel pulse beats both with his hand and his lips. Finding the curve of his neck vulnerable, Asher began to give him the same pleasure he was bringing her.

"I want to touch you," she complained. "I can't touch you this way."

But he continued to explore from where he was, enjoying the freedom his hands had over her body. The scent of the rich sauce still lingering in the air, and the zing of champagne clung to two tongues as they joined. The mattress groaned quietly as she shifted. Then she was on her knees, pressed body to body. In a quick move she had stripped the robe from him so he was as naked as she. With a half laugh, half sigh, she ran her palms up his strong back.

Entwined, enchanted, neither noticed that the rain had ceased. Inside the quiet room, pleasure built. Strong thigh pressed against strong thigh, hungry lips sought hungry lips. Their passion was equal, their needs the same. Together, they lay down.

Soft sighs became moans. Before long, gentle caresses became demanding. Both seemed desperate to touch and be touched, to have their own weaknesses exploited. With instinctive understanding they held back the final gift. The inner fire built, dampening their flesh, but still they lingered over each other. There was so much to make up for, so much time to recapture.

Though passion was flaring, this thought hovered in the back of both their minds. Tonight was a fresh beginning. They wanted all of it.

Asher thought her lungs would burst. The combination of wine and passion buzzed in her head. A laugh, smoky with desire, floated from her as he gasped her name. She wanted to tempt him, torment him, give to him. His stomach was hard and flat with muscle, yet the touch of her fingertip could make it quiver. Asher had forgotten this sense of power and exulted in it. Her small hands could make him weak. Her shapely, serious mouth could drive him wild.

The power shifted so abruptly, she was helpless. He found her greatest vulnerability and used his tongue to destroy her last vestige of control. Half wild, she called for him, struggling to have more, desperate to have all. Arching, she pressed him closer, cresting on a wave of delight that had no chance to recede. She thrashed as if in protest, yet arched again in invitation. As she built toward a higher peak, Ty slid up her body. Greedy, she drew him inside of her, hearing his gasp for breath before there was only feeling.

Later, they still clung together, damp, spent, fulfilled. He shifted only to turn out the light. In the midnight darkness they molded to each other, drifting toward sleep.

"You'll move in with me."

The murmur was a statement rather than a question. Asher opened her eyes before she answered. She could just see the outline of his face. "Yes, if you want me."

"I never stopped wanting you."

Without the light he didn't see the flicker of doubt in her eyes before he slept.

Chapter 7

She was afraid of London. Lady Wickerton had lived there—hostessing parties in the elegant three-story house in Grosvenor Square, attending the ballet at the Royal Opera House, the theater in Drury Lane, shopping in the West End. Lady Wickerton had played bridge with members of Parliament and had sipped tea at Buckingham Palace. Lady Wickerton had been a quiet, dutiful wife, a woman of intelligence, breeding and control. She had nearly suffocated in London.

Perhaps if Ty hadn't come between Jim Wolfe's daughter and Eric Wickerton's wife, Asher would have accepted her role with ease. She'd wanted to, had struggled to. Too much passion simmered inside her. It had been there all of her life, but the months with Ty had liberated it. Controlling something dormant was entirely different from harnessing something that pulsed with life. There had not even been her profession as an outlet for the energy that drove her.

Coming back to London was the most difficult step yet. There she would not only have to face memories of Ty, but the ghost of a woman she had pretended to be. It was all so familiar—Westminster Abbey, Trafalgar Square, the smells, the voices. Even the anticipation of Wimbledon couldn't block them out. There would be faces here that would remember the coolly elegant Lady Wickerton. And there would be questions.

Publicly she would remain aloof, distant and uninformative. Asher felt she owed Eric that much. She would simply refuse to discuss her marriage or its demise. Her early training, her years of following her father's rules, would serve her now more than ever.

She would give them tennis. With two straight championships now under her belt, Asher would have been spotlighted in any case. It was up to her to sway the press away from her personal life toward her professional resurgence. What was growing between her and Ty was still too fragile to be shared.

Happiness. She had nearly forgotten how simple and overwhelming the feeling was. Lazy midnight talks, crazy loving, quiet walks. They shared a hotel room and made it home for the days and nights they were there. She felt as much a gypsy as he, and was content to be so. Once she had looked for roots, stability, commitment. She'd learned that they meant nothing without the fullness of love. His spontaneity had always fascinated her. This time Asher would resolve the lingering fear of it and enjoy.

"Aren't you dressed yet?"

At the question Asher stopped tying her tennis shoe

and glanced up. Ty stood in the doorway between the small parlor and bedroom. Fully dressed, impatient, he frowned at her. His hair fell over his forehead as unruly as ever and still slightly damp from his shower. Waves of love radiated through her.

"Nearly," Asher tossed back. "Not everyone can move quickly in the morning, you know—especially on six hours' sleep."

The frown became a grin. "Something keep you up?" He caught the shoe she hurled at him in one hand, his eyes never leaving her face. Apparently the late night hadn't affected him. He looked well rested and full of barely controlled energy. "You can always take a nap after morning practice."

"Awfully pleased with yourself this morning, aren't you?"

"Am I?" Still grinning, he came toward her, tossing her shoe lightly. "It probably has something to do with trouncing that British kid in the quarter-finals yesterday."

"Oh?" Lifting a brow, Asher looked up at him. "Is that all you're pleased about?"

"What else?"

"Let me have my shoe," she demanded. "So I can throw it at you again."

"Did you know you have a poor morning attitude?" he asked, holding the shoe out of reach.

"Did you know you've been insufferable ever since you won the French?" she countered sweetly. "Remember, it's only one quarter of the Grand Slam."

He moved the shoe farther out of reach as she made a grab for it. "For you too, Face," he reminded her.

"The rest's on grass." In an attempt to hold him still, Asher grabbed the waistband of his warm-up pants.

"The woman's insatiable," he sighed. Diving, he pinned her beneath him on the bed.

"Ty! Stop!" Laughing, Asher pushed against him as he nuzzled at her neck. "We'll be late for practice."

"Oh. You're right." Giving her a quick kiss, he rolled away from her.

"Well," Asher muttered as she sat up, "you didn't take much persuading." Even as she started to tidy her hair, she was spun back into his arms. Her startled exclamation was smothered by his lips.

Long, deep, infinitely tender, smolderingly passionate. His arms circled her. Asher felt her bones soften, then dissolve. Her head fell back, inviting him to take more. Cradling her, Ty went on a slow exploration of her mouth. For the moment he enjoyed the sense of total domination. If they continued, he knew she would begin her own demands. Then it would be power for power. The knowledge excited him. Still, he laughed against her lips. There was time. A lifetime.

"You awake yet?" he asked her as he ran a hand lightly over her breast.

"Mmm-hmm."

"Good. Let's go." After setting her on her feet, he gave Asher's bottom a friendly pat.

"I'll get you for that," she promised. Needs stirred inside her, not quite under control.

"I certainly hope so." With an easy smile Ty slipped an arm around her shoulders. "You need to work on your backhand volley," he began as they walked from the room.

Insulted, Asher tossed her head back. "What are you talking about?"

"If you'd shorten your swing a bit more—"

"Shorten your own swing," she retorted. "And while you're at it," she continued, "you weren't exactly Mr. Speed yesterday."

"Gotta save something for the finals."

Asher snorted as she punched the elevator button. "Your conceit never wavers."

"Confidence," Ty contradicted. He liked seeing her this way—relaxed, but ready to laugh or to slap back. Briefly he wondered if she realized she was even more beautiful when she forgot caution. "What about breakfast?"

"What about it?"

"Want to grab some eggs after practice?"

She slid her eyes to his as the doors opened. "Is that your best offer?"

Ty lifted a brow as he followed her into the elevator. Asher exchanged a polite nod with a middle-aged couple in tweed. "Maybe you'd like to take up where we left off last night?" Ty lounged against an elevator wall as Asher gaped at him. "What did you say your name was again?"

Asher could feel two pairs of shocked and interested eyes boring into her back. "Misty," she replied, allowing a trace of cockney to color her voice. "Will you spring for champagne again, Mr. Starbuck? It was ever so good."

He recognized the light of challenge in her eyes and grinned. "So were you, sweetie."

When the doors opened to the lobby, the older couple moved out reluctantly. Asher punched Ty in the arm before she followed.

In less than an hour they were both concentrating on form and speed and the capricious bounces a ball could take on grass. Was she playing better? Asher wondered as she sprang for Madge's slice. She felt looser, less encumbered. Indeed, she felt as though losing were not even a possibility. At Wimbledon she could forget the city of London.

Instead, she could remember the qualifying games at Roehampton, with their anything-goes attitude. Both bad language and rackets had flown. It was a contrast to the elegance and glamour of Wimbledon. Here both the players and the crowd were steeped in tradition. Hydrangeas against a backdrop of rich green grass, ivy-covered walls, limos and chauffeurs. Colors were soothing, mauve and green, as if time itself had sobered them.

Here spectators would be well-mannered, quiet between points, applauding after them. Even those in standing room would behave, or the chair judge would tell them politely to quiet down. No one hung from the scoreboards at Wimbledon. It was as revered as the changing of the guards, as English as double-decker buses.

There was no doubt, as one gazed around the immaculately tended velvet lawns, the pampered roses, the dollhouse kiosks and the stands that could accommodate more than twenty-five thousand, that Wimbledon *was* tennis. It was here former players migrated to. It was here future players aspired to. Asher remembered Ty telling her about watching the matches one long-ago July Fourth and making a vow. He had kept it, not once, but four times. More than anything she had wanted before, Asher wanted them to both walk away from Centre Court as champions.

Behind the baseline, Asher stood with a racket and a ball, staring off into space.

"Had enough?" Madge called out.

"Hmm…what?" Asher's head snapped around. Seeing Madge standing with her legs spread, hand on hips, had her laughing. "I suppose I have, I was daydreaming."

From opposite ends of the court, they walked toward their bags and jackets. "No sense asking if you're happy," Madge began conversationally. "You look absolutely miserable floating two inches off the ground."

"That obvious, huh?"

"I won't pretend not to be pleased," Madge added smugly. "I've always thought you two made a great team. Going to make it official?"

"I— No, we're just taking it one day at a time." Asher kept her eyes lowered as she packed her racket. "Marriage is just a formality, after all."

"And pigs fly," Madge countered calmly. When Asher glanced up with a cautious smile, she went on. "For some, yes, you're right. Not for you, Face. Why did you stay in an unhappy marriage for three years?" When Asher started to speak, Madge lifted a hand. "Because to you marriage is a promise, and you don't break promises."

"I failed once," she began.

"Oh, all by yourself? Isn't that being a bit self-absorbed?" Impatient, Madge settled her hands on her hips again. "Listen, you aren't going to let one mistake keep you from being happy, are you?"

"I am happy," Asher assured her, punctuating the statement by touching Madge's shoulder. "Ty's all I've ever wanted, Madge. I can't risk losing him again."

Her brow puckered in confusion. "But you left him, Asher, not the other way around."

"I'd already lost him," she said flatly.

"Asher, I don't—"

"It's a new day," she interrupted, then took a deep breath of scented morning air. "A fresh start. I know what mistakes I made and have no intention of repeating them. There was a time in my life that I thought I had to come first, before this." Holding up the small white ball, Asher examined it. "Before anything. I looked on tennis as a competitor, his family as a rival. That was stupid." Dropping the ball into a can, Asher closed it.

"That's funny," Madge mused. "There was a time in my life I thought The Dean's work came first. He thought the same about me. It wasn't true in either case."

With a smile Asher slung her bag over her shoulder. "Ty won't ever forget that tennis took him out of that tenement. Maybe he shouldn't. That's the thing that brings fire to his game."

She knows him so well in some ways, Madge thought, and not at all in others. "And what brings the ice to yours?"

"Fear," Asher answered before she thought. For a moment she gave Madge a blank look, then shrugged. Saying it aloud made it seem rather unimportant. "Fear of failure, or exposure." Laughing, she began to walk. "Thank God you're not a reporter."

The gravel crunched underfoot as they moved down the path. It was a sound Asher associated with the tidiness of English courts. "Remind me to tell you sometime what goes through my head five minutes before a match."

With a sigh Asher hooked her arm through her old partner's. "Let's hit the showers."

There was no dream. Asher slept as deeply as a child, with no worries, no nagging fears. The curtains were drawn closed so that the afternoon sun filtered through lazily. Traffic sounds muffled through it, coming as a quiet drone. She wore only a short terry robe and lay on top of the spread. Ty would come back to wake her so that they could spend some time sight-seeing before nightfall. Because they were both scheduled to play the following day, they would go to bed early.

The knock on the door wakened her. Sitting up, Asher ran a hand through her tousled hair. He'd forgotten his key, she thought groggily. She stepped from the dim bedroom into the brighter parlor, wincing against the change of light. Absently she wondered what time it was as she opened the door. Shock took a moment to penetrate.

"Eric," she whispered.

"Asher." He gave her what was nearly a bow before he elbowed his way into the room. "Did I wake you?"

"I was napping." She closed the door, trying to recover her scattered wits. He looked the same, she thought. Naturally he would. Eric would see no reason to change. He was tall, slim, with a military carriage. He had a sharp-featured European face, a bit haughty and remote. Dark blond hair was cut and groomed to indicate wealth and conservatism. Light eyes in a pale face—both romantic, yet intelligent and cold. Asher knew that his mouth could twist into a hard line when he was crossed. As a suitor he had been charming, as a lover, meticulous. As a husband he'd been unbearable. She drew herself straight. He was no longer her husband.

"I didn't expect to see you, Eric."

"No?" He smiled. "Did you think I wouldn't drop by while you were in town? Lost a bit of weight, Asher."

"Competition tends to do that." Years of training had her gesturing toward a chair. "Please, sit down. I'll get you a drink."

There was no reason to be upset by him now, she told herself. No need to feel fear or guilt. Divorced couples managed to be civilized more often than not. Eric, Asher thought with a grim smile, was a very civilized man.

"Have you been well?" She poured his scotch neat, then added ice to Perrier for herself.

"Quite well. And you?"

"Yes. Your family?"

"Doing wonderfully." Eric accepted the glass she offered, then eyed her over the rim. "And your father?" He watched for the flash of pain, and was satisfied.

"As far as I know, he's fine." Quite consciously Asher drew on the mask as she sat.

"Still hasn't forgiven you for giving up your career."

Her eyes were level now and expressionless. "I'm sure you're aware he hasn't."

Mindful of the crease in his pants, Eric crossed his legs. "I thought perhaps now that you're competing again…" He allowed the sentence to die.

Asher watched the bubbles rise in her glass, but left them untasted. "He no longer acknowledges me," she said flatly. "I'm still paying, Eric." She lifted her eyes again. "Does that satisfy you?"

He drank leisurely for a moment. "It was your choice, my dear. Your career for my name."

"For your silence," Asher corrected. "I already had your name."

"And another man's child in your belly."

Ice clinked against ice as her hands shook. Quickly she controlled the tremor. "One would have thought it would have been enough that I lost the child," she murmured. "Did you come all this way to remind me?"

"I came," Eric said as he leaned back, "to see how my ex-wife was adjusting. You're victorious on the courts, Asher, and as lovely as ever." She didn't speak as his eyes roamed the room. "Apparently you didn't waste too much time picking up with your old lover."

"My mistake was in leaving him, Eric. We both know that. I'm very, very sorry."

He sent her an icy look. "Your mistake was in trying to pass his bastard off on me."

Furious and trembling, Asher sprang to her feet. "I never lied to you. And by God, I'll never apologize again."

He remained seated, swirling liquor. "Does he know yet?"

Her color drained dramatically enough to make him smile genuinely. Hate ate at him. "No, I see he doesn't. How interesting."

"I kept my word, Eric." Though her hands were laced tightly together, Asher's voice was strong. "As long as I was your wife, I did everything you asked of me."

He acknowledged this with a slight nod. Her honesty

hadn't been enough—nor had her three years of penance. "But you're not my wife any longer."

"We agreed. The marriage was intolerable for both of us."

"What are you afraid he'd do?" Eric mused, frowning up at the ceiling. "He's a very physical man as I remember, with a primitive sort of temper." Lowering his eyes, he smiled again. "Do you think he'd beat you?"

Asher gave a short laugh. "No."

"You're very confident," he murmured. "What exactly are you afraid of?"

Wearily she dropped her hands to her sides. "He wouldn't forgive me, Eric, any more than you have. I lost the child, I lost my father. My self-esteem. I'll never lose the guilt. I hurt nothing but your pride, Eric, haven't I suffered enough for that?"

"Perhaps...perhaps not." Rising, he stepped toward her. She remembered the scent of his crisp, dignified cologne very well. "Perhaps the most perfect punishment might be in never knowing your secret is safe. I'll make you no promises, Asher."

"It astonishes me that I was ever naïve enough to think of you as a kind man, Eric," she said softly.

"Justice," he returned, toasting her.

"Revenge has little to do with justice."

He shrugged an elegant shoulder. "All in your viewpoint, my dear."

She wouldn't give him the satisfaction of breaking down—of weeping, of screaming or begging. Instead, Asher stood perfectly still. "If you've said all you've come to say, I'd like you to go."

"Of course." After finishing off the liquor, he set down the glass. "Sleep well, darling. Don't bother, I'll let myself out." Eric turned the doorknob and found himself face-to-face with Ty. Nothing could have pleased him more.

Ty noted his cold, satisfied smile before his gaze shifted to Asher. Standing in the center of the room, she seemed frozen. There was anguish, and, he thought, fear in her eyes. Her face was dead-white and still. Even as he wondered what it was she feared, Ty took in the rest of her appearance. The tousled hair, the brief robe and exposed skin had rage boiling in him. Asher could feel it from where she stood.

His eyes whipped back to Eric's. There was murder in them. "Get the hell out of here."

"Just on my way," Eric said equably, though he had inched back against the door in instinctive defense. His last thought as he shut it behind him was that Asher would bear the brunt of the fury in Ty's eyes. That alone had made it worth the trip.

The room vibrated with the silent storm. Asher didn't move. It seemed Ty would stare at her for eternity. The trembling was difficult to control, but she forced herself. If she made light of the incident, perhaps so would he.

"What the hell was he doing here?"

"He just dropped by...I suppose to wish me luck." The lie sliced at her.

"Cozy." Crossing to her, Ty caught the lapel of her robe in his hand. "Don't you usually dress for visitors, Asher? Then again, I suppose it isn't necessary for ex-husbands."

"Ty, don't."

"Don't what?" he demanded. Though he struggled against the words, the accusations, the feelings, he knew it was a losing battle. Against the unknown he would always attack. "Wouldn't it be better form to meet him somewhere else? It's a little sticky here, isn't it?"

The cold sarcasm hurt more than his fury would have. With so much to hide, she could only shake her head. "Ty, you know there's nothing between us. You know—"

"What the hell do I know?" he shouted, grasping the other lapel. "Don't ask, don't question. Then I walk in and find you entertaining the bastard you left me for."

"I didn't know he was coming." She gripped his arms for balance as he nearly lifted her off her feet. "If he had called, I would have told him to stay away."

"You let him in." Enraged, he shook her. "Why?"

Despair rather than fear clutched at her. "Would you be happier if I had slammed the door in his face?"

"Yes, damn it."

"I didn't." She pushed at him now, as furious as he. "I let him in, I gave him a drink. Make what you like of it. I can't stop you."

"Did he want you back?" he demanded, ignoring her struggles. "Is that why he came?"

"What does it matter?" Impotently she slammed her fists into his chest. "It's not what *I* want." She threw back her head, her eyes burning.

"Then tell me, tell me now why you married him." When she tried to pull away, he dragged her back. "I'll have that much, Asher, and I'll have it now."

"Because I thought he was what I needed," she cried out. Roaring in her ears was the anger, the fear she had felt for Eric.

"And was he?" To prevent her from striking out, Ty grasped her wrist.

"No!" She jerked but couldn't free herself. Frustration added to an almost unreasonable fury. "No, I was miserable. I was trapped." Her voice was both strong and harsh. "I paid in ways you can't imagine. There wasn't a day I was happy. Does that satisfy you?"

She did something he had never seen her do before. She wept. His grip on her wrists loosened as he watched tears flood her eyes and spill onto her cheeks. Never in all the years he'd known her had he seen that kind of torment on her face. Tearing herself from his grip, Asher fled into the bedroom, slamming the door at her back.

She wanted peace. She wanted privacy. The grief had hit her unexpectedly. If the tears hadn't clogged her throat, she would have told him about the baby. The words had been there, ready to spill out in anger. Then speech had been impossible. Now she needed to weep it out.

Ty stared at the closed door for a long time. The wrenching sound of sobbing came to him. It was a reaction he hadn't expected. His anger was justified, as were his questions. Anger for anger he could have comprehended, but the pain he heard was altogether different. Having come from a family of women, he understood a woman's tears. Over the years he'd done his share of comforting and soothing. But these sobs were hot and bitter—and Asher never wept.

Jess cried easily, quiet, feminine tears. His mother wept with joy or silent sadness. These he could handle. A shoulder could be offered, a few sympathetic words, a teasing comment. Instinctively he knew none of those were the prescription for raw grief.

He still had questions. He still had anger. But the sounds from the bedroom forced him to put them aside. Ty recognized when tears were used as a weapon or a defense. These were being torn from her unwillingly. Dragging a hand through his hair, he wondered if it was Eric or himself who was responsible for them. Or something he knew nothing about. Cursing softly, he went to the door and opened it.

She lay curled on the bed in a ball of misery. Her body shook. When he touched her she jerked away. Saying nothing, Ty lay down beside her, gathering her close. For another moment she fought him. *Alone.* Her tears were not to be observed, not to be shared. *Private.* Ty dealt with her struggles by merely holding her tighter in arms that were both strong and gentle.

"I'm not going anywhere," he murmured.

With no more protest, Asher clung to his comfort and let her grief run its course.

It had grown dark and her body was weak. There were no more tears left in her. Ty's arms were strong around her. Beneath her damp cheek she could hear the steady beat of his heart. Gently, almost absently, his fingers stroked the base of her neck.

She'd nearly told him. Asher closed her eyes, too weary to feel fear or regret. If she could have summoned up the energy, she would have been grateful for the tears that had prevented her confession.

I lost your baby. Would he be holding her now if those words had spilled out? What good would it do to tell him? she asked herself. Why make him grieve for something he had never known? And grieve he would, she knew, after the anger passed. It came to her suddenly that it wasn't only fear that kept the secret locked inside her. She couldn't bear to see Ty hurt as she had hurt.

How could she explain to him about Eric without

dragging up old bitterness, opening old wounds? Ty hadn't wanted her any longer—Jess had made that abundantly clear. But Eric had. It had been her pride that had turned to Eric, then her sense of duty that had kept her with him. Perhaps if she had been stronger after the accident she would never have made those promises to him....

Asher had floated to consciousness on a wave of pain. What reason was there to wake up and hurt? she thought groggily. Sleep, sleep was so peaceful.

She remembered the shouting, the fall, the swimming darkness. The baby...Ty's baby. Panic—the panic pierced by lethargy. Her eyelids seemed weighted with lead, but she forced them open even as she reached a protective hand to her stomach. Stern and cold, Eric's face floated in front of her eyes.

"The baby," she managed through dry lips.

"Dead."

Tearing, burning grief replaced the pain. "No." Moaning, she closed her eyes again. "Oh, God, no. My baby, not my baby. Ty—"

"Listen to me, Asher." Eric spoke briskly. For three days he had waited while Asher drifted in and out of consciousness. She had lost the baby and a great deal of blood. Once she had nearly slipped away, but he had willed her to live. The love he had once felt had turned to resentment that bordered on hate. She had deceived him, made a fool of him. Now he would have his payment.

"My baby..."

"The baby's dead," he said flatly, then gripped her hand. "Look at me." She obeyed with eyes glazed with sorrow. "You're in a private clinic. The reason for your being here will never be known beyond the front doors. If you do what I say."

"Eric…" A spark of hope flickered. With what strength she had, Asher tightened her fingers on his. "Are they sure? Couldn't there be a mistake? Please—"

"You miscarried. The servants will be discreet. As far as anyone knows, we've slipped away for a few days."

"I don't understand." She pressed her hand against her stomach as if to make the truth a lie. "The fall…I fell down the stairs. But—"

"An accident," he stated, making the loss of the child sound like a broken glass.

Insidiously the pain slipped through. "Ty," Asher moaned, shutting her eyes.

"You're my wife, and will remain so until I say differently." Eric waited until her eyes focused on him again. "Would you have me call your lover and tell him you married me while carrying his child?"

"No." She could only whisper the word. *Ty.* She ached for him. He was lost to her—as lost as the child they'd made together.

"Then you'll do as I say. You'll retire from professional tennis. I won't have the press speculating about the two of you and dragging my name through the mud. You'll behave as I expect Lady Wickerton to behave. I will not touch you," he continued with a trace of disgust. "Any physical desire I felt for you is gone. We will live in the manner I designate or your lover will hear from me about this game you played. Is this understood?"

What did it matter how she lived? Asher asked herself. She was already dead. "Yes. I'll do whatever you want. Please, leave me alone now."

"As you wish." He rose. "When you're stronger, you'll give an official press release on your retirement. Your reason will be that you have no more time for tennis or any desire for a career that would take you away from your husband and your adopted country."

"Do you think it matters to me?" she whispered. "Just let me alone, let me sleep."

"Your word, Asher."

She gave him a long last look before she wearily closed her eyes. "My word, Eric."

And she had kept it. She had tolerated Eric's pleasure when her father had turned away from her. She had ignored his discreet but frequent affairs. For months she had lived like a zombie, doing as she was bid. When the layers of grief began to peel away, his hold remained through guilt and threats. When she had begun to come to life again, Asher had bargained for her freedom. Nothing was more important to Eric than his reputation. She held his many women in one hand, he held the knowledge of Ty's child in the other. They'd made an uneasy agreement.

Now he was back, Asher mused. Perhaps because she was making a success of her life again. Still, she felt he would keep his silence, if only to ensure a hold over her. Once he spoke, all ties were severed. Or if she spoke…

She remembered the look on Ty's face when he had seen her with Eric. Explanations would never be accepted now. Perhaps the day would come when they fully trusted each other, when the memory of betrayal would be dimmed.

She'd been silent for some time. By the steadiness of her breathing she might have been sleeping. Ty knew she was awake and thinking. What secrets was she hold-

ing from him? he wondered. And how long would it
be before the air between them was finally cleared?
He wanted to demand, but her vulnerability prevented
him. More than anything else, he didn't want to risk
her slipping behind the wall she could so easily erect.

"Better?" he murmured.

She sighed before he felt the faint movement of her
head as she nodded. There was one thing she could
settle between them, one thing she could make him
understand. "Ty, he means nothing to me. Do you believe that?"

"I want to."

"Believe it." Suddenly intense, she sat up and leaned
against his chest. If she could give him nothing else, she
could give him this. "I feel nothing for Eric, not even
hate. The marriage was a mistake. From the start it was
nothing more than a façade."

"Then why—"

"It's always been you," she said before she crushed
her mouth to his. "Always you." She pressed her lips to
his throat, passion erupting in her as swiftly as the tears.
"I stopped living for so long and now…" Her mouth ran
wildly over his face. "I need you now, only you."

Her mouth met his fervently, saying more than words.
Her ardor touched off his own. There was no need for
questions now, or for answers. She pulled the shirt from
him, eager to touch. Pressing her lips to heated flesh,
she heard him groan. Though her hands moved swiftly
to undress him, her lips loitered, lingering to arouse.
With her tongue she left a moist trail of fire.

His body was a pleasure to her—hard muscle, long
bones, taut flesh. Delighting in him, she sought new
secrets. If she nibbled at his waist, his breathing grew

shallow, his fingers gripped her hair. If she moved her palm along his thigh, his moan vibrated with need. Giddy with power, she ran a crazed trail from stomach to chest, her lips hungry and seeking.

He struggled to pull the robe from her as she caught his earlobe between her teeth. Low, sultry laughter drove him wild. Neither heard the seam rip as he tugged the terry cloth from her. Limber and quick, she made it impossible for him to grant them both the final relief. Her lovemaking tormented and thrilled him while her agility held him off.

"Now," he demanded, grasping her hips. "Asher, for God's sake."

"No, no, no," she murmured, then cut off his oath with a searing kiss. She found the torture exquisite. Though her own body begged for fulfillment, she wanted to prolong it. As his hands slid over her damp skin, she arched back, reveling in his touch. She belonged, and always would, to the man who could release her fires.

Neither was in control, each a slave to the other. She wanted nothing more than to be bound to him—here, in a dark room with the sound of her own breathing raging in her ears, in the sunlight with the secrets of the night still humming between them. For always.

Beneath her, his body was hot and moist and moving. The rhythm seduced her. Everything warm, everything giving, flowed through her. Thoughts vanished, memories dimmed. Now—there was only now—the all-powerful, greedy present.

This time when he gripped her hips she made no attempt to stop him. Her head fell back in complete abandonment as they joined. The moan was rich and deep, and from both of them. As one, they were catapulted up, beyond pleasure, into ecstasy.

Chapter 8

Asher had driven in limousines all her life. As a child she'd ridden behind a chauffeur named George in a shiny maroon car with smoked glass and a built-in bar. George had remained the family driver though the cars had changed—an elegant white Rolls, a sturdy blue Mercedes.

Lady Wickerton's driver had been Peter and the car had been an old discreet gray Daimler. Peter had been as silent and as efficient as the car. Asher felt no thrill at being driven in the long black limo toward Wimbledon.

As they passed through Roehampton, she watched the scenery. Tidy, healthy trees, trimmed shrubs, orderly flowers. In a few hours, she would be in Centre Court. Aching, sweating…and winning. This was the big prize. Credibility, prestige, press. They were all at Wimbledon.

Once before she and Ty had taken the championships and led the dancing at the Wimbledon Ball—in that year of her life that had brought complete joy and complete misery. Now she would play her old foe Maria Rayski with all the verve and all the cunning she had at her disposal.

Though she'd thought her life had begun to come to order with her first win, Asher now realized she'd been wrong. The turning point was today, here in the arena that was synonymous with her profession. She would play her best here, on the surface she knew best, in the country in which she had lived like a prisoner. Perhaps true confidence would begin after this match was over.

She thought of Ty, the young boy who had once vowed to play and win. Now, in the lush interior of the limo, Asher made a similar vow. She would have a championship season. Reestablish Asher Wolfe *for* Asher Wolfe. Then she would be ready to face the woman. The woman would face the only man who mattered.

The crowds waited for her and other arriving players. The greetings were enthusiastic. Roaming spectators sipped champagne and nibbled on strawberries and cream. Signing autographs, Asher felt light, confident, ready. Nothing, she thought, could mar such a day. The Fourth of July, the brilliant sunshine, the scent of garden flowers.

She remembered other Wimbledons. So little had changed. Fans mingled with players, chatting, laughing. The atmosphere was one of an informal tea party with the promise of a spectacle. But she could feel the nerves. They were there, just under the bonhomie, in the young players, the veterans, doubles and singles fi-

nalists. Mixing among them were rock stars and celebrities, millionaires and landed gentry.

Asher saw faces from the past, players from her father's generation. For them it was a reunion, nostal-
gia, tradition. There were people she had entertained
in Grosvenor Square. For them it was a social event.
The dress was summer-garden-party chic—picture hats
and pastels. Because yesterdays had to be faced, Asher
greeted former acquaintances.

"Asher, how lovely to see you again...." "What a
sweet little outfit...." "How strange it is not to see you
at the club anymore...." There was speculation, thinly
veiled by stretched manners. She dealt with it calmly,
as she had during her three years of marriage.

"Where's that old man of yours?"

Turning, Asher clasped two large hands warmly.
"Stretch McBride, you haven't changed a bit."

Of course he had. When he'd first tickled Asher's
chin, he'd been thirty. His face had been unlined, his
hair untouched with gray. He'd won nearly every major
championship there was to win twice around. Though
he was still tall, and nearly as lean as he had been in his
prime, the twenty years showed on his face.

"You always told a lie beautifully." Grinning, he
kissed her cheek. "Where's Jim?"

"In the States," she answered, keeping her smile
bright. "How have you been, Stretch?"

"Just fine. Got five grandchildren and a nice string
of sporting goods stores on the East Coast." He patted
her hand. "Don't tell me Jim isn't going to be here? He
hasn't missed it in forty years."

It was a struggle not to show the pain, much less not
to feel it. "As far as I know, he won't be. I'm awfully

glad to see you again. I haven't forgotten that you taught me the dump shot."

Pleased, he laughed. "Use it on Maria today," he advised. "I love to see Americans win at Wimbledon. Tell your old man hello for me."

"Take care, Stretch." Her smile evaded the promise she couldn't give. With a parting kiss, he moved away.

Turning, Asher found herself face-to-face with Lady Daphne Evans. The striking brunette had been one of Eric's more discreet dalliances, and one of Asher's more difficult trials. Her eyes automatically cooled, though her voice was scrupulously polite.

"Daphne, you look exquisite."

"Asher." Daphne skimmed cool eyes over Asher's brief tennis dress, down long bare legs to her court shoes. "You look different. How odd to find you an athlete."

"Odd?" Asher countered. "I've always been an athlete. Tell me, how is your husband?"

The thrust was parried with a quick laugh. "Miles is in Spain on business. As it happens, Eric escorted me today."

Though her stomach churned, her face remained composed. "Eric's here?"

"Yes, of course." Meticulously Daphne adjusted the brim of her rose-pink hat. "You don't think he'd miss this Wimbledon, do you?" Long mink lashes swept down, then up again. "We're all very interested in the results. Will we see you at the ball, darling?"

"Naturally."

"Well, I must let you mingle, mustn't I? That's traditional. Best of luck." With a flash of a smile Daphne swirled her skirts and was gone.

Asher fought the nausea, but began to nudge her way through the crowd. All she wanted was the comparative peace of the A locker rooms. The day ahead promised to be enough of a fight without contending with ghosts. With a few smiles and mechanically gracious greetings, she made her way out of the main throng. A few moments to herself—that was what she needed before the stands began to fill, before her strength and abilities were put to the test.

She knew Eric well enough to be certain he had asked Daphne to seek her out. Yes, he would want to be sure she knew he was there—before the match. As she slipped into the locker room, Asher noticed her hands were shaking. She couldn't allow it. In thirty minutes she would have to be in complete control.

When she walked onto the court Asher was careful not to look into the crowd. It would be easier on her nerves if the people who watched and cheered remained anonymous. As she attempted to empty her mind of all but the first game, Asher watched Maria Rayski.

On her own side of the court, Rayski paced, gesturing occasionally to the crowd, tossing comments. Her nerves were undisguised. It was always so, Asher mused. Rayski chewed her nails, cracked her knuckles and said the first thing that came into her mind. In a wary sort of fashion Asher had always liked her. At five foot ten, she was tall for a woman and rangy, with a deadly stretch. Fatalistically Asher recalled she had a habit of badgering her opponent.

Well, she decided as she chose her game racket, Rayski's histrionics might just keep her mind off who was, and who was not, in the stands. She eyed the television camera dispassionately. With the wonder of technol-

ogy, the match would be relayed to the States with only
a brief delay. Would her father even bother to watch?
she wondered. Silently she walked to the baseline for
the first serve.

There was no cautious testing in the first games.
Rayski went straight for the jugular. Both were fast players, and while Rayski was more aggressive, Asher was
a better strategist. A ball could take ungodly bounces
on grass, particularly the lush grass of Wimbledon's
Centre Court. To defend, to attack, required instinct
and timing. It also required complete concentration.

The lead jockeyed back and forth during the first set
as the players gave the fourteen thousand spectators the
show they'd come to see. Over the elegant, century-old
court, they sweated, gritted their teeth and scrambled,
not for the enjoyment of those who paid to see, but for
the game. Rayski tossed an occasional taunt over the
net between rallies. Asher might have been deaf for all
the response she gave. She had her rhythm—nothing
was going to interfere with it. She placed her ground
strokes with deadly precision, charged the net for short
angling volleys. Both her form and her energy seemed
at perfect peak.

Everything changed when the women took their seats
for the towel-off before the third set.

Because she had forgotten about everything but the
game, Asher's defenses were lowered. An inadvertent
glance up in the stands had her eyes locking with Eric's.
A slow, icy smile spread over his face as he lifted a hand
in salute—or reminder.

What the devil's wrong with her? Ty asked himself. He shifted closer to the edge of his seat and studied Asher with narrowed eyes. She'd just dropped two

games straight, the second one on a double fault. True, Rayski was playing superbly, but so was Asher—until the third set. She was playing mechanically now, as if the life had gone out of her. Too often she was missing basic shots or failing to put anything extra on a return. Rayski's serve was not her strongest weapon, yet she was repeatedly breezing service winners past Asher.

If he didn't know her better, he would have sworn Asher was tanking the match. But Asher wasn't capable of deliberately losing.

Carefully Ty watched for signs of an injury. A strained muscle or twisted ankle would explain the change in her. She gave no sign of favoring a leg. The composure on her face was as perfect as a mask. Too perfect, Ty reflected as the third game went to fifteen-love. Something was definitely wrong, but it wasn't physical. Disturbed, he quickly scanned the crowd.

There were dozens of faces he knew, some by name, some by reputation. There was an award-winning actor he'd once played a celebrity tourney with. Ty had found him an earthy man with a credible forehand. He recognized the ballet star because Asher had once dragged him to see *The Firebird.* Beside the ballerina was a country-western singer with a crossover hit. Ty passed over them, looking for an answer. He found it sitting near the Royal Box.

There was a cool, satisfied smile on Eric's face as he watched his ex-wife. Beside him, a thin, flashy woman in a rose-colored hat looked bored. Rage rose in Ty instantly. His first instinct was to yank Eric up by his five-hundred-dollar lapels and rearrange the expression on his face with his fists.

"Son of a bitch," he muttered, already rising. The hand that grasped his wrist was strong.

"Where are you going?" Madge demanded.

"To do something I should've done three years ago."

Still clinging to his arm, Madge twisted her head to follow the direction of his eyes. "Oh, boy," she said under her breath. Through her fingertips she could feel Ty's temper. Only briefly did she consider the personal satisfaction she would gain from letting Ty do what he wanted. "Hold on," she snapped between her teeth. "Listen to me. Punching him out isn't going to do anything for Asher."

"The hell it won't," he retorted. "You know why he's here."

"To upset her," Madge managed calmly enough. "Obviously he's succeeding. Go talk to her." A strong man might have cringed from the blazing look Ty turned on her. Madge merely arched a brow. "You want to start a fight, Starbuck, do it after the match. I'll referee. Right now, use your head."

His control didn't come easily. Madge watched him struggle for it, lose it, then finally win. Though his eyes were still stormy, the hand under hers relaxed. "If talking doesn't work," he said flatly, "I'm going to break him in half."

"I'll hold your coat," she promised before Ty slipped away.

Knowing he'd have only a moment, Ty decided to use words sparingly—and make them count. After losing the game without making a point, Asher slumped into her chair. She didn't see Ty waiting for her.

"What the hell's wrong with you?"

Her head jerked up at the harsh tone. "Nothing."

She was tired, already defeated as she mopped at the sweat on her face.

"You're handing the match to Rayski on a platter."

"Leave me alone, Ty."

"Going to give him the satisfaction of watching you fall apart in front of fourteen thousand people, Face?" There was sarcasm without a trace of sympathy in his voice. He noted the quick, almost indiscernible flash in her eyes. He'd wanted to see it. Always, she played better if there was anger beneath the ice.

"I never thought I'd see you tank a match."

"Go to hell." Whirling, she stalked back to the baseline. Nobody, she thought as she waited for Rayski to take position, nobody accused Asher Wolfe of tanking. Rayski crouched in her pendulum receiving stance while Asher gave the ball a few testing bounces. Tossing it, she drew back her racket and lunged. The effort of the serve came out in a force of breath. The finely pulverized chalk at the baseline rose on contact. Without giving the ace a thought, Asher took her stance for the next serve.

Her anger had teeth. She could feel it gnawing at her. A photographer zoomed in on her face and captured the contradictory placid expression and frosted eyes. Temper was energy. Asher flew across the court, striking the ball as if it were the enemy. Yet her battle was sternly controlled. No one watching her would realize that she cursed Ty with each stroke. No one but Ty himself. Satisfied, he watched her turn her fury on her opponent.

Oh, she was fabulous to see, he thought. Those long, slim legs, the strong shoulders. Her form was so smooth, so precise, yet beneath was that excitement, that smoldering passion. She was as she played, he mused, and wanted her. No one but he knew just how reckless she could be, just how abandoned. The thought had desire moving through him. She was the woman all men fantasized about—part lady, part wanton. And his, Ty told himself fiercely. Only his.

After watching Asher fire a backhand volley past Rayski, he glanced up. Eric's smile was gone. As if sensing the scrutiny, the Englishman looked down. The two men studied each other as the crowd applauded Asher's game. Ty laughed, softly, insolently, then walked away.

Though the match held close to the last point, the impetus Ty had instilled in her carried Asher to the win. She was polite, even charming as she accepted the Wimbledon plate. Inside she was raging. The joy of victory couldn't penetrate the fury and resentment she was feeling. Ty had turned the tide of her emotions away from Eric and onto himself.

She wanted to shout. She smiled and raised her trophy for the crowd to see. She wanted to scream. Politely she allowed the army of cameras to snap her. Fatigue didn't touch her. The ache in her arm might not have existed.

At last freeing herself from the press and well-wishers, she simmered under the shower and changed. Determination made her remain at Wimbledon to watch Ty's match. Stubbornness made her refuse to admire his game. Eric was forgotten. Asher's only thought was to vent her fury at the first possible moment. It took five hard sets and two and a half hours before Ty could claim his own trophy.

Asher left the stadium before the cheers had died.

* * *

He knew she'd be waiting for him. Even before Ty slipped the key in the lock, he knew what to expect. He looked forward to it. His adrenaline was still flowing. Neither the shower nor the massage had taken it from him. Wimbledon always affected him this way. As long as he played, winning there would be his first goal.

Now, the demanding games behind him, the win still sweet, he felt like a knight returning home victorious from the wars. His woman waited. But she wouldn't throw herself into his arms. She was going to scratch at him. Oh, yes, he was looking forward to it.

Grinning, Ty turned the knob. He had no more than shut the door behind him than Asher stormed out of the bedroom.

"Congratulations, Face," he said amiably. "Looks like I get first dance at the ball."

"How dare you say those things to me in the middle of the match?" she demanded. Eyes glittering, she advanced on him. "How dare you accuse me of tanking?"

Ty set his bag and rackets on a chair. "What do you call what you were doing?"

"Losing."

"Quitting," he corrected her. "You might as well have put up a sign."

"I've never quit!"

He lifted a brow. "Only for three years."

"Don't you dare throw that in my face." Raising both hands, she shoved him. Instead of being offended, he laughed. It pleased him enormously that he could rattle her control.

"You did good," he reminded her. "I couldn't take a

chance on your losing." He gave her cheek an affectionate pinch. "I didn't want to open the ball with Maria."

"You conceited, overconfident louse!" She shoved
him again. "Gramaldi almost took you. I wish he had."
She shouted the lie at him. "You could use a good kick
in the ego." With the intention of storming back into
the bedroom, she whirled. Catching her wrist, Ty spun
her back around.

"Aren't you going to congratulate me?"

"No."

"Aw, come on, Face." He grinned appealingly. "Give
us a kiss."

For an answer Asher balled her hand into a fist.
Ducking the blow, Ty gripped her waist and slung her
over his shoulder. "I love it when you're violent," he
said huskily as she pulled his hair.

To her own surprise—and annoyance—she had to
choke back a laugh. "Then you're going to get a real
charge out of this," she promised, kicking wildly as he
threw her on the bed. Even though her reflexes were
quick, Ty had her pinned beneath him in seconds.
Breathless, she struggled to bring her knee up to his
weakest point.

"Not that violent." Wisely he shifted to safety.

She twisted, squirmed and struggled. "You take your
hands off me."

"Soon as I'm finished," he agreed, slipping a hand
under the blouse that had come loose from her waistband.

Refusing to acknowledge the sensation of pleasure,
Asher glared at him. "Don't you touch me."

"I have to touch you to make love to you." His

smile was reasonable and friendly. "It's the only way I know how."

I will not laugh, she ordered herself as the gurgle rose in her throat. She was angry, furious, she reminded herself.

Ty recognized the weakening and capitalized on it. "Your eyes get purple when you're mad. I like it." He kissed her firmly shut mouth. "Why don't you yell at me some more?"

"I have nothing more to say to you," Asher claimed haughtily. "Please go away."

"But we haven't made love yet." Lightly he rubbed his nose against hers.

Refusing to be charmed, she turned her head away. "We aren't going to."

"Wanna bet?" With one swift move he ripped her blouse from neck to waist.

"Ty!" Shocked, Asher gaped at him, her mouth open.

"I nearly did that when you were on Centre Court today. You should be glad I waited." Before she could react he tore her shorts into ragged pieces. Thinking he might have gone mad, Asher stayed perfectly still. "Something wrong?" he asked as his hand moved to cup her breast.

"Ty, you can't tear my clothes."

"I already did." Soft as a feather, his hand roamed down to her stomach. "Want to tear mine?"

"No." Her skin was beginning to quiver. She tried to shift away and found herself held prisoner.

"I made you angry."

Her head cleared long enough for her to glare at him. "Yes, and—"

"Angry enough to win," he murmured, trailing his

lips along her throat. "And when I watched you I nearly exploded from wanting you. All that passion simmering just under the surface. And only I know what it's like when it escapes."

She gave a little moan as his fingers stroked the point of her breast but tried to cling to reality. "You had no business saying I was tanking."

"I didn't say that, I only planted the idea." When he lifted his head, the look in his eyes had her drawing in a quick breath. "Did you think I'd stand by and watch him get to you like that? No man gets to you, Asher, no man but me."

With a savage kiss he cut off all words, all thoughts.

It always surprised Asher that Ty could project such raw sexuality in black tie. Conservative, formal dress could do nothing to alter his air of primitive masculinity. The material could cover the muscles, but it couldn't disguise the strength. There had been times Asher had wondered if it was his earthiness that had drawn her to him. Glimpsing him in a room filled with elegantly attired men and women, she knew it was more than that. It was all of him, every aspect, from temper to humor, that had made her his.

The Wimbledon Ball was as traditional as the tournament. The music, the lights, the people. It was always an evening to remember for its beauty and tastefulness. Asher counted the hours until it would be over. Scolding herself, she tuned back in to the conversation of her dance partner. She'd always enjoyed a party, always found pleasure in quiet well-run affairs. But now she wished she and Ty could have shared a bottle of wine in their room.

She didn't want the spotlight this evening, but candlelight. Over the heads of the other dancers her eyes met Ty's. It took only one brief glance to know that his thoughts mirrored hers. Love threatened to drown her.

"You're a lovely dancer, Miss Wolfe."

As the music ended, Asher smiled at her partner. "Thank you." Her smile never wavered as it ran through her head that she had completely forgotten the man's name.

"I was a great fan of your father's, you know." The man cupped a hand under her elbow to lead her from the dance floor. "The Golden Boy of Tennis." With a sigh he patted Asher's hand. "Of course, I remember his early days, before you were born."

"Wimbledon has always been his favorite. Dad loved the tradition...and the pomp," Asher added with a smile.

"Seeing the second generation here is good for the soul." In a courtly gesture he lifted her hand to his lips. "My best to you, Miss Wolfe."

"Jerry, how are you?"

A stately woman in silk brocade swept up to them. Lady Mallow, Eric Wickerton's sister, was, as always, elegant. Asher's spine stiffened.

"Lucy, what a pleasure!"

She offered her fingers to be kissed, sending Asher a brief glance as she did so. "Jerry, Brian's been searching for you to say hello. He's just over there."

"Well then, if you ladies will excuse me."

Having dispatched him, Lucy turned to her former sister-in-law. "Asher, you're looking well."

"Thank you, Lucy."

She gave Asher's simple ivory sheath a brief survey, thinking that if she had worn something so basic, she would have blended in with the wallpaper. On Asher, the muted color and simple lines were stunning. Lucy gave her a candid stare. "And are you well?"

A bit surprised, Asher lifted a brow. "Yes, quite well. And you?"

"I meant that as more than small talk." Lucy's hesitation was brief, as was her glance to determine if they could be overheard. "There's something I've wanted to say to you for a long time." Stiffening, Asher waited. "I love my brother," Lucy began. "I know you didn't. I also know that throughout your marriage you did nothing to disgrace him, though he didn't return the favor."

The unexpected words had Asher staring. "Lucy—"

"Loving him doesn't blind me, Asher," she continued briskly. "My loyalty is with Eric, and always will be."

"Yes, I understand that."

Lucy studied Asher's face a moment, then she seemed to sigh. "I gave you no support when you were my brother's wife and I wanted to offer my apologies."

Touched, Asher took her hand. "There's no need. Eric and I were simply wrong for each other."

"I often wondered why you married him," Lucy mused, still searching Asher's face. "At first I thought it was the title, but that had nothing to do with it. Something seemed to change between you so soon after you were married, hardly two months." Asher's eyes clouded for only a moment under Lucy's direct gaze. "I wondered if you'd taken a lover. But it became very obvious in a short time that it was Eric, not you, who was…dallying. Just as it's become obvious that there's been only one man in your life." Her gaze shifted. Asher didn't have to follow it to know it rested on Ty.

"Knowing that hurt Eric."

"Knowing that, Eric should never have married you."
Lucy sighed again, a bit indulgently. "But then, he's always wanted what belonged to someone else. I won't speak of that, but I'll tell you now what I should have told you long before—I wish you happiness."

On impulse, Asher kissed her cheek. "Thank you, Lucy."

Smiling, she glanced over at Ty again. "Your taste, Asher, has always been exquisite. I've envied it, though it's never been right for me. It's time I joined Brian."

As she turned away, Asher touched her hand. "If I wrote you, would you be uncomfortable?"

"I'd be very pleased." Lucy moved away, silks rustling.

Smiling, Asher realized she had been right. Wimbledon was her turning point. Another layer of guilt had been lifted. She was coming closer to discovering who she was, and what she needed. Feeling a hand on her arm, she turned to smile at Ty.

"Who was that?"

"An old friend." Asher lifted a hand to his cheek. "Dance with me? There's no other way I can hold you until we can be alone."

Chapter 9

Asher knew she had made great strides when pressure from the press no longer tightened her nerves. Her habitual terror of saying the wrong thing, or saying too much, faded. She still had secrets. Before coming to Australia she'd promised herself a moratorium. Whatever decisions had to be made would wait. For the moment she wanted to concentrate on happiness. Happiness was Ty—and tennis.

There were good memories in Australia—wins, losses. Good tennis. The people were relaxed, casual. The friendliness was exactly what Asher needed after the tension of England. Aussies remembered The Face, and welcomed her. For the first time since her comeback Asher found the winning taking second place to the enjoying.

The change in her was noticeable even during the early rounds. Her smiles came more frequently. Though her play was no less intense and concentrated, the air of being driven was fading.

From the first row of the stands Ty watched her in early morning practice. He'd just completed two hours of his own. Now, his legs stretched out, he studied her from behind the protection of tinted glasses. She'd improved, he mused...not only as an athlete. He remembered how important athletic ability was to her. The fact that she was a strategist and a craftsman had never been enough. Always, she had striven to be recognized as a good athlete. And so she would be, he thought, as she raced to the net to slap a return with her two-fisted backhand. Perhaps in some ways the years of retirement had toughened her.

His face clouded a moment. Consciously he smoothed the frown away. This wasn't the time to think of that or to dwell on the questions that still plagued him. Whys— so many whys hammered at him. Yet he recognized that she was grabbing this time to be carefree. He'd give her that. He would wait. But when the season was over, he'd have his answers.

When her laughter floated to him he forgot the doubts. It was a rich, warm sound, heard all too rarely. Leaning back, Ty chugged down cold fruit juice and looked around him.

If Wimbledon was his favorite stadium, the grass of Kooyong was his favorite surface. It was as hard as a roadbed and fast. A ball bounced true here, unlike other grass courts. Even at the end of the season, when the courts were worn and soiled, the surface remained even. Even after a deluge of rain, the Australian grass was resilient. Kooyong was a treasure for the fast, for the aggressive. Ty was ready for just such a match.

Through half-closed eyes he watched Asher. She was ready, too, he decided. And ever more ready to enjoy it. A smile touched his mouth. Whatever questions there were, whatever answers, nothing could harm what was between them now.

Noting the practice session was winding up, Ty jumped lightly down to the court. "How about a quick game?"

Madge shot him a look and continued to pack up her rackets. "Forget it, hotshot."

He grabbed a racket from her, bouncing a ball lightly on the strings. "Spot you two points."

With a snort Madge snatched the ball, dropping it into the can. "Take him on, Asher," she suggested. "He needs a lesson."

Catching her tongue between her teeth, Asher studied him. "Head to head," she decided.

"You serve."

Asher waited until he had taken his receiving position. Cupping two balls in her hand, she sent him a smile. "Been a while, hasn't it, Starbuck?"

"Last time we played you never got to game point." He gave Madge a wink. "Sure you don't want that handicap?"

Her ace answered for her. As pleased as he was surprised, Ty sent her a long look. Removing the tinted glasses, he tossed them to Madge. "Not bad, Face." His eyes followed the trail of the next serve. He sent it to the far corner to brush the service line. Ty liked nothing better than to watch Asher run. The range of her backhand was limited, but perfectly placed. He was on it in a flash. The last time they had played he had beaten her handily even while holding back. Now he scented challenge.

Asher lined the ball straight at him, hard and fast. Pivoting, Ty slammed it back. The ball whistled on her return. With a powerful swing Ty sent her to the baseline, then nipped her return so that the ball brushed the net and died in the forecourt.

"Fifteen-all." Ty feigned a yawn as he went back to position.

Narrowing her eyes, Asher served. The rally was a study in speed and footwork. She knew he was playing with her, moving her all over the court. Aware that she was no match for his power, she chose to catch him off guard. The ball thudded. She raced. It soared. She followed. The sounds of rackets cutting air had a steady, almost musical sound. A rhythm was set. Patiently she adhered to it until she sensed Ty relaxing. Abruptly she altered the pacing and slapped the ball past him.

"Getting crafty," he muttered.

"Getting slow, old timer," she retorted sweetly.

Ty slammed her next serve crosscourt. After the bounce, it landed somewhere in the grandstands. Under her breath Asher swore pungently.

"Did you say something?"

"Not a thing." Disgusted, Asher shook her hair back. As she readied to serve, she caught the look in Ty's eyes. They rested not on her ball or racket, but on her mouth.

All's fair, she mused with a secret smile. Slowly and deliberately she moistened her lips with the tip of her tongue. Taking a long, preliminary stretch, she served. Distracted, Ty was slow to meet the ball. Asher had little trouble blowing the return past him.

"Game point," she said softly, sending him an intimate smile. Keeping her back to him, she bent to pick up a fresh ball, taking her time about it. She could almost feel Ty's eyes run up the long length of her legs. Smoothing a hand down her hip, she walked back to the baseline. "Ready?"

He nodded, dragging his eyes away from the subtle sweep of her breasts. When his eyes met hers, he read an invitation that had his pulse racing. His concentration broken, he barely returned her serve. The rally was very short.

Victorious, Asher let out a hoot of laughter before she walked to the net. "Your game seemed to be a bit off, Starbuck."

The gibe and the laughter in her eyes had him wanting to strangle her...and devour her. "Cheat," he murmured as he walked to meet her at the net.

Asher's look was guileless and she was faintly shocked. "I have no idea what you're talking about." The words were hardly out of her mouth when she was pulled against him, her lips crushed under his. Laughter and desire seemed to bubble in her simultaneously. Without being aware of it, she dropped her racket and clung to him.

"You're lucky I don't toss you on the ground here and now," he mumbled against her mouth.

"What's lucky about that?" Enchanted, Asher strained against him. How was it possible for one kiss to make her head swim?

Ty drew back, inches only. His whole body was throbbing for her. "Don't tempt me."

"Do I?" she asked huskily.

"Damn you, Asher. You know just how much."

His voice shook, delighting her. She found she

needed him to be as vulnerable as she. "I'm never sure," she whispered, dropping her head to his chest.

His heart was beating too rapidly. Ty tried to fight down the impossible surge of need. Not the time, not the place, his sanity stated. Control was necessary. "You were sure enough to use a few tricks to distract me."

Lifting her head, Asher smiled at him. "Distract you? How?"

"Took your time picking up that ball, didn't you?"

She seemed to consider a moment. "Why, I've seen Chuck do the same thing playing against you. It never seemed to make any difference." She let out a whoop of surprise as he lifted her up and over the net.

"Next time I'll be ready for you, Face." After giving her a brief, bruising kiss, he dropped her to her feet. "You could play naked and I wouldn't blink an eye."

Catching her lip between her teeth, she sent him a teasing glance. "Wanna bet?" Before he could connect his racket with her bottom, she dashed away.

The locker room wasn't empty as Asher walked in, but the crowd was thinning. With the fifth rounds completed, there were fewer contenders, and therefore fewer bodies. She was looking forward to her match that afternoon with a hot newcomer who had hopped up in the rankings from one hundred and twentieth to forty-third in one year. Asher had no intention of strolling into the finals. Even the pressure of Grand Slam potential couldn't mar her mood. If ever there was a year she could win it, Asher felt it was this one.

She greeted a towel-clad Tia Conway as the Australian emerged from the showers. Both women knew they would face each other before the tournament was over. Asher could hear a laughing argument taking place over the sound of running water. As she started to remove her warm-up jacket, she spotted Madge in a corner.

The brunette sat with her head leaning back against the wall, her eyes shut. She was pale despite her tan, and there were beads of perspiration on her brow. Asher rushed over to kneel at her feet.

"Madge."

Opening her eyes slowly, Madge sighed. "Who won?"

For a moment Asher went blank. "Oh, I did. I cheated."

"Smart girl."

"Madge, what's wrong? God, your hands are like ice."

"No, it's nothing." She let out a breath as she leaned forward.

"You're sick, let me—"

"No, I've finished being sick." After a weak smile Madge swiped the sweat from her brow. "I'll be fine in a minute."

"You look terrible. You need a doctor." Asher sprang to her feet. "I'll call someone." Before she could move, Madge had her hand.

"I've seen a doctor."

Every sort of nightmare went through Asher's head. In stark terror she stared at her friend. "Oh, God, Madge, how bad?"

"I've got seven months." As Asher swayed, Madge caught her arm tightly. "Good grief, Asher, I'm pregnant, not dying."

Stunned, Asher sank to the bench. *"Pregnant!"*

"Shh." Quickly Madge glanced around. "I'd like to keep this quiet for a while. Damn morning sickness catches me off guard at the worst times." Letting out a shaky breath, she relaxed against the wall again. "The good news is it's not supposed to last long."

"I don't—Madge, I don't know what to say."

"How about congratulations?"

Shaking her head, Asher gripped both of Madge's hands in hers. "Is this what you want?"

"Are you kidding?" On a half laugh, Madge leaned against Asher's shoulder. "I might not look too happy at the moment, but inside I'm doing cartwheels. I've never wanted anything so badly in my life." She sat silently for a moment, her hand still in Asher's. "You know, during my twenties all I could think about was being number one. It was great being there. The Wrightman Cup, Wimbledon, Dallas—all of it. I was twenty-eight when I met The Dean, and still ambitious as hell. I didn't want to get married, but I couldn't live without him. As for kids, I thought, hell, there's plenty of time for that. Later, always later. Well, I woke up one morning in the hospital with my leg screaming at me and I realized I was thirty-two years old. I'd won just about everything I thought I had to win, and yet something was missing. For the better part of my life I've floated around this old world from court to court. Team tennis, pro-am tourneys, celebrity exhibitions, you name it. Until The Dean there was nothing but tennis for me. Even after him, it was the biggest slice of the pie."

"You're a champion," Asher said softly.

"Yeah." Madge laughed again. "Yeah, by God, I am, and I like it. But you know what? When I looked at the snapshot of Ty's nephew I realized that I wanted a baby, The Dean's baby, more than I'd ever wanted a Wimbledon plate. Isn't that wild?"

She let the statement hang in silence a moment as both women absorbed it. "This is going to be my last tournament, and even while that's hurting, I keep wishing it was over so I could go home and start knitting booties."

"You don't know how to knit," Asher murmured.

"Well, The Dean can knit them then. I'll just sit around and get fat." Twisting her head to grin at Asher, Madge saw the tears. "Hey, what's this?"

"I'm happy for you," Asher muttered. She could remember her own feelings on learning of her pregnancy—the fear, the joy, the nausea and elation. She'd wanted to learn to sew. Then it had been over so quickly.

"You look overjoyed," Madge commented, brushing a tear away.

"I am really." She caught Madge to her in a viselike hug. "You'll take care of yourself, won't you? Don't overdo or take any chances?"

"Sure." Something in the tone had the seed of a thought germinating. "Asher, did you... Did something happen when you were married to Eric?"

Asher held her tighter for a moment, then released her. "Not now. Maybe someday we'll talk about it. How does The Dean feel about all this?"

Madge gave her a long, measuring look. The non-answer was answer enough, so she let it lay. "He was all set to take out a full-page ad in *World of Sports*," she stated. "I've made him wait until I officially retire."

"There's no need to retire, Madge. You can take a year or two off, lots of women do."

"Not this one." Stretching her arms to the ceiling, Madge grinned. "I'm going out a winner, ranked fifth. When I get home, I'm going to learn how to use a vacuum cleaner."

"I'll believe that when I see it."

"You and Ty are invited to my first home-cooked dinner."

"Great." Asher kissed her cheek. "We'll bring the antacid."

"Not nice," Madge mused. "But wise. Hey, Face," she continued before Asher could rise. "I wouldn't want this to get around but—" her eyes were suddenly very young, and she looked very vulnerable "—I'm scared right out of my socks. I'll be almost thirty-four by the time this kid makes an appearance. I've never even changed a diaper."

Firmly Asher took Madge's shoulders and kissed both of her cheeks. "You're a champion, remember?"

"Yeah, but what do I know about chicken pox?" Madge demanded. "Kids get chicken pox, don't they? And braces, and corrective shoes, and—"

"And mothers who worry before there's anything to worry about," Asher finished. "You're already slipping right into the slot."

"Hey, you're right." Rather pleased with herself, Madge rose. "I'm going to be great."

"You're going to be terrific. Let's get a shower. You've got a doubles match this afternoon."

With feelings mixed and uncertain, Asher rode the elevator to her hotel room late that afternoon. She had won her round with the young upstart from Canada in straight sets. Six-two, six-love. There was little doubt that Asher had played some of the finest tennis in her career in court one. But she didn't think of that now. Her mind kept drifting back to her interlude with Madge, and from there back to her thoughts on learning of her own pregnancy.

Would Ty have wanted to take out full-page ads, or

would he have cursed her? Like Eric, would he have accused her of deceit, of trickery? Now that they were being given a second chance, would he want marriage and children? What was it Jess had said that day? she wondered. *Ty will always be a gypsy, and no woman should ever expect to hold him.*

Yet Asher had expected to hold him, and, despite all her vows, was beginning to expect it again. Her love was so huge, so consuming, that when she was with him, it was simply impossible to conceive of doing without him. And perhaps because she had once, briefly, carried his child inside her, the need to do so again was overwhelming.

Could a woman tame a comet? she asked herself. Should she? For that's what he was—a star that flew, full of speed and light. He wasn't the prince at the end of the fairy tale who would calmly take up his kingdom and sit on a throne. Ty would always search for the next quest. And the next woman? Asher wondered, recalling Jess's words again.

Shaking her head, she told herself to think of today. Today they were together. Only a woman who had lived through change after change, hurt after hurt, could fully appreciate the perfection of a moment. Others might not recognize it, but Asher did. And the moment was hers.

She unlocked the door to their suite and was immediately disappointed. He wasn't there. Even had he been sleeping in the other room, she would have sensed him. The air was never still when Ty was around. Tossing her bag aside, she wandered to the window. The light was still full as the sun had only just began to set. Perhaps they would go out and explore Melbourne, find one of the tiny little clubs with loud music and laughter. She'd like to dance.

Twirling in a circle, Asher laughed. Yes, she would like to dance, to celebrate for Madge…and for herself. She was with the man she loved. A bath, she decided. A long, luxurious bath before she changed into something cool and sexy. When she opened the door to the bedroom, Asher stopped and stared in astonishment.

Balloons. Red, yellow, blue, pink and white. They floated throughout the room in a jamboree of color. Helium-filled, they rose to the ceiling, trailing long ribbons. There were dozens of them—round, oval, thin and fat. It was as if a circus had passed hurriedly through, leaving a few souvenirs. Grasping a ribbon, Asher drew one down to her while she continued to stare.

They were three layers deep, she saw in astonishment—at least a hundred of them bumping against one another. Her laughter came out in a quick burst that went on and on.

Who else would think of it? Who else would take the time? Not flowers or jewelry for Ty Starbuck. At that moment she could have floated to the ceiling to join the gift he had given her.

"Hi."

She turned to see him lounging in the doorway. In a flash Asher had launched herself into his arms, the single balloon still grasped in her hand. "Oh, you're crazy!" she cried before she found his lips with hers. With her arms wrapped around his neck, her legs around his waist, she kissed him again and again. "Absolutely insane."

"Me?" he countered. "You're the one standing here surrounded by balloons."

"It's the best surprise I've ever had."

"Better than roses in the bathtub?"

Tossing her head back, she laughed. "Even better than that."

"I thought about diamonds, but they didn't seem like as much fun." As he spoke he moved toward the bed.

"And they don't float," Asher put in, looking up at the ceiling of colorful shapes.

"Good point," Ty conceded as they fell together onto the bed. "Got any ideas how we should spend the evening?"

"One or two," Asher murmured. The balloon she held drifted up to join the others.

"Let's do both." He stopped her laugh with a soft kiss that became hungry quickly. "Oh, God, I've waited all day to be alone with you. When the season's over we'll find someplace—an island, another planet—anyplace where there's no one but us."

"Anyplace," she whispered in agreement while her hands tugged at his shirt.

Passion soared swiftly. Ty's needs doubled as he sensed hers. She was always soft, always eager for him. If the pounding of his blood would have allowed, he would have revered her. But the force of their joined desire wouldn't permit reverence. Clothes were hastily peeled away—a blouse flung aside, a shirt cast to the floor. Overhead, the balloons danced while they savored each other. The scent of victory seemed to cling to both of them, mixed with the faint fragrance of soap and shampoo from the post-game showers. Her lips tasted warm and moist, and somehow of himself as much as of her.

When there was nothing to separate them, they tangled together, their bodies hot and throbbing. With questing hands he moved over territory only more exciting in its familiarity. He could feel reason spin away into pure sensation. Soft here, firm there, her body was endless delight. The warmth of her breath along his skin could make him tremble. Her moan, as he slipped his fingers into her, made him ache. With open-mouthed kisses he trailed over her, seeking the hot heady flavor of her flesh. It seemed to melt into him, filling him to bursting.

When she arched, offering everything, Ty felt a surge of power so awesome he almost feared to take her. Too strong, he thought hazily. He was too strong and was bound to hurt her. He felt he could have lifted the world without effort. Yet she was drawing him to her with murmuring pleas.

There was no control in madness. She stole his sanity with her smooth skin and soft lips. There were no more pastel colors from frivolous balloons. Now there was gleaming silver and molten reds and pulsing blacks whirling and churning into a wild kaleidoscope that seemed to pull him into its vortex. Gasping her name, Ty thrust into her. The colors shattered, seeming to pierce his skin with a multitude of shards. And in the pain was indescribable pleasure.

When he was spent, nestled between her breasts, Asher gazed up at the darkening ceiling. How could it be, she wondered, that each time they were together it was different? Sometimes they loved in laughter, sometimes in tenderness. At other times with a smoldering passion. This time there had been a taste of madness in their loving. Did other lovers find this infinite variety, this insatiable delight in each other? Perhaps the two of them were unique. The thought was almost frightening.

"What are you thinking?" Ty asked. He knew he should shift his weight from her, but found no energy to do so.

"I was wondering if it should be so special each time I'm with you."

He laughed, kissing the side of her breast. "Of course it should, I'm a special person. Don't you read the sports section?"

She tugged his hair, but tenderly. "Don't let your press go to your head, Starbuck. You have to win a few more matches before you wrap up the Grand Slam."

He massaged the muscles of her thigh. "So do you, Face."

"I'm only thinking as far ahead as the next game," she said. She didn't want to think of Forest Hills, or the States—or the end of the season. "Madge is pregnant," she said half to herself.

"What!" Like a shot, Ty's head came up.

"Madge is pregnant," Asher repeated. "She wants to keep it quiet until the Australian Open is over."

"I'll be damned," he exclaimed. "Old Madge."

"She's only a year older than you," Asher stated defensively, causing him to laugh again.

"It's an expression, love." Absently he twined one of Asher's curls around a finger. "How does she feel about it?"

"She's thrilled—and scared." Her lashes lowered, shielding her expression a moment. "She's going to retire."

"We're going to have to throw her one hell of a party." Rolling onto his back, he drew Asher close to his side.

After a moment she moistened her lips and spoke casually. "Do you ever think about children? I mean, it would be difficult, wouldn't it, combining a family with a profession like this?"

"It's done all the time, depends on how you go about it."

"Yes, but all the traveling, the pressure."

He started to pass it off, then remembered how she had lived her childhood. Though he had never sensed any resentment in her, he wondered if she felt a family would be a hindrance to her career. Physically a baby would prevent her from playing for some time. And she'd already lost three years, he reflected with an inner sigh. Ty pushed the idea of their children out of his mind. There was time, after all.

"I imagine it's a hassle to worry about kids when you've got a tournament to think of," he said lightly. "A player's got enough trouble keeping track of his rackets."

With a murmured agreement, Asher stared into space.

In the thin light of dawn she shifted, brushing at a tickle on her arm. Something brushed over her cheek. Annoyed, Asher lifted her hand to knock it away. It came back. With a softly uttered complaint she opened her eyes.

In the gray light she could see dozens of shapes. Some hung halfway to the ceiling, others littered the bed and floor. Sleepy, she stared at them without comprehension. Irritated at having been disturbed, she knocked at the shape that rested on her hip. It floated lazily away.

Balloons, she realized. Turning her head, she saw that Ty was all but buried under them. She chuckled, muffling the sound with her hand as she sat up. He lay flat on his stomach, facedown in the pillow. She plucked a red balloon from the back of his head. He didn't budge. Leaning over, she outlined his ear with kisses. He muttered and stirred and shifted away. Asher lifted a brow. A challenge, she decided.

After brushing the hair from the nape of his neck, she began to nibble on the exposed flesh. "Ty," she whispered. "We have company."

Feeling a prickle of drowsy pleasure, Ty rolled to his side, reaching for her. Asher placed a balloon in his hand. Unfocused, his eyes opened.

"What the hell is this?"

"We're surrounded," Asher told him in a whisper. "They're everywhere."

A half dozen balloons tipped to the floor as he shifted to his back. After rubbing his face with his hands, he stared. "Good God." With that he shut his eyes again.

Not to be discouraged, Asher straddled him. "Ty, it's morning."

"Uh-uh."

"I have that talk show to do at nine."

He yawned and patted her bottom. "Good luck."

She planted a soft, nibbling kiss on his lips. "I have two hours before I have to leave."

"'S okay, you won't bother me."

Wanna bet? she asked silently. Reaching out, she trailed her fingers up his thigh. "Maybe I'll sleep a bit longer."

"Mmm-hmm."

Slowly she lay on top of him, nuzzling her lips at his throat. "I'm not bothering you, am I?"

"Hmm?"

She snuggled closer, feeling her breasts rub against his soft mat of hair. "Cold," she mumbled, and moved her thigh against his.

"Turn down the air-conditioning," Ty suggested.

Brows lowered, Asher lifted her head. Ty's eyes met hers, laughing, and not a bit sleepy. With a toss of her head Asher rolled from him and tugged on the blanket. Though her back was to him, she could all but see his grin.

"How's this?" Wrapping an arm around her waist, he fit his body to hers. She gave him a shrug as an answer. "Warmer?" he asked as he slid his hand up to cup her breast. The point was already taut, her pulse already racing. Ty moved sinuously against her.

"The air-conditioning's too high," she said plaintively. "I'm freezing."

Ty dropped a kiss at the base of her neck. "I'll get it." He rose, moving to the unit. It shut off with a dull mechanical thud. With a teasing remark on the tip of his tongue, he turned.

In the fragile morning light she lay naked in the tumbled bed, surrounded by gay balloons. Her hair rioted around a face dominated by dark, sleepy eyes. The faintest of smiles touched her lips, knowing, inviting, challenging. All thoughts of joking left him. Her skin was so smooth and touched with gold. Like a fist in the solar plexus, desire struck him and stole his breath.

As he went to her, Asher lifted her arms to welcome him.

Chapter 10

"Asher, how does it feel being only three matches away from the Grand Slam?"

"I'm trying not to think about it."

"You've drawn Stacie Kingston in the quarter-finals. She's got an oh-for-five record against you. Does that boost your confidence?"

"Stacie's a strong player, and very tough. I'd never go into a match with her overconfident."

Her hands folded loosely, Asher sat behind the table facing the lights and reporters. The microphone in front of her picked up her calm, steady voice and carried it to the rear of the room. She wore her old team tennis jacket with loose warm-up pants and court shoes. Around her face her hair curled damply. They'd barely given her time to shower after her most recent win at Forest Hills before scheduling the impromptu press conference. The cameras were rolling, taping her every movement, recording every expression. One of the print reporters quickly scribbled down that she wore no jewelry or lipstick.

"Did you expect your comeback to be this successful?"

Asher gave a lightning-fast grin—here then gone—something she would never have done for the press even two months before. "I trained hard," she said simply.

"Do you still lift weights?"

"Every day."

"Have you changed your style this time around?"

"I think I've tightened a few things up." She relaxed, considering. Of all the people in the room, only Asher was aware that her outlook toward the press had changed. There was no tightness in her throat as she spoke. No warning signals to take care flashing in her brain. "Improved my serve particularly," she continued. "My percentage of aces and service winners is much higher than it was three or four years ago."

"How often did you play during your retirement?"

"Not often enough."

"Will your father be coaching you again?"

Her hesitation was almost too brief to be measured. "Not officially," she replied evasively.

"Have you decided to accept the offer of a layout in *Elegance* magazine?"

Asher tucked a lock of hair behind her ear. "News travels fast." Laughter scattered around the room. "I haven't really decided," she continued. "At the moment I'm more concerned with the U.S. Open."

"Who do you pick to be your opponent in the finals?"

"I'd like to get through the quarters and semis first."

"Let's say, who do you think will be your strongest competition?"

"Tia Conway," Asher answered immediately. Their duel in Kooyong was still fresh in her mind. Three exhausting sets—three tie breakers—in two grueling hours. "She's the best all-around woman player today."

"What makes you say that?"

"Tia has court sense, speed, strength and a big serve."

"Yet you've beaten her consistently this season."

"But not easily."

"What about the men's competition? Would you predict the U.S. will have two Grand Slam winners this year?"

Asher fielded the question first with a smile. "I think someone mentioned that there were still three matches to go, but I believe it's safe to say that if Starbuck continues to play as he's played all season, no one will beat him, particularly on grass, as it's his best surface."

"Is your opinion influenced by personal feelings?"

"Statistics don't have any feelings," she countered. "Personal or otherwise." Asher rose, effectively curtailing further questioning. A few more were tossed out at random, but she merely leaned toward the mike and apologized for having to end the meeting. As she started to slip through a rear door, she spotted Chuck.

"Nicely done, Face."

"And over," she breathed. "What are you doing here?"

"Keeping an eye on my best friend's lady," he said glibly as he slipped an arm around her shoulders. "Ty thought it would be less confusing if he kept out of the way during your little tête-à-tête with the members of the working press."

"For heaven's sake," Asher mumbled, "I don't need a keeper."

"Don't tell me." Chuck flashed his boy-next-door smile. "Ty had it in his head the press might badger you."

Tilting her head, Asher studied his deceptively sweet face. "And what were you going to do if they had?"

"Strong-arm 'em," he claimed while flexing his muscle. "Though I might have been tempted to let them take a few bites out of you after that comment about nobody beating Ty. Didn't you hear they were naming a racket after me?"

Asher circled his waist with her arm. "Sorry, friend, I call 'em like I see 'em."

Stopping, he put both hands on Asher's shoulders and studied her. His look remained serious even when she gave him a quizzical smile. "You know, Face, you really look good."

She laughed. "Well, thanks...I think. Did I look bad before?"

"I don't mean you look beautiful, that never changes. I mean you look happy."

Lifting a hand to the one on her shoulder, Asher squeezed. "I am happy."

"It shows. In Ty too." Briefly he hesitated, then plunged ahead. "Listen, I don't know what happened between you two before, but—"

"Chuck..." Asher shook her head to ward off questions.

"But," he continued, "I want you to know I hope you make it this time."

"Oh, Chuck." Shutting her eyes, she went into his arms. "So do I," she sighed. "So do I."

"I asked you to keep an eye on her," Ty said from behind them. "I didn't say anything about touching."

"Oh, hell." Chuck tightened his hold. "Don't be so selfish. Second-seeds need love too." Glancing down at Asher, he grinned. "Can I interest you in lobster tails and champagne?"

"Sorry." She kissed his nose. "Somebody already offered me pizza and cheap wine."

"Outclassed again." With a sigh Chuck released her. "I need somebody to hit with tomorrow," he told Ty.

"Okay."

"Six o'clock, court three."

"You buy the coffee."

"We'll flip for it," Chuck countered before he sauntered away.

Alone, Asher and Ty stood for a moment in awkward silence while an airplane droned by overhead. The awkwardness had cropped up occasionally on their return to the States. It was always brief and never commented on. In the few seconds without words, each of them admitted that full truths would soon be necessary. Neither of them knew how to approach it.

"So," Ty began as the moment passed, "how did it go?"

"Easily," Asher returned, smiling as she stood on tiptoe to kiss him. "I didn't need the bodyguard."

"I know how you feel about press conferences."

"How?"

"Oh…" He combed her hair with his fingers. "*Terrified*'s a good word."

With a laugh she held out her hand as they started to

walk. "*Was* a good word," Asher corrected him. "I'm amazed I ever let it get to me. There was one problem though."

"What?"

"I was afraid I'd faint from starvation." She sent him a pitiful look from under her lashes. "Someone did mention pizza, didn't they?"

"Yeah." He grinned, catching her close. "And cheap wine."

"You really know how to treat a woman, Starbuck," Asher told him in a breathless whisper.

"We'll go Dutch," he added before he pulled her toward the car.

Twenty minutes later they sat together at a tiny round table. There was the scent of rich sauce, spice and melted candles. From the jukebox in the corner poured an endless succession of popular rock tunes at a volume just below blaring. The waitresses wore bib aprons sporting pictures of grinning pizzas. Leaning her elbows on the scarred wooden table, Asher stared soulfully into Ty's eyes.

"You know how to pick a class joint, don't you?"

"Stick with me, Face," he advised. "I've got a hamburger palace picked out for tomorrow. You get your own individual plastic packs of ketchup." Her lips curved up, making him want to taste them. Leaning forward, he did. The table tilted dangerously.

"You two ready to order?" Snapping her wad of gum, the waitress shifted her weight to one hip.

"Pizza and a bottle of Chianti," Ty told her, kissing Asher again.

"Small, medium or large?"

"Small, medium or large what?"

"Pizza," the waitress said with exaggerated patience.

"Medium ought to do it." Twisting his head, Ty sent the waitress a smile that had her pulling back her shoulders. "Thanks."

"Well, that should improve the service," Asher considered as she watched the woman saunter away.

"What's that?"

Asher studied his laughing eyes. "Never mind," she decided. "Your ego doesn't need any oiling."

Ty bent his head closer to hers as a defense against the jukebox. "So what kind of questions did they toss at you?"

"The usual. They mentioned the business from *Elegance*."

"Are you going to do it?"

She moved her shoulders. "I don't know. It might be fun. And I don't suppose it would hurt the image of women's tennis for one of the players to be in a national fashion magazine."

"It's been done before."

Asher conquered a grin and arched her brows instead. "Do you read fashion magazines, Starbuck?"

"Sure. I like to look at pretty women."

"I always thought jocks tended to favor other sorts of magazines for that."

He gave her an innocent look. "What sorts of magazines?"

Ignoring him, Asher went back to his original question. "They're playing up this Grand Slam business for all it's worth."

"Bother you?" As he laced their fingers together, he studied them. There was an almost stunning difference in size and texture. Often he'd wondered how such an elegant little hand could be so strong…and why it should fit so perfectly with his.

"A bit," Asher admitted, enjoying the rough feel of his skin against hers. "It makes it difficult to go into a match thinking of just that match. What about you? I know you're getting the same kind of pressure."

The waitress brought the wine, giving Ty a slow smile as she set down the glasses. To Asher's amusement, he returned it. He's a devil, she thought. And he knows it.

"I always look at playing a game at a time, one point at a time." He poured a generous amount of wine in both glasses. "Three matches is a hell of a lot of points."

"But you'd like to win the Grand Slam?"

Raising his glass, he grinned. "Damn right." He laughed into her eyes as he drank. "Of course, Martin's already making book on it."

"I'm surprised he's not here," Asher commented, "analyzing every volley."

"He's coming in tomorrow with the rest of the family."

Asher's fingers tightened on the stem of her glass. "The rest of the family?"

"Yeah, Mom and Jess for sure. Mac and Pete if it can be arranged." The Chianti was heavy and mellow. Ty relaxed with it. "You'll like Pete; he's a cute kid."

She mumbled something into her wine before she swallowed. Martin had been there three years ago, along with Ty's mother and sister. Both she and Ty had gone into the U.S. Open as top seeds; both had been hounded by the press. The two of them had shared meals then, too, and a bed. So much was the same—terrifyingly so. But there had been so much in between.

There'd been no small boy with Ty's coloring then. No small boy with that air of perpetual energy to remind her of what was lost. Asher felt the emptiness inside her, then the ache, as she did each time she thought of the child.

Misinterpreting her silence, Ty reached over to take her hand. "Asher, you still haven't spoken to your father?"

"What?" Disoriented, she stared at him a moment. "No, no, not since… Not since I retired."

"Why don't you call him?"

"I can't."

"That's ridiculous. He's your father."

She sighed, wishing it were so simple. "Ty, you know him. He's a very stringent man, very certain of what's right and what's wrong. When I left tennis I did more than disappoint him, I…wasted what he'd given me."

Ty answered with a short, explicit word that made her smile. "From his viewpoint that's the way it was," she went on. "As Jim Wolfe's daughter I had certain responsibilities. In marrying Eric and giving up my career I shirked them. He hasn't forgiven me."

"How do you know that?" he demanded. His voice was low under the insistent music, but rich with annoyance. "If you haven't spoken to him, how can you be sure how he feels now?"

"Ty, if his feelings had changed, wouldn't he be here?" She shrugged, wishing they could have avoided the subject for a while longer. "I thought, at first, that when I started playing again it might make the difference. It hasn't."

"But you miss him."

Even that wasn't so simple. To Ty, family meant

something warm and loving and eternal. He'd never understand that Asher looked not so much now for her father's presence or even his love, but simply his forgiveness. "I'd like him to be here," she said finally. "But I understand his reasons for not coming." Her brow clouded for a moment with a realization that had just come to her. "Before, I played for him, to please him, to justify the time and effort he put into my career. Now I play for myself."

"And you play better," Ty put in. "Perhaps that's one of the reasons."

With a smile she lifted his hand to her lips. "Perhaps that's one of them."

"Here's your pizza." The waitress plopped the steaming pan between them.

They ate amid noise and their own casual chatter. Even the pressure of the upcoming matches had no effect on Asher's mood. The cheese was hot and stringy, making Ty laugh as she struggled against it. The contents of the squat bottle of Chianti lowered as they drank leisurely, content to let the meal drag on. Tennis was forgotten while they spoke of everything and nothing at all. A group of teenagers poured in, laughing and rowdy, to feed another succession of quarters into the jukebox.

Why am I so happy to be in this loud, crowded room? she wondered. The cooling pizza and lukewarm wine were as appealing as the champagne and caviar they had shared in Paris. It was Ty. The place never mattered when she was with him. Abruptly it occurred to Asher that it was herself as well. She was being herself. There weren't any guards, or the need for any. Ty was the only man she'd ever been close to who required none from her.

Her father had wanted her to be perfect—his glass princess. All through her youth she had done everything in her power to please him. With Eric, she had been expected to be the cool, well-mannered Lady Wickerton, a woman who could discuss art and politics intelligently. She was to have been like crystal, many-faceted, elegant and cold.

All Ty had ever expected her to be was Asher. He accepted her flaws, even admired them. Because he had wanted her to be herself, she'd been able to be just that. Not once in all the time she had known him had he ever demanded that she fit a pattern or requested that she conform to any standards but her own. Impulsively she reached over to take his hand, then pressed it to her cheek. There was warmth against warmth, flesh against flesh.

"What's this for?" he asked, allowing his fingers to spread.

"For not wanting glass."

His brows drew together in confusion. "Am I supposed to know what that means?"

"No." Laughing, Asher leaned closer. "Have you drunk enough wine that your resistance is down and you'll be easily seduced?"

A slow smile spread. "More than enough."

"Then come with me," Asher ordered.

It was late when Ty lay sleepless beside Asher. Curled close, her hand caught loosely in his, she slept deeply, drugged with loving and fatigue. Her scent hung in the air so that even in the dark Ty could visualize her. A small alarm clock ticked monotonously at his left, its luminous dial glowing. Twelve twenty-seven.

His mind was far too active for sleep. He sensed, as he knew Asher did, that the idyll was nearly over. They were back where they had once ended, and questions would not be put off too much longer. Impatience gnawed at him. Unlike Asher, Ty looked for the end of the season. Only then would the time be right for answers and explanations. He was not used to biding his time, and the strain was beginning to tell. Even tonight under the laughter he had understood her wordless request that he not probe.

The question of her father, Ty mused, shifting the pillow to brace his back. She was more unhappy about the estrangement than she admitted. It showed in her eyes. It was incomprehensible to him that members of a family could turn away from one another. His thoughts drifted to his mother, to Jess. There was nothing either of them could do he wouldn't forgive. He'd never be able to bear the thought of being responsible for their unhappiness. Could a father feel any different about a daughter? An only daughter, a much-loved daughter, Ty reflected.

He could remember Jim Wolfe's pride in Asher. Ty had often sat beside him during one of Asher's matches in her early days as a pro, then consistently during her last year. Even in such a private man the adoration had showed. It wasn't possible to believe it had been only for the athlete and not for the woman.

Surprisingly Jim had accepted Ty's relationship with his daughter. No, Ty corrected, approved. He'd seemed to enjoy seeing them together. Once, Ty recalled, he had gone as far as outlining his expectations to Ty of their future. At the time Ty had been both amused and annoyed at the fatherly interference. What plans he had

had for a future with Asher had still been vague. Then, when they had crystalized in his mind, it had been too late. Frowning, Ty glanced down at her.

In the pale shaft of moonlight her face seemed very fragile. Her hair was a silvery, insubstantial cloud around it. A wave of longing swamped him so that he had to fight the need to wake her and satisfy himself that she was there for him. His feelings for her had always been mixed—wild desire, unbearable tenderness, traces of fear. There had been no other woman who had ever brought him such sharp and conflicting emotions. Watching her sleep, he felt the need to protect. There should be no shadow of unhappiness in her eyes when they opened.

How many obstacles would they have to overcome before they were really together? he wondered. There was one he might remove himself. Perhaps the time had come to take the first step. On impulse, Ty slipped from the bed and into the sitting room.

It took only moments by phone to travel from coast to coast. Dropping into a chair, Ty listened to the faint crackling on the wire before it began to ring.

"Wolfe residence."

In the two words, Ty recognized the trained voice of a servant. "Jim Wolfe please. It's Ty Starbuck."

"One moment please."

Ty sat back, keeping one ear trained on the adjoining bedroom. He heard two distinct clicks as one extension was lifted and the other replaced.

"Starbuck."

The quiet, cautious voice was instantly recognizable. "Jim. How are you?"

"Well." A bit surprised by the late night call, Jim

Wolfe settled behind his desk. "I've been reading quite a bit about you."

"It's been a good year. You were missed at Wimbledon."

"That makes five for you there."

"And three for Asher," he returned pointedly.

There was a moment of complete silence. "Your slice volley's cleaner than it once was."

"Jim, I called to talk about Asher."

"Then we have nothing to say."

For a moment the cool, calm statement left Ty speechless. In a flood, fury took over. "Just a damn minute. I have plenty to say. Your daughter's battled her way back to the top. She's done it without you."

"I'm aware of that. Do you have a point?"

"Yes, I have a point," Ty retorted. "I've never seen anyone work as hard as she has these past few months. And it hasn't been easy, dealing with the pressure, the press, the constant questions on why her father isn't in the stands while she wins championship after championship."

"Asher knows my feelings," Jim said flatly. "They're no concern of yours."

"Whatever concerns Asher concerns me."

"So…" Jim picked up a slim gold pen from the desk and carefully examined it. "We're back to that."

"Yes, we are."

"If you've decided to resume your relationship with Asher, it's your business, Ty." He flung the pen back onto the desk. "And it's my business if I don't."

"For God's sake, Jim," Ty began heatedly, "she's your daughter. You can't turn your back on your own child."

"Like father, like daughter," Jim murmured.

"What the hell does that mean?" Frustrated, Ty rose to pace, dragging the phone with him.

"Asher wiped her child out of existence. I've done the same."

All movement stopped. Ty felt something freeze in him as his knuckles turned white on the receiver. "What child?"

"She turned her back on everything I taught her," Jim went on, not hearing Ty's harshly whispered question. "The daughter I knew couldn't have done it." The words, and the anger that accompanied them, had been held in for years. Now they came bursting out. "I tried to understand why she married that pale excuse for a man, even tried to resign myself to her throwing away her career. But some things I won't forgive. If the life she chose to live was worth the price of my grandchild, she's welcome to it."

Enraged at letting his feelings pour out so openly, Jim slammed down the receiver.

Three thousand miles away Ty stood, staring at nothing. With infinite care he placed the phone back on the table. Too many thoughts were whirling in his head, too many questions and half-answers. He had to think, to take his time. Silently he walked back into the bedroom and dressed.

He wanted to shake her awake and demand an explanation; he wanted to wait until he had a grip on himself. Torn, Ty sat on a chair and stared at the still form in the bed. Asher slept so peacefully, her quiet breathing hardly stirred the air.

A child? Asher's child? But there was no child, Ty reasoned. If Lord and Lady Wickerton had produced an offspring, there would have been some mention of it in the press. An heir was never kept secret. Dragging a hand through his hair, Ty shifted. Besides, he reasoned, if Asher had had a child, where was it? Struggling to overcome the jealousy at imagining Asher's bearing another man's child, Ty went over his conversation with Jim Wolfe again.

Asher wiped her child out of existence....

His fingers tightened on the arms of the chair as he stared at her sleeping form. Abortion? Without warning, a storm of emotion took over that he had to systematically fight back until his pulse leveled. All attempts to think of the word with an open mind were futile. He couldn't rationalize it, not when it was Asher, not when the child was part of her. Could the woman he thought he knew have made that kind of choice? For what purpose? Was it possible that the social life she had sought had been more important than...

As bitterness filled him, Ty shook his head. He wouldn't believe it of her. Controlled, yes. There were times Asher could be infuriatingly controlled. But never calculating. Jim had been talking in riddles, he decided. There'd never been a child. There couldn't have been.

He watched Asher stir. With a soft murmur she shifted toward the emptiness beside her where Ty should have been. He sensed the moment she woke.

The moonlight gleamed on her arm as she lifted it, brushing her fingers at the hair that curled around her face. She placed her hand on his pillow, as if testing it for warmth.

"Ty?"

Not trusting himself, he said nothing. If only she would go back to sleep until he had resolved his feelings. He could still taste the bitterness at the back of his throat.

But she wouldn't sleep. Although groggy, Asher sensed tension in the air. Ty's emotions were always volatile enough to be felt tangibly. *Something's wrong, something's wrong,* hammered in her brain.

"Ty?" she called again, and a hint of fear touched the word. Asher had struggled to a sitting position before she saw him. The moonlight was enough to allow her to see that his eyes were dark and fixed on her face. It was also enough to let her see that they were cold. Her pulse began to race. "Couldn't you sleep?" she asked, struggling to convince herself it was all her imagination.

"No."

Asher laced her fingers together as she swallowed. "You should have woke me."

"Why?"

"We—we could have talked."

"Could we?" Cold anger filled him. "We can talk as long as I don't ask any questions you don't want to answer."

She'd been expecting the showdown, but not like this. His resentment was already wrapping around her. Still, he had a right, and she'd put him off too long. "Ty, if it's answers you want, I'll give them to you."

"Just like that?" he snapped, rising. "Just ask and you'll answer. Nothing more to hide, Asher?"

Stung by his tone, she stared up at him. "It wasn't a matter of hiding, Ty, not really. I needed time—we needed time."

"Why was that, Asher?" he asked in a tone that was uncharacteristically cool. She felt a shudder zip down her spine. "Why was time so important?"

"There were things I wasn't sure you'd understand."

"Like the baby?"

If he had slapped her, Asher couldn't have been more stunned. Even in the moonlight he could see her face go white. Her eyes grew huge and dark and desperate. "How…" The words wouldn't form. Though they raced around in her mind, Asher seemed incapable of forcing any through her lips. How had he found out? Who had told him? How long had he known?

"Eric," she managed, though the name threatened to strangle her. "Eric told you."

Sharp disappointment cut through him. Somehow he had hoped it hadn't been true that she had conceived and rejected another man's child. "So it's true," he exclaimed. Turning from her, Ty stared through the window at the darkness. He found he couldn't be logical or objective. It was one thing to understand the concept of freedom of choice, and another to apply it to Asher.

"Ty, I…" She tried to speak. All of her worst fears were hurtling down on her. The gulf between them was already tangible and threatening to widen. If only she had been able to tell him in her own way, in her own time. "Ty, I wanted to tell you myself. There were reasons why I didn't at first, and then…" Asher shut her eyes. "Then I made excuses."

"I suppose you thought it was none of my business."

Her eyes flew open again. "How can you say that?"

"What you do with your life when you're married to one man isn't the concern of another, even when he loves you."

Simultaneous flashes of pain and joy rushed through her. "You didn't," she whispered.

"Didn't what?"

"You didn't love me."

He gave a brief laugh, but didn't turn back to her. "No, of course I didn't. That's why I couldn't stay away from you. That's why I thought of you every moment."

Asher pressed the heel of her hand between her eyes. Why now? she thought wildly. Why is it all happening now? "You never told me."

This time he turned. "Yes, I did."

Furiously she shook her head. "You never said it. Not once. Even once would have been enough."

In concentration, his brows drew together. She was right, he decided. He'd never said the words. He'd shown her in every way he knew how, but he'd never said the words. "Neither did you," he blurted, speaking his thoughts.

She let out a breath that was perilously close to a sob. "I was afraid to."

"Damn it, Asher, so was I."

For a long, tense moment they stared at each other. Had she been that blind? Had she needed words so badly that she hadn't seen what he'd been giving her? The words would never have come easily to him because they meant everything. For Ty, a declaration of love wasn't a casual phrase but a declaration of self.

Asher swallowed a tremor, wanting her voice to be strong. "I love you, Ty. I've always loved you. And I'm still afraid." As she held out a hand he glanced down at it, but made no move to accept it. "Don't turn away from me now." She thought of the child she had lost. "Please, don't hate me for what I did."

He couldn't understand, but he could feel. It seemed love for her justified anything. Crossing to her, Ty took the offered hand and brought it to his lips. "It'll be better when we've talked this out. We need to start clean, Asher."

"Yes." She closed her hand over their joined ones. "I want that too. Oh, Ty, I'm so sorry about the baby." Her free arm wrapped around his waist as she dropped her head on his chest. The relief, she thought. The relief of at last being able to share it with him. "I couldn't tell you before, when it happened. I didn't know what to do. I didn't know how you'd feel."

"I don't know either," he answered.

"I felt so guilty." She shut her eyes tight. "When Jess showed me that picture of your nephew, I could almost see how the baby would have looked. I always knew he would have had your hair, your eyes."

"Mine?" For a moment nothing seemed to function. His mind, his heart, his lungs. Then, in a torrent, everything came together. *"Mine?"* Asher gave an involuntary cry as he crushed her fingers in his. Before she could speak he had her by the shoulders, digging into her flesh. His eyes alone brought her ice-cold terror. "The baby was mine?"

Her mouth moved to form words, but nothing came out. Confusion and fear overtook her. But he'd already known, she thought desperately. No, no, he hadn't. Eric's baby, her mind flashed. He'd thought it was Eric's baby.

"Answer me, damn you!" He was shaking her now, violently. Limp as a rag doll, Asher made no protest and sought no defense. Both would have been futile. "Was it my baby? Was it mine?"

She nodded, too numb to feel the pain.

He wanted to strike her. Looking at her face, Ty could almost feel the sensation of his hand stinging against it. And he'd want to keep striking her until rage and grief could no longer be felt. Reading his thoughts in his eyes, Asher made no move to protect herself. For an instant his fingers tightened on her arms. With a violent oath he hurled her away. Hardly daring to breathe, she lay on the bed and waited.

"You bitch. You had my child in you when you married him." He flung the words at her, struggling not to use his fists. "Did he make you get rid of it when he found out? Or did you take care of it so you could play the lady without encumbrances?"

She wasn't aware that her breathing was ragged, or that she was trembling. Her mind was too numb to take in more than half of his words. All she understood was the fury of his feelings. "I didn't know. I didn't know I was pregnant when I married Eric."

"You had no right to keep this from me." Towering over her, he reached down to yank her to her knees. "You had no right to make a decision like that when the child was mine!"

"Ty—"

"Shut up. Damn you!" He shoved her away, knowing neither of them was safe if they remained together. "There's nothing you can say, nothing that could make me even want to look at you again."

He strode from the room without a second glance. The sound of the slamming door echoed over and over in Asher's mind.

Chapter 11

Ty took the quarter-finals in straight sets. Most said he played the finest tennis in his career on that hazy September afternoon. Ty knew he wasn't playing tennis. He was waging war. He'd gone onto the court full of vengeance and fury, almost pummeling his opponent with the ball. His swing was vicious, his aim deadly.

The violence showed in his face, in the grim set of his mouth, in the eyes that were nearly black with emotion. It wasn't the winning or losing that mattered to him, but the release of the physical aspect of the temper that he'd barely controlled the night before. When he struck, he struck brutally, always moving. The motion itself was a threat. He'd often been called a warrior, but the description had never been more true. As if scenting blood, he hounded his opponent, then ground him mercilessly into the ground.

Ty's only disappointment was that the match didn't last longer. There hadn't been enough time to sweat out all of his fury. He wondered if there would ever be enough time.

In the stands there were differing reactions as he stalked off the courts.

"Name of God, Ada, I've never seen the boy play better." Martin Derick beamed like a new father. His voice was hoarse from cheering and cigarettes. A pile of butts lay crushed at his feet. "Did you see how he massacred that Italian?"

"Yes."

"Oh-ho, two matches more and our boy's going to have a Grand Slam." Martin squeezed Ada's workworn hands between his two smooth ones. "Nothing's going to stop him now!"

In her quiet, steady way, Ada stared down at the court. She'd seen more than Ty's victory. There'd been fury in her son's eyes. Outrage, hurt. She recognized the combination too well. She'd seen it in a little boy who'd been teased because his father had deserted him. Then, he'd used his fists to compensate. Today, Ada mused, he'd used a racket. As Martin recounted every serve and smash, Ada sat silently and wondered what had put that look back in her son's eyes.

"Mom." Jess leaned close so that her voice wouldn't carry. "Something's wrong with Ty, isn't it?"

"I'd say something's very wrong with Ty."

Jess rubbed her cheek against Pete's, wishing his powdery scent would calm her. Giggling, he squirmed out of her arms and dove toward his father. "Asher wasn't in the stands today."

Ada lifted her eyes to her daughter's. Jess had mentioned, perhaps too casually, that Ty was seeing Asher Wolfe again. Ada had hardly needed the information. Once she had heard Asher was competing again, she'd known what the results would be.

The only time she had ever seen Ty truly devastated had been when Asher had married the polished British lord. His rage and threats had been expected. But they turned to a brooding that had concerned her a great deal more.

"Yes, I noticed," Ada replied. "Then, she's got a match of her own."

"On the next court, and not for a half hour." Jess cast another worried glance around at the people who filled the stands. "She should have been here."

"Since she wasn't, there must be a reason."

A fresh tremor of unease ran up Jess's back. "Mom, I've got to talk to you—alone. Can we go get a cup of coffee?"

Without question, Ada rose. "You fellas keep Pete entertained," she ordered, tousling her grandson's hair. "Jess and I'll be back in a few minutes."

"You're going to tell her?" Mac spoke softly as he touched his wife's hand.

"Yes. Yes, I need to."

Bouncing his son on his knee, he watched them melt into the crowd.

After they had settled at a table, Ada waited for her daughter to begin. She knew Jess was marking time, ordering coffee, speculating on the chances of rain. Ada let her ramble. An orderly, even-tempered woman, she had learned the best way to deal with her emotional offspring was to ride out the storm. Eventually Jess stopped stirring her coffee and lifted her eyes to her mother's.

"Mom, do you remember when we were here three years ago?"

How could she forget? Ada thought with a sigh. That was the year Ty had won the U.S. Open, then barely had time to savor it before the world had crumbled around his ears. "Yes, I remember."

"Asher left Ty and married Eric Wickerton." When Ada remained silent, Jess lifted her coffee cup and drank as if to fortify herself. "It was my fault," she blurted out.

Ada took the time to taste her own coffee, deciding it wasn't half bad for restaurant brew. "Your fault, Jess? How?"

"I went to see her." In quick jerks Jess began to shred her napkin. She'd thought it would be easier now that she had told Mac everything, but with her mother's gaze steady and patient on hers, she felt like a child again. "I went to her hotel room when I knew Ty wouldn't be there." After pressing her lips together, she let the confession come out in a burst. "I told her Ty was tired of her. I told her he—he was bored."

"I'm surprised she didn't laugh in your face," Ada commented.

Quickly Jess shook her head. "I was convincing," she went on. "Maybe because I was convinced it was the truth. And I—I was sympathetic." Remembering how well she had played the role of reluctant messenger tore at her. "Oh, God, Mom, when I look back and remember the things I told her, how I said them…" Anguished, her eyes met her mother's. "I told her Ty thought she and Eric were suited to each other. There was enough truth in that, but I turned it around to give her the impression that Ty was hoping Eric would take her off his hands. And I defended Ty, telling Asher he'd never want to hurt her, that he was really very concerned that she'd gotten in over her head. I—I made it seem as though Ty had asked my opinion on the best way to untangle himself from an affair he had no more interest in."

"Jess." Ada stopped the movement of her nervous daughter's hands with her own. "Why did you do such a thing?"

"Ty wasn't happy. I'd talked to him just the night before, and he was so down, so unsure of himself. I'd never seen Ty unsure of himself." Her fingers began to move restlessly under her mother's. "It seemed so clear to me that Asher was wrong for him, hurting him. I was convinced I had to save him from being hurt more."

Leaning back, Ada let her gaze drift. The West Side Tennis Club was respectfully dingy, very American. Perhaps that was why she'd always liked it. It was noisy. The Long Island Railroad ran alongside, competing with helicopters, planes and road traffic. Ada had never completely gotten used to the relative quiet of suburbia after a lifetime in the inner city. Now she sat back, absorbing the noise, trying to think of the right words. It occurred to her that parenting didn't stop when children became adults. Perhaps it never stopped at all.

"Ty loved Asher, Jess."

"I know." Jess stared down at the shredded paper napkin. "I didn't think he did. I thought if he'd loved her, he would have been happy. And if she had loved him, she would have…well, she would have acted like all the other women who hung around him."

"Do you think Ty would have loved her if she had been like all the other women?"

Jess flushed, amazing herself and amusing her mother. It was a bit disconcerting to think of the tiny, white-haired Ada Starbuck, mother, grandmother, knowing about passion. "It wasn't until after I met Mac that I realized love doesn't always make you smile and glow," Jess went on, keeping her eyes lowered. "There are times when I was miserable and confused over my feelings for Mac and I began to remember that last talk I had with Ty before I went to see Asher. I realized how alike Ty and I are, how the stronger our feelings are, the more moody we can become."

On a deep breath she met her mother's gaze levelly. "I tried to rationalize that Asher wouldn't have left Ty, that she wouldn't have married Eric if she had really cared. And that if he had, Ty wouldn't have let her go."

"Pride can be just as strong as love. The things you said to Asher made her feel unwanted, and betrayed, I imagine, that Ty would have spoken to you about it."

"If the situation had been reversed, I would have scratched her eyes out and told her to go to hell."

Ada's laugh was a warm, young sound. "Yes, you would. Then you'd have gone to the man you loved and used your claws on him. Asher's different."

"Yes." Miserable, Jess pushed her untouched coffee aside. "Ty always said so. Mom, when they got back together, I was so guilty and frightened. Then I was relieved. And now, I can tell something's gone wrong again." As she had as a child, Jess gave her mother a long, pleading look. "What should I do?"

Strange, Ada mused, that her children wanted to pamper her on one hand, thrusting dishwashers and fancy jewelry on her, while on the other, they still looked to her for all the answers. "You'll have to talk to both of them," Ada said briskly. "Then you'll have to back off and let the two of them work it out. You might be able to heal what you did three years ago, but you can do nothing about what's between them now."

"If they love each other—"

"You made a decision for them once," Ada pointed out. "Don't make the same mistake again."

She hadn't been able to sleep. She hadn't been able to eat. Only the promise she had made to herself never to quit again forced Asher onto the court. Purposely she remained in the dressing room until the last moment to avoid the fans who wandered the walkways and mingled with players. It would take more effort than she could have summoned to smile and make small talk.

When she came outside the humidity hit her like a fist. Shaking off the weakness, Asher went directly to her chair. She heard the applause, but didn't acknowledge it. She couldn't afford to. Even before she began, Asher knew her biggest problem would be concentration.

Her arms ached, her whole body ached and she felt bone-deep exhausted. Pain was something she could ignore once the match was under way, but she wasn't sure she could ignore the jellied weakness inside her, the feeling that someone had punched a yawning hole in the center of her life. Still wearing her warm-up jacket, she took a few experimental swings.

"Asher." Cursing the interruption, she glanced over at Chuck. Concern touched his eyes as he stepped toward her. "Hey, you don't look good. Are you sick?"

"I'm fine."

He studied the shadowed eyes and pale cheeks. "Like hell."

"If I come out on the court, I'm well enough to play," she returned, exchanging one racket for another. "I've got to warm up."

Baffled, Chuck watched her stalk onto the court. It took only a moment of study to see that she wasn't in top form. Chuck moved away to find Ty.

He was in the showers, his eyes closed under the spray. He'd been curt and brief with the press and even briefer with his colleagues. He wasn't in the mood for congratulations. Anger lay curled inside him, undiminished by the physical demands he had placed on himself. He needed more—a sparring match, a marathon run—anything to pump the poison out of his system. Though he heard Chuck call him, Ty remained silent and kept his eyes shut.

"Ty, will you listen to me? Something's wrong with Asher."

Taking his time, Ty stepped back so that the water beat on his chest. Slowly he opened his eyes. "So?"

"So?" Astonished, Chuck gaped at him. "I said something's wrong with Asher."

"I heard you."

"She looks sick," Chuck continued, certain that Ty didn't comprehend. "I just saw her. She shouldn't be playing today. She looks awful."

Ty fought the instinctive need to go to her. He could remember vividly the scene the night before. With a flick of the wrist he shut off the shower. "Asher knows what she's doing. She makes her own decisions."

Too stunned to be angry, Chuck stared at him. He'd

never seen Ty look cold any more than he'd ever seen Asher look furious. Until today. "What the devil's going on here?" he demanded. "I just told you your woman's sick."

Ty felt the tightening in his belly and ignored it. "She's not my woman." Grabbing a towel, he secured it lightly around his waist.

After dragging a hand through his hair, Chuck followed Ty into the locker room. He'd known since that morning when he and Ty had practiced together that something was wrong. Accustomed to his friend's mercurial moods, he had dismissed it, assuming Ty and Asher had had a lover's quarrel. But no lover's quarrel would make Ty indifferent to Asher's health.

"Look, if you two have had a fight, that's no reason—"

"I said she's not my woman." Ty's voice was deadly calm as he pulled on jeans.

"Fine," Chuck snapped. "Then if the field's clear, I might just try my luck." He was slammed back against the lockers, feet dangling as Ty grabbed his shirt in both hands, jerking him up. Coolly, Chuck looked into the stormy eyes. "Not your woman, friend?" he said softly. "Tell that to somebody who doesn't know you."

Breathing hard, Ty struggled against the need to strike back. The hours of violent tennis hadn't drained the anger or the grief. Without a word he dropped Chuck to his feet, then snatched a shirt from his locker.

"Are you going out there?" Chuck demanded. "Somebody should stop her before she makes whatever's wrong with her worse. You know damn well she isn't going to listen to me."

"Don't push me." Ty dragged the shirt over his head

before he slammed the locker door. This time Chuck kept his silence. He heard the tremor in Ty's voice and recognized that the emotion wasn't anger. Only once before had he seen his friend this torn apart. It had been Asher then, as it was obviously Asher now. With warring loyalties, he reached out.

"Okay, you want to talk about it?"

"No." Clenching his fists, Ty fought to regain his control. "No, just go on out…keep an eye on her."

She was fighting, and losing. Asher had used almost all her reserve of energy to take the first set to a tie breaker. The ultimate loss had taken its emotional toll. Kingston was a crafty enough player to sense her opponent's flagging stamina and capitalized on it. Precision was nothing without strength. Asher's strength was ebbing quickly.

The noise played havoc with her concentration. Already playing below par, she needed the sound of the ball hitting the racket. Engines drowned it out, denying her the sense of hearing. On the brittle grass the ball jumped, skidded and stopped. Top speed was necessary, and she didn't have it.

Unable to prevent himself, Ty came to the edge of the tunnel to watch. Immediately he could see that Chuck hadn't exaggerated. She was too pale, too slow. Instinctively he took a step forward. Restraining himself was more difficult than going on, but he stopped, cursing her even as he cursed himself. She'd made her own choice. She herself had cut off any right he had to influence her. From where he stood he could hear her labored breathing, see the strain she fought to keep from her face. At the twinge of fresh pain he turned away from the court.

With a blind determination that was more nerves than power, Asher had taken the second set to three-all. Her face shone with sweat. Weakened, Asher knew that she would have to find a hole in Kingston's game soon, and have the wit and stamina to exploit it. Grit was a weapon, but not weapon enough against power, precision and cunning.

At double break point Asher prepared to serve again. If she could pull this one out, she'd have a chance. If Kingston broke her serve, the match was as good as over. *Concentrate, concentrate,* she ordered herself as she gave the ball a few testing bounces. She counted each one, trying to calm herself. Ty's furious, accusing words hammered in her brain. His face, enraged and stricken, floated in front of her eyes. Tossing the ball, Asher drove at it with her racket.

"Fault."

She shut her eyes and cursed. Control, she ordered herself. If she lost control now, she lost everything. As she took an extra moment, the crowd began to hum in speculation.

"Come on, Face, let's see what you're made of!"

Gritting her teeth, Asher put everything she had left into the serve. The ace brought a roar of approval. She wasn't beaten yet.

But her next serve was soft. Slapping it back to her, Kingston incited a hard, punishing rally. Asher battled by instinct, all reserve depleted. Her eyes, her mind, were fixed on the ball and the ball only. Dodging after a slice, she skidded, barely meeting it with her racket as she stumbled. She went down to her knees, crumbling into a ball of exhaustion and pain.

Someone's hands hooked under her armpits, pull-

ing her to her feet. Asher pushed them away blindly to
stagger to her chair.

"Come on, Asher." Chuck toweled off her streaming face, talking to her as she drew in ragged, straining
breaths. "Come on, babe, you're not in any shape to be
out here today. I'll help you inside."

"No." She shook off his hand. "No, I won't forfeit."
Rising, she dropped the towel to the ground. "I'm going
to finish."

Helpless, Chuck watched her fight a losing battle.

Asher slept for almost twenty-four hours straight.
Her body recharged as she lay motionless in the bed
she had shared so recently with Ty. The loss of the
match—and the Grand Slam—meant little. She'd finished. Her pride was whole because she had refused to
give up, because she had managed to face the reporters after the match and give them a calm accounting.
When they had speculated on the state of her health,
she'd told them she'd been fit to play. She would give
no excuses for losing. If there was blame, it lay within
herself. That was the primary rule of the game.

On returning to her room, Asher only took time to
strip to her underwear before falling exhausted onto
the bed. Sleep came immediately. Hours later she didn't
hear the door open or Ty's footsteps as he crossed to the
bedroom to look at her.

Asher lay flat on her stomach across the spread—
something he knew she did only when absolutely depleted. Her breathing was deep, a heavy sound of
fatigue. The hands he had thrust in his pockets balled
into fists.

His emotions were pulling in too many directions.

She shouldn't be allowed to do this to him, he thought furiously. She shouldn't make him want to hurt and protect at the same time. Walking to the window, he remained silent for a quarter of an hour, listening to her breathe. Before he left her, Ty drew the drapes closed so that the sunlight wouldn't disturb her.

When Asher awoke, a full day had passed. The aches made themselves known.

Keeping her mind a blank, she ran a hot bath. As the water lapped over her, she slipped into a half doze. Asher heard the knock on the door, and ignored it. The phone rang, but she didn't open her eyes.

Disturbed, Jess replaced the receiver after ten full rings. Where could Asher be? she wondered. She knew Asher was still registered at the hotel, but she hadn't answered the phone or the door in more than a day. She'd tried to tell Ty, but he simply wouldn't listen. Any more than he'd listened to her attempts at confession.

Her conscience plagued her. She hadn't tried hard enough, Jess berated herself. She'd been so afraid of losing Ty's love, she had allowed him to brush her off when she tried to talk to him. Well, no more, she determined.

Checking her watch, Jess calculated that Ty would be preparing for the day's match. She cursed, then fretted, then made herself a promise. When it was over, win or lose, she was going to corner her brother and make him listen until she'd told him everything.

Now that the vow had been made, Jess discovered that the waiting wasn't easy. In the stands she marked time. Ty played with the same fierce anger she had observed in his quarter-final match. It was just as effective.

Beneath her pride in him was the constant thought

that her brother might turn away from her after he'd heard her out. But Jess sat patiently through the match and through the press conference. She'd left it to her mother to persuade Martin to go back to the hotel instead of dragging Ty off for a replay of the match. Like a tennis groupie, Jess waited for Ty to emerge from the locker room, then pounced.

"Ty, I need to talk to you."

"I'm talked out, Jess." He patted her hand, then removed it from his arm. "I want to get out of here before the next sportswriter latches on to me."

"Fine, I'll drive. You'll listen."

"Look, Jess—"

"Now, Ty."

Annoyed, Ty stalked to the car. For the first time in his life he wished his family hadn't come. He'd managed to avoid them for the most part, using fatigue or practice as excuses. His mother knew him too well, and her silence questioned him constantly. Martin was ecstatic, wanting to analyze every volley and shower praise. And the hardest of all was watching Pete, darting here and there, babbling, laughing, reminding Ty of something that might have been.

"Look, Jess, I'm tired—"

"Just get in," she interrupted tersely. "I've already put this off for too long."

They slammed their doors simultaneously. Not a very auspicious start, she mused as she merged with traffic, but she'd never finish if she didn't begin. "Okay, I've got some things to tell you, and I'd like you to hear me out before you say anything."

"Unless I want to hitch a damn ride back, I don't have much choice, do I?"

She sent him a worried look. "Don't hate me, Ty."

"Oh, come on, Jess." Ashamed of wishing her away, he gave her hair a quick tousle. "I might be mad at being shanghaied, but I'm not going to hate you."

"Just listen," she started. Staring straight ahead, she began.

At first, Ty paid little attention. She was hopping back to the summer he had first been with Asher. He started once to interrupt, not wanting to be reminded. Jess shook her head fiercely and silenced him. With strained patience Ty sat back and watched the passing scenery.

When Jess told him that she had gone to see Asher, his brows lowered. His concentration focused. Listening to her pouring out the things she had said—*Ty's tired of you.... He doesn't know exactly how to end things without hurting you*—his rage built swiftly. Jess felt the fury swirling, and barely paused for breath.

"She seemed to have no reaction to anything I said. She was very cool, totally in control of herself. It just seemed to reinforce what I thought of her." Stopping for a light, Jess swallowed quickly. "I didn't understand how anyone could have strong feelings and not express them, not then. After I met Mac I realized…" When the light changed she gunned the motor with a jerk of her foot, then stalled the engine. On a frustrated oath she started the car again as Ty remained silent.

"When I look back on it," Jess continued after a shaky breath, "I remember how pale she got, how quiet. It wasn't indifference, but shock. She listened to everything I said, never raising her voice or shedding a tear. I must have hurt her terribly."

Her voice broke and she waited for him to speak,

but there was nothing but thick, vibrant silence. "I had no right, Ty," Jess continued quickly. "I know that. I wanted—I wanted to help, to pay you back somehow for everything you'd done for me. At the time, I thought I was telling her the things you couldn't bring yourself to. I'd convinced myself... Oh, I don't know." Jess made a quick gesture with her hand before she gripped the gear shift. "Maybe I was even jealous, but I didn't think you loved her and I was so sure she didn't love you. Especially when she married so quickly."

Because tears were forming, she pulled over to the side of the road. "Ty, to tell you I'm sorry isn't enough, but I don't have anything else."

The silence in the car vibrated for the space of three heartbeats. "What made you think you could play God with my life?" Ty demanded in a sudden burst that had her jolting. "Who the hell put you in charge?"

Forcing herself to meet his eyes, Jess spoke quietly. "There's nothing you can say to me I haven't said to myself, but you're entitled."

"Do you have any idea what you did to my life?"

She shuddered involuntarily. "Yes."

"I was going to ask Asher to marry me that night, the night I got back and found you in our room. The night you told me she'd gone off with Wickerton."

"Oh, God, Ty." Choking back a sob, Jess laid her head on the steering wheel. "I never thought...I never realized she meant that much to you."

"She was everything I wanted, don't you understand? Everything! I was half crazy because I wasn't sure she'd say yes." He drummed his fist against the dash. "And, God, I'm still not sure. I'll never be sure." The anguish in his voice made Jess straighten.

"Ty, if you'd go see her. If you'd—"

"No." He thought again of the child. His child. "There are other reasons now."

"I'll go," Jess began. "I can—"

"No!" The word whipped out at her, causing Jess to swallow the rest of the sentence. "Stay away from her."

"All right," she agreed unsteadily. "If that's the way you want it."

"That's the way I want it."

"You still love her?" Jess asked.

Ty turned his head so that his eyes met his sister's. "Yes, I love her. That isn't always enough, Jess. I don't think I'd ever be able to forget…"

"Forget?" she prompted when he trailed off. "Forget what?"

"Something she took from me…" Angry energy built up again, grinding at his nerves. "I've got to walk."

"Ty." Jess stopped him with a tentative hand on the arm as he jerked open the door of the car. "Do you want me to go away—back to California? I can make up an excuse, even leave Pete and Mac here for the rest of the tournament. I won't stay for the finals if it upsets you."

"Do what you want," he told her shortly. He started to slam the door of the car when he caught the look in her eyes. He'd protected her all of his life, too long to change now. Love was rooted in him. "It's history, Jess," he said in calmer tones. "Past history. Forget it."

Turning, Ty walked away, hoping he'd be able to believe his own words.

Chapter 12

Asher sat on the bed to watch the men's singles championship. The television commentary barely penetrated as she judged and dissected each stroke and volley for herself. She couldn't go to the stadium, but nothing would prevent her from watching Ty compete.

On the close-ups, she studied his face carefully. Yes, some strain showed, she noted, but his concentration was complete. His energy was as volatile as ever, perhaps more so. For that she could be grateful.

Each time they replayed a shot in slow motion, Asher could fully appreciate the beauty of his form. Muscles rippled as he stretched; feet left the turf in a leap for more power. He was a raw athlete with anger simmering just under the discipline. The graphite racket was no more than an extension of the arm that was whipping the ball harder and harder. As always, his hair flew around the sweatband, dramatic and unruly. His eyes were dark with a rage barely contained. Was it the game that drove him? she wondered. The insatiable thirst to win? Or were there other emotions pushing him this time?

If there were, it was easy to see that they added to the impetus. He was an explosion heating up, a storm rumbling just overhead. Asher knew him well enough to recognize that his control balanced on a very thin edge, but it made his game all the more exciting.

His topspin drove to Chuck's backhand and was returned, power for power. A slice, a lob, an overhead. Turned the wrong way, Chuck pivoted, sprinted, but had no chance to return. The call was late, judging Ty's ball long.

His head whipped around to the judge, his eyes deadly. Asher shuddered when the camera zoomed in so that the undisguised fury seemed aimed directly at her. For a moment they seemed to stare into each other's eyes. Disgust warred with temper before he turned to resume his receiving stance. Crouched like a cat, his eyes intense, he waited. Asher let out an unsteady breath.

Ty was judging the bounce with uncanny accuracy. If it threatened to die, he was under it. When it chose to soar, he got behind it. With unrelenting challenge he charged the net. He baited Chuck, dared him, and, time after time, outwitted him. His game was all aggression and power—Starbuck at his best, she thought with undiminished pride. He could demoralize even a seasoned pro like Chuck with a lightning-fast return that lifted chalk from the service line. With each swing she could hear the grunt of exertion and the swish of air. How she wanted to be there.

He wouldn't want her. She wouldn't soon forget that look of rage and disgust he had turned on her—too much like the one his video image had projected. A man like Starbuck had no ambivalent emotions. It was love or hate; she'd felt them both.

She'd been cut out of his life. She had to accept that. She had to…quit? Asher asked herself. Suddenly her chin rose. Was that what she was doing again? She looked back at the screen as the camera zoomed in on Ty's face. His eyes were opaque and dangerous before he went into a full stretch for his serve. The force of her feelings attacked her. She loved and wanted and needed.

No, damn it! Rising, Asher cursed him. No, if she was going to lose, she was going down fighting, just as she had on the courts. He wouldn't brush her out of his life so easily this time. Briefly she'd forgotten that she no longer aimed her actions at pleasing those around her. Perhaps he didn't want to see her, but that was just too bad. He would see her…and he would listen.

Just as she snapped off the set, a knock sounded on her door. Battling impatience, Asher went to answer. Her expression changed from grim determination to wonder.

"Dad!"

"Asher." Jim met her stunned expression with an unsmiling nod. "May I come in?"

He hadn't changed, she thought wildly. He hadn't changed at all. He was still tall and tanned and silvery-blond. He was still her father. Her eyes filled with love and tears. "Oh, Dad, I'm so glad to see you." Grasping his hand, she drew him into the room. Then the awkwardness set in. "Sit down, please." While gesturing to a chair, Asher sought something to fill the gap. "Shall I order up something to drink? Some coffee?"

"No." He sat as she suggested and looked at his daughter. She was thinner, he noted. And nervous, as nervous as he was himself. Since Ty's phone call, he'd done little but think of her. "Asher," he began, then sighed. "Please sit down." He waited until she settled across from him. "I want to tell you I'm proud of the way you've played this season."

His voice was stiff, but she expected little else. "Thank you."

"I'm most proud of the last match you played."

Asher gave him a small smile. How typical that it was tennis he spoke of first. "I lost."

"You played," he countered. "Right down to the last point, you played. I wonder how many people who watched knew that you were ill."

"I wasn't ill," Asher corrected him automatically. "If I came on court—"

"Then you were fit," he finished, before he shook his head. "I drummed that into you well, didn't I?"

"A matter of pride and sportsmanship," she said quietly, giving him back the words he had given her again and again during her training.

Jim lapsed into silence, frowning at the elegant hands that lay folded in her lap. She'd always been his princess, he thought, his beautiful, golden princess. He'd wanted to give her the world, and he'd wanted her to deserve it.

"I didn't intend to come here to see you."

If the statement hurt, she gave no sign. "What changed your mind?"

"A couple of things, most particularly, your last match."

Rising, Asher walked to the window. "So, I had to lose to have you speak to me again." The words came easily, as did the light trace of bitterness. Though love had remained constant, she found no need to give him unvarnished adulation any longer. "All those years I needed you so badly, I waited, hoping you'd forgive me."

"It was a hard thing to forgive, Asher."

He rose, too, realizing his daughter had grown stronger. He wasn't sure how to approach the woman she had become.

"It was a hard thing to accept," she countered in the calm voice he remembered. "That my father looked at me as athlete first and child second."

"That's not true."

"Isn't it?" Turning, she fixed him with a level stare. "You turned your back on me because I gave up my career. Not once when I was suffering did you hold out a hand to me. I had no one to go to but you, and because you said no, I had no one at all."

"I tried to deal with it. I tried to accept your decision to marry that man, though you knew how I felt about him." The unexpected guilt angered him and chilled his voice. "I tried to understand how you could give up what you were to play at being something else."

"I had no choice," she began furiously.

"No choice?" His derision was sharp as a blade. "You made your own decision, Asher—your career for a title—just as you made it about the child. My grandchild."

"Please." She lifted both hands to her temples as she turned away. "Please don't. Have you any idea how

much and how often I've paid for that moment of carelessness?"

"Carelessness?" Stunned into disbelief, Jim stared
at the back of her head. "You call the conception of a
child carelessness?"

"No, *no!*" Her voice trembled as it rose. "The loss.
If I hadn't let myself get upset, if I had looked where
I was going, I never would have fallen. I never would
have lost Ty's child."

"What!" As the pain slammed into his stomach, Jim
sank into the chair. "Fallen? Ty's child? *Ty's?*" He ran a
hand over his eyes as he tried to sort it out. Suddenly he
felt old and frail and frightened. "Asher, are you telling
me you miscarried Ty's child?"

"Yes." Wearily she turned back to face him. "I wrote
you, I told you."

"If you wrote, I never received the letter." Shaken,
Jim held out a hand, waiting until she grasped it. "Asher,
Eric told me you aborted his child." For an instant, the
words, their meaning, failed to penetrate. Her look was
blank and vulnerable enough to make him feel every
year of his age. "A calculated abortion of your husband's child," he said deliberately. When she swayed
he gripped her other hand. "He told me you'd done so
without his knowledge or permission. He seemed devastated. I believed him, Asher." As she went limp, he drew
her down to her knees in front of him. "I believed him."

"Oh, God." Her eyes were huge and dark with shock.
Her father's fingers trembled in hers. "He phoned me
from London. He sounded half mad—I thought with
grief. He said that you hadn't told him until after it was
done. That you had told him you wanted no children

to interfere with the life you intended to build as Lady Wickerton."

Too numb for anger, Asher shook her head. "I didn't know even Eric could be so vindictive, so cruel."

It all began to make horrid sense. Her letters to her father hadn't been answered. Eric had seen that they were never mailed. Then, when she had phoned him, Jim had been cold and brief. He'd told her that he could never resolve himself to her choice. Asher had assumed he meant her rejection of her career.

"He wanted me to pay," she explained as she dropped her head on her father's lap. "He never wanted me to stop paying."

Gently Jim cupped her face in his hands. "Tell me everything. I'll listen, as I should have a long time ago."

She started with Jess, leaving nothing out including her final stormy estrangement from Ty. Jim's mouth tightened at her recounting of the accident and the hospital scene with Eric. Listening, he cursed himself for being a fool.

"And now, Ty..." As realization struck her, she paled. "Ty thinks—Eric must have told him I'd had an abortion."

"No, I told him."

"You?" Confused, Asher pressed her fingers to the headache in her temple. "But how—"

"He called me a few nights ago. He wanted to convince me to see you. I told him enough to make him believe the lie just as I'd believed it."

"That night when I woke up," Asher remembered. "Oh, my God, when he realized it had been his baby... The things he was saying! I couldn't think at the time." She shut her eyes. "No wonder he hates me."

Color flooded back into her face. "I have to tell him the truth and make him believe it." Scrambling up, she dashed for the door. "I'll go to the club. I have to make him listen. I have to make him understand."

"The match must be nearly over." Jim rose on unsteady legs. His daughter had been through hell, and he had done nothing but add to it. "You'll never catch him there."

Frustrated, Asher looked at her watch. "I don't know where he's staying." Releasing the doorknob, she went to the phone. "I'll just have to find out."

"Asher…" Awkward, unsure, Jim held out his hand. "Forgive me."

Asher stared into his face as she replaced the receiver. Ignoring the hand, she went into his arms.

It was nearly midnight when Ty reached the door of his room. For the past two hours he'd been drinking steadily. Celebrating. It wasn't every day you won the Grand Slam, he reminded himself as he searched for his keys. And it wasn't every day a man had a half dozen women offering to share their beds with him. He gave a snort of laughter as he slid the key into the lock. And why the hell hadn't he taken one of them up on it?

None of them was Asher. He shook away the thought as he struggled to make the doorknob function. No, he simply hadn't wanted a woman, Ty told himself. It was because he was tired and had had too much to drink. Asher was yesterday.

The hotel room was dark as he stumbled inside. If he was right about nothing else, he was right about having too much to drink. Through glass after glass Ty had told himself the liquor was for celebrating, not for forgetting. The kid from the Chicago slum had made it to the top, in spades.

The hell with it, he decided, tossing his keys into the room. With a thud they landed on the carpet. Swaying a bit, he stripped off his shirt and threw it in the same direction. Now if he could just find his way to the bed without turning on a light, he'd sleep. Tonight he'd sleep—with enough liquor in his system to anesthetize him. There'd be no dreams of soft skin or dark blue eyes tonight.

As he fumbled toward the bedroom, a light switched on, blinding him. With a pungent curse Ty covered his eyes, balancing himself with one hand on the wall.

"Turn that damn thing off," he muttered.

"Well, the victor returns triumphant."

The quiet voice had him lowering the hand from his eyes. Asher sat primly in a chair, looking unruffled, soft and utterly tempting. Ty felt desire work its way through the alcohol.

"What the hell are you doing here?"

"And very drunk," she said as if he hadn't spoken. Rising, she went to him. "I suppose you deserve it after the way you played today. Should I add my congratulations to the host of others?"

"Get out." He pushed away from the wall. "I don't want you."

"I'll order up some coffee," she said calmly. "We'll talk."

"I said get out!" Catching her wrist, he whirled her around. "Before I lose my temper and hurt you."

Though her pulse jumped under his fingers, she stood firm. "I'll leave after we talk."

"Do you know what I want to do to you?" he demanded, shoving her back against the wall. "Do you know that I want to beat you senseless?"

"Yes." She didn't cringe as his fury raged down on her. "Ty, if you'll listen—"

"I don't want to listen to you." The image of her lying exhausted on the bed raced through his mind. "Get out while I can still stop myself from hurting you."

"I can't." She lifted a hand to his cheek. "Ty—"

Her words were cut off as he pressed her back into the wall. For an instant she thought he would strike her, then his mouth came down on hers, bruising, savage. He forced her lips apart, thrusting his tongue deep as she struggled. His teeth ground against hers as though to punish them both. There was the faint taste of liquor, reminding her he had drink as well as anger in his system. When she tried to turn her head, he caught her face in his hand—not gently, in the touch she remembered, but viselike.

He could smell her—the soft talc, the lightly sexy perfume. And the fear. She made a small, pleading sound before she stopped fighting him. Without being aware of what he did, he lightened the grip to a caress. His lips gentled on hers, tasting, savoring. Mumbling her name, he trailed kisses over her skin until he felt the essence of her flowing back into him. God, how he'd missed her.

"I can't do without you," he whispered. "I can't." He sank to the floor, drawing her down with him.

He was lost in her—the feel, the taste, the fragrance. His mind was too full of Asher to allow him to think. Sensation ruled him, trembling along his skin to follow the path of her fingers. It was as if she sought to soothe and arouse him at once. He was helpless to resist her—or his need for her. As if in a trance, he took his lips over her, missing nothing as his hunger seemed insatiable. Her quickening breaths were like music, setting his rhythm.

The air grew steamier as his hands homed in on secrets that made her moan. Her body shuddered into life. No longer gentle, but demanding, she tangled her fingers in his hair and guided him to sweet spaces he'd neglected. Then ever greedy, ever giving, she drew him back to her mouth. Her tongue toyed with his lips, then slid inside to drink up all the flavors. His head swimming, he answered the kiss.

The need for her was unreasonable, but Ty was beyond reason. Without her there'd been an emptiness that even his fury couldn't fill. Now the void was closing. She was in his blood, in his bone, so essential a part of him he had been able to find no place of separation. Now there was no will to do so.

Under him, she was moving, inviting, entreating. He whispered a denial against her mouth, but his pounding blood took control. He was inside her without being aware of it. Then all sensations spiraled together in an intensity that made him cry out. And it was her name he spoke, in both ecstasy and in despair.

Drained, Ty rolled from her to stare at the ceiling. How could he have let that happen? he demanded. How could he have felt such love, found such pleasure in a woman he had vowed to amputate from his life? He wondered now if he'd ever find the strength to stay away from her. Life with her, and life without her, would be two kinds of hell.

"Ty." Reaching over, Asher touched his shoulder.

"Don't." Without looking at her he rose. "Get dressed,

for God's sake," he muttered as he tugged on his own jeans with trembling hands. Who had used whom? he wondered. "Do you have a car?"

Sitting up, Asher pushed her hair out of her face. Hair, she remembered, that only moments before he had been kissing. "No."

"I'll call you a cab."

"That won't be necessary." In silence she began to dress. "I realize you're sorry that this happened."

"I'm damned if I'll apologize," he snapped.

"I wasn't asking you to," she told him quietly. "I was going to say that I'm not sorry. I love you, and making love with you is only one way to show it." She managed, after three attempts, to button her blouse. When she looked up, he was at the window, his back to her. "Ty, I came here to tell you some things you must know. When I'm finished, I'll go and give you time to think about them."

"Can't you understand I don't want to think anymore?"

"It's the last thing I'll ask of you."

"All right." In a gesture of fatigue she rarely saw in him, he rubbed both hands over his face. The liquor had burned out of his system—by the anger or the passion, he wasn't sure. But he was cold sober. "Maybe I should tell you first that what Jess said to you three years ago was her own fabrication. I didn't know anything about it until the other day when she told me what she'd done. In her own way, she was trying to protect me."

"I don't understand what you're talking about."

Turning, he gave her a grim smile. "Did you really think I was tired of you? Looking for a way out? Won-

dering how I could ditch you without raising too much
fuss or interfering with my career?"

Asher opened her mouth to speak, then shut it again.
How strange that the words still hurt and made her defensive.

"Obviously you did."

"And if I did?" she countered. "Everything she said
fit. You'd never made a commitment to me. There'd
never been any talk about the future."

"On either side," he reminded her.

Asher pushed away the logic. "If you'd once told
me—"

"Or perhaps you were uncertain enough of your own
feelings that when Jess dumped that on you, you ran
right to Wickerton. Even though you were carrying my
baby."

"I didn't know I was pregnant when I married Eric."
She saw him shrug her words away. In fury she grabbed
both of his arms. "I tell you I didn't know! Perhaps if
I had known before I would have simply gone away. I
don't know what I would have done. I was already terrified you were growing tired of me before Jess confirmed it."

"And where the hell did you get a stupid idea like
that?"

"You'd been so moody, so withdrawn. Everything
she said made sense."

"If I was moody and withdrawn, it was because
I was trying to work out the best way to ask Asher
Wolfe, Miss Society Tennis, to marry Starbuck, from
the wrong side of the tracks."

Asher took an uncertain step toward him. "You
would have married me?"

"I still have the ring I bought you," he answered.

"A ring?" she repeated stupidly. "You'd bought me a ring?" For some inexplicable reason the thought of it stunned her more than anything else.

"I'd planned to try a very conventional proposal. And if that didn't work, maybe a kidnapping."

She tried to laugh because tears were entirely too close. "It would have worked."

"If you'd told me you were pregnant—"

"Ty, I didn't know! Damn it!" She pounded once against his chest. "Do you think I would have married Eric if I had known? It was weeks afterward that I found out."

"Why the hell didn't you tell me then?"

"Do you think I wanted to get you back that way?" The old pride lifted her chin. "And I was married to another man. I'd made him a promise."

"A promise that meant more than the life of the child we'd made together," he retorted bitterly. "A promise that let you walk into one of those antiseptic clinics and destroy something innocent and beautiful. And mine."

The image was too ugly, the truth too painful. Flying at him, Asher struck him again and again until he pinned her hands behind her back. *"And mine!"* she shouted at him. "And mine, or doesn't my part matter?"

"You didn't want it." His fingers closed like steel as she tried to pull away. "But you didn't have the decency to ask me if I did. Couldn't you bear the thought of carrying part of me inside you for nine months?"

"Don't ask me what I could bear." She wasn't pale now, but vivid with fury. "I didn't have an abortion," she spat at him. "I miscarried. I miscarried and nearly died in the process. Would you feel better if I had? God knows I tried to."

"Miscarried?" His grip shifted from her wrists to her shoulders. "What are you talking about?"

"Eric hated me too!" she shouted. "When I learned I was pregnant and told him, all he could say was that I'd deceived him. I'd tried to trick him into claiming the baby after you'd refused me. Nothing I said got through to him. We argued and argued. We were near the steps and he was shouting. All I wanted to do was get away." Her hands flew up to cover her face as she remembered again, all too clearly. "I didn't look, I only ran. Then I was falling. I tried to stop, but my head hit the railing, I think. Then I don't remember anything until I woke up and the baby was gone."

Somehow he could see it as vividly as though it were being played on film in front of his eyes. "Oh, God, Asher." When he tried to take her in his arms, she pulled away.

"I wanted you, but I knew you'd never forgive me. It didn't seem to matter anymore, so I did what Eric wanted." To force back the tears, she pressed her fingers to her eyes. "I didn't want you to know, I couldn't have stood it if you had known when you didn't want me." Lowering her hands, she looked at him, dry-eyed. "I paid for losing your baby, Ty. For three years I did without everything that mattered to me, and I grieved alone. I can't mourn any longer."

"No." Going to the window, he flung it up as if he needed air. There was no breeze, nothing to relieve the burning that he felt. "You've had years to deal with it. I've had days." And she'd had no one, he thought. Years with no one. Ty took several long breaths. "How badly were you hurt?"

Puzzled by the question, she shook her head. "What?"

"Were you badly hurt?" The question was rough and turbulent. When she remained silent he turned. "When you fell, how bad was it?"

"I—I lost the baby."

"I asked about you."

She stared without comprehension. No one had asked her that, not even her father. Looking into Ty's ravaged face, she could only shake her head again.

"Damn it, Asher, did you have a concussion, did you break any bones? You said you almost died."

"The baby died," she repeated numbly.

Crossing to her, he grabbed her shoulders. *"You!"* he shouted. "Don't you know that you're the most important thing to me? We can have a dozen babies if you want. I need to know what happened to you."

"I don't remember very much. I was sedated. There were transfusions..." The full impact of his words penetrated slowly. The anguish in his eyes was for her. "Ty." Burying her face against his chest, she clung. "All that's over."

"I should have been with you." He drew her closer. "We should have gone through that together."

"Just tell me you love me. Say the words."

"You know that I do." He cupped her chin to force her head back. "I love you." He saw the first tear fall and kissed it away. "Don't," he pleaded. "No more tears, Face. No more grieving."

She held him close again until the fullness left her chest. "No more grieving," she repeated, and lifted her face.

He touched it gently, fingertips only. "I hurt you."

"We let other people hurt us," she contradicted. "Never again."

"How could we be stupid enough to almost lose it all twice?" he wondered aloud. "No more secrets, Asher."

She shook her head. "No more secrets. A third chance, Ty?"

"I work best under pressure." He brushed his lips over her temple. "Double break point, Face, I'm on a winning streak."

"You should be celebrating."

"I did my share."

"Not with me." She gave him a light kiss full of promise. "We could go to my place. Pick up a bottle of champagne on the way."

"We could stay here," he countered. "And worry about the champagne tomorrow."

"It is tomorrow," she reminded him.

"Then we've got all day." He began to pull her toward the bedroom.

"Wait a minute." Snatching her hand away, she stepped back. "I'd like to hear that conventional proposal now."

"Come on, Asher." He made another grab for her hand, but she eluded him.

"I mean it."

Flustered, he stuck his hands into his pockets. "You know I want you to marry me."

"That's not a conventional proposal." She folded her arms and waited. "Well," she began when he remained silent, "should I write you a cheat sheet? You say something like, Asher—"

"I know what I'm supposed to say," he muttered. "I'd rather try the kidnapping."

Laughing, she walked over and twined her arms around his neck. "Ask me," she whispered, letting her lips hover an inch from his.

"Will you marry me, Asher?" The lips held tantalizingly near his curved, but she remained silent. His eyes dropped to them, lingered, then rose to hers. "Well?"

"I'm thinking it over," she told him. "I was hoping for something a bit more flowery, maybe some poetry or—" The wind was knocked out of her as he hefted her over his shoulder. "Yes, that's good too," she decided. "I should be able to let you know in a few days."

From the height he dropped her, she bounced twice before she settled on the bed.

"Or sooner," she decided as he began unbuttoning her blouse.

"Shut up."

She cocked a brow. "Don't you want to hear my answer?"

"We'll get the license tomorrow."

"I haven't said—"

"And the blood tests."

"I haven't agreed—"

His mouth silenced her in a long, lingering kiss as his body fit unerringly to hers.

"Of course," Asher sighed, "I could probably be persuaded."

* * * * *